THE

DARK BRIDE

ecco

An Imprint of HarperCollins*Publishers*

THE

DARK BRIDE

a novel

LAURA RESTREPO

Translated by Stephen A. Lytle

HarperCollins books may be purchased for educational, business, or sales promotional use. For information please write: Special Markets Department, HarperCollins Publishers Inc., 10 East 53rd Street, New York, NY 10022.

FIRST EDITION

Designed by Claire Vaccaro

Library of Congress Cataloging-in-Publication Data has been applied for.

ISBN 0-06-008894-X

02   03   04   05   06   DC/BG   10   9   8   7   6   5   4   3   2   1

Fiction

Restrepo, Laura.

Dark bride

I am as dark — but lovely,
O daughters of Jerusalem,
As the tents of Kedar,
as the curtains of Salma.

SONG OF SONGS

But who would know the way
to enter her heart?

SAINT-JOHN PERSE

one

 Then slowly the night would open and the miracle unfold. Far off in the distance, against the immense, silky darkness, strings of colored lights would appear in La Catunga, the barrio of *las mujeres,* the women. Men, freshly bathed and splashed with cologne, would pile into trucks on payday and come down the mountain from the oil fields to the city of Tora, drawn like moths to a flame by those twinkling electric lights that held the greatest promise of earthly bliss.

"To see the lights of La Catunga from a distance? That was heaven, *hermano,*" recalls Sacramento, who has suffered a great deal because of his memories. "For that, just for that, we would break our backs working in the cruel jungle, the four hundred workers of Campo 26. Thinking of that sweetness, we withstood the rigors of Tropical Oil."

Day after day they waded through swamps and malarial dampness, until finally the moment arrived, at the far reaches of hope, when they would glimpse the lights of La Catunga, that barrio baptized by *las mujeres* in honor of Santa Catalina—la Santacata, the loving Catica, the compassionate Catunga—in accordance with their devotion to her, whether for her chastity, her martyrdom, her beauty, or her royal status as a princess.

"She had enormous castles and inheritances," relates the elderly Todos los Santos of her princess and patron saint, "herds of elephants and three rooms overflowing with jewels that had been given to her by her father the king, who was proud to have a daughter more beautiful and pure than sunlight itself."

On foot and hatless, almost reverently but snorting like calves and jingling the coins in their pockets—that is how on each payday the men entered those narrow, brightly lit streets they had dreamed of in their barracks, Mondays with hangovers, Tuesdays with the longing of orphans, Wednesdays with the fever of lonely males, and Thursdays with the ardor of the lovelorn.

"*Llegaron los peludoooos!* Here come the shaggy men!" Sacramento says in falsetto to imitate a woman's shout. "They called us the shaggy men because an oil worker was proud of arriving in La Catunga looking tough, tan, hairy and bearded. But clean and smelling fine, wearing leather boots and a white shirt, with a good gold watch, necklace, and ring to show off his salary. And always, as if it were a medal, his company ID visible on his lapel. The ID that identified you as an *obrero petrolero*, an oil worker. That, *hermano*, was our badge of honor."

"*Llegaron los peludoooos!*" laughs Todos los Santos, showing the teeth she no longer has. "It's true, that was the war cry. Tough and shaggy, that's how we liked them, and when we saw them arriving we also shouted: *Ya llegó el billete!* Here comes the money!"

Back then Tora was distinguished in the great vastness of the outside world as the city of the three p's: *putas, plata,* and *petróleo,* that is, whores, money, and oil. *Petróleo, plata,* and *putas.* Four p's really, if we remember that it was a paradise in the middle of a land besieged by hunger. The lords and ladies of this empire? The *petroleros* and the *prostitutas.*

"We didn't call them *putas* or *rameras* or other offensive names," remembers Sacramento. "We just called them *las mujeres,* because for us there were no others. In the oil world, *amor de café* was the only recognized form of love."

"Understand that Tora was founded by *prostitutas* according to our own law, way before the wives and fiancées arrived to impose their rights of exclusivity," Todos los Santos tells me, regal and handsome despite her advanced age, as she finishes a glass of *mistela* with the manners of a countess and smokes a fat, odoriferous cigar of the traditional brand Cigalia, with gestures worthy of the equerry of that same countess.

"Have a little smoke, *reina*," she offers me, reaching out the hand holding the cigar a little toward where I am not sitting, and I realize that she can't see very well.

"How could you think of that, doña, can't you see I'm choking?" I say, and she laughs; she seems to think I've said something funny.

"The ones who hold back are the most vice-ridden." She laughs and covers her mouth with her hand, like a little girl. "If you won't smoke, then have a *mistela*. It's refreshing and pleasant. Please don't refuse me."

In its early days word spread to the four winds that La Catunga was the optimal marketplace for love because of the abundance of money and availability of healthy males, so beauties all over the world packed their beads and baubles and came here to try their luck.

"Extraordinary beauties came here, improving upon what was already here," says Todos los Santos dotingly, then coquettishly begging forgiveness for the lack of modesty. "There were some real ladies, all so very elegant and pious. The candleholders in the sanctuary of the Sagrado Corazón never had an empty slot. One didn't go around brusquely or soil her mouth with foul words, or display poor manners as occurred later, two women fighting over a man and things of the sort. None of that. Vulgarity had no place among us."

Since there were women from so many different places, tariffs were established based upon how exotic and distant a woman's nationality was, or how sonorous her name and unusual her customs. Those who charged the most were the French: Yvonne, big and beautiful, the languid Claire, pale as the moon, and Mistinguett, who before coming to contend with the *petroleros* was a favorite of the painters in Montmartre.

"She always dreamed of returning to her country, that Mistinguett; she said that there she was paid just for allowing herself to be painted in the nude. There was also a painter who came here and used her as a model in a painting, but he was a modern painter, a lover of bright colors and foolish lines. She didn't approve the portrait and scolded him: 'That's not me, it looks like a chicken. I should have charged you more for wasting my time. Where do you see feathers on me, fool? Go and paint chickens and see if they turn out like women.' She said all that and then to add insult to injury she told him that he painted unholy messes and had reawakened her anxiousness to leave the country, because in France painters truly knew their trade."

In the strict classification by nation, after the French came the Italians, ill-tempered but professional in their work, and as the scale descended came the girls from surrounding countries such as Brazil, Venezuela, or Peru, then came the *colombianas* from the various regions in general, and on the bottom rung the native Pipatón Indians, who were at a disadvantage because of racial prejudices and because they were the most abundant.

Men of varying talent and diverse plumage made the trip to this utopian place to taste a mouthful of olive flesh, or blond, or *mulata* — of every kind and in willing abundance, without reproach or commitment, in a harmonious blend of *guaracha*, tango, and *milonga* music. There's nothing like the vice of sweet love to kill longings and loneliness with tender kisses at the edge of a river, between sips of champagne or rum, with words whispered in one's ears perhaps in Italian, or maybe Portuguese, nearly always in baby talk.

"They were sincere words, don't think that we let out an 'I love you' if we didn't intend for it to mean something. For every man there was a pretty phrase, 'handsome daddy,' 'my little piece of caramel,' 'light of my eyes,' and other flattering words like that. But 'I love you' was only used for the *enamorado* that each woman had, the one for whom her heart remained faithful."

So as not to generate misunderstandings with the business of the international tariffs and so that the male clientele would know exactly what to go by, the custom of hanging a lightbulb of a different color in each house was established: green for the blond French women; red for the Italians, so temperamental; blue for all the women from neighboring countries; yellow for the *colombianas*; and common, ordinary white — vulgar Philips bulbs — for the *pipatonas*, who only aspired to a crust of bread to feed their brood of children. At least that's how it was until the startling Sayonara made her appearance. Startling? Made of shadow and wonder, her name charged with good-byes.

Sayonara, the aloof goddess with oblique eyes, more revered than even the legendary Yvonne and Mistinguett, and the only one in the history of the barrio whose window glowed with a violet-colored bulb.

"The violet light, that was the key," affirms Todos los Santos. "It was a new color, unnatural, never before imagined. Because green lights are seen in stoplights, in lightning bugs, and reds and blues are at the circus, in bars, in shooting stars, on Christmas trees. But violet? Violet is a mystical color. A violet light in the dark of night produces anxiety and motivates uncertainty. And to think that we owe it to Machuca, may God protect her despite the barbarities she says about Him; it was Machuca, the blasphemer, who obtained that violet lightbulb, so one of a kind. She stole it from a traveling carousel that had stopped in town at the time."

Sacramento, the cart man, was the first to see Sayonara arrive in Tora.

"Sayonara, no; the girl that would become Sayonara and that later would stop being Sayonara to become another woman," emphasizes Sacramento, and I begin to understand that I have entered into a world of performances where each person approaches or retreats from his own character.

The river floated along in a lethargy of idle crocodiles, and the *champán*, the raft, that brought travelers and hustlers, *tagüeros* and *caucheros* — gatherers of ivory palm wood and rubber — lively men and those dying of hunger from every port along the Magdalena, was taking longer than usual to arrive. Sacramento was waiting for a client who might solicit his service of human-powered transport for cargo or passengers, and as he waited he grew drowsy watching the spirals of brown water, frothy with oil, twisting and untwisting as they glided lazily by. He says he didn't know when, light as a memory, she climbed into his cart with her two cardboard boxes and her battered suitcase, because he was startled from his nap by her voice ordering him:

"Take me to the best bar in town."

He looked at her through still foggy eyes and he couldn't see her face, which was covered by a tangle of wild, dirty hair. But he did see her beat-up luggage and the poplin dress that left uncovered some skinny and dark extremities. This girl isn't even thirteen, nor does she have a peso to pay for the ride, he thought, as he yawned and took a handkerchief from his pocket to wipe away the sleep that was still hanging from his eyelashes.

"Wake up, man, I'm in a hurry."

"Haughty little girl."

Sacramento stood up, walked to the river, making a show of not being in a hurry, drew a little muddy water in a can, dampened his head and T-shirt, took a mouthful, and spat it out.

"The world's all fucked up," he sputtered. "The water tastes like gasoline."

"What is the best bar in this town?" she insisted.

"The most famous one is the Dancing Miramar. Who are you looking for there?"

"I'm going there to look for work."

Intrigued and finally awake, Sacramento inspected the bony, tangled creature who had climbed into his cart without warning or permission.

"Do you know who works there?" he asked her. "Bad women. Very bad women."

"I know that."

"I mean very, very bad. The worst. Are you sure you want to go there?"

"I'm sure," she said with a certainty that left no room for doubt. "I'm going to be a *puta*."

Sacramento didn't know what to say, so he simply diverted his gaze to a portion of the slow journey of a log with reptilian wrinkles that was being carried along by the river's current.

"You're too skinny," he said finally. "You won't have much luck in the business. Besides, you need manners, a little elegance, and you look like a hick from the mountains."

"Take me there now, I can't waste time arguing with you."

Sacramento doesn't know why he ended up obeying; he tells me that perhaps he was stirred by the freshness of the fruity lips and healthy teeth that he thought he saw beneath the tangles.

"To think that I was the one who took her to La Catunga," he says to me. "You can't count the number of sleepless nights that regret has robbed me of."

"You took her because she asked you to," I tell him.

"For years I thought I could have dissuaded her that first day when she was still such a young girl and so newly arrived. Now I'm sure I couldn't have."

"Everything was already written." Todos los Santos exhales smoke from her Cigalia. "Eager creatures like her bargain with the future and shape it to their fancy."

Weaving among the crowd, dodging tables and chairs, Sacramento the cart man pulled his old wooden wagon through the smell of oil reheated a hundred times emanating from stands crowded along the *malecón* that were selling greasy, delicious catfish stew and fried fish. The girl weighed so little that in an instant they were passing the main entrance to the Tropical Oil Company's facilities, where several guards armed with rifles were busy feeding their pet iguana.

"What does it eat?" asked Sacramento as he walked by.

"Flies," answered one of the men, without lifting his head to look.

Floating among cloying organic vapors, Sacramento took a shortcut through the municipal slaughter yard.

"Get me out of here quick; I don't like this smell of guts," protested the girl.

"Do you think I am your horse that you can just guide anywhere you want?"

"Get up, horse!" she said, laughing.

Then they crossed diagonally across the Plaza del Descabezado, so named because enthroned in its center was the decapitated statue of some important person whose identity was long forgotten by the townspeople, and that had turned green from stray dogs urinating on it each time they passed.

"Why doesn't he have a head?" she wanted to know.

"It was knocked off years ago, during a labor strike."

"The man's, or the statue's?"

"Who knows?"

They crossed themselves as they passed the church of Santo Ecce Homo and ended up on Calle de la Campana, better known as Calle Caliente, then Sacramento announced, with chauvinistic pride, their arrival in La Catunga.

"The most prestigious *zona de tolerancia* on the planet," he said.

The girl climbed out of the cart, straightened her poplin dress, which was wrinkled like wrapping paper, and raised her nose into the air, trying to sniff the winds that the future had reserved for her.

"This is it?" she asked, although she already knew.

In the vertical heat of midday, winding through the dust, a neighborhood lined by dirt alleyways made narrower on each side by blossoming scarlet *cayenos* and irregular dwellings made of packed dirt topped with tin roofs, each one with a door open to the street, revealing a minimal interior without mystery or secret and featuring an armoire, a slowly turning fan, a pitcher and washbasin, and a tidily made bed. Outside were mingled stray animals, little boys who wanted to be *petroleros* when they grew up, little girls who dreamed of becoming teachers, women in slippers shouting to one another as they swept their doorways or sat in rocking chairs in the shade, fanning themselves with the lid of a pot.

A poor barrio, like any other. Except for the colored lightbulbs, now extinguished and invisible, that hung from the facades as the only sign of the difference, the great, unfathomable difference. As soon as the girl tried to take a step forward, the brutal current that struck violently at her legs made her realize, once and for all, that La Catunga was enclosed within an imaginary cordon that burned like the lash of a whip.

"Once inside you will never leave," she heard Sacramento's voice warning, and for an instant her resolved heart knew doubt.

"Where is the Dancing Miramar?" she asked in glassy syllables that tried to hide her twinges of panic.

"At the end of that passageway, against the Troco's fence."

"Take me to the Dancing Miramar."

"I can't, the cart won't fit in there. Besides, it's too early; no café opens until five in the afternoon."

"Then I'll wait at the door," she said, once again in conformity with the design of her destiny. She picked up the suitcase and the two cardboard boxes with excessive energy for the fragile twig that was her body and began walking, without paying or thanking the cart man, toward that territory marked with red steel, where it was fitting that everything outside was execrable, where life revealed itself in reverse and love fought against God's mandates.

"It's nice to say thank you!" shouted Sacramento.

"You're welcome," she answered, brusquely turning her head back to reveal her face for the first time, and Sacramento felt the dark and ancient gaze of Asiatic eyes fall upon him. The boldness with which her eyebrows had been plucked until they disappeared and were replaced by a pencil line, and one or another scar left by the acne on her cheeks, made him think that she might not be as young as she had first seemed. One of the girl's cardboard boxes fell to the ground and she started kicking it up the street as Sacramento, sitting on his cart, watched her and wondered what that skinny, ill-mannered girl had that would make a man like him, who already had his *cédula* of citizenship, work for free and then stand rooted there, admiring the decisiveness and aplomb with which she kicked the box, as if the world were tiny compared to the force of her will.

"Wait, *niña*!" he shouted. "If you're going to stay here you're going to need a *madrina*. A veteran of the trade to teach and protect you."

"I don't know any."

"Well, I do. Come," he said, springing to his feet. "I'm going to take you to a friend of mine. If you don't work out as a *puta*, maybe she'll keep you to help with the pigs and other chores."

Sacramento's friend was none other than this matron, Todos los Santos, who is now drinking her *mistela* with birdlike sips, sucking on her cigar like a Jewish man from Miami Beach, and delving into the past to reveal to me the particulars of a love story that is both bitter and luminous, like all love stories. The old woman tries to study me, but her eyes reflect the smoke from her Cigalia, clouding her gaze and condensing it into a milky opaqueness, and I now realize that Todos los Santos has cataracts and can't see me. She knows by heart the corner of the world that shelters her and she moves about it as if she can see, which makes me the only thing around her that she doesn't know by sight. So I move closer to her, speak right into her ear; she raises her hand, knotted with arthritis, and feels my face with the soft pats of an old dove that can no longer fly.

"*Ah, sí. Muy bien, muy bien,*" she approves, satisfied at making certain that my nose isn't missing and that I only have two eyes.

"*Mira, madre,*" says Sacramento, "the sun is setting."

"Yes, I see it, I see it!" she says enthusiastically and plunges her white eyes into the rosy air.

"The sky is turning red with specks of gold," he tells her.

"With specks of gold, you say? How pretty, how pretty! And as impressive and red as it is today, I'll bet there's a broad violet edge."

"Well, yes, more or less. If you really look at it, you can see a little violet."

"I knew it! And are there any birds flying across?"

"Four, five, six, seven . . . seven ducks flying north to south."

"Ay!" she sighs. "How I love the sunset."

I have been told that Todos los Santos was conceived by a cook and a landowner from Antioquia one Palm Sunday while the wife and children were waving dry palm leaves in solemn mass. Because of her beauty and the European whiteness of the skin she inherited from her father, she became a prostitute, following the path drawn from the instant of her conception.

"There was no place for me either in my father's house or in Medellín society. Bastard male children became peons on the haciendas and that took care of the problem," she tells me. "But with females it was more complicated. There were illegitimate daughters of landowners, like me, and then others that were called daughters of a slip who were the product of a well-bred girl's sin. The daughters of a slip had it worse, hidden in the cupboards of the big house or behind curtains, while we illegitimate girls grew up loose in the countryside, like little animals. When we were able to use our brains, some of us were buried alive with the cloistered nuns until adolescence, when a few accepted the habit and the rest did what I did, escaped the convent and landed in a bordello."

Clandestine paths, sometimes sweet and sometimes bitter, took her from love to love and from street to street until she reached the heavily brothel-ridden city of Tora, where she was so admired and desired in her youth and maturity that she was able to know, for moments, material well-being and even the glitter of fame and fortune. Without a hint of avarice, her beauty burned with a sublime, cunning fire, and guided by a scrupulous sense of pride and decorum, the moment she saw the first ugly signs of old age she moved into a period of discretionary retirement, which she didn't hesitate to interrupt, from time to time, each time her soul demanded satisfaction and her insides, heat. She was feared and recognized as a pioneer and founder of the barrio of La Catunga: the defender of the girls' rights against the Troco, the Tropical Oil Company, and its deputy, the Colombian government; the efficient *celestina,* the instructor of young novices; now close to blindness, to her centenary, and to the most impeccable poverty, she has been elevated to the category of sage and holy mother.

Today, the morning undulates innocent and warm and there is no trace of evil in this clear sky that Todos los Santos can't see but can guess, as she also guesses the pansies, the *caracuchos* and the *cayenos* that explode in reds, violets, and tongues of yellow fire. She says that more than hearing the ruckus the parrot is making in his cage, and the rainwater dripping into the cistern, she is longing for them. And the striated green of the croton leaves? She says yes, she sees it, that she keeps it very much alive and flowering in her mind's eye, just like each and every one of her memories.

She tells me that on that afternoon, when Sacramento appeared at her house with the aspiring *prostituta,* just one look at the wild and disheveled creature standing in front of her, half challenging and half imploring, was enough for her to recognize in the girl that singular mixture of helplessness and arrogance that fueled male desire better than any aphrodisiac, and since she knew from years of experience it was a virtue that was hard to find, she said that it was all right, she could stay, that she was going to put the girl to the test to see if she would work out.

When she limped onto the patio, Olguita, who had had polio, was surprised to see the scrawny novice that Todos los Santos had adopted, and thought that the *madrina* was losing her marbles, surely due to menopause.

"I've still got plenty of bleeding to do," Todos los Santos said, and asked Olguita why she thought the student was so lacking.

"She's a malnourished and wretched girl," replied Olguita, "and you're going to lose what's left of your money trying to save her from anemia."

"You don't have an eye. When this girl becomes a woman all the men are going to love her. There won't be one who can resist her. You'll see; it's just a question of applying some willpower and knowing how to wait."

Todos los Santos and Sayonara were brought together by chance, but they were united by urgency. They needed each other, like a fish needs the cloud that will later become water, for obvious and complementary reasons. To prosper in the pursuit of survival, Todos los Santos had everything except youth, and youth was the only thing the girl wasn't lacking.

"Work wasn't so good for me anymore and I often went around fearing that old age would drag me to the verge of starvation, because it's well known that no one can retire off of prostitution, if it's exercised honestly. When I saw her come through the door of my house, I had a whiff of intuition and knew that it was me, thirty years earlier, stepping across the threshold at that moment. Patience and a willing spirit, I told myself, because we're going to start all over again here, from the very beginning, as if the wheel were beginning to turn anew. Here comes love again with all its pains, which after everything is said and done are more tolerable than this nothingness that is bogging down my days. That's what I thought. And, in all frankness, I also thought: God is sending me what I have been asking Him for, the fount of my subsistence in this last stretch of life."

Todos los Santos served Sacramento a bit of lunch and dismissed him with a few coins.

"A few, no; seven coins exactly," corrects Sacramento. "They were ten-centavo coins, which in those days bore the image of a large-nosed and plumed Indian on one side. They burned in my hand like hot oil because they were the payment I received for selling an innocent into a life of vice. I felt myself falling and I thought it was my own profile, with a crown of feathers and a Judas nose, stamped onto the coins. No, señora, I told her, you don't have to give me anything, but she insisted with the justification that she was paying for the ride in my cart. It was the only money I had earned that morning and there was very little work available in the afternoons, so I speculated that if she was giving them to me for my honest work it was valid compensation, and that my conscience had no reason to be afraid."

Sacramento went out into the street without daring to look at the girl, and the heat of an afternoon drowned in its own light fell upon him with the full weight of guilt. He didn't see a soul around. The barrio had taken refuge in the dark, cooler interior of the houses for a siesta, and he, who had no house, consoled himself thinking that he was holding in his hand triple what he needed to ask for a cold beer in the bar across the street. He lost the impulse at the mere idea of abandoning the shade to cross the colorless fringe where the sun beat mercilessly and he sat down right there, on the ground, leaning against the door that had just closed behind him, his eyes fixed on the cool drops that were condensing on the bottle of beer the bartender was going to take out of the refrigerator when he gave her his money. But he kept his ears tuned to what might be happening inside Todos los Santos's house, where an ominous silence was vibrating, which he interpreted as a signal that the girl who wanted to be a *puta* had already been swallowed up by calamity.

The sting of regret attacked again and Sacramento thought he heard the voice of his conscience ordering him to renounce the wicked money. Terrified that he might be discovered in his secret act, like a dog hiding a bone, he scraped the earth with both hands until he had opened a hole and in it he buried the seven coins, one after the other. Once he had covered the hole he breathed with relief, now rid of the evidence of the crime; he squatted very still to slow the beating of his heart and hummed a popular song that lulled him to sleep. He tells me that he dreamed about the cold beer that another man, less punctilious than he, would be drinking at the bar across the way.

Meanwhile, in the house, alone now with the girl, Todos los Santos proceeded to roll up her sleeves, put on rubber gloves, and tie her hair back with a cord: the necessary preparation for a first-class skirmish.

"Well, then, let's begin your education," she announced in solemn initiation.

To tame the girl and give her some luster she had to start by pulling the hunger out of her, little by little, in a gradual, calculated nutritional plan that would take months, beginning with potato broth with parsley, followed by a mixture of oatmeal or pearl barley, and evolving gradually to green beans, lentils, and lima beans, because a creature that has learned to feed herself on air, like a bromeliad, can't be terrorized with sausage and tripe stew unless she's been carefully conditioned; otherwise she'll burst.

Todos los Santos served the girl some broth in a pewter cup and set it on the table with a piece of bread. Without waiting for it to cool or using a spoon, the girl guzzled it down and as soon as the señora had turned her back, she hid the bread in the pocket of her dress.

"I'm done," she announced. "I want more."

"Please, *madrina*, may I have another serving?" enunciated Todos los Santos in a didactic tone, inviting the proper formula.

"If you want another serving, go ahead, but give me some more."

Since a thorough bath was the next step to be imposed, Todos los Santos took the girl to the patio and stripped her: She was a frog, a cricket, an incredibly young kitten, dark and savage, her nose blocked with dried mucus and giving off a dense smell of smoke and loneliness. Cruz soap in hand, the señora attacked the lice crawling over the girl's head, and then, with suds and scouring pad, she started ridding the young body of the obstinate shell of ancient dirt that she wore like armor, until finally she appeared, dazed and blue, in the defenselessness of her tender skin. She chattered with cold as if she had just been born, alert and glistening as she dripped cool water like the threads of stars that appear at night in the reflection of a pool. There wasn't much of an inventory that could be made: a tumult of hair sprouting from her head, two skinny arms, two dark, elongated legs, two tiny hints of breasts, and a minimal sweetness of moss, pleated and secret, under her arms and between her legs.

"She was a bundle of scared chicken bones, anxious to find a connection to the world," says Todos los Santos. "I dried her with a towel, put a large cotton nightgown on her, and told her not to be afraid. 'I am going to treat you well,' I promised her."

"This dress is too big and ugly," protested the girl. "Give me a tight, shiny one, because I don't look like a *puta* in this one."

"What are you going to show off, tadpole?" retorted Todos los Santos. "Wait until you get a little flesh and then you can squeeze it into tight clothing."

The sun's edge had advanced, striking full upon the front of the house and falling mercilessly on the sleeping ball that was Sacramento, who awoke suffocated by the discomfort of a sweaty body and a dry mouth. If she wants to be a *puta*, let her, he thought, the devil with guilty consciences. He burrowed in the earth again and recovered his coins, but only six; the seventh had disappeared, swallowed by the dust. With his money in his pocket he crossed the street with determination and entered the bar.

"A good, cold beer," he asked in a man's voice, as he heard the first howl come from the house across the street.

Inside, the *madrina* was trying to get into the girl's hair strand by strand with an orthopedic comb with very close teeth, in order to eradicate any trace of knots or critters, and with each pull the girl shrieked, tried to bite the señora and wriggled away to take refuge under some piece of furniture. The *madrina* drove her back out with swats of a broom, grabbed her by the collar, and subjected her again to the torture until the girl bit her again and the struggle recommenced. When Sacramento and the owner of the bar decided to enter Todos los Santos's house, they found both women staring at the ceiling, vanquished and exhausted, and reigning over them, unconquered like a corsair's flag, the black mane still filled with its crop of lice.

"Sacramento had a cruel childhood and Olguita believes for that reason one must try to understand him," Todos los Santos tells me, "but I say to her that she'd better not come to me with speeches about psychology, because lots of people have come around here lately to see if I have been traumatized by this prostitution business, and I've sent them all packing. Blessed Sacramento, I say to Olga, he had a difficult childhood, but the rest of us didn't have one or even know what it was."

One afternoon when he isn't present, the *madrina* tells me that Sacramento was born one day to a girl in the neighborhood who left him in the care of some friends while she traveled to the coast to settle accounts with the man who had deserted her. Since she never came back, the infant was raised from house to house and from one woman's arms to another's, like so many other children that belong to everyone and to no one, until the Franciscan monks arrived in Tora to evangelize. They opened the only school in the barrio and accepted him as an errand boy and kitchen helper and gave him a scholarship.

"This was a land where the normal thing was to be a *puta,* and to be an *hijo de puta*—the son of a *puta*—was the logical and painless consequence," Todos los Santos informs me. "Sacramento would have grown up as sad or as happy as anyone else if the monks hadn't taken it upon themselves to convince him of his shame."

"To remind him of his origins they goaded him, calling him *hijo de* La Catunga or *hijo de los callejones,* son of the alleys, and when he turned seven years old they christened him with the name Sacramento," adds Olga.

Sacramento was the name they gave all the bastard children, dousing them with baptismal water and condemning them to that distinction, which couldn't be erased because it had been inflicted in a solemn blessing. The illegitimacy remained stamped on their birth certificates, on their *cédulas de ciudadania*—the official government-issued identity cards—and on their military cards, but people arranged to ignore these and various other punishing scars. According to Christian tradition, the priests baptized any child with a string of three or more names and they did the same with the bastards—Juan Domingo Sacramento, Sacramento Luis del Carmen, and Evelio del Santo Sacramento—and that made it easier for others, out of compassion, to remove the punitive moniker and to call them just Domingo, Luis del Carmen, Evelio, and so on. But this Sacramento, the cart man, ended up with the hard luck of being given only that name, or if it was accompanied by others, they were no longer remembered, and because of that he was the only *hijo de* La Catunga whom the entire barrio called by that name, Sacramento, which was the same as calling him *hijo de* La Catunga, or *hijo de los callejones.*

As if that punishment weren't enough, the Franciscans filled his soul with a horror of the sins of the flesh and with a visceral mistrust of women, above all of his *puta* of a mother, who had abandoned him to chase after her instincts, like a lowly animal. Some time later the monks left Tora, and Sacramento, who ended up in the streets, had to accept the coarse and spontaneous tenderness with which the women of La Catunga offered him a bowl of soup, cured a wound with gentian violet or a sore throat with methylene blue, let him sleep at the foot of their beds, taught him sad love songs, and terrorized him with ghost stories. They did the same, out of maternal instinct, generous and indiscriminate, for all of the many boys and girls who roamed the barrio in need of affection and were unsure of their parentage. And so the boy grew up with twisted thoughts, troubled about work, tortured, loving what he hated and hating what he loved, always finding a spur for the turmoil boiling in his head, where adoration and gratitude toward the women was mixed with a painful rancor for their many sins and deep down a chronic incapacity to forgive them.

I asked Sacramento if by chance he remembered what had happened to the infamous coins. Of course he remembered; the most minute, decisive details are the last things lost by our memory.

"The first one was swallowed by the earth," he told me.

"That I already know."

"With the second and third I paid for the beer I never drank, because the shouting made me return to Todos los Santos's house. I put the other four in my pocket, but the girl looked so humbled, so gentle in that shirt that looked like a straitjacket, that I thought it was only fair to give her at least half of what was left of the profit, so I gave her two coins, which she accepted without question. I kept the last two, which got mixed up with others that a man gave me that same afternoon for moving some things, a little extra work that came to me."

Then I asked Sacramento if he had ever gone back to look for the buried coin. He laughed with surprise and said it had never even occurred to him, but he was piqued by the idea and twenty minutes later we were in front of a storehouse that had been built on the lot that had belonged to Todos los Santos. An entire lifetime had passed from the day when Sacramento's minuscule treasure had been buried, and although the houses and people had changed, the street was still the same: a narrow passageway with no sewer or pavement. With a garden trowel, we began to scrape around the spot where he calculated the door had been. We removed dirt in no particular hurry, he for a while and then I, conversing in the meantime, very conscious that we were wasting our time. Several bottle caps turned up, and a rusted nut, a casing that looked like it was from a bullet, pieces of glass and rubber, and some other foolishness. And then, suddenly, a ten-centavo coin appeared, one of the ones with an Indian head that had stopped circulating a long time ago.

From that moment on Sacramento looked at me differently. In his eyes appeared a hint of perplexity and suspicion that I think made the existence of this book possible, because from then on he didn't dare keep any secrets from me, as if I were a sibyl and knew everything before he told me. Of course, I didn't want to take advantage of the situation to pry information from him, so I told him not to give too much importance to what had happened, that we had just found an old coin and it probably wasn't his. He didn't look at me with disappointment, as I had expected, but with incredulity and something close to anger.

"This is my coin," he assured me. "I would recognize it anywhere."

Faced with his emphatic tone, I had to admit my flippancy and ask for forgiveness. Then I tried to explain that I had invited him to look for the coin because those of us who make a living by writing live for the hunt of minute coincidences and subtle proofs that reassure us that what we write is, if not necessary, at least useful. Because it responds to currents that flow beneath what is ordinarily apparent, currents that turn back upon themselves and twist fate in circles. I also told him that a blind poet named Jorge Luis Borges believed that every casual meeting is an appointment. The more I talked, the more I got tangled up and the more magical my words seemed, and he listened to them, hypnotized, as if they were being spoken in some archaic tongue. Afterward, with the passing days and interminable conversations, during which he told me his whole life story, and I, something of mine, a sort of serene confidence developed between us that dispelled the magic in favor of friendship. But there was something that Sacramento never lost after that episode: the conviction that literature is a means for conjuring and that it can reveal secret clues. He, who had been anything but a reader, began to become interested in books.

two

 Todos los Santos arranged for the girl to sleep on a straw mattress spread out beside her own bed. Before she lay down to sleep she turned off the light in the bedroom and checked to make sure that the perpetual candle was burning in its red glass holder beneath the picture of the Sagrado Corazón de Jesús. Just as she had always done and would keep on doing, she tells me, until the day she dies.

Colombia is known as the country of the Sacred Heart. He is our patron saint and in that capacity has tinged our collective spirit and our national history with the same romantic, tormented, and bloody condition. The only common element in all of the homes of the poor in Colombia — it was removed from the houses of the rich a few generations back — is the image of this Christ who looks you in the eyes with doglike resignation while he shows you his heart, which isn't found inside his body as one would expect, but has been extracted and is held in its owner's left hand, at chest level, beneath a carefully tended chestnut beard. But it's not an abstract heart, rounded, in a pretty rose color and of a less than remote likeness to the original, as it appears in Valentine's messages. The one our Christ displays is an impressive organ, throbbing, a proud crimson, with a stunningly realistic volume and design. A true butcher's prize, with two disturbing attributes: From the top a flame is burning, while the middle is encircled by a crown of thorns that draws blood.

The girl couldn't sleep a wink in that foreign, unfamiliar room filled with unknown smells. She uncovered herself, then covered up again, unable to find a comfortable position. She felt besieged by the presence of that kind and mutilated young man who never stopped looking at her from the wall, and on whose face the candle cast dancing shadows and reflections of bloodletting. In her own bed, Todos los Santos was uncomfortable with the heat of a fitful and choking sleep, until without warning she began to snore with a sudden bubbling of mucus only to then completely suspend breathing altogether, without releasing her breath inward or outward for an entire minute, her throat closed by a plug of still air, two minutes, three, until the girl was convinced she had died. Then it returned, like waves on the ocean, that rhythmic snoring . . .

"*Madrina*," the girl dared to call out, "*madrina*, that man scares me."

"What man?" asked Todos los Santos, half asleep.

"The one with the beard."

"That's not a man, it's Christ. Trust in him. Ask him to watch over your sleep."

Trust in the enemy? She'd rather die. Maybe if she didn't look at him . . . she covered her head with the pillow and closed her eyes, but she immediately guessed that Christ had stopped smiling and was making horrendous faces at her. Uncovering her eyes quickly, she tried several times to catch him in the act, but he was clever and never let her. He smiled at her, the hypocrite, and no sooner than she had closed her eyes, he began to threaten her again with evil faces.

"*Madrina*, Christ is making faces at me."

"Hush, child. Let me sleep."

The girl put the pillow where her feet had been, turned on her mattress, and lay with her face toward the other wall, which had no portraits. But the palpitations of the candle reached even the far wall, wavering in slowly burning veils. Despite her struggles to stay alert, waves of sleep began to cloud her eyes. From time to time she turned quickly, to keep Christ under control, but he only looked at her with that melancholy smile and with his wounded heart in his hand.

"*Madrina*, don't you think it hurts?"

"Hurts?"

"Christ, don't you think his heart hurts?"

Then Todos los Santos got up and, blowing out the candle, made Christ disappear. With him went the red shadows and the sad smiles, and at last, in the darkness of the calm room, the two women slept soundly.

The sun came up very early and began marking the days of a new existence for both of them. The girl began not only to lose her fear of Christ, but to approach him with a strange familiarity and an attempt at dialogue that to Todos los Santos seemed theatrical and excessive.

"You must pray, child, but not too much," she recommended.

One day when she was cleaning the image of the bleeding Jesus with a feather duster, she found wedged between the canvas and the frame several small, strange lumps, like tiny cocoons but made of paper. She decided to unravel one and was half startled, half amazed to see that it was covered with a tight, microscopic writing that she decided to try to read with a magnifying glass. But she found no legitimate letters there, no known alphabet, just scribbling, elongated in some places, flat in others, but always with a lot of curlicues.

"Come here," she called out to the girl. "Can you explain this to me?"

"They are messages that I write."

"To whom?"

"To the man with the beard."

"I've told you that's Christ."

"To Christ, then."

"And what kind of writing is this?"

"One that he knows how to understand."

"You never went to school?"

"No."

"You don't know how to write like other people?"

"No."

"I'm going to start teaching you right now. Get a pencil and some paper."

Many tense and fatiguing hours were dedicated to reading and writing lessons with the square-ruled notebook that Todos los Santos used to keep accounts, with an old chart they bought at the apothecary, with a number-two Mirado pencil, and with disastrous results. The girl looked around the room, she rocked nervously in her chair, she bit her fingernails and cuticles, she wouldn't concentrate for anything in the world. She had no idea, it seemed, what Todos los Santos, who was clenching her teeth in order not to lose control and give her a whack, was saying.

"Just teach me how to work, *madrina*. I can't waste any time."

"All in due time, now settle down and read here: The dwarf im-itates the mon-key."

"What dwarf?"

"Any dwarf, it doesn't matter."

Lunchtime came and the girl, who hadn't read a single syllable, was still asking about the dwarf, so Todos los Santos put off the lesson until the next day at the same hour and shut herself up in the kitchen to calm her nerves by peeling potatoes and chopping vegetables.

Everything changed one unforgettable afternoon when the *madrina* was drinking *mistela* with her disciples Machuca and Cuatrocientos while they gossiped about a famous debt between two neighbors that had erupted in gunfire. The girl was nearby, sitting on the floor, entertaining herself with pencil and paper, without anyone paying her any attention. Until one of the women realized that if they said "bullet," the girl would write "bullet" with large, clear, round letters; if they said "bank," she wrote "bank"; if they said "greedy," or "Ana" or "mandarin," she wrote that too.

"What!?" exclaimed Todos los Santos, taking the paper in her hands. "This is incredible! Yesterday you didn't know how to write and today you do . . ."

"Because yesterday I didn't want to and today I do."

Had Todos los Santos kept any of those invented, tight scribbles on little rolls of paper? I insinuate that perhaps the girl's initial disinterest in conventional writing had to do with an unnecessary duplication.

"Maybe she didn't need to learn, because in her own way she already knew . . . ," I say, then wonder whether I should have. I was the one who needed to learn: not to get on the wrong side of Todos los Santos.

"Don't think I didn't consider that," she responds. "Instead of forcing her, I should have learned her way of writing so we could have sent messages to each other, or better yet, to Christ, because no one else would have understood us."

Encouraged by the miracle of the sudden dominion over letters and taking care not to destroy her student's initiative and temperament, the *madrina* took upon herself the painstaking task of polishing the most offensive edges of the girl's rebelliousness. She trained the child in the healthy customs of brushing your teeth with ashes; saying good morning, good night, and thank you very much; listening patiently to the troubles of others and keeping her own quiet; taking sips of anise tea in a glass, pretending it was *aguardiente,* the strong licorice-flavored liquor; chewing cardamom seeds to freshen her breath; letting down her hair every day and brushing it in the sun to infuse it with warmth and brilliance.

The child, for her part, approached the lessons with the tenaciousness of a mule that surmounted any obstacle, with a few unyielding exceptions, such as using silverware, which her manual clumsiness converted into deadly weapons, or the habit of speaking loudly and stridently at any hour and on every occasion, including when she prayed.

"Sacred Heart of Jesus, I confide in you!" the girl shouted at the painting, overcome with fervor.

"Don't shout at him so, you'll make him lose his hair. My holy God, how this creature howls!" complained the *madrina*, who knew from personal experience the advantages of a discreet and velvety tone, although the habitual consumption of tobacco had turned hers gravelly.

She begged the girl to lower her voice, then she ordered and exhausted herself with chastisements, but it was beyond the girl's control, and despite all of her attempts, she continued bellowing and raising a ruckus like the vegetable sellers in the market.

"Let her have a taste of her own medicine," decided Todos los Santos. And she took the girl to a loud and imposing waterfall formed by the Río Colorado near Acandai. There she made the child recite at full volume the poem "La Luna" by Diego Fallon, until her voice could be heard over the roar of the water, with the hope of filing down her vocal cords a bit. The goal was to tire her of shouting, but she tired first of Diego Fallon, so her teacher familiarized her with Neruda's despairing song, Bécquer's dark swallows, Valencia's languid camels, and assorted pages of a popular collection of romances that was much in vogue at social gatherings in La Catunga.

Day after day the girl made her voice rise over the sound of the cascade, which was polishing it in tune with the musical scale and modulating its diverse gradations of volume. Once, Todos los Santos opened the book to a certain poem by Rubén Darío and indicated for the girl to begin her exercises by reading it at the top of her voice. It was about a princess who steals a star from the sky.

"Isn't this princess Santa Catalina, our protectress?" asked the girl excitedly.

"Don't get off track. This is a book of poems, not prayers. Don't confuse the earth with the sky, just keep on reciting."

"I can't, *madrina*, it's too beautiful."

"Nonsense. Give it to me," said the veteran, and she began reading about the king's great anger at the theft.

"You must be punished," brayed the sovereign. "Go back to the sky and what you have stolen you must now return."

"The princess grows sad over her sweet flower of light," Rubén Darío went on, "but then, smiling, good Jesus appears."

"From my fields I offered her that rose," clarified Jesus. "They are flowers for the girls who think of me in their dreams."

"I think this good Jesus is the same one who lives in our bedroom," said the girl. "He gave me a rose too the other day."

"Hush, you're mixing things up and making me lose the rhythm. Religion in excess makes good nuns and miserable *putas*," warned Todos los Santos.

"The princess is beautiful, because now she has the brooch in which verse, pearl, feather, and flower shine, along with the star," rhymed Rubén Darío. The girl was suddenly overwhelmed by a sighing that was foreign to her temperament and she moved away to cry. It was then that Todos los Santos discovered in her disciple an inclination for poetry and a fascination with sad stars that alarmed her and seemed to her a dangerous symptom in a promising apprentice of the most merciless profession known to man.

"It's not a game, child," she said. "Prostitutes, like boxers, cannot allow themselves a weakness or they'll get knocked out. Life is one thing and poetry is another; don't confuse shit with face cream."

When it became necessary to hasten the training of the girl's voice, the two women went to stand at the edge of the brand-new Libertadores highway, where ravaging progress entered Tora, and to subject themselves to the ultimate test of infernal noise that rose up to the heavens from the river of vehicles.

"Sailors kiss and then leave!" shouted the girl to the roar of the passing trucks that in their stampede almost tore off her clothing and left reduced to wind the already volatile sailors' love.

After such a din, when the girl returned home she appreciated being back amid the imperceptible sounds of silence, never before noticed: the faint song of the hummingbird, the whistle of light as it passes through the lock of a door, the buzzing of neighbors on the other side of the wall, the brushing of bare feet against the patio tiles. She had managed to break the tyranny of noise and in recompense was given the calming gift of intimacy, which allows one to pray in secret, to hum boleros, recite sonnets, and whisper phrases in someone's ear with the purr of a stuffed toy tiger.

"That's better," said Todos los Santos. "Now you have the tone and you are ready to acquire the timbre. Your voice should sound like the great bell of the Ecce Homo. Listen to it. Look at it. The bell tower was built on top of the first derrick in Tora's oil field. Listen to it now as it calls to Ángelus, and tomorrow also when it rings the morning prayers. Listen to it always because that is how your voice should sound, deep and tranquil, just like the great bell in your pueblo."

"But, *madrina*," objected the girl, "this isn't my pueblo."

"But it will be, as soon as your voice sounds like its great bell."

Also arduous was the challenge imposed upon them by the girl's chronic skinniness, which was like that of a malnourished cat, because the more she ate the thinner she looked for her size, with hollow cheeks, scanty bust, and inordinately long extremities. Todos los Santos maintained that all of the food the girl ate went to her hair, which, at the expense of the rest of her body, grew robust and out of control, and if she were to cut it she would gain the pounds it had snatched from her.

"It's alive," said Olguita, enthralled, as she combed it into braids. "And I think it bites."

They knew that cutting it would be a hideous crime, so they decided instead to force its owner to consume a double ration of soup, bread, and fruit, one for her and the other for her hair, which in all honesty was the only party that benefited from the overeating and ended up becoming a cascade of dark, murmuring waters.

"Since God limited you to such poverty of flesh, you have no other choice but to study dance," recommended Todos los Santos, resolved to find a way out by another means, and she revealed the secrets of a certain dance that wasn't performed with footsteps, wiggling, or shaking hips but with undulation, absences, and stillness. She told the girl that

Salomé had managed to bewitch John the Baptist because she knew the magic of moving without movement.

The girl embraced those words, never needing to have them repeated, and surprised her teacher with the engrossed naturalness with which she let herself sway with a deep, measured rhythm that wasn't *cumbia* or merengue, but the ebb and flow of her own blood along the clandestine paths of her body.

"I enjoyed watching her dance," Todos los Santos tells me. "And at the same time it terrified me, because I understood then that we were losing her. Only when she danced did she give herself license to visit the land of her own memories and to escape into the enormity of the vault that was inside her. She danced and I knew she was swimming in distant waters, as if visiting other worlds, perhaps worse, or perhaps better."

Perhaps worse or perhaps better, but never shared. From the beginning it was obvious that the young girl was no friend of commentary or gossip, even less so if it were about her, and that she maintained the hermeticism of a statue about her past, which made one think of the painful or guilt-ridden reasons that caused her to hide it. When they asked her where were you born, what is your name, how old are you, she slipped away with nonanswers into a silent void of memories, or sometimes just the opposite, she would overflow with words, filling the house with mindless chatter that was even more concealing than her muteness.

"Were you born yesterday?" asked Todos los Santos. "Spit out your past, child, or it will rot inside you."

That negation of memory made her the pure vibration of a present that burned in front of your eyes the instant that it was contemplated, like a scene illuminated by the flash of a camera. Although at times things escaped from her, now and then she would carelessly reveal little fragments.

"Do you like my new skirt?" asked Tana.

"Cecilia had one just like it," she said. "Except yellow, not green."

So they quickly asked her who Cecilia was, perhaps your mother, or an aunt, maybe a friend of your mother's? Can you answer us, for the love of God, who was Cecilia?

"What Cecilia?" was her reply, surprised at all the insistence, as if she had never uttered such a name.

One day an old client and lover of Todos los Santos asked for a date to say good-bye; tired of going daily to the offices of the Troco to collect a perpetually delayed payment for an accident, he had decided to leave for Antioquia to help his son start a coffee farm. It was an evocative and nostalgic occasion and Todos los Santos was busy exquisitely attending to her friend while the girl, wearing her oversized blouse, devoted herself to pestering Aspirina, Tana's dog, tying red ribbons around her ears, not paying any attention to the visit, or at least so it seemed, and without interrupting. Until at the end, when the gentleman was about to leave, she caught up with him at the door and stopped him.

"If somewhere you run across a woman from Guayaquil that they call La Calzones," she ventured, "tell her that her niece asked you to tell her that she's doing fine."

Just like that, like a cannon shot, Todos los Santos learned that her student was happy in La Catunga and that in some part of the country she had an aunt with a vulgar nickname, by which she deduced that the girl's vocation came to her by family tradition.

"That explains something," I tell her, "but not much. Really it explains almost nothing."

"That's right."

Not even during the hardest stages of training did the student give signs of defeat or weakening; she didn't complain, she didn't express pleasure or sadness, heat or cold, nor did she soften even one millimeter the military discipline she had imposed upon herself, as if responding to a sense of duty that was greater than she herself. Only once did she refuse to obey, when Todos los Santos asked her to clean the pigsty that was fairly buzzing with a horrendous stench at the rear of the house.

"I decided to became a *puta* so I wouldn't have to clean up *caca* ever again," grumbled the girl.

"Well, you made a mistake. You should know that here you will earn more from washing a gringo's laundry than from going to bed with a man. In order to survive, a woman of the profession must also apply herself as seamstress, cook, fortune-teller, and nurse, and she must not be repelled by any task that life imposes on her, no matter how humbling or difficult it may be. So go back and get the bucket and brush and make that patio clean as a whistle."

One night of supernatural clarity, Todos los Santos awoke in the middle of a coughing fit and, between gasps, asked for a glass of water. The girl didn't respond because she wasn't on her mattress but instead was sitting at the front door in her nightshirt and barefoot, framed in the moonlight and absorbed in the slow amazement descending from the highest abysses. Her perplexity was so deep, so vibrant that, touched, the *madrina* scoured the cellars of her memory looking for an explanation that had been with her a long time ago, before years and years of struggling and scratching for her daily bread had taught her to live without explanations.

"Up there in the sky, the seven planets spin and sing around the Earth," she said, pulling up a stool to sit beside the girl in the brilliant darkness. "The Moon, Mars, Mercury, Jupiter, Venus, Saturn, and the Sun. Each one has a corresponding musical note, a metal from the chart of elements, and a day of the week. The moon that robs you of your sleep is made of solid silver, whistles songs in the key of C, and reigns over Mondays. The great buzzing produced by the universe is what wise men call the music of the spheres, and the primary voice in this excellent concert is our Earth's."

"If that's true, why can't I hear it?"

"You do hear it, you were listening to it just now when I found you."

"What is our Earth singing?"

"A song of the wind, made with your breath and mine and that of all men and women, alive, dead, and yet to be born."

"We'd better go back inside, *madrina,* or all that tremendous wind will catch you and you'll start coughing again."

three

 I ask what had happened in Sacramento's life during all this time and they tell me that in the afternoons, after five o'clock, he would visit the girl and play with her.

"Play?" I ask. "Wasn't he a little old to be playing?"

"But he was just a boy . . ."

"You told me that by then he had been given his *cédula de ciudadanía.* He must have been at least eighteen."

"Yes, he had his *cédula,* but that doesn't mean anything. He got it four or five years early from some crooked politicians who falsify *cédulas* to get minors or nonexistent or dead people to vote for them in the elections."

Sacramento and the girl played barefoot with the other children in the dusty alleys of the barrio of the *putas.* London Bridge, hot potato, jump rope. But those traditional, organized games weren't their favorites; more than anything else they liked to play war. The girl was famous on the streets for being a rough-and-tumble scoundrel. There was no one more expert than she at executing flying kicks, spitting at a greater distance, throwing bone-crushing punches, knocking the wind out of someone with a fist to the solar plexus. Other handy diversions of

hers were urinating in jars, tormenting the enemy by putting chili powder in their eyes, and playing violent games of red rover.

"The heart of the pineapple is winding and winding, is winding and
winding, all the children are falling and falling," sings Sacramento, and
he's remembering and remembering. "It was called the heart of the
pineapple and it was a rough game that left everyone injured. And me?
The heart of the pineapple crushed my soul."

The heart of the pineapple was winding, the speeding chain of children holding hands, pressing tighter and twisting until it formed a
human knot, a true pineapple heart that squeezed and asphyxiated and
finally ended up with a pile of crushed children on the ground. One day
several older boys from another neighborhood joined the game and the
pineapple, devilish and frenetic, began to twist ankles and knock heads,
and more than one kid came out bruised from the crush. But the older
ones weren't there to play, they only incited the jumble and took advantage of the confusion to touch the girl, knocking her to the ground and
grabbing her hair to steal kisses and to lift her skirt. She defended herself with sharp jabs and dolphin kicks and had already managed to get
them off of her and to quickly escape, when Sacramento learned of the
offense and a surge of wounded dignity electrified his heart.

"At that moment I felt that the pain stabbing me was the strongest I
could ever know. Boy, was I wrong. It was a child's pain compared to
those that were to come."

"Over the years, Sacramento grew and filled out," tells Todos los
Santos, "but at the time he was just a skinny boy, a head shorter than the
girl, with wiry hair and sweet little eyes that inspired laughter and compassion. Without taking time to realize that the others were greater in
number and size, he rushed at them, avenger and executor of justice, and
he managed, of course, to be beaten to a pulp and left half broken."

"Why do you defend her," they shouted at him as they watched him
bleeding on the ground, "when she's just going to turn out to be a *puta*."

"That's work, stupid bastards. We were just playing!" he shouted in
a voice broken with tears that even to him sounded lamentably infantile,

and to try to turn around this sorry ending, he summoned up strength from his crushed pride and rushed at them again.

"He was lucky that the second time they knocked him down with a single blow and ran off."

Sacramento and the girl spent hours and hours on Todos los Santos's patio, busy stretching the last sunny days of their childhood, playing that they were already grown up and inventing and acting out episodes and dramas with dialogues, never-ending like life itself. You could say that they were growing up as they played being grown up, like when they decided to pretend to be brother and sister who were leaving home to travel around the world in search of fame and fortune, but first they had to have breakfast, let's pretend that this is bread and that's milk, bread, no, I was eating eggs for breakfast, now we have to pack the suitcases, you're the woman and you have to take care of that, no, you're the man, you take care of it and I'll sharpen our swords, let's pretend that these are your clothes, these are mine and this box is the trunk where we keep them, but before we go we have to give hay to our horses. These railings are our horses! Okay, but let's pretend that yours is sick with a tumor and we have to heal him with this bandage, and so on, and from one preparatory step to another the shadows of night were falling on the patio. Todos los Santos served them real bread and real glasses of milk, the game was over and the two adventurous siblings hadn't even crossed the threshold of their house.

Todos los Santos started to notice that some of her clothes were missing, first stockings, then handkerchiefs embroidered with her initials, then a short-sleeved blouse, then some other article.

"In which trunk have the traveling brother and sister put my silk stockings?" she grew tired of asking, and as they swore that they hadn't seen her stockings, pillowcases and hand towels began to disappear.

One morning, as she was cleaning the kitchen, Todos los Santos perceived a strong, rancid odor whose origin she couldn't pinpoint no matter how diligently she rummaged through boxes looking for rotten food and moved furniture to see if it was coming from dead mice. The following day the odor was even more intense and the *madrina* stood up on a stool to clean off the top shelves, from which she took down a reeking basket filled with dirty rags. Rags that weren't rags; they were her lost stockings, her blouses, her pillowcases, and her handkerchiefs, twisted into knots, wadded up and stained with dried blood.

"Girl, come here!"

"What happened now, *madrina*?"

"What is this?"

"Who knows?"

"This is the clothing that I was missing."

"How nice that you found it."

"Who stuffed it up there all dirty?"

"You probably did and you just don't remember," said the girl as she scurried away.

"Girl, come here!"

"Yes, *madrina*?"

"Tell me why this clothing is stained with blood."

"Because of a cut I have on my arm that bleeds a lot."

"Show it to me."

"It's already healed now, *madrina*. It was here, on my knee."

"Wasn't it on your arm?"

"One on my knee and another on my arm."

"But you don't have any scabs or scars . . ."

"It was a pretty small cut."

"Then why did it bleed so much . . . ?"

"It was very deep, I think."

"Could it have been a bullet wound?"

"More likely from a knife, a very sharp one . . ."

"Did you get it in the war? Or was it the police?"

Then the girl covered her face and moved away to cry and Todos los Santos, after closing the kitchen door to be alone with her, sat the girl on her lap and began to repeat the same complicated saga about the pollination of flowers that she herself had heard from the nuns dozens of years earlier and under similar circumstances, with the protagonist of a bee who buzzed around a rose to accomplish an incomprehensible and loving mission, in the midst of a great anatomical mixing of stamens, corollas, and pistils, until by some miracle of God, who is merciful, finally, at the end of all this dancing, a beautiful peach was born.

"God's baby or the bee's?" asked the girl.

"The bee and the flower's baby. Something like that is happening to you. Now do you understand? That's why you shouldn't feel ashamed about your blood or hide it in a basket as you have done, even though they tell you it stains and poisons. What you have to do is collect it every month in some little cloths that I will give you and show you how to wash with warm water so they won't smell bad, and you shouldn't worry because it's something natural that happens to all women. Do you understand?"

"Yes, *madrina*," said the girl, starting to cry again, but this time with more momentum.

"Then why are you crying?"

"It hurts, *madrina*, every time the blood comes out. My insides burn. Do you think I'm injured inside? Do you think the bee you were talking about got inside me and stung me there, inside? That's what it feels like, *madrina*, like a wasp sting."

"It's a wound that opens in all women once a month and that never heals because it's a wound of love. But you'll see, when you start going with men, how much happiness the red roses inside you will bring you every time they appear, because it will be the signal that you aren't pregnant. I can already see you, like the others, counting the days that your blood is late in staining your clothes."

"Does it happen to men too?"

"No. It is God's will that it only happens to women. That's why we love more, too, because our insides hurt."

"Like Jesus' heart?"

"Yes. Just like that."

Then the girl stopped crying, wiped her nose on her sleeve, and went back out to the patio to resume playing brother and sister, who were now facing the problem of not having any blankets for the tremendously cold nights they would encounter on their long journey, and from that day forward the sister adventurer could look for fame and fortune without panicking at the onset of her menstrual cycle, which was no longer a sin that had to be hidden on the top shelf, and she learned how to use white cloths that she washed later in warm water, scrubbed with a pumice stone and hung to dry in the sun, knowing that if she ever had a daughter, she would calm her by patiently explaining the mystery of how the blood that appears in her underwear, which is the bee's blood, makes it possible for fruit to be born from a flower.

"Do you remember the treasure chest?" Todos los Santos asks Sacramento.

Frequently the two children would entertain themselves with a cookie box that they called the treasure chest. It contained a delightful collection of items such as broken necklaces, buttons, loose stones, old brooches, and fairy-tale earrings, and it made the children's eyes shine with sparkles of emerald green, ruby red, French pink, depending on the color of the beads they were looking at.

"How wonderful!" exclaimed the girl, completely absorbed, and she would begin to tell Sacramento lies, as big as a house, that he would pretend to believe.

"She made up that the box contained the jewels that Santa Catalina had been given by her father the king, and she made me promise that I would defend them with my life, property, and honor against anyone who tried to steal them."

Sacramento swore on his knees, she tapped him on the shoulder a couple times with a sword that was really a stick and named him Knight of the Order of the Holy Diamond. He was ashamed that the older kids would see him playing like that and he wouldn't let her name him a knight unless there were no witnesses; after all, he was already a man who worked and supported himself and he found that game—like so many things of hers—shamefully simple. Poor Sacramento, he never suspected that that title would be, by a long shot, the most honorable that he would ever have bestowed upon him in his life.

"To have been named Knight of the Order of the Holy Diamond by her . . . ," he says to me, "I think when I die that will be the best memory I leave behind."

four

 I've been told that a miracle prevented the infidels from sawing in half, with a cogged wheel, Santa Catalina virgin and martyr, and that they had to limit themselves to decapitating her and were unable to stem the flow of milk that ran from her wounds instead of blood, nor the curative aroma exhaled by her bones for the benefit of the sick who happened to be nearby. I've also been told that the anniversary of this horrifying episode is the date favored by the *mujeres* of La Catunga for being initiated into their professional life, their baptism by fire, as they themselves call it. I have noticed that prostitution promotes tendencies and fixations similar to those that in other instances I have observed in *sicarios* from communes in Medellín, truck drivers who have to pass through regions of *violencia*, the *bazuco* dealers on Calle del Cartucho in Bogotá, mafiosos, judges, witnesses, bullfighters, guerrillas, antiguerrilla commandos, and so many other Colombians who risk their lives on a routine basis. To begin with, they all wear one or several medals featuring the Virgen del Carmen, whom they familiarly call La Mechudita because of her thinness, her wit, and her characteristic long hair, and whom they venerate as the patron saint of difficult professions.

Like the others, the *mujeres* of La Catunga know that those who fully embrace their profession risk their skin; unlike others, the *mujeres* know that they also risk their souls. Hence the meticulous, manic way in which they perform self-imposed purifying rituals, hence the importance that they bestow upon a saint like Catalina; they, who in some dark way also become martyrs, yield to tragedy and accept the notion of life as a sacrifice.

Four months remained before the celebration of the fiestas of Santa Cata, just enough time to round out the girl's education in love. But, as I had heard said so many times in Tora, man proposes and hunger imposes. Todos los Santos's savings, which were diminishing, wouldn't last until the date she had set for the girl's initiation into the profession. So Todos los Santos decided to force her hand and release the artist into the game while she was still a little wet behind the ears, short on training, unpredictable in conduct, and psychologically immature.

"You don't make a man fall in love with you through gymnastics in bed or tricks in the bedroom," was her first strictly professional lesson. "Leave that to those who don't have other skills. What you should do is spoil him and console him as only his mother ever has."

One midnight in La Catunga, with the song of the cicadas particularly intense, a council of advisers was assembled at Todos los Santos's house. Over *mistelas*, Pielroja cigarettes, and sweet *pastelitos de gloria* they argued without reaching agreement on any of the details of the mise-en-scène. The greatest polemic centered around the choosing of the girl's *nombre de guerra*, which in this case would also have to serve as her Christian name, because she swore she didn't remember having been baptized.

"At least tell us what they called you before you came here," said Tana the Argentine, a veritable rattle of bracelets and necklaces, given to her by her lover, an engineer for the company.

"They didn't call me anything," she lied, or perhaps she was confessing true abandonment.

What she did tell them was that she would like to be called La Cal-zones, the underwear girl, in homage to her aunt, for whom she seemed to profess some admiration or affection.

"Over my dead body!" shouted Todos los Santos. "I have never heard a name so coarse and devoid of style."

"But if that name brings the girl good memories," Olguita dared to venture, her nature made velvety by the polio that had withered her legs.

"Good memories don't exist. All memories are sad," Todos los Santos said, ending the discussion.

"Let's call her María, Manuela, or Tránsito, for God's sake, they were all important women and heroines in novels," proposed Machuca, the blasphemer, who was a high school graduate with a diploma, and a devoted reader.

"What does that have to do with anything? None of them had to offer up their asses."

"Well, if that's the requirement, then call her Magdalena."

"Don't even mention that renegade, first she sinned, then she spent the rest of her life crying with regret."

"Then what about Manón or Naná, who made history in Paris?" suggested Machuca, her mouth watering.

"Paris and Tora can't be mentioned on the same day."

"Why not Margarita, then?"

"Margaritas also cry too much. And they fall in love with money, and die spitting blood. I tell you, names of flowers bring bad luck."

"Well, Flor Estéves, who was my aunt on my father's side," offered Delia Ramos, "was said to have found heaven in a sailor's love."

"Sailors kiss, then they leave," Todos los Santos recited the only line of poetry her memory had retained.

"Rosa la Rosse always sounded so sweet to me . . . ," sighed Olguita. "I would have loved to have been called that. But I got tangled up in this profession without realizing it and when I opened my eyes I was already a consecrated *puta* and they just kept calling me Olguita, like when I was good. They say that God doesn't forgive those who work under the names they were baptized with. They say it sullies the holy name and takes it in vain."

"God has gotten so old and he still hasn't stopped inventing sins."

"It doesn't do me any good to give you ideas, if you don't pay any damn attention," said Machuca testily, but she tried again anyway. "Call her Filomena, who was the winner in a tournament of beautiful breasts."

"Maybe that Filomena had hers very much in order," interjected Delia Ramos, "but on this child they're barely showing, and you can tell that as an adult they'll sprout scant and pointed, like a Turkish slipper."

"I heard about an incredibly extraordinary *puta* who was called Cándida . . . ," mused Olguita.

"Don't even think about it," said Machuca. "That Cándida deserves a place among the gods of Olympus for bearing eternal torture chained to a bed, like Prometheus to his rock. Cándida is a myth of sublime flight and this poor little girl of ours is nothing more than a vile mortal."

"You read so many books and invent so many beautiful things," said Tana to Machuca, "and just look at the sad name you've got."

"I use it because that's what a poet I once loved called me," said the latter in self-defense, then became lost in the shadows of days gone by.

They got tangled up in meditations without reaching a satisfactory solution and instead ended up postponing other urgent decisions, like fixing the fee and selecting the corresponding color of lightbulb in accordance with the standing hierarchies and conventions in La Catunga. The girl was as copper-colored and Indian-looking as the *pipatonas*, and according to that she should have been accorded a minimal remuneration, but Todos los Santos aspired to the highest destiny for her student and she wouldn't resign herself to condemn the girl to a lowly white lightbulb.

"It can't be," she lamented. "With those beautiful almond eyes she's got, like a Japanese princess's!"

"That's it." From the haze of her *mistelas* Delia Ramos saw the light.

"Japanese! Let her be the only Japanese girl in this red-light district, and that way she can charge an exclusive fee."

"Such nonsense! The Japanese are yellow like chickens . . ."

"It doesn't matter, nobody around here would know the difference because they've never seen one."

"Besides, coloring can be lightened with rice powders . . ."

"But she doesn't speak Japanese."

"And you think, mother, that these French women of ours speak French? If they ever knew it, they forgot it a long time ago. And nobody complains; after all, the profession has a universal language."

Olguita suggested the name Kimono, the only word she knew in Japanese, and Delia Ramos came up with another possibility:

"I say that it would be best to call her Tokyo."

"What's that?"

"A big city in Japan."

"It won't do, it'll scare off the gringo clientele."

"Despite everything, Tokyo sounds very good to me."

"In that case Kyoto would be better."

"Why not Sayonara?"

"Kimono or Sayonara," declared Todos los Santos. "Either of the two would work."

"Sayonara is more beautiful, it means good-bye."

"Good-bye forever?" sighed Delia Ramos tragically, already drunk.

"It just means good-bye."

"Let the girl choose."

Without even thinking about it, the girl chose Sayonara and from then on she clung to that word, which she had never heard before, as if in it she had finally found the stamp of her identity.

"Then let it be Sayonara. Sayonara. You will no longer be the girl, but Sayonara," they approved unanimously, and there descended over them, leaving their hair gray, that drizzle of soot that falls from the ceiling every time a childhood ends before its time.

"Four months," said Delia Ramos between hiccups. "Only four months and she would have been an adult."

"It's all the same," said Todos los Santos, "four months more or less. Which of us didn't start too early? Childhood doesn't exist, it's a luxury invented by the rich."

Today, despite her eyes being bathed in clouds, Todos los Santos tells me she can see with perfect clarity that upon adopting that name with the flavor of good-bye, Sayonara unknowingly—or perhaps she did know it—sealed her own fate and that of all of La Catunga.

On one thing Todos los Santos, Olguita, Delia Ramos, Tana, and Machuca did agree that night, which was to select señor Manrique as the girl's first client, the one who would initiate her in the profession prior to her social and official presentation at the Dancing Miramar. He was a soft, kind man of some fifty years, all reverence and old-fashioned courtesies, one of those who breaks bread with his hands so he won't have to plunge a knife into it. He worked as the quartermaster general of the commissary at the Troco, where he earned a good living, and visited the *chicas* of La Catunga every night to have eventual and insignificant sex with them, dispersed among dozens of games of dominoes, imperative, long, and impassioned.

"What do you think, girl? After all, you are the interested party . . ."

"I don't care."

Señor Manrique would have been accepted unanimously if a bilious blonde named Potra Zaina hadn't planted a tempting worry at the last moment:

"Let her first time at love be with Piruetas, he really knows how to dance and make a woman feel alive."

None of them, not even Todos los Santos, was immune to the difficult charms of Piruetas, who came in and out of their lives with a dancer's agile moves. Unpredictable, incomprehensible, slick, he made them all suffer with his snubs; from all of them he obtained benefits of bed and kitchen in exchange for gazes from his lying eyes; they all loved him without charging him a peso so that he, in return, would teach them tango steps and the latest pirouettes in the dancing salons of Pereira and the capital.

"Hey, Piruetas!" they would shout competitively at him when they saw him pass, a figure of ambiguous temperament, malevolent hat, and patent-leather shoes. "Slay me with those eyes! Come, love, show me a new number, one of the ones only you know."

"*Prostitutas*, like bullfighters, try to ease sorrows with superstitions," Todos los Santos assures me. "One of their many beliefs says that the man who breaks a woman in marks her life from then on. That's why the selection of the first client was a delicate matter and why a melancholy man would be rejected, for example, or a glutton or a sick man. All the pains, of the body and the soul, are transmitted through the sheets."

"Piruetas for Sayonara?" shot Tana. "Don't even think about it, he's a fancy man who plays crooked."

"Life is short and you have to know how to enjoy it, and we aren't going to condemn the girl to bitterness by starting her out with a tattered old man," interjected Machuca.

"On the contrary, she shouldn't become accustomed to thinking work is idleness and the salary is enjoyable, because later there's no way to rid her of the habit."

"Who said such foolishness! If she is going to live off of her body, then let her at least shake it out and enjoy it. Sanctimoniousness will only bring you communion wafers!"

"Death is always crouching somewhere and the trick is to discover where before it lashes out at you." Todos los Santos uttered those somber words and the other women didn't understand what they had to do with anything. "I'll say just one thing: In this barrio death dances around, so very slyly, in Piruetas's shoes."

An uncomfortable silence descended and the women pressed against one another, seeking the antidote to that shivering thought.

"I am not one to prohibit the girl from dealing with Piruetas," continued Todos los Santos. "You all know that for years he has been in and out of my bed as he chose. He casts his net over all of us and sooner or later she too will have to feel the brush of his effeminate fingernails, sparkling with polish. But it's preferable that it be later rather than sooner."

The dawn fell thick with humidity and shrouded in the screaming of seagulls over the gentleness of the river, and the girls went each one to her own home, grateful along the way for the existence of affable men like Manrique, who soften the ominous fascination that they all, without exception, felt toward cruel men like Piruetas.

When he learned that the girl's hour had arrived, and that the chosen *novio* for her first time was old Manrique, Sacramento's spirit crashed to the ground and shattered into a thousand pieces.

"So even then you loved her?" I ask.

"Loved her, no. Love, what people call love, not sleeping at night or eating during the day thinking about a woman, señorita Claire inspired something like that in me, always solitary even when she was accompanied, with that mystery of hers, made of dark circles under her eyes and pale skin under her dress. Or señora Machuca, with her thirty years of life so well lived that there was nothing beautiful or ugly in this world left for her to discover. Or even Olguita, so compassionate, her legs useless, like a mermaid, who half frightened me and half fascinated me with those steel orthopedics pressing against her flesh. I loved and desired all of them until I was crazy and even beyond. But the girl? No one falls in love with a wild-haired, slippery, surly tadpole. At that time she was to me something worse and much stronger than love. She was the pain of my conscience."

Since he knew about señor Manrique, Sacramento was attacked by a frenzy of labor that was incomprehensible to the neighbors who always caught him taking a siesta in the shade of some tree and who now saw him slaving away under the broiling sun like a mad ant, thumping his cart along the streets of the pueblo from dawn well into night to carry cans of gasoline from the docks to the sawmill and lumber from the sawmill to the docks, to carry recently arrived travelers from the train station to the Hotel Pipatón and travelers about to depart, from the

Hotel Pipatón to the train station, to haul cement or bricks to construction sites, cans of water to the higher barrios, sacks of rice and grain from the river to the cooperative and from the cooperative to the Troco's kitchens. They even saw him dragging up to the peak of Cristo del Pronto Alivio sick people who were going there to beg for their health and the recently healed who were going to give thanks for the miracle of their healing. At the end of a week of maximum output he presented himself in Todos los Santos's house with his pockets filled with coins, which he dumped on the table in the kitchen.

"I have come to pay for the girl's thing."

"What thing?"

"Her first night of love."

Olguita, Tana, Machuca, Delia Ramos, all of them had gathered to prepare tamales for the leper colony bazaar, with corn *masa* and pork wrapped tightly in banana leaves, then tied with string, and they all stiffened with their hands in the *masa* when they saw the boy's expression of pathetic solemnity as he delivered his capital; the wind of life or death ruffling his hair; the lyric tenor's ardor with which he had burst onto the scene of tamale preparation, trying to prevent the inevitable by presenting his petition; his delicate supplication that broke into stammering when the chuckling started and he saw the women doubled up with laughter over the yellow corn flour, and their laughter slid like liquid fire through his ears, ulcerating his body inside, burning even more because of the presence of his idolized Claire, who wasn't making tamales with the others, of course, but was sitting there in the background painting her fingernails killer red, and who, like the others, threw the boiling flood of her laughter in his face.

"Come here, my precious child," said Machuca, still shaking from the hilarity of it, crushing his face against her soft breasts. "This boy is worth his weight in gold."

"Such beautiful curly eyebrows!" said Olguita, kissing his eyes. "When he grows up he's going to be a considerate man, God bless him."

Once again able to be serious, Todos los Santos gathered up the coins on the table, put them in a paper bag, took some more coins from her savings drawer, and put them in the bag too.

"Take this," she said to Sacramento, giving him the bag. "Take the girl to the movies. Buy some chocolates and cotton candy, you'll have more than enough there."

The two kids went to the movies together and saw a few westerns in which a riled-up John Wayne didn't leave an Indian standing. But when they got back to Todos los Santos's house, Sacramento said he didn't want to go inside and stubbornly insisted on saying good-bye at the door.

"I'm leaving Tora, girl," he announced. "I am going to sign up as a *petrolero* to come back bronzed by the sun, shaggy and with a lot of money, so the *mujeres* of La Catunga won't ever laugh at me again."

"Okay," she said, "we were going far away; I was going to be a *petrolero* too and we were going through the jungle with our horses and . . ."

"No more silly games; this time it's for real. *Adiós.*"

The girl just stood there against the falling sunset, devoid of sorrow or glory, featuring an invisible sun with insipid tones of gray and brown, and watched Sacramento's tiny figure as it moved away into the distance, along the edge of the Tropical Oil Company's fence, toward the point at which the underbrush swallowed the path, where the pueblo ended and the Carare-Opón jungle began.

"*Adiós, hermano mío.* I hope you come back rich and powerful!" she shouted, waving her hand, and it was the first of many times that he would hear her say good-bye without a trace of sadness in her voice.

five

The girl became an adult on that afternoon of insipid twilight when Sacramento departed. In accordance with the new name she had been given, she was no longer called Girl, rather Sayonara. She was never again seen engaged in childish brawls in the barrio, and if from time to time she opened the treasure chest, it was to adorn herself with jewelry and gaze at herself in the mirror.

"The mirror, always looking at yourself in the mirror," Todos los Santos reproached her, seeing her absorbed and distant as if it were she who had left Tora. "You should know that the mirror is not an object of confidence because it is inhabited by Vanity and Deceit, two evil creatures that swallow everything they reflect. He who looks a lot in the mirror will end up spending a lot of time alone."

She no longer paid attention even to her friend Christ, or to Aspirina, who anxiously followed her everywhere; nor to the conversations of *las mujeres* on the patio, which she as a girl had followed as if hypnotized and without missing a single word.

" 'Run along, girl! Go play, adult problems aren't to be heard by tender ears,' that's how we had to shoo her away, but later came a time when she wouldn't join us even when we especially invited her."

One day in May her state of stupefaction reached such a point that she threw to the pigs, instead of potato peels, the rose petals they had prepared for the passing of the Virgin in the procession.

"That's what you call throwing pearls before swine," joked the others. "If you continue in this manner, you're going to end up throwing potato peels to the Virgin."

Only her hair seemed to keep her company during that period of isolated adolescence when she could spend the entire day bringing out its shine with a brush and arranging it into all kinds of styles: crazy woman, a Phrygian cap, Medusa, ragpicker, Policarpa Salavarrieta, or Ophelia drowned in the well, based on the characters that Machuca described in her stories.

"Her hair purred like a contented cat when she brushed it," Olga recalls.

Sometimes she would steal a cigarette and smoke it in front of the mirror, breathing deeply and practicing slow gestures, elegant ways of lighting the match or exhaling the smoke, walking around in tight skirts and sitting with her legs crossed.

"What are you dreaming about, girl?"

"I'd like to have a herd of elephants and to see snow, and for my father to be a king so I could smoke cigarettes in the salons of his palace."

One torrential afternoon, Todos los Santos announced it was time for her to start working: señor Manrique had already been summoned, he had been informed that he would be meeting a young girl recently arrived from Japan who had not yet mastered the Spanish language, and he had shown himself to be in agreement with everything. Sayonara said all right, that it was all right by her, and Todos los Santos set about preparing the proper costume as must be done for *amor de café*, where illusion, theater, and duplicity predominate.

"Hadn't señor Manriquito seen the girl?" I ask.

"Many times. But since adults often look at children without seeing them, he had seen her scurrying around without ever really noticing her."

So the name, the client, and the date had already been chosen and now they needed to physically transform the girl into Sayonara, or rather into an authentic Japanese woman, or more precisely into a fake Japanese woman but superior to an authentic one. In a glorified junk store called El Pequeño Paris, the *madrina* bought a black silk skirt, long and tubular, with a deep slit rising to mid-thigh. Then she marched twenty yards down Calle Caliente under the shade of her parasol to reach the Bazar Libanés.

"Let me see that Japanese blouse," she asked Chalela the Turk, indicating a red satin top with a gold dragon embroidered on the back that was being displayed on a mannequin.

"That blouse is Chinese, not Japanese," Chalela the Turk advised her.

"What's the difference?"

"The Japanese lost the war."

"Too bad for them . . ."

"Too bad."

"Good thing you told me. Then show me another one just like it, but in another color."

"I only have red and white left."

"White, then."

"But the white one is Chinese too . . ."

"Yes, but at least it's discreet. You wouldn't go around in red if your country had lost the war."

"Very well, then," said Chalela the Turk, and he wrapped the white blouse without understanding anything.

They brushed the girl's hair back, tied it in a ponytail, and yanked so tight they made her cry.

"Loosen it a little, *madrina*," asked the girl.

"That wouldn't do. This way it pulls your eyes and they really look Oriental."

Tana loaned her some cultivated pearl earrings, they duly hung the violet lightbulb that certified her Japanese nationality, and Olguita brought a reliquary that contained fragments of a martyr's bones, assuring her that it protected young girls their first time.

"There have already been other times," said the girl, which she had never mentioned before.

"It doesn't matter, keep the reliquary; it'll protect you anyway," answered Olga, kneeling at Sayonara's feet as she adjusted the hem of her skirt.

When señor Manrique was at the door fantasizing over the delights that the date promised, Todos los Santos took her disciple aside to deliver the final piece of advice.

"Never, never let yourself be tempted by an offer of matrimony from any of your clients. Don't forget that the pleasures of *amor de café* aren't the same as the pleasures of the home. Señor Manriquito, I leave you with my adopted daughter," she went on to say. "Daughter, this is Señor Manrique, treat him with affection, he is a good man."

When the old man was alone with the quiet, slender girl who had been assigned to him, he glimpsed such rapturous faraway places in her dark glances and high cheekbones, and perceived such warm apple and cinnamon well-being in her skin, that he didn't know what else to do but to propose matrimony.

"No, thank you," she responded with the silky voice, the good manners, and the discernment she had been taught.

Todos los Santos slept in the kitchen that night and before dawn entered the bedroom, making her way through the air saturated with the scent of intimacy. Sayonara was no longer there and señor Manrique slept in the beatific placidity of satisfied dreams, naked, soft, and white like cottage cheese. His usual blue suit waited for him neatly at the ready on a chair, rigid and carefully laid out to allow its owner to resume his human form when he put it on again. The *madrina* made a silent inspection of the room and then rushed out to the patio like a madwoman, shouting to Sayonara. The girl, now without her goddess disguise, was disheveled and barefoot, bucket in hand, feeding the pigs.

"Sayonara, come here!"

"Yes, *madrina*?"

"Where is the fountain pen?"

"What fountain pen?"

"What do you think? Señor Manrique's gold fountain pen . . ."

"I haven't seen it."

"He always wears it in the pocket of his jacket and now it's not there."

"Maybe he lost it, who knows?"

"You listen carefully to what I am going to say. For fifteen years señor Manrique has been coming to La Catunga with his gold fountain pen, for fifteen years he has fallen asleep in any of these houses, for fifteen years he has left without losing anything. Right this minute you will go, without waking him, and leave the pen where he had it. Being a *puta* is a profession, but being an evil *puta* is filth. If I haven't been able to make you understand that, then I've wasted my time with you."

The sun burned bright, radios were already chattering, and the heat was mature when señor Manrique, rejuvenated by the cistern, gave Todos los Santos the agreed upon sum and said good-bye, stamping a kiss on her fingers; she saw in his face an expression as clear as a medal of merit, which she had never seen before.

"You look magnificent today, señor," she said, probing the terrain.

"Not to boast, señora, but last night I devoted myself completely to the mission you bestowed upon me, and I believe that my performance as initiator and guide in matters of love was favorable. Of course, I don't imagine that a girl so young could have taken a fancy to me . . ."

"I understand, señor."

"Suffice it to say that I don't aspire to so much. But be that as it may, and you know better than I, a woman never forgets her first man and all those who pass through her bed afterward she compares to him . . ."

"Of course, señor, of course," she said condescendingly. "Of course."

We all have our vanities and cling to our illusions, thought Todos los Santos, and she stood there watching Manrique walk down the street toward the Plaza del Desacabezado, innocent of all suspicion and puffed up in his circumspect blue suit, carrying with him, as always, his gold fountain pen in the left breast pocket of his jacket.

six

Today I am visiting Todos los Santos in her bedroom because she is feeling ill and has been in bed since the day before yesterday. It's strange to find her like this, giving in to old age, propped up among the pillows on her bed and covered to the tip of her nose with a blanket despite the fact that the heat is killing the rest of us. It's the first time I have seen her with her hair uncombed, devoid of her earrings, with no appetite for her Cigalias and *mistelas*.

"I'm tired of going around driving away shadows," she tells me when I ask her why she hasn't gotten out of bed. Then she takes my hand, places it over her tired eyes, and assures me that it makes her feel better, that it is very cool.

"Did many women take up the profession out of hunger?" I ask after a long conversation about everything and nothing. She remains pensive.

"No, not many, just the opposite, very few."

She is quiet for a while and seems to have forgotten about me, but later she continues with the subject.

"Mostly the *indias*. I saw *pipatonas* become *putas* out of physical hunger, and the proof was that once they had enough money for food, they left and went back to their people. As for the rest of us, we couldn't go back, because for our families it was as if we were dead. With the Indians things were different; maybe it's because the missionaries never really fully explained sin to them. Or because their sins were different from ours, who knows? But it wasn't the same. Nor were their reasons and ours the same for getting into this life. If we had been motivated only by hunger, we would have done what they did, earn a little money, then leave, spend the money, and come back, then leave again, and keep the wheel turning that way. But our motives are more lasting." Todos los Santos lets out a harsh laugh, devoid of happiness. "They are so lasting that they endure our whole lives, because for us, once we become a *puta* there's no way back. It's like becoming a nun. A woman with this life dies being a woman of this life, although she no longer even remembers what the thing that hangs between a man's legs is called."

"What are those lasting motives you're talking about?"

"Take Correcaminos, for example," she answers, resorting to a quirk I have learned to expect from them—they speak of others when they don't want to speak about themselves. "It happened to Correcaminos, as it did with so many others, who in twenty-four hours go from being virgins to being *putas*. She was a decent, illiterate girl from a poor family who one day lost her virginity, became pregnant, and was transformed into the dishonor of her family. You are no longer my daughter, she heard her very Catholic father say, and the next minute she saw herself alone in the street without hope for pardon or return, with a baby in her belly and no roof over her head. Everything that had been hers suddenly wasn't anymore: father, mother, siblings, barrio, friends, bread on the table, morning sun, afternoon rain."

"Can you imagine that?" said Olga indignantly, listening to us as she chopped parsley to add to a compress for Fideo, who lay in a hammock due to her chronic illness. "Everything was taken from her and her child with only six words: You are no longer my daughter. Like a damning curse. To hear that, as if he had said 'abracadabra,' and to have everything disappear, absolutely everything, forever and ever. As if by a spell."

"To be so evil to her, her own father!"

"Delia Ramos was raped by her stepfather and when her mother found out, she burned with such jealousy that she punished Delia, throwing her out of the house," shouted Fideo from her hammock, who by now had ascertained that we were talking about misfortune.

"Of course, when we asked Delia Ramos if it was true, she denied it. She never wanted to confess to anyone. The old man didn't even remember what he had done and Delia, in contrast, martyred herself with guilt and regret. I knew about it because her sister told me, a girl named Melones who was also in the business, not here in Tora but in San Vicente Chucurí, and was crushed to death in an accident involving two buses on the Libertadores highway," interrupted Olguita, who is fond of going into detail. "Do you remember that horrendous accident? They made Delia Ramos go identify the body and she came back telling that she knew it was her sister because of a burn mark she had on her upper thigh ever since hot depilatory wax spilled on it."

The three interrupt each other, remembering the misadventures of Melones, and meanwhile I think to myself that between being cast out of her home and reaching La Catunga, Delia Ramos and Correcaminos, whose name literally meant "road traveler," must not have gone down too many roads. All they had to do was take a step, because La Catunga is around the corner from any street, and the difference between calling oneself Rosalba or Anita and nicknaming oneself Puta is a single word.

"When others refuse to offer a hand, mother prostitution receives you with open arms," says Olguita, "although afterward she swallows you alive and she makes us all pay for it."

"Opposite sides of the same coin," I think out loud, "virgin and *puta*. Honor and shame."

"That's right, opposite sides of the very same coin. And let the devil throw it into the air to see which you end up with."

"Did Correcaminos's father ever forgive her? Or Delia Ramos's mother?"

"Not them or anyone," shouted Fideo. "You can go from there to here, but from here to there all the doors are locked."

"All," adds Olga, "except those of your memories."

I have convinced Todos los Santos to get up and take a walk, and as we stroll, with me supporting her arm, the river turns red and the herons fly just above its surface, brushing the burning water with their wings. The momentary freshness of a breeze off the mountain abruptly ceases and the heat seizes the opportunity to fall upon us and crush us.

"The river blushed, didn't it?" asks Todos los Santos. "That's why it got hot, because the river turned red."

"And out of pleasure?" I continue. "Has anyone joined the profession because she liked it?"

Todos los Santos laughs in that peculiar manner of *las mujeres* when they are really amused, throwing their heads back and striking their thighs with the palms of their hands.

"It is a profession that has its compensations," she says, "that cannot be denied. Sometimes you sing and sometimes you cry, as with everything, but I will tell you one thing, a girl in this life has more opportunities for happiness than, let's say, a dentist. Or a locksmith, for example."

"Oh God, yes," assures Olguita, laughing, as she walks behind us.

seven

 Any worthwhile life is woven with white ceremonies and black ceremonies, in an inevitable chain where some justify the others. Although the easy encounter with señor Manrique floated by, inoffensive, among Sayonara's days, the following Tuesday Todos los Santos was forced to introduce her disciple to the murky ceremonies of a shameful routine. Every Tuesday by law, week after week, the prostitutes of La Catunga had to appear at dawn in the center of town, on Calle del Comercio, and stand in line in front of the antivenereal dispensary to have their health cards renewed.

"Only on that day," Todos los Santos tells me, "were they disrespectful and treated us like *putas*."

"Why do we need a card, *madrina*?" asked Sayonara, running behind the older woman, unable to match her steps.

"So the government will let us work. They require it of anyone in La Catunga who wears a skirt, even the nuns. They don't cure the sick women, they just charge them double to say they're healthy."

"But why, *madrina*?"

"The government officials pocket the fifty centavos that each of us pays for the validation."

"Well, if they're going to steal from us, why do we go?"

"So they'll let us live in peace."

"What happens if we don't have a card?"

"They kick our asses right into jail."

They found the others waiting in line beneath the rising sun, messy and gray, as if they had swallowed ashes. The collective disgust cut off any attempt at conversation and Sayonara knew instinctively that it was better not to continue asking questions, because putting words to grave matters only makes them graver. There was Yvonne, perched on a pair of red spiked heels; Claire, mortally beautiful; Analía, stealing sips of vodka from a poorly camouflaged bottle; the *pipatonas* suckling their babies; Olga with her legs in the armor plating of her orthopedic devices. Leaning against a wall, all identical in the eyes of the corrupt officials, with no preferred lightbulb status or nationality or fee differential, no color of skin better than any other. On Tuesdays the dignity of any of them was worth fifty centavos, not one more or one less.

"The infected women's cards were marked with crosses, one or several depending on the severity, and some women's had so many they looked like cemeteries," said Todos los Santos. "One cross meant thin blood; two, rotten blood; three, swollen flesh; four, irremediable situation."

"Off with the underwear!"

Men with white lab coats were giving orders and Sayonara was seized with a sudden anxiety attack and a growing foreboding of frozen forceps in her crotch. A strong whiff of cleaning fluids made her nauseous.

"It smells like a circus, *madrina*."

"It is a circus, and we're the clowns."

"Through here for genital inspection," indicated a doctor of dubious qualifications, so coarse in appearance and with a lab coat so stained that he looked more like a mechanic than a doctor.

Obeying orders like a frightened animal, the girl lay down on the examining table and began to tremble.

"Hold on, girl," encouraged Todos los Santos. "Think of Santa Cata, who withstood the cogged wheel without complaint."

"Some comfort you are, *madrina*."

The man with the stained lab coat performed the examination in view of all the others, with total disinterest, a cigarette in his mouth and without interrupting a conversation about the legitimacy of the elections, which he was carrying on with a tall, ungainly colleague who didn't look like a doctor either, or even a mechanic, but rather a giraffe from a zoo.

When he finished with the girl, the man moved over to a desk, signed and stamped a card of pink pasteboard, threw the fifty centavos in a drawer, and without washing his hands shouted:

"Next!"

Todos los Santos tried to climb onto the high table without losing her composure, but she got tangled in her skirts, suffered a sudden coughing attack, the leg that was supposed to rise wouldn't respond, the upper part of her body managed some success and reached the table but the other half failed and hung there, heavy and grotesque, while, completely humiliated, she begged the doctor's pardon for her lack of agility, explaining that in her youth she had been slender.

"Hurry up," said the man. "I'm not going to wait all morning."

"Can't you see the señora needs help?" said Sayonara, and her fear yielded to her fury.

"Up, señora, and open your legs."

"She is not climbing up or opening her legs, you shitty bastard," Sayonara spat out as she grabbed Todos los Santos by the arm, struggling to pull her out to the street.

"Don't be a rebel, *hija*, you'll leave me without a card," protested the *madrina*, who still hadn't picked up her purse or finished rearranging her hair, stockings, and skirt.

"Let her insult me, doña," said the doctor so loudly that the others outside could hear. "Next time the little brat is going to have to suck me off before I'll do her the favor of renewing her card."

"Why don't you suck this," shouted a woman from Cali who had been eating a mango; she threw the pit and hit him in the eye, letting out a hearty laugh that alerted the others and made them laugh too, first a little, then more, beginning as the chatter of schoolgirls, then becoming the harassment of mutinous *putas*, hurling insults, trash, and rocks at the dispensary doctors who, without knowing how, managed to lock the door and barricade themselves against the revolt that was mounting outside.

"Down with the pimping government!"

"Down!"

From the corner and a little apart from the rest, looking at all of this with the burned-out eyes of someone who has seen it before, Todos los Santos registered the novelty only as highlighted in insignificant details: the touch of color that the commotion brought out on Claire's translucent cheeks, the agility with which Yvonne ran on her red stilts, the wounded-deer urgency with which the group of *pipatonas* and their children fled, abandoning the uprising at the onset. But more than anything she noticed the metamorphosis that her adopted daughter underwent, having seized the first line of fire, hair on end like a wild beast, vociferous, and later scampering across the roofs with a diabolical agility to reach the skylight and attack from above.

"I watched her," she tells me, "and said to myself: Maybe it's better for me to never find out what this child's past is, or what mix of blood brought about such vigor and fury."

"Bastards, bloodsuckers!"

Delia Ramos, consumed with rage, incited battle with Walkyrian shouts, and a woman from the Pacific coast whom they called La Costeña harangued from the top of a wall.

"*Putas hijueputas!* Son-of-a-bitch whores!" answered masculine voices from behind the barricades. "Syphilis spreaders!"

"This is for all of our friends who were raped and abused in this dump!" trumpeted the vodka-soaked voice of Analía, and a bottle crashed against the window of the dispensary, shattering the glass.

"Filthy gonorrhea-infected whores!" responded the barricaded men.

"Death to corrupt officials!"

"Down with the pimping government!"

"Death!"

A flying orange buzzed through the broken window and stamped itself, yellow and juicy, on a cabinet, knocking over all the flasks, and then the roof fell in with a clatter of glass.

"They're burning us alive!" howled the besieged men, as a rain of burning paper and rags descended upon them, which Sayonara, angel of fire, young cat on a hot tin roof, was tossing onto their heads and which fell onto the spilled alcohol, spreading the fire. From her street corner Todos los Santos saw the smoke that was beginning to rise wispy and pale and noticed that it was becoming blacker and thicker, like the clouds that precede storms. She also saw the first flames peering out, seeking something to cling to, like long, mobile, hungry tongues, and she watched the heat smash, one by one, the rest of the windows in a frenzy of invisible punches reverberating through the air.

And she also saw, with the stupor of one contemplating someone else who has been reborn, her adopted daughter standing at the edge of the great fire, watching it, spellbound and ecstatic, captivated by the spectacle of its growing force and without retreating from her attacks or perceiving the heat building up in the iron skylight frames across which she was effortlessly balanced, as if suspended from the sky by invisible threads.

There was something irrational and challenging in the way that girl ignored the danger, and Todos los Santos suddenly understood that her adopted daughter couldn't, or, worse still, didn't want to separate herself from the fascination that wouldn't take much longer to envelop her in its burning arms.

"Down with the pimping government!" howled the women, feverish before the excitement of the fire.

"Down!"

"Out of Tora with the bloodsuckers!"

"Out!"

Asphyxiated by the smoke, their eyes reddened and teary, and their arms raised high, like freed puppets, the besieged doctors exited in surrender at the very moment that men in olive green appeared, jogging down the street, holding their weapons.

"Their reinforcements are coming!" Someone sounded the alarm and the rebels shot off in every direction, leaving the scene empty in a matter of seconds.

"Here come the cops!"

"Death to corrupt officials!"

"Death to the police who protect them!"

"Death to all the sons of bitches who exploit the women of Tora!"

Todos los Santos, the only woman who remained in the plaza, without vacillation crossed the tense silence of thistles and porcupines that electrified the air to approach the dispensary as far as permitted by the fury of the blaze, which was now escaping through doors and windows, and she didn't know whether it was because of dizziness from the heat or hallucination from the gases, but as she looked up in the air she saw Sayonara advance serenely, like Christ on top of the waves, along a narrow open path among the flames, a vertiginous ballerina on the verge of disaster. And she swears to me that she saw too how the gusts of smoke delicately stroked her hair and how the fire approached, tame, to kiss her clothing and lick her feet.

As she contemplated this nerve, this display of irresponsibility on the part of the insolent child, Todos los Santos became greatly annoyed and was about to shout angrily for the girl to climb down from there that very instant and to cease her strange behavior, but just as she was about to open her mouth she heard her instincts give her a countermand.

"Suddenly I realized that her own foolishness was what would save her," she tells me, "and that if I called out to her I would startle her and once she awakened the fire would swallow her up, because her only protection lay in her dazed state of mind. You see, if I shouted, it would break the spell, the skylight would suddenly collapse, and she would fall into the center of the burning embers. Then I looked at her calmly, without reproach, as if approving her shadowy passage over that hell, and I told her with the softest voice in my throat, in just this tone, without insulting, without haste, I told her quietly, lovingly: 'Let's go, child, it's late and we should be getting back to the house.' I don't know how, but she heard me; somehow she descended from the roof as effortlessly as she had climbed up and the next instant was at my side, standing on the ground, urging me to run so the troops wouldn't grab us."

"Run, *madrina*! Give me your hand and run! Don't you see they're almost on top of us?" she shouted, just like that, as if it had all been a children's game and death didn't exist, soldiers didn't kill, sadness didn't strike or fire burn."

There was no time to run; down the street that emptied into the plaza came the crush of jogging boots hammering the dust, but when they arrived with their weapons at the ready, the only traces of the rebels' passage were Yvonne's abandoned red shoes and four or five fake doctors, stunned and banged up, who didn't know whether to open their mouths to curse their luck or to thank God who had saved them. Sayonara and Todos los Santos? They found a hiding place in the house of friends who had opened their doors to them.

"A French investigator who came around in those years made inquiries and threw out some figures that reflected that the *prostitutas* of Tora paid more to the state in health control and fines than the Tropical Oil Company did in royalties," Machuca tells me. Meanwhile, the girls struggled to ward off syphilis and gonorrhea with prayers and cloths dampened with warm water, and the crosses kept cropping up on *carnés* and in cemeteries.

eight

Sometime later, torrential rains came to quiet the fevers of the barrio and turned its narrow streets into rivers of mud. Nocturnal lightning flickered against the zinc roofs with fading discharges and Holy Week arrived, bringing with it a slow, sorrowful silence, in solidarity with the agonies of the crucified. Sayonara, who was once again fixated on the red Christ with the fanaticism of earlier days, tried to please him with flowers and candles and left him cigarettes and matches, plates of rice, glasses of rum, anything that would help to alleviate the bitter drink awaiting him.

The Maundy Thursday sky dawned, vaulted over with dark clouds, and the streetwalkers of La Catunga, following tradition, dressed in mourning, covered their faces with Spanish mantillas, and went barefoot, in a vow of humility. Olguita vulnerable without her steel braces, Tana stripped of her jewels, Claire drained of life, Yvonne voluptuous, Analía sober for the moment, Delia Ramos peaceful of spirit, and Machuca abstaining from cursing; the Italians, La Costeña, the Indians with their herds of children, and others, all filed barefoot along the narrow streets of sin, in voluntary penitence, which was heightened by the rain.

They emerged from the Dancing Miramar, leaving behind the barbershop, the apothecary, the billiard halls, the cantinas, the statue of the headless man, and the municipal slaughterhouse. When they reached Ecce Homo, the pealing of the bells exploded into the air and the interior of the church overflowed with lilies, while the altar was set for the last supper and the saints were clothed in purple raiment. But they kept walking.

"They didn't enter the church?"

"The parish had forbidden them to enter unless they had publicly renounced their profession."

"Did they really walk barefoot?"

"Barefoot and in a holy trance, without dodging mortifications or garbage heaps."

The black pilgrimage of penitents arrived at its destination, the Patria Theater, around eleven that morning and the early show, exclusively for them, was *Jesus of Nazareth* with Spanish subtitles and in Technicolor, which according to Olga was almost the same as real life.

"A sacred ceremony in an unholy temple," I comment.

"We *putas* were born to rub luck against the grain," assents Todos los Santos.

From the moment that the Christ child trotted behind his sheep on the screen of the Patria Theater, before he got into his predicament, much before the terrible denouement, the women of La Catunga burst into tears. They gave free rein to a cascade of warm and comforting tears, salty and sweet like sea and river currents. They cried because they weren't able to withstand so much death and love. They cried for the man who would pardon them on the cross, for his father Joseph's troubles and his mother Mary's lacerations. And they cried for themselves, for their mothers who they hadn't seen for so long, for their fathers who they had never seen, for their own children and for the children they would never have, for their sorrows as lonely women, for all the men who had gone and those to come, for the sins they had committed and those they would commit, for the past and for the future.

They didn't stop crying until they heard the celluloid Mary Magdalene swear and swear again that she had seen Christ resplendent, his wounds healed and gloriously resuscitated, and then they left the Patria Theater feeling lightened, free of guilt and empty of tears, prepared to bear another year of life without complaint or protest. Until the next Maundy Thursday, with its rain and tears, would come to bring the world purifying alleviation in the form of streams and torrents of water.

On the way back home along the Calle del Comercio, a few steps removed from the others, Todos los Santos and Sayonara walked arm in arm, one old and the other young, one pale-skinned and the other dark, one the mother and the other the daughter: both threatening and haughty in their black dresses, not looking back or greeting anyone.

"Mother whore, daughter whore, who does the blanket cover more?" commented the pious as they watched the pair pass.

"If the girl were hers," murmured others, "that procuress wouldn't have allowed her to work the street, she would have installed her in a convent school, in Bucaramanga or in Cúcuta."

"A convent?" says Todos los Santos, terrified. "Why would I leave her in the hands of nuns? Who are those señoras to educate her better than I?"

After living together for two years, everything that Sayonara knew she had learned from her *madrina*. She echoed her *madrina*'s expressions, had the same deep gaze, the identical habit of walking around barefoot, and of curing illnesses with infusions of parsley. She had even inherited the peculiar style of cleaning her teeth, scrubbing so hard that the brush barely lasted a month.

"Under my wing that girl was growing up beautiful and strong. In her steps I found my own footprint and in her mirror I could read the same traces of my youth.

"I taught her how to be a prostitute and not anything else because it was the trade that I knew, just as the shoemaker can't train a bricklaying apprentice nor should a viola player try to give piano lessons.

"I did what I did without doubting my conscience," Todos los Santos assures me, "because I have always believed that a *puta* can have a life that is just as clean as any decent housewife, or as corrupted as any indecent housewife."

nine

They say that at some moment in their itinerant existence the men from all the camps in the world, from the oil wells of Infantas to the vast fuel deposits of Iraq, passed religiously through the streets of sin in La Catunga, as if coming to fulfill a promise, because it was the heart and sanctuary of the extensive oil labyrinth. In La Catunga the circle was completed; it was the obligatory point of return for their travels.

"As a boy I had lived invisibly in Tora, leading a humble existence, hauling people and packages with my cart," says Sacramento. "Living that way it is difficult for anyone to notice you, especially the *majeres de café*, who were accustomed to rubbing elbows with engineers, contractors, trained personnel. That's why I left, thinking I would return with some distinction, which is the purpose of everyone who leaves."

"With what they gave him for selling the cart, Sacramento bought a pair of walking shoes and started walking," Todos los Santos tells me.

Where to? He didn't have to ask anyone; he took off walking by the compass of the wandering multitude, joining the great river of seekers of fortune until he arrived at the oil installations at El Centro, where he found a population drowning in a persistent downpour that lashed diagonally, soaking mankind to the bone and reminding them of their help-lessness. He arrived at dawn and immediately, without shrinking back from the weather's sudden attacks, took his place in the queue under the deluge, in front of the recruiting office. After hours of waiting, with his skin wrinkled under his soaked clothing, he gathered the courage to ex-change words with the man waiting behind him.

"Raindrops were falling from his hair too and running into his eyes, his mouth and his ears, as they were into mine. So I asked him: A lot of rain, isn't it? An insignificant question, just to find a subject, and he an-swered me: Yeah, except maybe for frogs in a pond. From there we could converse more seriously because his words and mine had already been intertwined, and he confessed that he had come from the city of Popayán to try out his luck. Popayán? Where in the hell is that? I asked him, again just for the pleasure of chatting, or the need to find an ac-complice, because I already knew more or less where the city of Popayán was."

"It's on the other side of the country," he answered.

"That's not so bad, there are several here who come from the other side of the planet. I've seen Armenians, Canadians, Jews, Greeks . . ."

"Well, I still had to walk three months to get here."

" 'Okay, Payanés' — I called him that because that's what they call people who are from Popayán, and I kept calling him Payanés through the many good days that we were close friends, and even afterward — 'now that you're here hold my place in line while I go take a leak,' I said eagerly and in confidence, like any timid guy who wants to hide his ur-gent condition. In truth I had decided to talk to him because I had to go badly and didn't want to lose my place in that line of men, winding long and nervous like a poisonous snake."

At noon, the rain gave way to a brilliant sun that dried the clothes on their backs, then around three in the afternoon it was finally their turn to face the recruiter, a robust man with the neck and disposition of an ill-tempered young bull.

"Show me your palms!" he bellowed, and they obeyed instantly.

"Those are the hands of a lady, aren't you ashamed? Get out of here, we don't need women!"

"Respect!" demanded Sacramento, but without much conviction, so the bull wouldn't charge him.

"Yeah, respect," echoed Payanés, and from that first adversity they became accomplices for all the others to come.

"I'll kill that son of a bitch," boasted Sacramento when the beast was no longer within earshot. "I'll choke him with my bare hands, then we'll see whether they're a lady's hands."

"You're not going to choke anybody, much less that giant," said Payanés, taking his new friend over to join a group of fellow rejects as they headed out to look for work as road laborers, to wield shovels until their hands were covered with calluses and they could return to the recruiting officer stronger and better prepared.

They penetrated the dense, hungry jungles of Carare through a tunnel they barely managed to open with slashes of their machetes and that snapped shut behind them like the jaws of a beast. They walked in the dark, feeling their way and withstanding scratches, roars, venom, and harassment from slimy fauna and hairy flora whose existence Sacramento had never dreamed of even in his worst nightmares, and that Payanés pointed out and classified according to their place in the animal, mineral, or vegetable kingdom.

"This is a *sarrapial,* those giant burning flowers are called *cámbulos,* those shouts you hear are from white-faced *maicero* monkeys, this must be the footprint of a *momano,* half ape and half human, who walks upright through the jungle, wary and nearly hairless, hiding from people because he's shy and ashamed of his nakedness."

Sacramento tore off a leaf and it turned out to be an insect, he was about to grab a stick but it was a snake, he heard the beautiful song of a bird and it too turned out to be a snake: a singing ophidian.

"I'm never going to learn," he said, disheartened. "Nothing here is what it seems and everything acquires the gift of transforming itself into its opposite. The only certain thing is the hungriness with which the jungle looks at you; let down your defenses for a second and you'll get swallowed up."

Eight days later, green, weak, and moldy from the humidity and lack of sun, their stomachs out of sorts from drinking amoebic broth and chewing *corozo* seeds, they found themselves on an old *camino real* opened by the conquistador Jiménez de Quesada along the Río Opón, upon which the Troco wanted to build a road to Campo Escondido and so was recruiting fresh blood for the work of leveling and moving earth.

They arrived around midnight and were greeted by the miracle of the river transformed into a bed of placid stars, which at the edge came away from the water and took off in flight.

"Those floating lights you see are female lightning bugs calling their mates," said Payanés.

"Such tireless vegetation, so many creatures giving off light, so many males trying to copulate," said Sacramento. "Nature is a very loving thing, *hermano*."

They removed their shoes and lay down among the rest of the men, beneath the immense sky and with their heads firmly resting on their shoes, which are the most cherished possession in the life of a foot traveler. Despite their precaution, they went to sleep with four and awoke with three: Payanés's two and only the right shoe belonging to Sacramento, who sat in a gully hugging his widowed shoe and began to cry. He cried from exhaustion and because he was an orphan and because of the desolation of his abandoned foot, which was condemned to the sharp edges of the rocks and to the itching from the ticks and chiggers that embedded themselves in the plants, where they lay their crops of eggs.

"Monday, Wednesday, and Friday you get the complete pair," Payanés said consolingly, handing him a tin can of hot coffee. "Tuesday, Thursday, and Saturday I'll have it. Two Sundays a month for you, two Sundays for me."

"Monday, Tuesday, Wednesday, Thursday, Friday, Saturday, and Sunday," corrected Sacramento, "the first son of a bitch who lets down his guard tonight will have to limp around, because I'm going to steal a left shoe."

"Why would they have only stolen one?"

"It must have been some damned one-legged thief."

"It won't be hard to recognize him then."

"What if the thief has all of his legs, and if someone else had stolen only one of his shoes too?"

"Then that means that a cycle has begun that not even God can end."

Sacramento and Payanés racked their brains trying to imagine what luck could befall two men with three shoes, when toward them came an old man, ill-humored and mumbling curses.

"I'm getting out of here," he said, chewing his words, as Sacramento studied the sturdy pair of raised-heel boots with leather straps the old man was wearing. "If you want my place you can have it. I'd rather die of hunger in my homeland than leave my bones buried in these shitty swamps. They're plagued with bugs, look, there goes one, and there's another. They say they bite, the filthy creatures. I'm getting out of here, yessir, before a fucking bug eats me."

"Well, if you're leaving, why don't you do me the favor of leaving me your boots?" proposed Sacramento, inspired by the muses of his desperation.

Astonished, Payanés looked at him.

"What do you mean, my boots?" the old man shot back. "Do you by chance have a million pesos to give me for them?"

"I don't have anything to give you for them, but look at my situation and you'll understand, somebody stole my shoe, which there is a great need for around here, and since you're going home and probably have another pair waiting for you there . . ."

"And how am I supposed to get home, fly? Stupid idiot. That's just what I need, some blockhead to start asking me for presents. Maybe you think I look like baby Jesus?"

Stubborn in his foolishness, Sacramento kept arguing reasons for mercy and heaping on descriptions of his misfortune, refusing to recognize that there is no human power that can convince a stranger to cross the mass of the Andes unshod, of his own will, for no good reason and without receiving anything in return.

"What do you mean that you're leaving us your place?" Payanés, who was sharper at this sort of dealing, asked the old man.

"There's plenty of work to go around here, what there's not enough of is willing men. The only requirement for a man is that he have two hands, bring his own tool, and be willing to work like an animal and leave the child's play behind. And your shovels? Where are your shovels?"

"We don't have shovels."

"They only hire personnel with tools."

"Serious problem, *hermano*," said Payanés to Sacramento, removing his red baseball cap to scratch his head.

"Well, if you want I'll sell you my shovel."

"Well, seeing that it's an old shovel, and I'm not exactly rich . . ."

The give and take of the negotiation started high, rapidly descended to midrange, and stagnated with the bartering of trifles—the shovel for the red cap, a pound of coffee and the shovel for the missal that Sacramento was carrying, the coffee for the red cap—until the old man convinced himself of the calamitous insolvency of his opponents and chose to move on to look for a higher bidder.

"Don't go," said Sacramento, grabbing him by the sleeve. "I'll give you my shoe for your shovel."

"What in the hell do I need with a single shoe?"

"In case someone steals one of your boots . . ."

"That would never happen, who's going to steal it?"

"These unfortunate things happen, look at me. Anyway, an extra shoe will certainly serve you more than a broken shovel on your journey."

The old man left for his homeland with Sacramento's shoe in his pack, while the two boys agreed to take turns with the endowment:

While one rested the other would work with the shovel and Payanés's shoes, and the next day they would exchange roles.

"Repeat after me: Pick, you are my father; shovel, you are my mother"—that was the only instruction given to them by the foreman before he exploded the dynamite that reduced a huge rock to gravel, sending monkeys and parrots to the moon.

That's how they started to work, and to suffer. They clung to their shovel as if it were the sword and shield of a wandering knight and with it they opened the way among the thousand torments of the jungle, paddling among the stagnant waters at the edge of the river, which boiled like a thick, rancid soup and gave off a fetid vapor that impeded their breathing.

"It's malaria," diagnosed someone. "This poisonous air is what they call malaria."

"Don't be ignorant, malaria doesn't fly around on its own, it spreads by mosquitoes," corrected someone else. "They're called anopheles. Only the female bites, and she lives only seven days, but in that time she can infect at least seven men."

"And those seven men are bitten by a hundred flies who then bite seven hundred more men, until there's not a healthy Christian in the whole *departamento* of Magdalena."

"Or in all of Colombia."

"Well, the truth is that yes, they are biting," complained Payanés, and the statement bothered Sacramento, because it made real a nuisance that until then he had managed to ignore.

"Hush, Payanés, don't court disaster. Don't think about the mosquitoes and they won't bite you; they're just like dogs, they only bite those who are afraid of them."

He hadn't finished speaking those words when he began to feel the stings on his cheek, on his hand, on his thigh through the cloth of his trousers. He hadn't seen them before and suddenly he saw them, in clouds, in battalions, forcing him to scratch himself until he drew blood, dodging their victims' swats and laughing at the foul-smelling smoke of some cigarettes the men called repellent. He tells me that of the many bites he received in the quagmire of the Carare, there was one that infected him, and he assures me he knows which one it was.

"I turned to look when that mosquito's sting lanced my neck, like a hypodermic needle, injecting into my veins that insatiable parasite that stayed on to live inside me, to devour my blood little by little. And look how things turn out: The day I contracted malaria was the same day I heard someone talk of her for the first time."

He heard someone talk about Sayonara, a girl in La Catunga whom the men that visited those streets said they had fallen in love with, and whose fame had begun to spread by word of mouth even among those who didn't know her, the thousands of seekers of destiny who walked along the roads of Magdalena after bread and work; after opportunities, as they themselves said to give a generic name to the future, to love, to their lucky star, the holy grail, the treasures of El Dorado, the philosopher's stone, a mother's compassion, a lover's sheets, the roar of black gold. Sacramento says:

"I think we were looking blindly for something that was worthy of all that searching; something, finally, that deserved to be sought out and that at the moment of death would allow us to say, that's what I lived for."

It often turned out, due to a breath of spontaneous winds, that the object of the collective search would take a woman's name, and then the chosen one would rapidly be converted into a legend, and her glory would extend everywhere the oil pipes ran. That happened with Sayonara, the slender girl. Sayonara, the *novia*, the lover, of everyone and no one, silent and dark: Each man who passed through Tora left the city dazzled by her. Whether it was true or just an empty boast, there was no man who didn't pride himself on having been with her.

"It's the simple things that we understand the least," Sacramento acknowledges. "How was I to imagine at the time that my scraggly, wild girl, my sister on those endless imaginary journeys, was the Japanese goddess that every voice spoke to me of? Or had I imagined it in the fires of my youthful longing?"

"Sayonara," Sacramento was heard to say one night when the heat nearly drove him mad, and the name refreshed him just by its repetition and it sounded like happiness. As the days passed he got to thinking that it was a talisman against the difficulties of life, and he began to tie himself to the memory of the woman, although it wasn't his own exclusive memory, because after all he had never seen her, or at least that's what he thought, but her fame was a patrimony diffused through those mountains and vast lands. Like the troubadour's mysterious and anonymous Lady of Provence, Sayonara had become, in *petrolero* land, the inspiration of every man proud enough to call himself one. At least that was the reasoning that called Sacramento to his senses, while his heart busied itself, stubbornly, in the belief that the beautiful woman he dreamed of belonged to him alone, because the others bought and used her, but he would adore her forever. He committed the error of letting his guard down and allowing the delirium of that woman's name to lodge in his bloodstream in the form of jealousy, which is as obstinate as malaria itself, and from then on he began to carry within him the two plagues, which embraced him like twin rivers of fever and fire, distinct yet confluent.

"That was the serious problem, that Sacramento was jealous of Sayonara even before he loved her," sighs Todos los Santos.

But the first symptoms of Sacramento's recently acquired double illness took months to incubate and manifest themselves, and they gave him respite from the putridness of the Río Opón's quagmire. Together with Payanés, after having bought a new pair of shoes, he went to try his luck as a repairman on the oil pipeline that flowed into the Bahía of Cartagena, and then they joined the railway workers on the section of line that stretched between Papayal and Espíritu Santo. Wherever they went they heard a pained sighing, a sort of prayer intoned by dozens of lonely men to the young *prostituta* from Tora.

"Maybe they grieved for many women, each man for his own," acknowledges Sacramento today, "but to me it was as if they only spoke of her. No other names entered my ears, only Sayonara, Sayonara, falling like snow onto the high treetops in the midst of the suffocating heat, and I couldn't believe that there was any greater passion than the one that emanated from her."

Without knowing how or when, Sacramento began to build his life upon the messianic obsession of rescuing the beautiful object of his fantasies from her wrong path, apparently without suspecting that he knew her in flesh and blood—very little flesh and blood—because that distant Japanese girl with the legendary wake who pursued and trapped him was the same skinny girl that he had personally taken to Todos los Santos to teach her how to be someone, before she had a rare and exotic name but was simply called "the girl," and she didn't come from the Orient, like the three wise men, but from some pueblo like so many others whose name nobody bothered to ascertain. And she held no fascination or mysteries, just the existence of a cornered, hungry animal, with such force of character, freedom of spirit, and mulish stubbornness, that if Sacramento had been an attentive reader of souls, like Todos los Santos, he also would have perceived—or did he perceive it?—that the ordinary girl could convert herself into a living relic of the oil world, with the sole requirement that she choose to do so.

Each time Sacramento came upon civilization, the first thing he did, even before using a washbasin to rinse his face, or sitting down in front of a plate of hot food, was to send a postcard addressed to the girl in Tora, via the occasional traveler, migratory workers, the river mail, or the comings and goings of the mule drivers. He did it just like that, out of an affectionate impulse, the natural inclination toward the only thing in his life that resembled rootedness. Without fully comprehending that a mocking fate, which amuses itself at the expense of mortals, obliged him to send missives to someone who he adored without knowing it, and forced him to pursue through the labyrinth of roads precisely that which he had left behind.

They were colorful postcards with photographs and motifs of unexpected themes and diverse nationalities, on the backs of which Sacramento scrawled a few gerunds bearing his greetings. Like a FAÇADE OF THE PANCHAYAT PALACE IN KATMANDU, CAPITAL OF NEPAL, which read: "Thinking of you and remembering you, nothing more for the moment, Sacramento." Or a LADIES FROM TOLEDO IN TYPICAL DRESS MAKING THE TRADITIONAL LACE OF THE REGION, with a note on the reverse that added adverbs to the usual gerunds: "Everything going well hoping the same for you remembering you affectionately and also señora Todos los Santos." Or Sayonara's favorite, PLATE AND VEGETABLE DISH IN DELICATE SEVRES PORCELAIN, on which was written, in blue ink, the following courtesy: "Hoping and wishing to see you again soon, yours respectfully Sacramento."

Sayonara received them with jubilant shouts as if they were what they actually were, updates on pasteboard that reached her hands through mysterious routes from other worlds to notify her that she wasn't alone in this one. She would interrupt whatever she was doing to take them from house to house, showing them to her friends, and after reading each one many times, she would stick them with tacks to the wall around the red Christ, forming a rhombus, a circle, a butterfly pattern, or other figures, sometimes geometrical, sometimes whimsical, that were covered with the vermilion reflections of the votives and in some impious way were integrated with the fascination and panic that the sacred space inspired in her.

Each time she received a new postcard, Sayonara disapproved of its corresponding place on the wall according to the old design. So she would pull them all down, taking advantage of the opportunity to read them again, shuffle and mix them, and arrange them again, one by one, letting herself be guided by impulses or whims. PLATE AND VEGETABLE DISH IN DELICATE SEVRES PORCELAIN now far from QUEEN ELIZABETH II OF GREAT BRITAIN and to the right of TORERO EXECUTING A PASS WITH CAPE ON A YOUNG BULL; DANCE CLASS, OIL PAINTING BY PIETRO LONGHI diagonally across from LACQUERED TABLE WITH CHI-

NOISERIE, DETAIL; SECTION OF THE GARDENS OF LUXEMBOURG next to
BALCONY OF THE QUINTA DE BOLÍVAR SANTAFÉ DE BOGOTÁ, and so on
indefinitely, in variable and cabalistic order that neither she nor anyone
else could interpret but that seemed to be foreshadowing the course of
the events of her life.

ten

 Through the American Frank Brasco, I came to know of Sayonara's fascination with snow, despite her never having seen it, or perhaps precisely because of that.

"You must be crazy, Sayo," Brasco said to her. "We're melting at ninety degrees in the shade and you're asking me about snow . . ."

To Sayonara, a woman of the tropics accustomed to the frenzy of a vegetation perpetually sprouting and blossoming, to a voracious and persistent green that in a matter of hours swallows anything that remains still, the immobile silence of snow-covered fields must have been very perplexing. That sleepy landscape, hidden beneath an immense whiteness, barely conceived from photographs and postcards, must have been pure magic to her, or merely the hoax of foreigners, as if someone were to swear to a European that in other latitudes the sky stretched in red and white squares, like a quilt.

"She was more than simply curious," Frank Brasco assured me. "That snow, which she had never seen, created a deep longing within her; it was something she needed urgently, who knows why."

Otherworldly and overwhelming—as if seen through Sayonara's eyes—the forests of this wintery Vermont appear before me, where

Brasco the engineer was born and later spent many winters, until he finally established himself here permanently, now retired and at the doorstep of old age, in the midst of an austerity and a voluntary isolation that one could say is almost hermetic. I've come here looking for him because I have learned that he treasures memories of the time he worked for the Tropical Oil Company as general supervisor of Campo 26. He was at the time a man with a liberal attitude, accustomed to conducting relationships with women within the scope of a university environment, to such a degree that the possibility of seeking love in the world of prostitution had never even occurred to him. Besides, a bad case of poorly tended hepatitis in his childhood had left his liver sensitive to and incompatible with alcohol, so he considered himself immune to what he thought were the reasons that pushed the rest of the men as a mass toward the barrio of La Catunga. For that reason, despite regularly going down from 26 to the neighboring city, Frank Brasco had never crossed the boundaries of the *zona de tolerancia* and certainly would never have if chance hadn't caused, for a few revealing and fascinating days, his path to cross with that of Sayonara, the dark lover of Tora.

"What was the first thing you noticed about her?"

"From the very first moment, I was shaken by her beauty and pained by her excessive youth, because she was practically a girl. A beautiful and frightened girl, like a feline, and dedicated to being a *puta*. But I also immediately perceived an unyielding temperament and a certain, unusually powerful intensity. How can I describe it? A human warmth that kept her capacity for expression intact. Not that she was always affectionate, or happy. Sometimes, it was just the opposite, she would walk past you so absorbed in her affairs that she didn't even notice that you were there. But at those moments her presence weighed on you, and you couldn't avoid it. Every movement of her body, every sentence she spoke, her way of looking at something or laughing, everything about her was naturally surprising and not premeditated, was sure, exact. As if the earth were a planet populated by extraterrestrials and she was the only one who had really been born here."

"Do you mean that she had a conclusive way of being there?"

"Exactly. How did you know?"

"I have heard that before."

"I remember a Colombian song that goes, more or less, I love my woman because she is pure reality. It must have been written about her."

Frank Brasco tells me that from the first day they met, Sayonara devoted herself to asking about snow and kept insisting on the subject even at the moment when they were saying good-bye forever.

"It was her obsession," he tells me. "And I still don't understand why I didn't bring her here so she could experience winter, which made her so anxious. I also wonder why snow interested her so much, why it tugged at her, to the point of a mania."

As he shovels away the dense layer of snow that obstructs the entrance to his cabin, engineer Brasco struggles to bring to mind the memory of the thousand tones of green of the verdant Colombian landscape, from the most fiery to those streaked with black, the fresh sprouts of bamboo shoots, the nocturnal leaves of the *yarumo* plant bathed in moonlight, the chatter of the parakeets after a downpour, the piquant aroma of the high pastures, the smell of lemons that refreshes the hours of suffocating heat in Tora.

"And the slices of green mango with salt that they sell on the corners," he adds. "How I would love to eat green mango with salt again!"

"Sayonara wasn't the only delirious one," I say. "In the middle of this cold air and sunk to the knees in snow, you're talking about green mango with salt . . ."

"I asked her: 'Why do you like the snow so much, Sayo, when you've never seen it?' "

"Yes, I have seen it, in my dreams. And in pictures. Look, *mister* Brasco," Sayonara said to him, handing him one of the postcards sent by Sacramento, the reproduction of a painting by Alfred Sisley that showed the sweet way in which winter covered a village street.

"Isn't it true that this is your pueblo, *mister*?" Frank Brasco tells me she asked him.

"No, this is a French village. Mine is in the far north of the United States, near the border with . . ."

"Okay, okay, don't explain to me where it is, just tell me if it is just like this one in the postcard."

"Only a little."

"I say it must be just the same, because all towns look the same when they are covered with snow. Do you know, *mister*, why it is that snow never comes to Tora?" she asked, and immediately started to talk about something else, without waiting for an answer.

The next day, at exactly six in the morning, when Brasco, still half awake and suffocated by a buzzing dizziness that had tormented him through the night, came out of his room and went to the bathroom to refresh himself by submerging his head in clear water, he saw her sitting there on a bench, already bathed and dressed, impatient, waiting for him.

"Is it true, *mister*," she said suddenly, without saying good morning first, "that sometimes the snow falls blue and clean like the sky, and other times gray and soiled like dirt?"

"It's almost always white, but there are so many shades that the Eskimos who live in the frozen lands of Alaska have a hundred different words for the color white. To live in Colombia you must know a thousand different words for green . . ."

"Green, green, you always talk about green and what I want to talk about is white. And is it true, yes or no, that when a lot of snow falls you shouldn't wear silk stockings because they get stuck to your legs and if you try to take them off you'll tear off your skin and everything? Is it true?"

"Where did you hear that . . . ?"

"Somebody was going around saying it."

"You must be crazy. In the middle of this dizzying heat you come to me talking about snow . . ."

"My friend Claire doesn't like it either."

"Doesn't like what?"

"Talking about snow. I asked her and she avoided the subject because she says it made her sad to remember it. Is it true that snow is sad, *mister* Brasco?"

"No, Sayo, it's not sad. It's white, and beautiful, and happy, and I do like to talk about it. It's just that it makes me laugh to see how anxious it makes you . . ."

And if I tell her to come with me to Vermont, wondered Frank Brasco, more as a pleasurable and irresponsible musing than as a real possibility. And if I tell her not to be afraid because she will like my village even though it's not just like the postcard and because her silk stockings won't adhere to her skin, he stopped to consider, and that the snow extends blue-white and radiant there because there's no one to walk in it.

"But I didn't tell her," he confesses to me, "because deep down I didn't have the slightest intention of taking on such a commitment and because it was evident that she wasn't there to ramble on about fate but to inquire about certain very concrete aspects of the snow problem that she was still unsure about."

So Sayonara sat there looking up, with her eyes lost in a sky reverberating with light and heat, and asked:

"What flies higher, *mister*, snow or an airplane?"

"Snow doesn't fly, it falls."

"Airplanes also fall, sometimes."

"Okay, okay. Let's say that airplanes fly higher, then, because they can go over the clouds. Snow falls from the clouds."

"Then snow is pieces of cloud? And when snow falls, does it stay there forever?"

"No, because it melts, like ice."

"It falls onto animals, and the animals turn white. It falls on the trees, and the trees turn white . . . oh, how I would like all the trees and roofs in Tora to turn white! It would be so pretty. And I would have a good wool coat to protect me from the cold," she assured him, and her dark body, embraced by the sun, shivered beneath her light cotton sleeveless dress. "Do you wear a coat, *mister* Brasco, back where you're from?"

"A coat lined with fur and high boots and gloves and a wool cap."

"That's what I would like! A red wool hat . . . Olguita, she knows how to knit, she could make me one . . . if snow ever falls in Tora, of course, because if not then, why . . . ? And is it true, *mister*, that snow burns?"

"It could be, yes. It's so cold that it burns."

"So cold that it burns!" she laughed, hitting her thighs with the palms of her hands. "The things this gringo says! It's a good thing, snow, and Claire wasn't right when she said it was sad. How I would like to have a little snow, even just a handful!"

"Some day, some day," he lied, as he thought, And if I tell her to come with me to Vermont and to bring Todos los Santos with her? And Olguita too so she could knit them red wool caps. It would be a folly the size of a mountain, he realized, so he didn't say anything and he felt falling upon his shoulders, soft and wilted like snowflakes, the words of love that he never said.

"Don't be a liar, *mister*!" Sayonara protested, as if she were reading his thoughts. "How am I going to feel snow if it's never going to snow in Tora? At the very most we might get hail, and that on Judgment Day, but snow, what you call snow, it only falls over there, where the big world is."

The big world, she had said, and those words were accompanied by a wide, circular gesture of her hand and arm, as if indicating a very long journey, impossible, unthinkable.

"But Tora is also part of the big world," he said, trying to cheer her up.

"Don't be ridiculous. The big world is faaaaar away, there, way away, where only airplanes go."

"What do you want to know about the big world? Ask me anything, I'll answer you."

"No lies?"

"Only the truth."

"Then tell me, *mister* Brasco, when the airplanes fly over us, what happens with the *caca* and *pipí* that the people inside make? Does it fall on our heads?"

"I don't know. I've always wondered the same thing."

"You see? Why should I ask you if you don't know anything. Just keep talking about the snow. What did you tell me it was made of?"

"What do you think?"

"Flour or sand. Or rice. Who knows, it must be some very white powder."

Frank Brasco clears the path that leads to his cabin, throwing to the side shovelfuls of flour, or sand, or rice, and meanwhile he describes to me Sayonara's animated black eyes, which keep searching, without seeing all the green shining uselessly around her, because she preferred to lose herself in white-painted dreams.

"Did you ever consider, señor Brasco, the possibility of staying in Tora to live?" I ask.

"When I lived there I had the sensation of belonging in an unavoidable way to this world here, and now that I live here it's the opposite, I feel that I have never felt as at home as I did there."

He never slept with her, he confesses to me, and not because of lack of desire, but because he arrived in La Catunga during the so-called rice strike, initiated by the workers of Campo 26, which broke out in a labor and civil action in Tora, and during which the entire population declared solidarity with the demands of the *petroleros*. The *prostitutas* struck too, joining the striking ranks by making the decision not to work until the strike succeeded, with the result that for nearly twenty days and nights they didn't go to bed for money, and if they made love, it was only out of love.

"I'll talk about the strike later, if you want, because it's a story that is well worth the trouble of telling. But now I want to concentrate on the memory of Sayonara, without interference. I want you to know that her body and mine never touched, but other things did, which were probably our souls—they caressed each other at will, accompanied each other and rocked to the same rhythm, like a boat on an ocean swell. And those were days so charged with energy and enthusiasm, because of the tremendous explosion of hope, of fear and solidarity that the strike awakened in all of us, that it seemed like you were making love without ever needing to."

"But there is something I don't understand, señor Brasco, and allow me to advance a single question about the subject of the strike. Which side were you on, the American boss's or the Colombian workers'?"

"The Colombian workers' side, of course. Why do you think my stay in Colombia ended so quickly? Since Tropical Oil couldn't prove charges of my collaboration with the enemy, the letter they sent asking for my resignation alluded to 'inconvenient relationships' with Colombian prostitutes, expressly prohibited to American employees, they said, to avoid infection with syphilis and other venereal diseases. It was an allusion to her, to Sayonara, because they had seen us together during the strike. That was the apparent motive of my dismissal, but things were as I am telling you: I never had physical contact with her, or any other woman. Now let me tell you about the last night I spent in your country, at Todos los Santos's house."

"I'm listening."

"There were about fifteen people sleeping there with me while outside the threat continued, because the company and the government, which had broken the strike by force, were merciless and continued to pursue the guilty."

In one of the rooms, on mattresses laid out on the floor, slept Sacramento, Frank Brasco, and the other men, and the women were scattered around the rest of the house: Sayonara, Todos los Santos, Machuca, Analía, and a few others. Brasco tells me that despite the tension and the overpopulation, there was harmony in the sleeping house, and that the warmth of close bodies staved off any danger. Every now and then a cough, a somnambulant sigh, a creaking of floorboards gave testimony to the affinity of the human flock when it finds itself gathered, pacified, protected by a roof and a door that isolate it from the rest of the world. In his sleeplessness, Brasco happily realized how much it pleased him to feel like a member of a clan, linked by unspoken affections to those who lay next to him on this side of the wall, inside the protecting and hermetic circle that is a family and a home.

"The only feeling of well-being that can compare with the one I felt that night in the midst of so much company," he tells me, "is this cozy solitude in which I now live."

Early the next morning, before four o'clock, he had to leave overland for Bogotá, where he would take an airplane back to his homeland, so he got up while it was still dark, among the clamor of crickets and other nocturnal animals he couldn't identify, and he began to urinate, trying not to make any noise that would disturb the others. But Sayonara was already up and she approached him, barefoot, with sleep tangled in her hair and her body wrapped in a sheet to protect her from the cool dawn air.

"That's right, better urinate now, *mister*," she ordered him, laughing. "That way you won't spray us from the air."

"I will never forget you," he promised her.

"You're never going to forget me? Listen to the things that occur to this gringo! Don't speak useless words, *mister* Brasco. Memories melt, like snowflakes."

eleven

 One elusive morning, bathed in the perplexing light of an eclipse, beautiful Claire, the ethereal traveler, left this world into which she had perhaps never finished arriving. Her passing through Tora was sad and fleeting, like the shadow of someone who is present without really being there and who is not aware of the laws of gravity. Her death, however, fell upon La Catunga with the full weight of the calamity. It took everyone by surprise, leaving the barrio suspended between horror and shock and bringing to the fore how little we natives know of the foreigners who live among us. It doesn't matter that ten years, or twenty, pass: The outsider is still a stranger—in good measure suspicious—who has just arrived. Of Claire one could think, in accordance with her pale beauty and the fleeting lines of her character, that she rose in body and soul to heaven in the ecstasy of an assumption, like the Virgin Mary. But it wasn't thus; hers was an earthly and brutal death.

"One foul day Claire threw herself into the path of the train," Todos los Santos tells me. "Don't be alarmed, it was a common means of death among the *prostitutas* of Tora. Many of them killed themselves by the train out of despair, or loneliness, or indifference. Sometimes simply out of weariness or pure drunkenness. Never before three in the morning or after five, and all at the same spot: the corner they call Armería del Ferrocarril, in the poorer part of the barrio Hueso Blanco."

Now there's a gas station located there, and a car repair shop and a stand that sells newspapers, snacks, and drinks, just like on any other corner on the planet. But Todos los Santos assures me that if you watch carefully, you can see people still making the sign of the cross as they pass that corner, because they know they are stepping on unholy ground: the site of immolation.

According to tradition, Claire's remains were gathered up in a cart and taken to the place where she had lived, located in the miserable Calle de los Veinte Cuartos—the Street of Twenty Rooms. Todos los Santos was summoned to the deceased's room, one of the twenty that was squeezed along that alley saturated with the smell of excrement and rancid fruit. She was to carry out the compassionate act of arranging the cadaver's parts as lifelike as possible inside the coffin, officiate over the ceremony of closing the eyelids, and, to the degree it was possible, cross the arms over the chest, wrap the body in a shroud, and cover the head with a veil of silk lace.

"My heart shriveled when I entered that place," she tells me. "Claire was one of those who earned the most from her work; she saved what she earned and had become a rich woman. If she didn't live like a queen it was because she didn't want to, and because she always believed that she was here temporarily."

Despite having lodged Claire for a dozen years, the little room was still a poor and transient-looking place, with scarcely any furnishings. Not a single animal, not a single plant, nothing incompatible with the desolate impersonality of a boardinghouse, nothing that couldn't be packed up from one moment to the next, nothing that would involve delays when it was time to leave.

"Afterward, tying up loose ends, we came to a realization. Not even the train's passing could cure Claire of the broken promise that was always strangling her, like a hand pressing on her throat," Todos los

Santos recalls. "During the ten years Claire had lived in Colombia she agonized under false hope; now we know for certain that there was no other motive that pushed her toward her end."

From time to time throughout those ten years of anxiety and waiting they would hear her sigh for a certain Mariano, who, however, had never been seen in Tora. They all suspected that Claire languished in a distracted haze because she had given her heart to this Mariano. Rumors of him arrived, but he never did. His letters, staggered, also arrived, inside fine envelopes of Kimberly paper with Claire's name and address handwritten in sepia ink and beautiful nineteenth-century script; and the rumor circulated through the pueblo that he sent his lover funds in the form of money orders.

"Yes, there were money orders, but they weren't from him to her, it was the reverse," clarifies Fideo, as she travels in her hammock as if on a riverboat.

"How's that?"

"Just as it sounds. It was Claire who sent money to Mariano in the capital to support his electoral campaigns, because he was a politician."

According to the news that Mistinguett had spread around, with who knows what basis, Claire left her native France and came to America in the footsteps of this man, who had promised to marry her one spring night on the Pont des Arts. But clearly it was not her who he finally married, as the women of La Catunga would learn on the day of Claire's funeral.

The beautiful French woman was mourned, like so many fellow *prostitutas* who had died before her, in the red hall of the Dancing Miramar, surrounded like a bride by carnations and tapers; the face—miraculously spared by the impact and still beautiful—was enveloped in the silk lace veil; definitive was the paleness of her death and delicate the shadow cast by her eyelashes on her cheeks of soft Sevres porcelain, like that depicted on the postcard sent by Sacramento.

Except for Sayonara, who wasn't anywhere to be found, all of La Catunga was there, accompanying in grief someone who had died by her own hand and far from her homeland. The main hall of the Miramar—with its rows of mirrors, its Venetian chandeliers, its red and black velvet upholstery—in the semidarkness of midnight glistened dreamlike and splendid like a salon at Versailles, but beneath the indiscreet intrusion of the sun, it had more the look of a real funeral parlor: sad, faded, dusty, and airless.

The Dancing Miramar—doubly promiscuous?—was the unique and shared precinct for the rites of love and the rites of death, and not by choice but for lack of another alternative. Save for a few veterans, like Todos los Santos or Olguita, who were owners of houses with plots of land, the other women had only minuscule rooms in a jumble of precarious and collective buildings, with a common bath and kitchen. And those cubicles, which could scarcely hold a bed, certainly had no room for even a tenth of the huge crowd that generally appeared at funerals.

On the other hand, by decree of the parish priest, not even a dead prostitute, literally speaking, could enter the church, which provided an opportunity for La Negra Florecida, owner of the Dancing Miramar, who charged each girl ten pesos a night to dance in her establishment and snag clients, and a hundred and twenty for a funeral service, taking into account that the latter fee was paid only once. She made it available only during the day and as part of the deal she provided the tapers, the candelabras, black coffee in little cups for the ladies, rum in discreet quantities for the gentlemen, a sign at the entrance with a black emblem and the name of the deceased written in gothic letters, along with four dozen white, sweet-smelling flowers.

That afternoon, as they mourned Claire, those present witnessed the arrival of an imposing funeral wreath, the size of a truck wheel, into which at least two hundred roses of spectral whiteness had been intertwined and across which was a purple cloth ribbon with gold letters reading: MARIANO AZCÁRRAGA CABALLERO Y SEÑORA. The girls of La Catunga read the pompous name and were left breathless; fifteen months earlier Mariano Azcárraga Caballero, electoral baron of high caliber and kingpin of the reigning political party, had been elected senator. And "Señora"? Three months earlier there had been news of the existence of that wife, by way of the daily newspaper *El Tiempo*, which published a photograph of her on her wedding day with the same Mariano in whom Claire had deposited, until that day of irreparable sorrow and supreme anguish, all of her faith, her hope, and the better part of her charity.

"That's what she got for not mistrusting power, which is always poisonous and treacherous and disdainful of people," notes Fideo from the sidelines.

Dragging her trailing legs and bearing the wreath, Olguita approached Claire and placed it at her feet.

"Your Mariano wants you to know that he's with you at the hour of your death," she said quietly, rearranging a lock of limp, blond hair.

The Dancing Miramar no longer exists, but La Negra Florecida does and today she's the mother, grandmother, and great-grandmother of a tribe of men and women who are university graduates. She is very ill from an intestinal infection that they call, as she told me, the seventeen types of fecal material, and when I asked her, most likely with a look of surprise on my face, to repeat the name of her illness, she told me that if I didn't believe her she would show me the lab results, to which I quickly responded that that would not be necessary, that I had really come to ask her about something else.

"A hundred twenty pesos per dead person wasn't much to charge," she told me, "if you take into account that after the funeral I had to pay a *rezandero* to cleanse the place, because it would be contaminated after four or five hours of sheltering a tearful, moaning crowd. Around here there has always been a belief that after a funeral the walls are still in grief. If they aren't cleaned no one will want to come back at night to fall in love, sing, and laugh."

The Dancing Miramar: dual shelter of love and of death? No, an entire universe, and threefold, like the Trinity: birth, love, and death.

"I didn't just take care of death," La Negra Florecida told me, looking at me through her glasses, thick as the bottom of a bottle, as the seventeen types of fecal material ravaged her intestines. "I also handled births: I had set up a delivery room on the second floor, because there were many girls who ended up pregnant. When the time came I sent someone to fetch Cuatrocientos, who helped with the deliveries."

On her way to Claire's funeral, Todos los Santos stopped at her house to get Sayonara, but she couldn't find the girl. She asked around the block if anyone had seen her, but no one had. Claire was buried at sunset in a field where cows were grazing, free of crosses or tombstones, removed from the village and at the edge of the Río Magdalena, a place they called the Other Cemetery. It was there, with no shelter other than a flight of herons and no monument other than a weeping willow, that suicide victims, masons, unbaptized babies, women who had had abortions, and *prostitutas* went to find eternal rest—all unredeemable sinners to whom the priests refused burial in the Cementerio Mayor. At least with the double stigma of prostitution and suicide, Claire's unlucky star marked her for exile in death, just as it had in life.

"Claire wasn't a sad woman," says Todos los Santos in an elegiac tone, "she was sadness itself disguised as a woman. I have never known a more helpless soul in all the days of my life. However, it was she who brought to our attention that in the France of the Louis we, the courtesans, triumphed and we proudly let ourselves be called daughters of happiness."

I always imagined this beautifully surreal scene: a group of women wrapped in black clothes yet immune to the suffocating and shadowless midday heat, standing in front of a fresh hole in the red dirt of Tora in the middle of a vast nothingness of high pastures. A couple dozen Cebu cattle with several herons perched on their backs watching with infantile curiosity and slowly forming a circle around the field's unusual visitors.

Months later, when I myself had to attend a burial in the same place and under similar circumstances, I was able to verify that there in fact was a heat that was unbearable for me, tolerable for them, and the cattle also were there with their tick-removing herons, and the dead woman who yields docilely to the red earth. And yet, the foreshadowed image contained a double error that I will correct at once: There was shade after all, because the grave had been dug beneath the shelter of an enormous violet *guayacán* tree in full bloom, and the women weren't standing, solemn but at the same time eager to leave that place, as is often the case with the mourners in the Jardines del Recuerdo, the Tierra del Apogeo, the Valle de la Paz, and the rest of the cemeteries in our cities; instead they were idle and lying down in a clearing with the patience of rocks, as placid as if they had come to stay, chatting among themselves openly about the deceased's virtues, about her bad habits, about the illness that led her to the grave, about anything in general and in particular, and about the chicken stew that they were going to cook right there and consume with rum in complicity with the traveler to the next world and as a means of invoking her well-being.

As the stew was eaten and beautiful Claire was remembered, and afterward too, during the shoveling of dirt on the coffin, Todos los Santos looked from time to time toward the path leading to the pueblo with a presentiment of her adopted daughter Sayonara's arrival, which nevertheless didn't occur then or later, while they waited at home until after eleven that night without receiving word that she was at the Dancing Miramar, the neighborhood cafés, the home of one of her friends, the rocks at the river with the laundresses, the Arab's shops, the Acandai waterfall, or other usual places; they grew so worried that toward midnight Todos los Santos, Olga, and Machuca went looking for her at the hospital, the police station, and finally the morgue, but all without result.

"She isn't injured, sick, or dead," concluded Todos los Santos, who refused to keep looking for the girl and ordered the others to go to bed. "She left because she wanted to."

Why had Sayonara left? It wasn't easy to deduce the motive for her fleeing, which had occurred just when her life was going splendidly. She had become a golden legend, surrounded by the love of hundreds of *petroleros*, possessed of radiant youth and a wild beauty that was magnified a hundredfold by rumors. Loved and supported by her *madrina*, who was an imposing figure in La Catunga, and by the majority of the population of the barrio, who accepted without jealousy her clear professional supremacy. She was privileged also in the art of being a *puta*, in having so many aspirants that she could give herself the luxury of rejecting drunks, foul-smelling or virus-pocked clients, men with sour characters or exotic tastes in bed; she was so spoiled and blessed among all the other women that she only needed to appear briefly in the Dancing Miramar and to dance under the spotlights, somnolent and unenthusiastic, for the men who were in love with her to express their willingness to give her their paychecks just to caress her with a look.

The day after Sayonara's disappearance, Olguita, Delia Ramos, and the others devoted themselves to figuring what had happened to her and to finding her no matter where she was, and through inquiries and interrogations they managed to follow her trail to a tiny river port an hour and a half from Tora called Madre de Dios, where some fishermen confirmed they had seen her arrive alone, walking without bags and barefoot. Beyond Madre de Dios, all trace of her vanished.

"Maybe she boarded a *chalupa* and went downriver," said the fishermen without conviction. "Maybe, who knows?"

Isolated in her house, a perplexed and shaken Todos los Santos locked herself in her room and lit three candles of supplication on her altar.

"Tell me where she is, Jesucristo," she begged. "If you don't know, no one knows."

The Holy Christ smiled at her as pained as always, sweet and removed from human affairs, never uttering a word.

Then Todos los Santos began to study the postcards, remembering the faith with which Sayonara seemed to seek in them the key to some divine plan.

"Would she have gone off to look for Sacramento?" she asked herself, and the possibility seemed soothing to her, because it meant that the web of affection that they had woven together had not been broken, and that the girl wasn't wandering around lost, as feared, through the distant, unreachable shadows of her past. But no, it wasn't likely that she had followed after Sacramento, because the postcards gave no account of the location from which they had been sent.

Two things had occurred on the previous ill-fated day, mused Todos los Santos, wanting to tie up loose ends as she carefully examined the postcards to extract their secrets from them. Claire's death and Sayonara's disappearance: What did these two adversities have to do with this PALACE IN KATMANDU, opening its gardens to visitors, or with these two women, so absorbed in knitting their lace that to them the rest of the world doesn't exist? What the devil could be revealed by this QUEEN ELIZABETH II OF GREAT BRITAIN, if she seemed to be asleep with her eyes open beneath the weight of her enormous crown? What hidden thread could unite the FUNERAL URN, MUISCA CULTURE with the PORCELAIN JAR, MING DYNASTY, NINETEENTH CENTURY? Nothing, absolutely nothing, aside from the fact that both were thousand-year-old earthenware vessels. And so she continued to speculate, trying to make some sense of this nonsense, dazed with confusion, until dawn arrived, then she spent two days eating little and speaking even less, ruminating senselessly on the words on the postcards until she pushed them aside in disgust.

"No more silliness," she ordered herself. "We only know what our hearts tell us about people, and mine is shouting to me that this girl is going to come back. I just have to give her time."

With the first light of the fifth day, Todos los Santos, still not completely awake, saw Sayonara again. Or thought she saw the girl standing at the threshold of her vigil, there at her bedroom door. But she was shrunken, thin, and timid, just as she had appeared two years before when she arrived in Tora for the first time. The spectral apparition looked at her without smiling, once again looking more like a child than an adolescent, once again malnourished, suspicious, barefoot, and unkempt—smelling, as before, of smoke and helplessness. As if time had stagnated and everything were unreal and identical to the way it had begun.

"Are you a person or a memory?" whispered Todos los Santos.

Todos los Santos was on the verge of collapse when she was rescued by another sudden apparition in the doorway. This time it was the real Sayonara, the same smiling, beautiful girl who had left the house on the day of Claire's death.

"*Madrina*," she said, pushing forward the small replica of herself, "this is my younger sister, Ana. I have come to ask if she can live here with us."

On three other occasions over the course of the following year in similarly mysterious circumstances, Sayonara disappeared and reappeared without advising anyone of her intentions or telling anyone where she had gone, and always with identical results, and those three new opportunities also had their own names: Susana, Juana, and Chuza. So that by December the house was full and all five sisters were present, as Sayonara swore to Todos los Santos, promising her that she wouldn't be bringing any more. Sayonara was the eldest, then Ana, Susana, Juana, and finally Chuza, a very tiny, very dark little child with shining eyes, hair to her waist, and the reflexes of a lizard, who didn't speak Spanish or any other language and measured no more than twenty inches in height.

All five were installed full time and for life in Todos los Santos's house, all five having appeared out of nowhere, all swarthy, short-statured, and long-haired, one behind the other like those lacquered wooden dolls from Russia that you keep opening and inside you find another identical but smaller, and another and still another, in a descending line until you reach the tiniest, which in this case was little Chuza.

When she learned of sweet Claire's fierce death, a shadow, like a dead bird, fell across Sayonara's gaze and her expression froze into a mask, as if she had been told of a shame that was too much her own, that in some unsuspected way had something to do with her.

"My mother and my brother committed suicide," she said suddenly, five or six days later, making those who heard her shudder. "Until then my pueblo had known nothing about suicide; it had never occurred to a single one of those people to die that way. And suddenly two happened one after the other, with only a few hours between them, and both in my family."

After a period of silence she added: "I loved my brother very much."

Todos los Santos asked nothing, and she tells me that she had several reasons for doing so. First, because there is pain that doesn't allow questions or offer any answers. Second, to respect the memories of others, which are sacrosanct and private, and to avoid probing into the hidden story that had always been guessed at yet still eluded them, as if calling attention to it was a way of invoking it. And because of jealousy, I would add: I don't think that she wanted to admit the existence of another family and other love, different from her own, in Sayonara's life.

"I hadn't even been born when my mother died." The girl didn't make it any easier to find out much about her life, given her penchant for dropping false clues.

So the adopted mother didn't say anything to her adopted daughter but secretly began to watch Sayonara's every step, especially in the shifting hours between night and dawn, and if she saw the girl heading in the direction of the train tracks, she would take her by the arm, hastily inventing some pretext, and accompany her.

"I was afraid that her blood would pull her and throw her under the train," Todos los Santos confesses to me. "Ways of dying are inherited, you know? Like eye color or shoe size."

Like Todos los Santos and her friends, I too came to know in a single sentence of the existence of Sayonara's mother and brother and of their suicide. In a single instant they appeared, tied me to the enigma of their death, and disappeared, forcing me to spend that night awake, looking toward the river from the window of my room at the Hotel Pipatón. The formerly great Río de la Magdalena seemed to me like a long absence: slow, black, full of dredging boats—could those brown monsters that sank their feet in the water be dredgers?—and other metallic and orthopedic apparatuses that turned it into an extension of the refinery, which spread across the opposite bank, rusting the night sky with the perpetual combustion pouring from its tall smokestacks. An incongruent smell, feminine and sweet, came from those iron pipes. Don Pitula, the taxi driver who guided me around Tora—and who worked as a welder at the refinery for twenty-five years—had told me that afternoon that the perfumed smoke came from a factory that made aromatics, where they processed petroleum into shampoo, facial creams, and other cosmetics.

"The factory that smells the best is the most poisonous," he told me. "Working there is like signing a death sentence."

That frivolous, lethal fragrance seeped into my hotel room, a toxic effluvium of cheap cologne that rose through my nasal passages to my brain, where it sketched the image of Sayonara. Without ever having known or seen her, I had been trying to decipher her for several weeks, and with some degree of certainty, it had seemed until then, although perhaps I was forcing the missing pieces of her character a little to make them fit into a coherent whole. And now the specters of a mother and a brother killed by their own wills had made their brutal appearance, hopelessly exploding the puzzle that I had thus far managed to halfway assemble. Who were they? Why had they taken their lives? What deadly vocation had weighed so heavily on them? The day before, they hadn't existed in my awareness, and now they had loaded the image of Sayonara with a past so final, so turbulent that it threatened to bury the fragile blossom of her present beneath a river of sand. That mother and brother fell upon me from out of nowhere, bringing with them a worrisome guest I had not anticipated, at least not yet and not in such an excessive dose: the breath of death, which blended that night with the cloying smell of the aromatics factory.

"The big ugly bird hovered over Sayonara," Fideo told me, referring to death, with the lucidity and the edge that come only from the mouth of the dying. "There was no doubt about that. But she knew how to handle it. Don't pluck out my eyes, she commanded it, and the creature kept still. It didn't leave her alone, but it didn't harm her."

I learned that Todos los Santos was soon able to forget about her vigilance and fear with respect to a suicidal instinct in Sayonara, who seemed instead to be growing happier and more confident in the goodness of life, and about whom nothing aroused suspicion that she might belong to the group of those who are not comfortable on this side of heaven. If it was indeed true, as Fideo believed, that she carried the predatory bird of death on her shoulder, then it was also true that she had learned to feed it from her hand.

twelve

 Meanwhile, what was Sacramento up to? He was setting a course, together with his friend Payanés, along a rough road of old iron and broken machinery, which the birds resented and the vegetation didn't take long to devour. Ready now for the labor market with their hands and feet hardened with calluses, they had begun their pilgrimage to the Tropical Oil Company's famous Camp 26, which rose up from the indifferent jungle like a great industrial city, gray and repetitive in its metallic roar and closed off by barbed wire. Armed watchmen kept safe from any threat its treasure of beams and towers, machines, turbogenerators, gears, boilers, and fire-fighting units.

"I don't like this, *hermano*, it looks like a prison," protested Sacramento when they first saw it from afar.

"Cheer up and stop complaining," responded Payanés, "because that is the face of progress. Learn it well, because that's how every last corner of the world is going to look in fifty years: total development and entertainment for mankind."

A recruiter just like the one that had rejected them a year before hired them on this time, as *cuñero*'s helpers—Payanés with card number 29-170 and Sacramento with the next, 29-171.

"This is the most beautiful number, the one that belongs to my lucky star," Payanés said to Sacramento. "My mother died on the twenty-ninth, a blessed day."

"And the other numbers you were assigned, one, seven, and zero, do they also mean something?"

"Of course, man, zero is the universe, the symbol of eternity, and besides it's round like an asshole."

"And the one and the seven?"

"They're extra; they don't represent anything."

"I would have liked for my card to have had a five. Five is my favorite number."

"You don't have any reason to complain, yours has the number twenty-nine also, the anniversary of my blessed mother."

"But I didn't even know her . . ."

"You can be sure that she would have loved you like a son."

"Oh, well then, if that's so . . . ," said Sacramento, half consoled.

To have a contract at any of the camps, and particularly at 9, 22, and 26, the ones that produced the greatest number of barrels, was like knowing the password to heaven. There was no greater honor imaginable for a man, no better guarantee, and most of all it meant having found a port in the storm. "Now we are salaried employees," they repeated over and over, pronouncing the words with greater pride than if they had been named kings of Rome. In the middle of that vast, drifting humanity, to become a *petrolero* meant salvation.

Their joy was so great at finally having been awarded their cards and the salary that qualified them as members of the working class, as part of the heroic union of *petroleros*, they didn't even realize that they didn't know what a *cuñero* was, much less a *cuñero*'s helper.

"Look for skinny Emilia and ask for Abelino Robles, the gang leader. You just obey the orders he gives you, even if he tells you to put panties on a mermaid."

They assured and reassured him that of course, he could count on them, and they sailed off filled with enthusiasm, and without understanding much about exactly where they were going or what they would be doing.

"Can you tell me who skinny Emilia is? Where I can find her?" Sacramento asked a nearby worker with a kind face.

"Did you hear that?" the worker said to the others around him. "This guy's dying to meet Emilia."

"You don't want to fuck her because she'll rip your dick off," someone shouted, laughing, as the group walked away.

Since skinny Emilia turned out not to be skinny or even a woman, but one of the drilling towers in Camp 26, Sacramento and Payanés reddened with embarrassment at their naiveté and decided that from then on they would do things on their own, opening their eyes wide and biting their tongues before asking anything. Emilia, the oldest and most venerated tower in the oil territory—a 1912 Gardner Denver—stood solidly in the center of the camp like a ritual obelisk. Pachydermic and anachronistic but also imposing and all-powerful, Emilia was brutal in the merciless obsession with which she twisted her diamond bit to tear into the earth's heart, and famous not only for having worked day and night for decades without ever failing but also for her implacable temperament. It was said that if you handled her with intelligence and in full command of your five senses she treated you well, but the clumsy and the careless she made pay with their lives, as had already happened on two occasions, first with a pipe capper who she let fall fifty feet like a dove without wings, then, years later, a welder who she cut in two with the fulminating whip of a high-tension wire that suddenly broke without warning.

"Look at her carefully," Abelino Robles, the veteran cuñero, advised them. "Not only does she spin furiously, but the smallest part of her weighs as much as a man. All it takes is for you to drop a wrench on your foot to put you out of commission permanently, not to mention putting a hand where it doesn't belong."

"This Emilia; I've never seen such an incredible beast," said Payanés, impressed, looking at her deeply and lovingly as if she were a pagan

temple, delicately caressing the bluntness of her iron beams and uncon-
sciously making a pledge of fidelity that would be honored without fail
from that first encounter until the day death parted them.

"So, Payanés is dead?" I ask.

"Emilia is dead."

The alliance between the two of them was sealed that very night,
when Payanés was approached by a wandering peddler who professed
some skill in the art of tattooing and offered him the painless inscription
of the name of the woman he loved anywhere on his body.

"Put 'Emilia' here, on my chest. And put a little drawing beside it."

"How about a dagger or a swallow?"

"No, no daggers, and no swallows either."

"What about a rose?"

"That's it, a rose; a rose with a thorn and a drop of blood."

"The rose didn't turn out very well, it looked more like a carnation,"
Sacramento would say later, when he saw the drawing engraved forever
in blue and red ink on his friend's left pectoral. "The drop does look very
realistic. But the 'Emilia' . . . the 'Emilia,' I don't know, Payanés, it
seems risky. If they change your position you won't be able to take off
your shirt even to take a bath."

"They're not going to change my position," asserted Payanés, before
he fell asleep in his hammock. "I'm going to be the best *cuñero* in the
whole country, you'll see."

For three days—the three days of apprenticeship—the two young
men carried out the humble task of being the *cuñero*'s helpers, which consisted of clearing the mud off the platform as they watched, not missing
a thing, Abelino Robles and another seasoned worker execute the job of
petrolero with the precision of watchmakers and the mental concentration
of lion tamers and with Emilia's monumental and furious gears seem-
ingly calmed by their touch.

"Now it's your turn," announced Abelino Robles at the beginning of
the fourth day.

"Let's go!" shouted Payanés animatedly to Sacramento. "Let's put the panties on this mermaid."

The drilling pipe, which needed to penetrate the earth to a depth of three thousand feet, would grow longer as the *cuñeros*, from a low platform, screwed on more and more lengths of fifty-foot pipe. In order to do this, Sacramento would have to grip the new piece of pipe, which was hanging vertically through the center of the tower, with a precision wrench known as the scorpion, while Payanés capped the string of buried pipes with a 130-pound steel crown fitted with special bolts. Each time the bit wore out they had to remove the fitted pipes and disassemble them, reversing the fitting process.

"You're going to work as a team and each of you is going to depend on the other," the veteran fitter advised them. "Sacramento, if you slip with the scorpion, the pipe will sever your friend's hands; Payanés, if you don't fit the band well, the pipes will slide and the scorpion will spin around, kick Sacramento, and mess him up."

From the beginning Payanés showed natural ability, and even a certain happiness and ease of execution, and he proudly displayed on his naked torso, bathed in sweat, the throbbing *petrolero*'s rose, with its sharp thorn and drop of blood. Meanwhile, Sacramento seemed afraid and uncertain, gripped with nervous tension, as if counting every minute of every hour remaining before their shift ended without accident.

"Don't worry, *hermano*, I won't let you down," he shouted to Payanés above the deafening racket every now and then, as if to assure himself that what he was saying was true.

After eight hours of uninterrupted exertion, the whistle blew and the pair abandoned skinny Emilia to head for the barracks, arm in arm, exhausted, muddy from head to toe, and as giddy as a couple of boys who had just won a soccer match.

For only three weeks Sacramento was able to enjoy this occupational happiness, which for him meant, above all else, the possibility of getting closer to Sayonara. The illness, which had already infected him with its germ and dogged his steps, then fell upon him with all of its fury. The first manifestation was a dull, nagging pain, which made him dizzy and which he attributed to the eight hours a day that he spent focused on the bit.

"My thoughts were growing more and more confused and my love for Sayonara more tormented, and I blamed it on the noise of the machinery. But even when I had moved away from the drilling equipment, its roar pursued me; I heard it all night and its vibration rattled me to the bone.

"Later I lost my appetite and even when I'd had nothing to eat I vomited yellow, watery bile, for which I also found a justification, this time in the hardened balls of cold rice with lard that were passed around at lunchtime; they were so compact and inedible that we would use them as soccer balls."

Then he was overtaken by a waxy paleness and a pain in his temples, and a rising fever made its appearance. Sacramento, incapable of working and declared contagious by the medical staff, was moved to the camp's neat white hospital, where he came to share space and destinies with other lucky souls who were cured in fifteen or twenty days, and also with others less fortunate who were being consumed by mountain leprosy, malaria, intestinal infection, or tuberculosis and who represented nothing more to the company than financial loss.

Forgotten in that antiseptic corner of industrial paradise, Sacramento defended himself from the invading parasite with all of his available energy, and the ferocity of the internal combat began to produce extremely high fevers, combined with shivering and a trembling of his bones, which creaked in self-defense.

"I'm turning black, *hermano*," he said to a nurse called Demetrio.

"It's the melancholic fluids that are spreading through your body," explained Demetrio, who knew nothing of diplomacy when it came time to explain to his patients the symptoms of their illnesses.

"The black fluids, you mean?"

"Yes. They flow, little by little, blackening the liver, the spleen, the brain, the red blood cells. Well, just about everything; they turn everything black."

"*Hermano*, I'm burning alive," Sacramento complained to his friend Payanés, who came to visit whenever he could. "I'm burning with fever and with love and I'm roasting over a low fire. Don't I look black to you?"

"Black, no; just a little yellow. But it'll go away. Sooner or later everybody gets over it."

Despite Payanés's forced words of comfort, Sacramento felt weaker and weaker, more diminished, while a microscopic but audacious enemy was growing and multiplying inside him, assuming the frightening shapes of rings, clubs, and bunches of grapes.

Twice a day apathetic nurses went by the beds of those they called convalescents, among whom—with who knows what criteria—Sacramento had been placed. They performed their duties on the run, without paying much attention to anyone or asking any questions, distributing the only available medicine: quinine for fevers, aspirin for pain, brown mixture for infections, and white mixture for unknown ills.

"Don't get too excited about the medicine, it's more toxic than the illness is," Demetrio would say to Sacramento as he gave him his ration of quinine. "Look at these pills, they're pink and round like women. And hurtful like women."

Like a bad actor, Sacramento would perform the same brief, equivocal scene every morning. He would stand up on his trembling legs, splash water on his face, halfheartedly run a comb through his tangled hair, and announce that he was cured, that he wanted to be taken to skinny Emilia because he was ready to go back to work.

"Tell me where there's oil," he would rant, "and that's where I'll drill the hole."

The next minute, exhausted by the futile exertion, he would collapse back onto his bed, surrendering to the fever, renouncing his existence in this world and withdrawing into his delirious passion for Sayonara. He would spend hours immobile with his eyes rolled back, searching for her, pleading and whispering incoherently into her ear, his whole body lifeless, feeling the sweat cooling on his skin and turning into a fine film of salt, telling him that everything was useless, that his dreams had already been shattered forever.

"I started to think that letting myself die from love was the only course, and that the sooner it happened the better."

Resigned to the other side of hibernation, receptive now to the idea of nothingness, he noticed with annoyance how without his consent his body reinitiated the war against the parasite; how his army of white blood cells remobilized, infuriating once more the fevers and the deterioration, stirring up again the demands of life, which in spite of his wishes refused to surrender without attempting one last battle.

On his first free Friday, Payanés traveled to La Catunga but he was unable to get into the Dancing Miramar, which was overflowing with people, not to mention the line two blocks long formed by those waiting for the opportunity to enter. He settled for a few drinks in a third-rate bar in the company of a young thing called Molly Flan. He returned to the camp on Sunday night and the first thing he did was to run to the hospital to bring news of Sayonara to his bedridden friend.

"I didn't get to see her, *hermano*, but I heard what they were saying about her. That she's the most sought-after woman in Tora and that she's not a woman but a panther."

"Were you with her?"

"I told you I wasn't, she was too much in demand. They say she only goes with gringos, engineers, and administrative personnel. They say she has no interest in lowly laborers."

"Then it's true that she exists . . ." Spikes of fever turned a black spot in front of Sacramento's watery eyes into a cat, then a swamp, a woman, storm clouds, then a cat again.

"Tell me more," he asked Payanés, who noted his friend's hopeless thinness and the sickly color of his skin, wavering between yellow and green.

"I should go, Sacramento. I have to get some sleep before I go back to work tomorrow."

"Tell me once more and then you can go."

"What do you want me to tell you about?"

"The panther, tell me about the panther."

"What panther?"

"That woman, Sayonara; didn't you say she looks like a panther?"

"If I were you I would aim a little lower so you don't get disappointed. I met a woman they call Molly Flan, you can't imagine how bewitching her eyes are . . ."

"Hush, my head aches. Tell me about Sayonara."

"Again?"

"One last time."

"I already told you what they say about her, that she's dark and inspires fear. She smells like incense and she hypnotizes when she dances, like a snake."

The black spot in front of Sacramento's eyes changed shapes again and turned into a hairy snake, and then a panther without eyes or a tail, and then into a shapeless oil spot with golden highlights, a rapturous spot shaped with a waist and long, elastic legs, two legs that twisted like ribbons around his throat, choking and asphyxiating him with thirst.

"Give me some water, *hermano*."

"They say the camp's water is polluted and spreads sickness."

"Give me some water anyway. When are you going to see her again?"

"Who?"

"That woman . . ."

"Next Friday I'll take you with me so you can see her yourself. You'll be fine . . ."

"Don't talk shit, Payanés; I'm going to die."

"You're too mean to die."

"Listen carefully to what I am going to say. When are you going back down to La Catunga?"

"In about a month, I think."

"Take this money to a kid they call the girl," he said, and gave Payanés all the money from the only paycheck he had received. "She's like my sister and she lives with her *madrina*, Todos los Santos. You tell her that Sacramento sent this to her so she'll have money for food and can get away from the evil life. Then you look for Sayonara and say these words to her, just as I am saying them now: 'Don't worry, as soon as I get better I am going to marry you.'"

"You're crazy, *hermano*. Are you turning into a savior of derailed women? What if they don't want you to save them?"

"You just say what I told you; tell Sayonara that it's a message from a man named Sacramento. That I know she's suffering and as soon as I'm well I'm coming for her. Do you swear that you'll do it?"

"I swear."

Payanés left the convalescent pavilion deeply troubled after seeing his soul mate so lost. You're screwed, *hermano*, he thought painfully, angrily, helplessly. Like the footsteps of a mammoth, the pounding of the drill bent on breaking the planet's back echoed through the jungle, so no one heard him as he said out loud:

"They're letting him die, the damned bastards."

thirteen

 "Llegaron los peludoooos!"

Friday nights in La Catunga the call to arms spread from woman to woman: *Llegaron ya los peluuudoooos!* And so began, in dark splendor, the romantic costumed opera, opulent and miserable.

On weekdays, under the bright sun, in baggy, faded bathrobes, with bouncing breasts unrestrained by bras and the unkempt look of housewives, the women of Tora—when they weren't breast-feeding babies—followed a routine of indiscriminately servicing rubber harvesters, jungle hunters, riverboat men, or merchants in brief, monetary episodes in bed that meant no more to them than scrubbing pots or feeding the chickens.

"What did you think about in the meantime?" I ask Todos los Santos. "I mean, while you were with them . . . ?"

"I added up my accounts. I thought about the money they were going to give me and calculated what I could buy with it, depending on the price of potatoes, plantains, rent. While the man did his thing, I figured out my expenses."

But Friday was Friday, and its arrival was evident in the air from the sound of crying babies whose diapers no one had changed, the hordes of wandering chickens stealing crumbs, and the fluttering of women humming love songs as they washed their hair in basins and spread their silk stockings out to dry in the sun. Dusk fell on the barrio, gilding the poverty, and the streets and alleys glowed with electric lights like a Christmas tree. Tired of crying, the children fell asleep in corners while their mothers gave themselves up, fluttering like black butterflies, to the ritual of dance, flirtation, and drinks.

Around seven the women would begin to arrive at the Dancing Miramar in groups of twos and threes, a few unaccompanied. All unrecognizable, vastly different from the way they appeared every day, their bodies transformed by a riot of color and anxious to escape their costumes of blue polyester, emerald green sateen, sunflower-hued rayon; neck and ears glittering with tricks of costume jewelry and fake diamonds; Elizabeth Arden lips bright red like the ace of hearts. Painted, dramatic, dolled up like transvestites—an eager, coquettish swarm of cats not yet fully tame. Or foxes, fully conscious of being *putas*, like a bullfighter is conscious of his being only when he steps into the ring, or a priest as he offers communion at the altar.

From that moment on life would be interwoven with the illusions of alcohol and darkness that magically lengthened eyelashes, sweetened the most unforgiving folds of skin, and poisoned the night with the smell of sewers and orange blossoms. The Victrolas would play tangos that made even the cat purr, and inside the Dancing Miramar, floating in smoke like a spaceship, love sprouted among the tiles and the ammonia in the back room.

Fragments of moonlight, like bits of broken glass, would collect in the corners among cigarette butts and empty bottles, and at the end of the spree, along with dawn, sadness would descend over the couples that lay naked on the beds and would clothe them with the caress of an angel.

At eight o'clock on another last Friday of the month, somewhere between stupefied and amazed, Payanés found himself seated at a table in the Dancing Miramar. This is what heaven must be like, he thought. It must be just exactly like this. Never in his life had he seen such an abundance of luxury and splendor. The red and black velvet, the semidarkness, the smoke that dazzled his eyes, the clinking of glasses, the delirium of women in brightly colored dresses, the smell of expensive perfume, the huge orchestra blasting the music of Pérez Prado. And above all, the satisfaction produced by the knowledge that in his pocket he had the money to pay for it all; he, Payanés, who had earned it fair and square. So this is the *petrolero's* compensation, he thought finally. He sat Molly Flan on his lap and ordered a bottle of whiskey.

On a platform, higher than everything in the room, unaware of everyone else, and protected by the cage of light cast upon her by a spotlight, danced Sayonara, her furious mane cascading down her back. She was wearing the silk blouse fastened with a tight row of buttons that passed over her heart and ascended to her neck, and the narrow skirt the color of mourning with the slit up the side, through which her dark leg showed: the tip of her foot, the shin, the calf, the knee.

"Is that her?" Payanés asked Molly Flan.

"That's her. What does she have, anyway, that the rest of us don't?"

"She's skinny, but pretty," said Payanés, as if to himself.

"She's pretty, but skinny," corrected Molly Flan.

Lost in her own world, as if floating in her dreams, Sayonara undulated in the stream of light. In the middle of the noise and the pressing crowd, the space she occupied seemed set apart like a sanctuary, inaccessible and inviolable, steeped in the air of another world like a lunar landscape.

"No one can find a way to penetrate that woman's solitude," said Payanés, thinking out loud.

Should I approach the platform and shout congratulations to her, that it's her lucky day because my friend Sacramento sends her the good news that he's going to marry her? He downed a burning shot of whiskey and decided not to say a word to her. That way I'll save Sacramento from looking like a fool, he thought—at the same time, and more importantly, I'll save myself from the same fate. He would take the envelope with the money to the girl, but he would play dumb about the message to this woman.

"Would it be breaking a promise to only half fulfill it?" he asked Molly, speaking loudly to make himself heard over the deafening silence that was created around the girl on the platform.

"What did you say?"

"Nothing."

fourteen

I have often asked myself the same question that Molly Flan asked—what did Sayonara have that the others didn't? What was it, really, that transformed her at a certain moment in the history of La Catunga into a sort of cipher of that tight universe of oil workers, prostitutes, and love for pay? According to what several people told me, the answer could be traced to her defiant nature. They say that she had a peculiar ferocity that went beyond beauty and that attracted and intimidated. Certainly one could also talk about a notable hybrid vigor, stemming from the mixture of blood, that illuminated her youthfulness with the spirit and sparkle of a filly.

I speak blindly about all this because I never met Sayonara personally. I learned the details of her life through the stories and memories of her people, particularly those of Todos los Santos, one of those monumental beings whom life grants us the privilege of getting to know. I forged a wonderful friendship with her through our many afternoons of conversation on Olguita's patio, in the shade of the rubber trees, and because of that it would be absurd to call research, or reporting, or a novel, something that was a fascination on my part with a few people and their circumstances. Let's just say that this book was born out of a chain of tiny revealed secrets that stripped the leaves, one by one, from Sayonara's days, in an attempt to reach the pith.

Todos los Santos, Sacramento, Olguita, Machuca, and Fideo were extraordinary narrators, gifted with an astonishing ability to tell their tragedies without pathos and to speak of themselves without vanity, imprinting on the facts the intensity of those who are willing, for motives I still do not understand, to confess to a stranger for the sole reason that she writes, or because she's precisely that, a stranger, or maybe because of the simple fact that she listens. As if the act itself of telling their own story to a third party would stamp it with a purpose, would make it somehow lasting, would clarify its meaning.

It was by accident that I entered the world of La Catunga. I was working against the clock on a report about a completely unrelated matter, the theft and clandestine distribution of gasoline by a criminal organization called the gasoline cartel, and because of that I landed in Tora on a Tuesday at eleven in the morning aboard a small plane belonging to the airline Aces. By two o'clock that afternoon Sayonara had already crossed my path, by pure chance but with a frightening obstinacy.

I needed a photograph of Sergeant Arias Cambises for my weekly magazine. He had been murdered six months earlier because he knew too much about the cartel's operations, and I went to look for a photograph of him at the archives of the daily newspaper *Vanguardia Petrolera*. The young man in charge was just leaving for lunch, but he kindly allowed me to look around on my own.

"I'll be back in half an hour," he told me, and I went right to work.

I didn't find what I was looking for in the alphabetical files, so I started rummaging around in the piles of unclassified material, a veritable Pandora's box with a little of everything, except photos of Sergeant Arias Cambises: pictures of public disturbances, of *bambuco* composers hugging their guitars, teenage girls being presented to society, a demonstration in the twenties led by the famous labor leader María Cano, notable figures receiving awards, a native Charles Atlas called El Indio Amazónico, who swam underwater across the Río Magdalena. Even a litter of angora kittens playing with balls of yarn in a basket. Hundreds of photographs of all kinds and, suddenly, something that couldn't be passed over.

It was a close-up of a mestiza girl of dark, biblical beauty, without makeup or adornment, who breathed an air of virgin jungles and at the same time of unfathomed depths, a truly jarring photograph. She had the bearing of the Tahitian women painted by Gauguin. But not a drop of the ingenuousness of the noble savage. Hers were the softened features of an everyday *india*, but her expression, I didn't know why, hinted at urban wiles.

I lay the photograph aside to keep looking for my sergeant and before I realized it, I had it in my hands again and was looking at the vigorous fall of that strong hair, parted in the middle, the unmanicured perfection of her almond-shaped fingernails, the eyes of a girl who has seen too much, the vague manner in which her full lips were parted. "As beautiful as Jerusalem and as terrible as an army with battle orders": studying her I finally understood how Shulamite from the Song of Songs could be so beautiful and so terrible at the same time.

The back of the photograph was also a surprise. It was signed, without a date, by Tigre Ortiz, one of the great Colombian photographers, of whom it was said that he had photographed and loved the most beautiful women on the continent, among them the goddess María Félix. Beneath his signature and between quotation marks appeared a single word, "Sayonara."

"Did you find what you were looking for?" asked the young man in charge of the archives when he returned from lunch.

"No, but I found this," I said, as I handed him the photo of the girl. "Do you know who it is?"

"Everybody knows who she is. She was a famous *prostituta* here in Tora."

Sometime later in Santafé de Bogotá, I looked for Tigre Ortiz, now retired and in his eighties, to ask him to tell me the story behind that photograph, with little hope that he would remember, because he must have taken it so many years ago. Yes, he remembered that photo, and all the others; he had the memory of an elephant.

He told me that the Tropical Oil Company—the Troco—had hired him at some point to take a series of photographs for a catalog of its installations and for which he had had to travel to Tora, Infantas, and El Centro in search of oil towers, iron beams, and all kinds of machinery.

"I clearly remember," he said, "a famous Gardner Denver derrick from the beginning of the century, a museum piece that was still functioning like a Swiss watch and was a source of great pride. Several workers asked me to photograph them at the base of the tower."

At the end of two weeks of photographing, he went out with some engineers to celebrate the culmination of the work in Tora's red-light district. And he saw her there, toward the middle of the afternoon, barefoot, wearing a loose camisole and brushing her hair on the patio of her house.

"As soon as I saw her I thought of Santi Muti, a poet friend who used to talk about 'the definitive air of a beautiful *india.*' Because that was exactly what that girl had, the self-assurance of a beautiful Indian that could take your breath away."

He asked her to allow him to photograph her just as she was, and before answering, she sought the consent of an older woman, who according to Tigre must have been her mother. He thought the woman would want to charge him, but she simply said: "Go on, *hija,* let him take your picture, it won't hurt."

"I asked the girl where she was from," Tigre continued, "because I have always believed that women who are as forceful as Eve all come from Tolima. And I was right. First she told me she was Japanese, then she laughed and confessed that she had been born in Ambalema, Tolima.

fifteen

 Payanés spent thirty-six hours straight partying with his friend Molly Flan in a warm and forgettable drunken spree of Vat 69 liquor and well-paired merengue. And the next morning, levitating in the watery imprecision of his hangover, he went looking for his friend Sacramento's girl at the place where he was told he would find her, the house of a matron called Todos los Santos.

There she was, Sacramento's girl, who was no longer a girl but a woman, in the middle of a carefree moment, frozen in time, with Ana, Juana, Susana, and little Chuza, all five dressed in their Sunday best, with freshly ironed light-colored cotton dresses, lined up one behind another and each one braiding the hair of the one in front of her: Susana braiding Juana's; Juana, Ana's; Ana, Sayonara's; and Sayonara, Chuza's, who wouldn't stand still or even let her hair be brushed because she was busy trying to tie ribbons onto Aspirina's fur.

I don't know whether Payanés, dazzled by the blue highlights in the lustrous hair of the five girls, realized at that moment, or whether he already knew—surely from Molly Flan herself—that Sayonara and the girl were two different people and yet one and the same. It wasn't easy to reconcile the night beauty, product of her own fame and secure on her high pedestal in the love of many men, with this village girl on a Sunday morning; such a sister to her siblings and such a daughter to her *madrina;* so approachable and true in her simple dress, in her common, everyday gestures—just another girl among so many poor, anonymous people.

What is certain is that Payanés stood there in the arched entryway without knowing what to say, without wanting to interrupt that everyday ceremony of women in their cool and shaded patio in contrast with the iridescent heat of the street, and that he stayed there, less observing than remembering, as if dreaming about something he'd already seen before, in the privileged days of a more pious era. These girls could be my sisters, he must have thought, or any man's sisters, and Sayonara could be my wife, or my brother's girlfriend, and that lady Todos los Santos, or another just like her, could be my mother, and this house, why not, this house could have been my house.

"What about the violet light?" I asked Olga. "The violet light must have brought him back to earth . . ."

"The lights were turned off in the mornings, and an extinguished light is a silent light."

They say that Payanés felt invaded by a calmness that partially mitigated the ravages of his hangover, due to a sort of reencounter with his own insides and a sudden realization that despite everything the world was still the same as he remembered it from his childhood.

"Wake up, boy," Todos los Santos said suddenly, as if she had read his mind. "This isn't a house of sisters or girlfriends, this is a house of *putas.*"

"Tell Sacramento that I thank him, but I'm sending his money back to him because I'm not thinking about giving up this life, which hasn't turned out badly," Sayonara said to him when he gave her his friend's pay. "Tell him that while he's away to send me more postcards, because I haven't received any for a while and I miss them."

Then Payanés assured her that Sacramento hadn't sent postcards or come down to Tora because of work-related impediments, but that he always thought of her, that he was generally all right and in perfect health.

In perfect health: They assure me that was what he said. Why didn't he say a word about the malaria that was consuming Sacramento? Why didn't he talk about the white hospital where the nurses soothed the shadow that was left of him, of the constant shivering and fevers, of the faith deposited in quinine with side effects perhaps more noxious than the illness itself? Why did he, Payanés, always collaborative, solid, trustworthy, fail just now? So as not to give away his friend, perhaps; out of fear of being indiscreet, or in order not to worry them with bad news . . . or because of the same shame that causes all members of the male sex to be silent when dealing with that which deeply concerns human beings? As if loneliness, joy, weakness, pain, or malaria were shameful, nameless things that one should never admit, even in the confessional, or to a doctor, or even to oneself.

Although, truth be told, I think I can sense another motive for Payanés's having kept silent, which is that over time, as I got to know Sacramento better, I began to doubt that he truly had been sick. With malaria, I mean, because he was always sick: with anxiety. Hungry to love and to be loved, to forgive and be forgiven, whipped by guilt of his own and of others, a bird that was always lost in the clouds of other firmaments, incapable of being happy with what his eyes see and his fingers touch—raging with fever, yes, but with fever wavering between utopias and the certainties at hand; with mythical love, but only sworn before a notary. And the vomiting: Was he struggling to throw out a swollen soul that would no longer fit inside his body?

Was Payanés also a prisoner of this suspicion about his friend and therefore hid the information about the complaint of malaria? That might have been. Did he omit the matrimonial message to Sayonara out of pure precaution, thinking that Sacramento himself, who was unaware of the girl's double identity, wouldn't want—of that he was almost certain—to marry someone that he saw as a sister? That might have been. Or maybe not?

It is clear that the most overwhelming hypothesis—the only serious one—would hold that behind this sin of omission could be the hand of fate that was gradually beginning to raise the foundation of a tragedy. Although I doubt that there is a genre that could be called tropical tragedy: The excessive light of the tropics blurs the sharp contours of any drama, makes it more rounded, wraps it in dreams, and finally dissolves it in forgetfulness.

Moved by a force greater than himself and acting against his custom and his helpful nature, Payanés had acted in accordance with his own convenience, in his own favor, from the moment that Todos los Santos and Sayonara had welcomed him so effusively and joyously, with fresh lemonade and the *empanaditas* they had fried up, as if the recent arrival had been Sacramento himself. Payanés, always concerned about taking care of others, had fallen prey to the temptation of allowing himself to be taken care of, of resting in the hands of others, because they had made him feel at home, in a house with clean laundry drying on lines, with chattering parakeets on a mango branch, wood burning in the stove, and chickens in the yard, everything that must taste like heaven to a man returning from the uncaring harshness of a work camp.

Ana, Juana, Susana, and Chuza spied on him from their hiding place behind a plantain tree and, mute with shyness, lowered their eyes when he asked them their names. Did Payanés think that on that patio he felt the noise of the world calm, the smell of lemons invite him to breathe, even if it was all only borrowed? He must have secretly been thankful for Sacramento's absence, for the alignment of the stars that allowed him to fill the space the other man had left, to be for a while that other person who could not be there, to appropriate his air. And to fall in love with the woman to whom he is bringing someone else's message of love? It is not surprising in any case that on this occasion Payanés would speak so little and so vaguely about the distant sick man.

"There's an *orillada* today. Do you want to come?" invited Todos los Santos.

Sundays during the season when the river rose, when its waters were calm and full of fish, the women of La Catunga would organize what they called an *orillada*, an outing with grilled fish, rum, and a wood-wind band on *la orilla*, the shore, of the Magdalena, on one of the beaches of brown sand that would disappear a few months later, along with the fish, when the volume of flow would grow angry again and overrun the riverbanks.

"It's thirty pesos," Todos los Santos told him. "For that you get food, drink, music, and love."

"Only thirty pesos? Then happiness is cheap."

"Temporary happiness, maybe. The other kind doesn't exist."

When Payanés reached into his pocket to pull out his money, he realized that he had already spent all of his own and all he had left was Sacramento's, which burned his fingers when he touched it. He turned it over and over in his head while the old lady waited with her hand extended. Sacramento, *hermano*, don't take it wrong, he thought, trying to calm his stomach. I'll repay these bills with identical ones.

An hour later, as he followed the thread of the river aboard a *champán* festooned for the party and overflowing with music and people, Payanés was still navigating foreign waters. He didn't dance with the girls as the other men did, or drink rum straight from the bottle like the old women. Instead, he was quiet and took refuge from the sun under the roof of palm fronds and tanned hides, grateful for the north winds that tempered the morning air and helped disperse the antiquated tunes with which the band was trying to liven up the boat ride, but which in him stirred who knows what sharp sense of lack, like a needle in his heart. Olguita tells me this and I ask her if she isn't perhaps speaking of a desired and nurtured longing, like the thorn on the rose that Payanés had requested be tattooed on his chest.

"In that he was a man like any other, in love with his sadness. That's why he liked to get drunk every now and then, because it was the next day, during *el guayabo*, the hangover, when his troubles were dearest to him," replied Olguita, and I reflect on the fact that unlike other Spanish words for hangover like *cruda*, or *resaca*, the Colombian term *guayabo* has two meanings: It means both hangover and nostalgia.

Sayonara had sat next to Payanés and talked with him, placing her mouth near his ear to protect her words from being scattered by the wind, without realizing, perhaps, that her right arm brushed, just barely, his left arm. But Payanés noticed; what's more, he focused only on the solace of that touch.

"Look," she said as she pointed. "See that herd of wild pigs? They come down to the riverbank when they're thirsty. There, that's La Ciénaga de Doncella, if you look carefully you can see tracks from the turtles who come out at night to lay their eggs."

"And there, where those women are washing clothes?" he asked.

"That's La Ciénaga de Lavanderas," she said, without pulling away her body, which was pleasant and smelled nice and which he began to caress with his desire, as if the light contact were the promise of what was to come.

Afterward a cadaver floated by, solemn and swollen like a bishop, so close to the boat that one of the boatmen had to push it away with the tip of his pole so that it wouldn't flood them with its sweet smell of death.

"Was he killed by the good guys or the bad guys?" asked Payanés, while the others continued to dance as if they hadn't seen anything.

"You never know," answered Sayonara.

"Do a lot come by here?"

"More every day. I don't know why the dead look for the river; who knows where they want it to take them."

But with the closeness of that girl's warm, tanned skin, the rest of the world was a faded backdrop for Payanés: the thirsty pigs from the mountain, the cadaver with its shame on display, the turtles and their tracks, the rocks that give a surface for the women to wash on, the women who rinse their sheets in waters of death, the flutes with their racket, even the girl's voice that was stitching words and pointing out trifles, lesser inventions of God, who was above all else the Creator of that skin that was brushing against his with the same indulgence with which the bottom of the *champán* was licking the surface of the water.

"I too am from this river. But from another pueblo, further upstream," she confessed. "I too," she had said, wanting to say, "like these thirsty pigs, and these old musicians, and these even older turtles, and this ageless cadaver, and the women washing at the shore." Payanés, although he scarcely heard her, could never again in his life be near the Magdalena without remembering her.

"Not the Magdalena or any other river, or city, or mountain," Olguita assures me, who is the one most convinced of Payanés's great love for Sayonara. "From that day on he couldn't open his eyes again, or close them, without remembering her."

They found a wide sandy beach surrounded by meadows where they ran the *champán* aground, disembarked, unloaded the provisions, and proceeded to set up the *orillada*. The young women adorned their hair with flame-red *cayena* flowers and prepared a pot filled with a cool drink spiked with just a little alcohol, while the older women, drinking straight rum, started preparing a *viudo* according to the tradition of the people who inhabited the shores of the river. They dug a hole in the beach that would serve as an oven, covered it with *vihao* leaves, and placed catfish and smallmouth bass right on top, whole, almost alive, they were so fresh—pulled from the water by the boatmen during the ride—together with chunks of yuca and plantain, all bathed in a mixture of chopped onion, salt, and tomato. They covered the *viudo* with more *vihao* leaves and on top of the hole, level with the ground, they built a fire.

"Come, girl," ordered Todos los Santos, who was no friend of sentimentality during work hours, separating Sayonara and Payanés. "Come give some attention to these important gentlemen who are waiting for you."

Without even realizing when, Payanés was left alone, sitting on a tree trunk on the shore, absorbed in the flies buzzing before his eyes and drawing arabesques against the sky. Through his hazy senses, dulled by the memory of yesterday's intoxication, he observed the others with that air of incomprehension and absence that unfailingly mark foreigners. Now that contact with her skin had been broken, the world was flooded with smoke and broken into unconnected visions of a very old scene, taken from pagan times. Young women with flowers in their hair dancing to the rhythm of some forgotten music, in full abandonment to laughter and movement; other women, dark and wrinkled, squatting with their skirts gathered between their legs in front of the hole in the ground that gave off an overly strong smell of food, a smell that was perhaps pleasant, thought Payanés, if one were hungry, but which his ravaged stomach found nearly intolerable. He felt as though he were spying on the secrets of a foreign tribe, as though it were the remote ancestors of these women who were really dancing and their ancient mothers who were preparing the concoction of yucas and fish. Just a few hours ago everything was diaphanous and healthy in the freshness of the patio, then on the river the presence of the girl with the sweet-smelling skin had expanded his soul, but now, watching her laugh as she tolerated a fat man wearing a hat and kissing her on the neck, life for Payanés was broken into four parts: the smell of food that had no place in his lack of appetite, the brown sand that soiled his white pants and stuck to his shoes, a love that had been dying inside of him even before it was fully born, and finally, he himself, a stony guest of this strange party, and he couldn't seem to make those four parts add up to any whole.

The beating of drums had been added to the flutes, along with an accompanying choir and the voice of a drunk old woman who shattered the air every now and then with interjections, and at other moments with *ayes* and weeping. After a period of anxiously observing Sacramento's girl, who was now embracing another gentleman and disappearing with him into the underbrush, Payanés was finally able to understand something. This feeling of malaise like ground glass in my stomach is the same thing that is killing Sacramento, he must have thought, and at once he corrected the error of a worry that he knew instinctively was wrong.

"There, just as she is: a *puta*. That's how God wants me to love her," he said out loud, and felt drops of relief that mitigated the sensation of chewing glass.

When the food was ready, the old women served it on green plantain leaves and distributed it, inviting everyone to eat with their hands. Payanés, who was a man from the mountains and as such inexpert in the art of eating fish, choked on the bones, was repulsed by those round, staring eyes challenging him to gobble them up, and mistrusted that scaly, aquatic being as if it were poisoned.

"You look like you're eating a porcupine," laughed Sayonara, once again at his side, and she tried to show him. "You pull out the meat with your fingers and make a little pile, like this, then you squeeze it a little, you feel it, before you put it in your mouth so you can find the bones and remove them."

She picked up a piece, cleaned the bones from it just as she had explained, and tried to get him to eat it.

"I can't," said Payanés, pushing away that bit of meat that was too white, too soft. "I can't. I'm still thinking about that dead body."

"Come on," she said. "You have to eat and you have to live even though others have died."

"It would be a sin to eat this creature, cooked so strangely."

"Stop saying silly things."

They went into the underbrush and undressed. Payanés made love eagerly and at a certain moment even with happiness, but without recovering in that ordinary episode the strange splendor of burning waters that had made him tremble earlier on the river. On the other hand, Sayonara's voice and gaze sweetened as if she were a little girl again, or were able to be one for the first time, and she nestled into the refuge of that embrace, seeking warmth and rest. Looking for love, perhaps? Olguita assures me that it was so, that from that very first time Payanés's serenity had consoled her, his comforting words calmed her and his self-assurance anchored her.

"Those two, Sayonara and Payanés, were for us the authentic incarnation of the legend of the *puta* and the *petrolero*. If you ask me what the best moment in the history of La Catunga was, I would tell you that it was when they first met. Others would tell you their relationship was rife with problems, that it wasn't perfect, and this that and the other. I don't pay them any attention. For me love should be rough and hard, just as theirs was."

"Is Emilia your girlfriend?" asked Sayonara, running her finger along the vivid lines of the tattoo on his chest.

"No," he smiled. "She's just the drilling tower where I work. We call her skinny Emilia."

"I'm happy to hear that," said Sayonara with unfounded relief, still unaware that here was a man who was married to his work.

"I'm a *cuñero*, you know? I think that with time I can become the fastest *cuñero* in Colombia," he told her, and he released his hold on her to talk about his work.

"Will you stay with me tonight?" Sayonara interrupted him.

"I can't," he replied, without even thinking about it. "I have to get back to camp today because I have to start work at dawn."

"When are you coming back to Tora?"

"The last Friday of next month, God willing."

"Will you come see me?"

"Okay. But you have to leave that whole day for me. You have to swear that for that one day there won't be any other men."

"That's how it went," Olguita told me. "They were apart from the group and we couldn't see them, because everyone's privacy is respected, but also because they were hidden behind some *patavacales*, which abound there. *Patavacal?* The things you ask, all unimportant details. But I will tell you what you want to know; a *patavacal* is a tangle of prickly bushes that have a leaf in the shape of a cow's hoof, which leaves a print in the shape of a heart. I was saying that they were away from the rest of us and hidden, but that wasn't surprising, since it's normal with couples in love. You look for a half-hidden flat spot, throw a blanket on the ground, and there, that's it, you do your business. Then you go with your partner, or sometimes alone, to swim in the river and come out again as if nothing happened. I tell you that we didn't see Payanés and Sayonara, but we knew what was going on between them, and I could read from Todos los Santos's worried look that she was afraid the girl was going to get foolish with Sacramento's friend and forget about the rest of the group. Later we saw them swimming naked, she slender and dark and he powerful and cinnamon-colored, both standing waist-deep in that water that wavered between lilac and mauve, and even with our view hindered by the distance, it was easy to read on their faces that they were in love. Dusk was falling, the hour when the birds' singing ceases and the river's breathing quiets, and as we learned later, it was then that they made their promise. The promise that was the most serious vow possible according to the laws of *amor de café*. They sealed a promise of fidelity for a single day each month, whenever he would come to visit from his camp. Payanés and Sayonara swore the fidelity of husband and wife for the last Friday of every month of the year, and it is well known that in these parts a promise is sacred."

"Agreed?" he asked, pressing against him the one who from now on, by sworn promise, would be a little more his than any other man's, including Sacramento, and he felt his heart begin to beat again at the threshold of visions of the future: He saw the water light up again, the air shimmer with phosphorescence, and her hair burn gold like the crown worn by the Virgen de Guadalupe and formed by the day's final rays as they escaped the night in the blue liquid of her hair.

"Agreed."

"If someday you leave Tora . . . ," he ventured.

"I'm not leaving Tora."

"You never know where all this war could drive you. If you leave Tora, I mean, and you settle in any other corner, just wait for our date, then walk in a straight line until you reach the Magdalena and I will be waiting there by the shore."

"This river is very long," she pointed out. "It crosses the whole country . . ."

"You just look for the river, I'll know where to look for you."

"Later," Olguita continues, "as they were dressing and the rest of us moved the party back onto the *champán* for the return trip, came the part with the memento. In that too they acted according to custom, because *amor de café* doesn't recognize commitments that don't involve mementos. Other people sometimes call them amulets or tokens. And notice this detail, the male always wears it, never the female, unless the promise is constant and total, which also occurs. Otherwise no, because she has to continue working, you see? And no man likes to find a trace of the previous one."

With a small knife, Payanés cut a long wisp of her hair, braided it, wrapped it several times with hemp fibers, and tied it off, forming a necklace, and with childlike solemnity and the attitude of an altar boy he quickly blessed it, then kissed it and secured it around his neck.

"Tell me your real name," said Payanés.

"You already know it, Sayonara."

"That's just a nickname."

"I've already forgotten the real one."

"Come on, tell me. Just me."

"I can't. If my father finds out the life I've chosen, he'll come and kill me."

"All right, then."

It was already too late for Payanés to catch the truck back to the camp, so Sayonara accompanied him and waited for him to catch the train, which was much slower, at that fateful stop they call Armería del Ferrocarril, which is always swarming with diminutive angels of sorrow that remind one of flies.

"This is where my friend Claire said good-bye forever," she tried to tell him through the window at the last minute, but the train had already started to move.

sixteen

 "Se sentaban con recato," don Alonso Olmeda told me last night—a veteran of the Troco who frequented La Catunga in Sayonara's time and knew and respected the *mujeres de la vida*.

They sat with modesty, don Alonso had said of the *prostitutas* of those days, and his delicate observation took me by surprise, it hit me like a peculiar clue for deciphering that world, one with which this book should be in harmony and which forced me to rethink things I had written earlier. For example, "her flesh overflowed the low neckline of the blue satinette dress." But they sat *con recato*. A curious and archaic word, *recato*. I heard my grandmother use it often and then after she was gone, gradually less and less, as if it alluded to an extinct virtue. *Recato:* a magical term when it refers, as from don Alonso's mouth, to a *puta*. From the Latin *recaptare*—to hide what is visible—it seems to refer to a secret world that avoids exhibition and which is, significantly, contrasted with the Latin *prostituere*, to debase, put before the eyes, expose.

"How did they dress, don Alonso?"

"With the elegance of poor ladies who wanted to look beautiful."

"No cleavage or bright-colored fabrics?"

"Cleavage, yes, and bright-colored, showy dresses too, but nothing that would call attention with vulgarity. The famous striptease, now obligatory in any brothel, would never have occurred to anyone at the Dancing Miramar and the other cafés in La Catunga. Instead we enjoyed dance contests and there were prizes and celebrations for the couple who performed the best tango, rumba, or *cumbia*. It was another world and things gave off different colors, and prostitution, forgive me for expressing a personal opinion, wasn't disgraceful for the woman who practiced it or for the man who paid for it."

"Even though there was payment?"

"The *petrolero* worked hard and earned his money. The *prostituta* worked hard and ended up with the *petrolero*'s money. They say that love for money is a sin, but I say that it's nothing more than the law of economy, because bread doesn't fall from the sky for anyone. And don't believe what they tell you, that *amor de café* is pleasure and not love. When some fellow worker was smitten by a particular woman, the rest of us managed to stay away from her and not interfere."

"Were you always successful?"

"No, not always. There were a few crooked girls who made their men suffer until they drove them to their deaths. No one confronted them for it because they were within their rights, and anyone who fell in love with a woman from that world was at the mercy of his own good luck. But in general, love between couples was respected and there were numerous cases of sworn and upheld fidelity, by choice of the couple and not because of any other circumstance. I can tell you the names of *petroleros* who had children in common agreement with prostitutes, without the women leaving the profession. It was a simple world because it wasn't hypocritical. It wasn't hypocritical but that doesn't mean that it was heartless. It may sound ridiculous to you, but there was a certain feeling of chastity in all of that. A certain kind of chastity, you know, and a certain elegance. To understand it you had to have seen them, so proudly gathering their skirts when they danced a *pasodoble*."

"Were you in love with any of them, don Alonso?"

"It's a story that wouldn't be honorable to confess because I am the widower of a good and noble woman. Out of respect for the dead. But I will tell you one thing, many of us were in love with *prostitutas*, and with the passing of the years and a look back in time, now that we're closer to death, we have to recognize that they were the great passion of our lives."

seventeen

As a young boy, Sacramento wanted to be a saint. No one knows how long and dark the nights of a lonely, sleepless boy can be under the high, resonant ceilings of a monastery, his heart knotting and twisting as he begs forgiveness from God the Father, who sees everything because he's a great swollen eye, a voyeuristic, furious, and triangular eye that would blink with benevolence only toward those who become a model of chastity, humility, and sacrifice. No one can measure the depths of loneliness of a boy who wants to be a saint.

Especially when the mercy that this child pursues is not only for his sins but for the sins of the whole world, and above all for the shame of his mother, whose fruit is this very child, conceived by her in sin. At the charity school for orphans and abandoned children that the Franciscan fathers presided over in Tora, where Sacramento attended his first years of elementary school—the only studies he would complete in his life—the majority of the students dreamed of becoming *petroleros* when they grew up. One wanted to be a butcher like his father and grandfather and another spoke of training to become a fighter pilot. But Sacramento had decided to reach sainthood. I was told this by Father Nataniel, who was one of his teachers and spiritual mentors.

Sacramento himself still keeps alive the memory of the morning they sent him to the sacristy to collect the prayer book that the rector had left behind. He was about to complete the errand when he suddenly found himself alone in the deserted chapel, panic-stricken by the looks of so many saints scrutinizing him from their high, deep niches, shrouded in the quiet violet light filtering through the stained-glass windows.

"The saints were wooden and stared at me," he tells me, "from glass eyes that cast real gazes. The one that terrified me most was Saint Judas Tadeo, with his sharp ax gripped tightly in his right hand, the patron saint of criminals because he is the only one with a weapon. You understand that with all of the violence flourishing in those days, Saint Judas Tadeo was highly revered and favored with votive candles and offerings, but I suspected that he looked harshly at me, as if reproaching me, threatening me with his decapitating ax, and I attributed to him the ability, with those blue glass balls he had in his sockets, of being able to see deep inside me and observe that I was failing in my commitment to sacrifice and suffering."

Lent arrived rainy and charged with remorse, and every boy was supposed to choose, according to the dictates of his own conscience, the sacrifices he was willing to make, step by step along a stairway to heaven that began with privations like giving up the milk candies that were served for dessert or getting up to pray an hour earlier than was mandatory, and that ascended through fasts and vigils to reach self-inflicted injuries to the flesh, such as walking barefoot over the pebbles on the patio or tying the rough jute rope worn by the Franciscans around one's waist under his shirt. In the hands of the penitent orphans of Tora lay the power of enduring suffering in exchange for cleansing humanity of the stains of sin, and no one knows how much a charge like that weighs and overwhelms when it falls on the shoulders of a young boy.

"Don't be an idiot," Sacramento's friend Dudi Abdala, who was a

Turk and an atheist, said to him. "Go ahead and eat your milk candies, don't you see that if you don't the rector will eat them all himself?"

But Sacramento, determined to become a saint at any price, genuflected and ignored the temptation.

"If you're not going to eat them, at least give them to me," implored Dudi Abdala, who besides being Turkish and an atheist was a glutton. "It's all the same to God . . ."

"Because of you mankind is going to get screwed up," Sacramento reproached him, and left the candy on the tray.

At the entrance to the chapel the Franciscan brothers had placed a jar with garbanzo beans and they hung a little cloth bag around each boy's neck, in which he could place one garbanzo for each sacrifice he inflicted upon himself. The garbanzos were the irrefutable and tangible proof of the degree of goodness achieved, and the boys who suffered most would proudly display the heaviest bags.

"I struggled a great deal to be the best of all of them," Sacramento tells me. "I injured my feet on the pebbles and I wore the jute rope, because I knew that I, being the son of a sinner, had to do twice as much as the others to achieve the same result. But I was hiding an unconfessable sin, falseness and pride, because I allowed the devil to push my hand and place unearned garbanzos in my bag so that it would look especially bulky. The full terror of this fell on me that morning as I stood alone in the chapel, when Saint Judas let me know that he was aware of my lies, and from then on he tormented my nights, never letting me sleep. Hour after hour until dawn I could hear the rasping of his ax against the sharpening stone, and I expected that at any moment he would appear to chop off my head with a single blow. In those days I used to cry a lot, mostly over my mother, because I loved her, although I had never seen her again after she left me. The priests told me not to waste my suffering on her because she would never have God's forgiveness, she was already condemned and there was nothing I could do about it."

In the light of day it was possible to put aside temptation and advance without stumbling along the path of chastity, but night was the realm of Lucifer. After nine o'clock, after the final rattle of the electric generator, sin spread through the dormitories and plunged through the darkness into the boys' hearts, and that was when the color pictures emerged from their hiding places in the complicit glow of candlelight. They were pages from calendars, clippings from magazines, or postcards with women in bathing suits, in towels, in shorts, in underwear, that revealed unsuspected glimpses of nudity, the vertiginous secrets of the flesh, the strange wonders that the feminine sex hide under their clothes. The boys stared at them in amazement, and even God, who saw everything because He was everywhere, looked at those pictures surprised at the audacity of His own creation, incapable of preventing His eyes from gazing upon the softness of those thighs and those necks, the roundness of those knees and shoulders, the miracle of those breasts and buttocks, beside which the pleasure of milk candies and the torment of the pebbles on the patio were minor passions. The pictures showed beautiful light-skinned girls with pink nipples and beautiful dark-skinned women with purple nipples; there were timid ones who covered their chests with crossed arms and brazen ones who showed their underwear because they were sitting immodestly; blondes with equally blond pubic hair; dancers covered with feathers and tulle; beauties in garters, black silk stockings, and high heels.

In order not to be discovered, the orphans passed the pictures from hand to hand, barely gazing at them before hastily hiding them under the mattress. Then each one would retreat into the cave of his sheets to invoke, now alone and at ease, that mysterious happiness he had just glimpsed. Erotic activity was unleashed throughout the dormitory, and for several minutes the bunk beds shook with the frenzy of their actions. Little by little the scene dissolved into sighs and silence, and overcome by exhaustion, the eye of God closed and before ten o'clock the boys had already escaped—redeemed sinners—to the guilt-free land of their dreams, hand in hand with those beauties with red lips, black hair, and warm thighs of milk and honey. All the boys except Sacramento, who didn't dream about kisses from beautiful women but rather the rasping of Saint Judas Tadeo's ax of justice.

"Every now and then Brother Eligio, the one in charge of discipline in the dormitories, would enter without warning. He would tear the colored photographs from our hands and rip them to pieces, say that those women were *putas* and that we were going to roast in the fires of hell. *Putas*, just like my mother, I shuddered, and I would gush with tears of anger against Brother Eligio, who insulted them like that, and against my companions too and above all against myself, for desiring women like my mother so."

"Strange boy, that Sacramento," says Father Nataniel. "Obedient and pious, but he never learned how to tie his shoes."

I ask him what he is insinuating by that and as he replies he peels with a knife one of the sweet pears that he grows in the orchard of the presbytery in Puentepiedra, Cundinamarca, where he spends the long hours of his retirement.

"Nothing, simply what I am saying, that as much as I tried to teach him how to tie his shoes and in spite of the patience I invested in the endeavor, he couldn't pick it up and always went around with his shoes untied."

Days later, when I return to Tora and see Sacramento again, the first thing I do is look at his feet. Father Nataniel is right; Sacramento still walks around with his shoelaces untied.

"I didn't believe the priests at the school when they assured me that there was no salvation for my mother," he says to me. "I was convinced that if I got to be a saint, I could get God to forgive her and take her to His kingdom after she died, for all eternity. Whatever the cost, I was personally going to get God to forgive her, of that I was sure; what wasn't so clear was whether I myself could forgive her."

eighteen

Payanés traveled four and a half hours along the *petrolero* route to the end of the tracks, which stopped at Infantas, and from there he had to walk another two hours along with the rest of the lagging workers who were returning to Camp 26, splashing into undesirable swamps through a jungle as black and dense as the belly of a mountain. The whole way he daydreamed about the girl without a name to whom he had sworn his love every last Friday of the month; difficult, contradictory dreams that got out of control and ended up with evocations of Sacramento, who appeared to claim her and accuse him of betrayal. Either you die, or regret will kill me, Payanés said to him in his head, and this too: I propose a deal, Sacramento, brother, if you live she's yours, but if you die you leave her for me. And a little later he would rave about another deal that seemed less cruel: If she leaves her life behind and marries you, I won't see her again. But if she keeps on doing her thing, you will have to admit that I have as much right to go after her as you do. That's how he thought he would balance accounts with his sick friend, and he tried to pick up the thread of his memories again, thinking only of her, stretching the fingers of his memory as far as possible to get her back, but Sacramento, relentless, would reappear to prevent it.

He could see Emilia's silhouette in the distance, illuminated and cold in the middle of the lake of fog that flooded the camp, and was startled to have completely forgotten about her for so long. He ran to the hospital, which at night seemed to be floating amidst the somnambulant fluttering of the bats that lived under its eaves, and he slipped in surreptitiously, greasing the palm of the night watchman with a tip because visiting hours had ended much earlier. He tiptoed through the heavy, listless silence and had almost arrived at his destination when he ran right into Demetrio, the nurse. Payanés excused himself as best he could for being there after hours and asked about his friend's health.

"No better. That boy will probably go on to the other side . . ."

"Just a minute, what do you mean, to what other side?"

"Are you an idiot? Where are you from that you don't understand Spanish? I am saying that he will probably die."

"Then why the hell don't they operate on him! Give him some medicine, something, but don't just let him die!"

"Be quiet, you'll wake up the few of them that are asleep. And get used to the idea; we did what we could." The nurse took off his white lab coat and hurried off to get ready to go home.

"Did you convey my promise of marriage to her?" Sacramento spat the question at Payanés, scrutinizing him with yearning eyes, in whose depths the mist of the other shore could already be seen.

"Yes, *hermano*, I gave her your promise," assured the other man, careful with his words so as not to lie outright, and at the same time speaking to the dying man as if he were a child for whom he wanted to relieve a great pain with subtle deceit.

"Did she say yes?"

"Yes, she said yes."

"Okay, then. Now I will have to get better so I can fulfill my promise. But how do I know you're not lying to me?"

"She gave me a lock of hair as a pledge . . ."

"This is it," said Sacramento without a shadow of a doubt, ripping the amulet from Payanés's neck with a single pull and putting it to his nose to smell it, with a surprising eagerness for someone on the brink of dying. "Yes, this is it, this is her hair . . . now, please tie it around my neck."

Payanés obeyed without protest, because you don't deny a terminal patient his last elixir of hope; because deep down he knew he could recover his memento as soon as his friend expired and because he understood, in a subtle way that he didn't know how to put into words, that for several months and especially now, as they were about to say goodbye, he and his friend were like two parts of the same person, the part who stays and the part who goes away, and that the double confusion of the amulet—your neck, my neck—was another one of the many signs of the coming and going between two destinies that had become interwoven and merged together without fault on the part of either.

"And the girl," Sacramento continued to question his friend, "did you give her the money?"

"She didn't want to take it, *hermano*, she says she would rather you send her postcards."

There was a long, final silence, in rhythm with the rocky trickle of the waters of death, as they tossed themselves upon Sacramento's pillow.

"Those two, are they the same person?" asked Sacramento, speaking with tenderness what surely would be his last words.

"What are you talking about?" said Payanés, and he wished with his whole soul that his friend hadn't asked the question.

"That's why I sent you to see them both, so you could confirm what I always knew, that the girl and Sayonara are one. I put her in that world and now it's only right that I separate her from it. But if I can't, Payanés, *hermano*, you have to promise me that you will do it for me."

nineteen

 I know this book will have no soul as long as I find no trace of the desperation that led Sayonara's mother and brother to take their lives, and, above all, of the hopes that pushed Sayonara herself to continue living after what happened.

Looking for answers, I leave Tora on the Magdalena, a river of mercury waters that turn rusty with the sunset, aboard an anachronistic steamboat whose existence is a pure act of faith and whose improbable advance erases from the map each port as we leave it behind: Yondó, Chucurí, Puerto Parra, Barbacoas, El Paraíso, Puerto Nare, Palestina, El Naranjo, La Dorada, Santuario, Cambao, and at the end of the trip, Ambalema, Tolima, where Sayonara was born, according to Tigre Ortiz.

I have to trust that the Magdalena can take me to the knot of memory, but I'm not sure I can rely on it. It has become a self-engrossed river, forgotten by history, detached from its own shores, allowing itself to be carried along unenthusiastically by a present of tame currents that don't bring to mind their place of origin and that try to ignore where they are going.

For now its course has brought me to Ambalema, the once prosperous Ambalema, capital of a tobacco bonanza that has already ended and that left its planters wiped out and its inhabitants convinced that life runs backward, like memories.

"We lived through progress yesterday," says señor Mantilla, the owner of a small hotel in the center of town. "Since then we have only seen disintegration and abandonment."

In the main plaza, to the right of the church and to the left of a scandalous ice cream shop with an English name, walls of mirrors, and techno music, I find a place like the one I am seeking, from the past almost to the point of nonexistence and discreet to the point of being nearly invisible. It's called the Gran Hotel Astolfi and you could say that it was extracted from the same ancient dictionary as the steamboat that brought me up the river. It has been reduced to a hostelry for travelers by foot, "Weekly or monthly room rentals with common bath," and as a rendezvous by the hour for couples, but it still retains in the vestibule an Acme Queen salon organ and a certain solidity of finely crafted wood that speaks of better times. I ask for the owner, and although they tell me that his daughter is now in charge of the administration, I insist that I want to see him.

"The owner is don Julio Mantilla, that gentleman sitting at the front door," they tell me.

I see him leaning against the wall, facing the street in a cowhide chair, just under the letter G of the sign that reads GRAN HOTEL ASTOLFI, greeting passersby with a nod of his head as if done purposely to show the freckles that crown his bald head. I introduce myself, tell him my profession, and explain that I have come looking for traces of a sad story that happened years ago and of which I have only a vague impression.

"I thought that only here, in your hotel, would someone be able to tell me about it. If I ask at that ice cream shop, for example," I raise my voice above the blasting music flooding out of the neighboring business, "I'm sure they wouldn't be able to tell me anything."

"Well, you won't go wrong with me," he answers. "For a quarter of a century I've been watching what goes on in this town, from this spot, right here where you see me sitting."

"You must know a lot of things . . ."

"Things from the past, yes, and the people who have lived here all their lives, but the modern stuff I don't understand very well. The one who knows about the new things is my daughter Adelia. Surely you would like to know about modern things, because you are young too . . ."

"It's more about an old case," I say. "A strange occurrence that must have shaken Ambalema when it happened. A mother and a son who committed suicide. Do you remember something like that?"

"Are you talking about doña Matildita and her son Emiliano?"

"I don't know their names, not even their last name. I only know that they both committed suicide, the mother and the son, and that the boy must have had several sisters."

"That's Matildita and her son Emiliano," he assures me. "It has to be them, because you can count the suicides in this town with one hand and only in that case, that I know of, were there two in the same family and at the same time. Rosalba, my sister, had dealings with doña Matildita; she can tell you about that misfortune," he says, and he invites me to the rooms at the hotel's rear patio, where he lives among rosebushes with his daughter, his two grandchildren, and his sister Rosalba, an elderly lady who would be identical to don Mantilla if on her bald head she had freckles, like him, and not the white, volatile wisp that she organizes into a small bun, like a cloud floating on top of her head. Señorita Rosalba offers me black coffee with canna cookies and dispenses, like her brother, the cordial treatment and beautiful manners of a bygone era that despite the ravages of violence you still find everywhere in this country, even on the part of people who don't know a thing about you.

I praise the splendid roses that she grows in her garden, I talk about the old tobacco haciendas in the area, anything that doesn't touch on the purpose of my visit. I don't know why, but at the last minute I start thinking that it's indecent to uncover information about a past that Sayonara never wanted anyone to know about. I am filled with doubt about how appropriate it is to link, by asking a question that is about to be answered, two worlds that she kept separate and ignorant of each other.

Years have passed, I tell myself to calm down, yet I still go on talking about roses and other insignificant things until señor Mantilla forces the denouement by telling his sister what brings me here.

"The señora has come to ask about Matildita who killed herself, may she rest in peace."

"I hope so, although I don't think it is so, because they say there is no rest for those who commit suicide," says señorita Rosalba. She asks me if I am related to Matildita and crosses herself when I confess that I am not. "Those people had very sad lives. They were etched in the annals of the town because until then suicide was an outside affair here; yes, there had been killings, and murders, but none of us had ever known anyone who dared to leave this world by his own choice. People are afraid of the Third Brigade, also called the Home of the Pumas and the Heroes of Chimborazo, which are different names for the same brutality, because they say those men still haven't been able to cleanse themselves from the curse that doña Matildita cast on them with her death."

"There are a lot of bastards among those Heroes of Chimborazo," said señor Mantilla gravely. "The only consolation is to think that their consciences are being eaten away by the weight of those deaths, the mother's and the son's. The brigade's headquarters are just outside the town, as you take the highway to Ibagué. If you like we could go there, we would be happy to take you, because he who helps a traveler will be treated kindly in heaven."

Don Mantilla calls for Wilfredo, an old man whose lower jaw hangs loosely toward the left and who works in the hotel as a bellboy, waiter, and handyman, to drive the family automobile, a '59 Buick that has been maintained in adequate condition, to be able to take us to the nearby brigade.

"Look carefully," the señorita warns me. "Look as Wilfredo drives past it slowly, because this is a military zone and they threaten anyone who stops with bullets. It was there, right there, where they've put up that guardhouse with the sentry. They built it to distract everyone, to prevent them from continuing to bring flowers, imagine that, so many years have passed and you can still see the carnations people throw from the highway, because as I told you, they don't allow pedestrians to walk or cars to stop in front of the brigade. If they left people alone, they would already have torn down the guardhouse and built an altar in its place."

"Altar, no, we would have built a monument," contradicts her brother. "Many people have faith in Matilde's holiness and swear that she works miracles, but to me she's not a saint, more like a noble martyr for the nation, because through her sacrifice she tried to cleanse the evil she had seen in this town — France has its Joan of Arc, but we have our own martyr here in Ambalema."

"For months after the tragedy you could still see the burned circle where it happened," says the señorita. "A few years ago they whitened it with lime, then they built the guardhouse on top of it so that not even the memory of it would remain."

"Where she burned, right there, they posted a sentry," adds Wilfredo, opening his mouth so round and wide because of the defect in his jaw that his words seemed to emanate from it like soap bubbles. "He has orders to shoot anything that approaches. They say it's to maintain public order, but we all know that it's because they're terrified of her spirit."

Sayonara's mother burned to death? She immolated herself with fire like a Buddhist monk, like a Florentine monk, like a Maid of Orleans? Suicide by fire moves me more than any other kind. During a visit to Cuba I expressed my astonishment at a statistic that reflected that a large number of women die annually by incineration, and it was explained that it is the traditional way, since time immemorial, that women commit suicide on the island, and that the practice is still as alive as ever despite attempts by the revolution to eradicate it. I was told the disconcerting details of several cases and since then have been obsessed with the idea of a closed chain, both sacred and perverse, whose links would be fire, woman, death, and back to fire, which attracts whatever has been born of it.

We stop the Buick further on, ten minutes down the highway, at a stand where all kinds of fruits are sold: bundles of oranges, mandarins, and lemons hanging from the roof beams, piles of grapefruit, *guamas*, watermelons, cherimoyas, *anones, maracuyás, mamoncillos*, and papayas in a wild array of colors and smells that convince me that nothing bad could have happened here, because nothing bad can happen at a fruit stand in *tierra caliente*, in a region where the weather is perpetually hot.

"Before everything happened, this stand was a *merendero*, a makeshift roadside restaurant, called Los Tres Amigos," says señor Mantilla. "It was always full of tobacco merchants, hacienda owners, hacienda workers, soldiers, and even brigade officers. The owner was a man from Antioquia named Abelardo Monteverde, the husband of doña Matildita, a Guahiba Indian who had a gift for cooking and seasoning."

"There was a vulgar saying around town, if you'll forgive me for re-peating it," ventured Wilfredo, releasing more soap bubbles into the air, "and that is that Matildita's food tasted so good because she lit the stove with a flame that she took from her groin."

"That, Wilfredo, is ignorant gossip," says señor Mantilla with an-noyance.

"Because she was an *indígena*, people think she was a witch and say things like that," says the chastised Wilfredo in self-defense, and this time the bubbles burst before they float into the air.

"They used to say, señora, that don Abelardo was Matildita's hus-band, although husband was just a way of speaking, because they were never married in a church even though they produced offspring, a male and several females. Around here a white man gets together with an In-dian woman but he never marries her, and a white woman never marries or gets together with an Indian man. That is the custom."

"They say that Indian women are versed in witchcraft," insists Wil-fredo, exposing himself to being hushed again, "and I know men that won't eat food they've prepared so that they won't fall prisoner to their fire, which isn't healthy. So many men won't let go of their Indian women because they have fallen under her spell and have renounced the cross."

Like so many other *antioqueños* with colonizing blood, don Abelardo

Monteverde was drawn to Ambalema by tobacco fever, built this stand with his own hands, and set up his restaurant here. The coal stoves, the ceramic sink, and the room where the family lived were in the back, where today there is an orchard with fruit trees. I look around: This is where Sayonara was born. Her mother, the Guahiba Indian, must have given birth to her squatting over a basin and hidden behind the bushes, with no help, not even complaining or celebrating.

"Matildita cooked, washed dishes, and waited on the tables, and thanks to her the establishment became famous and attracted a lot of people who were fans of her roast pork *tolimense,* her *poteca de auyama,* her stuffed goat, and her liver and onions. As I said, everything Matildita touched turned out delicious."

"How did don Abelardo meet Matildita?" I ask.

" 'Meet' isn't the appropriate word. Let's say instead that he captured her in one of those hunting expeditions that the white colonists organized in the eastern plains. It wasn't vermin that they downed with their rifles or even mountain birds, but sometimes those too. They went out to *guahibiar,* that's what they called it, and it meant to shoot at the Guahibo Indians, chasing them over those immense flatlands that offered no refuge, because between the bullet and the Indians there wasn't a single tree in sight. They say that to prevent themselves from being killed," señor Mantilla says to me, "the Guahibos shouted that they too were *hiwi,* which in their native language means 'people,' but the white men didn't seem to understand."

She was coming back from gathering fronds from the palms scattered in the forests that grow along the shores of the Río Inírida, and Abelardo, the *antioqueño,* wanted to bring her back alive. Since she had a pagan name and spoke a savage tongue, he baptized her Matilde and taught her Spanish, which was a civilized language.

"Despite her training, Matildita kept her bad habits and because of that she earned reprimands from don Abelardo; one day I saw him with my own eyes forbidding her to eat worms. 'They're good, *moriche* worms,' she said with that difficult accent that she never lost. And she also said: '*Bachao* ants are delicious.' "

"Did she eat ants too?" The idea seemed hilarious to señorita Rosalba. "Maybe out of sight from her husband the little devil would stuff herself with ants! And why not, since up around Santander even the whites like ants roasted with salt. I remember that Matildita used to complain often about not being able to fry *terecay* turtles in oil. Matildita was also a bit of a scoundrel, and while everyone saw her as so self-sacrificing and submissive, she had her own character, she pitched fits and gave in to her habits, so while she may have prepared civilized food for her clients, she preferred for herself and her children wild yucca, sweet potatoes, yams, and red pepper, which are pig slop for white men and delicacies in the mouths of Indians."

"She was endlessly working to keep her house and the restaurant in order, and besides cooking, she wove cotton and made cloth to dress her children and herself."

"Don't exaggerate, Julio, remember she was dirty and kept her children naked. She sent the eldest, the boy, to school, but not the girls, because she made them work," says the señorita critically, and I imagine Sayonara and her sisters running around the place. I see them with their own faces and their long hair, but with the bodies of lizards, of cats, of dragonflies; dirty and illiterate, peeling potatoes and scrubbing dishes, as señorita Rosalba testifies, but agile and free, indomitable, capricious, and foul-mouthed.

"Hush, woman, don't say evil things," señor Mantilla reprimands his sister. "Don't disparage her soul. Besides, as if that weren't enough, doña Matildita was skillful at weaving baskets, mats, and hammocks, and by that I want to tell you, señora journalist, that she produced a lot of income for don Abelardo and no expense. And in his own coarse, rustic way he realized that; he set himself up with her and kept her as his only woman until the end."

The couple's daughters, the Mantillas tell me, were all thin like their mother, with dark, opulent hair, almond-shaped eyes, and skin the color of fired bricks. The oldest child and only male was more like his father, with light blue eyes, lighter hair, and barely tanned skin, but he stuck to his mother with such devotion that as a young boy don Abelardo threatened to send him to an orphanage if he didn't let go of her skirts and act his age. You're a man and you're white, he kept telling the boy, so don't go around sniveling.

"That boy, who was given the name Emiliano," says the señorita, "was the light of Matilde's eyes, her reason for being. The only luxury she permitted herself in that valley of tears was loving and taking care of that boy as if he were a real live prince, and she would have given her very life for him, as they say, only that in her case that's exactly what happened."

When he turned eighteen, Emiliano was caught in an army roundup and was enlisted as a recruit in the Third Brigade. Military life wasn't a bad choice and don Abelardo was satisfied that his pup would be given the opportunity to progress in the arms race. Doña Matildita resented it, because it took the object of her devotion from her side and at the same time deprived her of his help, because the boy was her right hand in the innumerable chores of Los Tres Amigos. Since his military service would be short and nothing would be gained by protesting, Matildita relented, saying that at least those fools should teach you how to write, and the day he left she caressed his face, a rare gesture for her, a woman who didn't know anything about such things, and she kept saying over and over, so it would be etched into his soul: Never forget that you are *hiwi*; don't let them treat you like an animal. In spite of their prejudices, at first things were tolerable, because the brigade's close proximity allowed the boy to stop by the restaurant frequently to see his parents and because doña Matilde secretly managed daily to send him a basket filled with food.

"But it is customary for officers and superiors to humiliate the recruits," señor Mantilla tells me, "and Emiliano was a man of rebellious pride. There was a sergeant who was more cruel than the others, that sergeant treated him brutally and shouted in his face: 'What can you learn, you're the son of a savage,' and he ridiculed the boy in front of the others, calling him the son of Tarzan and Cheetah. Until Emiliano, who was tall and strong, chose not to swallow any more humiliation and split open the sergeant's face with a powerful punch."

As punishment they took his clothes and buried him in a jail they called the tomb, a hole in the ground, lined with cement, deep and narrow, covered on top by a steel grate that left the prisoner exposed to the rain, which in this region is frequent, to the cold nights and to the sun's burning rays. "You're going to rot there, monkey, savage, humanoid," shouted the sergeant from above as he passed Emiliano, and so did other officers, spitting on him and insulting him: "Don't even dream that we are going to let you out. Why don't you just die and take advantage of already being buried."

Don Abelardo's attempts to secure his release were futile, as were the pleas of Matildita, who abandoned her duties, forgot about her daughters, and planted herself day and night in front of the entrance to the brigade, where she cried from the top of her lungs and begged for clemency from all the officers she saw coming and going.

In that hole of death, Emilano wallowed in dementia and his own excrement. He was riddled with fungus and larvae and perhaps managed to calm his hunger and anguish by eating ants and worms as he had seen his mother do. And he endured being spit upon by the Heroes of Chimborazo and urinated upon by the Pumas of the Andes. Could he at least see the moon from his dungeon? Yes, he could: the moon, the stars, and any meteor that passed compassionately over his head, and they say that he spent his nights as a prisoner in the bowels of the earth, penetrating, with his gaze and his desire, the deep bowels of the firmament. According to the Mantillas, you could hear his voice repeating: "*Soy biwi,*" I am a man, I am a man, sometimes softly, sometimes in prayer, and other times shouting clearly so he wouldn't forget that he was a man and not filth, that he was a living being and not a cadaver. A cadaver that rebels, that wants to ignore his own decomposition, that abhors the earth that weighs upon him?

"That is what he had become," confirms the señorita.

He managed to survive for forty-six days, stolen minute by minute from horror and death, and on the night of October 17, beneath the miserly moonlight that refused to illuminate him, he cut his veins with a piece of broken glass and agonized until dawn, when his condition was discovered by the cleaning personnel. Then they opened the steel grate and disinterred him, but he was no longer saying *hiwi* or anything else, and he arrived at the infirmary with his heart drained of its blood and still, finally truly dead after having been dead for so long in life.

When they came to tell her what had happened, doña Matildita, who was barefoot and still hadn't braided her hair, was lighting the stove as she did every day at that hour, drenching the coal with liquid fuel before lighting it with a match. The bearers of the news hadn't finished saying what they had come to say before she took off running up the highway with the gallon of fuel in her hand, and in front of the brigade she up-turned it on herself and lit a match. Her hair was the first thing to burn, that sumptuous blue-black mantle that had been her only excess; it glowed red-white like a torch against the innocence of the sky until her lean body of dry wood was engulfed in flames. Her eyeballs melted and the intense fire of a mother's mourning began, the combustion of her infinite pain that wasn't of the flesh, and by the time the soldiers had put out the fire, her being had already been turned into a miserable heap of bereaved coals.

"And the girls?" I ask. "Matilde's daughters? What happened to the girls?"

But the Mantillas know little of them, not even their names, and Wilfredo shrugs his shoulders, excusing his ignorance.

"They were very little," the three justified themselves, "and they were all so alike that we never learned how to distinguish them."

"But the girls?" I insist. "You must know something of them . . ."

In Ambalema they only knew that they kept living with their father for a while, very unkempt and on the verge of starvation, until the

restaurant was closed, because after Matildita's death there were no pa-
trons, and the father brought from San Miguel Abajo, in the *departmento*
of Antioquia, a white woman whom he married in church and according
to law. That woman already had her own children who were also white
and she didn't want to have anything to do with the fruit of the previous
cohabitation arrangement. I didn't come here to take care of jungle children, she announced to her new husband, and Matildita's daughters
were turned over to God's care.

"We never heard about them after that . . ."

I thank the Mantillas and Wilfredo for the kindness they have shown
me with a basket of fruit and I say good-bye. I present myself at the Third
Brigade as a journalist, ask for an interview with the commanding officer,
General Omar Otoya, and I sit for a half hour in a windowless, air-
conditioned waiting room, imagining that Matildita's suffering soul must
wander scorched and howling through this military base at night until
the darkness is filled with the smell of fear, because the Heroes of Chimborazo, who are not afraid of death, are terrified of the vengeance of the
dead against the living who mistreated them. Is that the flicker of an old
anxiety I see in the alert eyes of these soldiers I watch coming and going
as if nothing had happened, but who know that their rifles are useless
against the ash that is settling in their lungs?

An officer takes me to General Otoya's office. It is large and well
ventilated, without a trace of torture or any reminder of horror, its doors
open to a balcony overflowing with ferns.

"People's imaginations are limitless," says the general, who is tall and
handsome and smells like cologne and looks like he just shaved with
Gillette Platinum Plus, when I ask him about soldier Emiliano Monteverde and the circumstances of his death. "There is no burying alive
here, nor has there ever been, no walling in or throat slashing, or anything of the sort. Cells like tombs? Don't tell me that you allowed yourself to be duped by those horror movies."

With the general's permission I look out over the railing on the green balcony, straining my eyes in search of the nonexistent cell, and suffice it to say that I don't see it anywhere.

The officer who led me a few minutes ago to the general's office now accompanies me back toward the reception area, and as he is returning my identification documents he gives me a sly look.

"It wasn't a disciplinary action, the thing with Emiliano Monteverde. There was a girl involved," he says, when no one can hear us.

"What? Then you do know about it?"

"The only one who knows is my general, and you already heard him, nothing happened here."

"But you just said . . ."

"Forget about what I said. You mentioned that you were in Tora before, right? Well, go back. Ask around there for a *prostituta* they call the Soldier's Widow. Ask her."

The Soldier's Widow? It's not a name that is easy to forget. And then there's the coincidence that I have heard it before.

Heading downriver during my return trip to Tora, I wring my memory trying to identify who I heard mention the Soldier's Widow for the first time. Todos los Santos, no, not Olguita either. Sacramento maybe? Or Fideo? No.

The river is so docile, so still in its course, that it seems philosophically feasible to be able to bathe twice in it. I can't stop thinking about Sayonara's mother, so close to those sorceresses who burn with inner heat, whose existence Mircea Eliade mentions, saying that they carry fire hidden in their genitals and that they use it to cook with. The mother, an Indian and a witch, the daughter, an Indian and a witch: One knew how to rub wood together to ignite the fire that feeds, the other, to rub the sex organs to ignite the fire of love.

An old man wearing a bright yellow shirt is rowing his *chalupa* in the opposite direction, propelling it forward with the strong strokes of a single oar, and I become absorbed in the brilliance of that yellow sparkling against the motionless river. Now I remember: It was Machuca, the ed-

ucated *puta*, the learned reader and heretic of the seventh circle that pro-
claims the death of God, it was she who mentioned the Soldier's Widow
to me. I see her sitting behind her Olivetti Lettera 22 in a corner of the
town hall in Tora, where she now works as a copier of notices, writings,
and documents, taking puff after puff on her eternal cigarette without
worrying about the ashes that fall, like bits of time, onto her blouse, her
papers, her lap, anywhere except the tin ashtray. I also see her shoes
sticking out from underneath the desk, wide and antiquated like Daisy
Duck's, her fingers stained with nicotine, her poorly embalmed
pharaoh's face, her crazy squirrel eyes, her enormous mouth that tells
me shocking stories about the inhabitants of the former barrio of La
Catunga, among which she mentions, only in passing and without emotion, the Soldier's Widow. I think I asked her about that woman with an
operatic name because I remember her assuring me that she wasn't anyone worth the trouble of investigating and except for her nickname was
a common, vulgar woman.

As soon as I reach Tora, before stopping by my hotel to leave my
knapsack, I run to the town hall to look for Machuca; it's five o'clock
and luckily they still haven't closed.

"Machuca," I ask, "did you know the Soldier's Widow? Does she
still live in Tora? Do you know where I can find her?"

"Why are you so interested. The Soldier's Widow came to La
Catunga after the best times had passed and it had succumbed to the
worst times. She never became a friend of ours."

"Why not?"

"Out of embarrassment. She was a gloomy *puta*, a spoilsport, a wet
blanket who was in the business by obligation and not by vocation.
More candle-sucking and prayerful than a blind zealot; I think she
would have liked to service her clients behind the altar so she wouldn't
have to lose sight of the Holy Child, who she had turned blue from asking so many things. For health, for money, for comfort for such a lonely
woman, for this and for that, because she was unhappy with this life,

that one, the Soldier's Widow. She wasn't anyone we would like, and you wouldn't like her either if you got to know her. An inspired *puta,* touched by the muses, that was Todos los Santos. Oh, yes! I wish you could have seen her in her splendor; she had the strength of a tractor and the happiness of a pair of castanets. Such a joy for life! On the other hand, the poor Widow was always a spiritless, downhearted woman.

"Why did they call her the Soldier's Widow?"

"It's a long story."

She arrived in La Catunga already in service and a veteran of the profession, with her hair dyed blond, an inconsolable air of abandonment, and dressed in the shroud of her own legend, according to which as a young woman she had been loved by a noble and gallant soldier who her brother, a sergeant in the same battalion, was pushing toward death to destroy their love.

The version of events that Machuca knows doesn't contradict that of the Mantillas. On the contrary, it raises the volume and adds two glorious elements that fill it with meaning: passion and heroism. There was no variation in the other ingredients: the same dungeon, the same boy buried in it, the same vengeful, insulting sergeant, his racial disdain, and his abuse of authority. But this time there's a woman, the sergeant's sister, who is the soldier's love. The differences in race and class are more notable and injurious because the recruit is the son of an Indian and a colonist, while the sergeant and his sister belong to an established, well-off family.

"I'll let you out of that hole if you swear you'll never see her again," bribes the sergeant, but the soldier, steadfast and faithful, refuses to renounce his loved one in spite of the torments of his corner of hell, and he advances so far in his unbreakable resistance that he can't withdraw again, even as he begins to rot alive in his grave.

"Will you swear now?"

"I won't swear anything."

"Do you swear? I will give you one last chance?"

"Let your fucking mother swear, that's why she gave birth to you."

"Then you'll stay there forever, because you're a bastard, a cretin, and an Indian."

This second version also details the reaction of the soldier's father — don Abelardo Monteverde, according to the Mantillas — who fulfills a decisive role in the tragedy's denouement.

"The soldier's father," Machuca tells me, "was an astute and cunning *antioqueño* who believed that the sergeant would tighten the tourniquet up to the end without his son giving in an inch, so he looked for the boy's girlfriend and managed to convince her to write in her own hand a false letter confessing that she no longer loved him, saying good-bye forever, and which she was to put in an envelope and deliver to her brother with some memento that was irrefutably hers. The purpose was to make the boy, faced with his love's change of heart, finally renounce his devotion to her so that the sergeant would lift the punishment and set him free."

"You can see with your own eyes, you wretch," the sergeant had said to the soldier, passing the false letter through the bars along with a medal of the Virgen del Carmen that the girl always wore pinned to her bodice. "My sister doesn't love you. Don't let yourself die because of her, she's going to marry someone more civilized than you, someone from her own class."

In both versions the soldier takes his own life by opening his veins — in the first, overwhelmed by desperation and suffering, in the second, destroyed by the evidence of his loss of love. When the girlfriend learns what happened, she fights bitterly with her brother and leaves her parents' house forever. Her refusal to forgive causes her to confront life on her own and to subsist by turning to prostitution. That is how, after much fighting, much wandering, she comes to live in La Catunga.

"No matter what else she is, the Widow was the protagonist of an intense story," I say to Machuca.

"There are people whose own story is too big for them."

"Why do you say that so harshly, Machuca, if she made the noble gesture of leaving her family for . . ."

"Yes, she made the gesture," she interrupts, "and from there on she let herself drown in indifference. It's better not to undertake those defiant stances worthy of bullfighters, they're so exhausting they just leave us empty."

"What about Sayonara and the Widow? Were they ever friends?" I test the terrain cautiously to see if Machuca suspects the close relationship that existed between them.

"There was something between them, but I never really knew what, because it wasn't friendship. I couldn't say. It was more like mutual compassion, as if they shared some dark, bitter secret. Only God knows! Too bad he doesn't exist."

"Only God knows," I agree. "Well, Machuca, if you'll forgive me, I would like to speak with the Soldier's Widow. Just because of her name she deserves my respect, and besides, she must have a lot of things to say."

"All she says is Hail Marys as she counts off the beads of her rosary, because she took refuge in a cloistered convent, the Clarisas' convent at Villa de Leyva, in Boyacá. She finally found her true destiny, which she had misplaced, but which was right there at the end waiting for her. You'll find her very happy there, sucking the Holy Child's tunic night and day, which is the only thing that she knows how to do. They say that the Clarisas refused to accept her because of her past, but in the face of the miracle of influence and money there is no door that can't be opened, nor any Clarisa that can resist. They say her family paid good money to lock her up with her shame, to grow old behind walls that are heavier than tombstones. So you see, you're not going to be able to get any further with that story, because what the Widow knows is cloistered right along with her."

twenty

 "You have beautiful eyes," Dr. Antonio María Flórez said to Sayonara the third or fourth time she entered his office.

"What do you mean by that, Doc?" she asked, shaking the blue brilliance of her hair and looking at him suspiciously.

"Just that, that you have beautiful eyes. Your problem is you can't stand people saying only that to you."

Olguita tells me that Sayonara couldn't understand when men weren't crazy in love with her. She couldn't accept that there was anyone who wasn't smitten by her, accustomed as she was to awakening love at first sight and stirring up desire with the mere brush of her skirt. If a man appeared and shuffled the cards for a game that didn't involve passion, she would focus her interest on him for that simple fact, watching him without believing, scrutinizing him from head to foot in an attempt to decipher the mechanisms that made him immune, then she would gnaw and scratch at his indifference with the claws of a rat, until she gouged and destroyed it. To finish the job she would deploy all the splendid plumage of a seductive female, because nothing unsettled her more than not unsettling others.

"It didn't happen only with humans," reports Todos los Santos. "It was her stubborn way with all God's creatures. She was so pampered in those days, and so haughty! My poor girl, she never suspected how hard things really are . . ."

Sayonara the dispossessed, the child prostitute of Tora, orphaned and dark-skinned, wandered the alleyways of her poor neighborhood in no particular hurry to get anywhere, ignoring the loneliness of stray dogs and the smell of fried fish and urine that enveloped everyone else, with a battery-operated radio in her hand and humming the romantic ballads of La Emisora Melodía, eating sweet oranges with clean bites and tossing the peels on the ground, sipping cool beer straight from the bottle and kicking the bottle cap down the street, freshly bathed and with her hair dripping wet, decked out in the only bit of elegance she knew, that narrow skirt with the slit up the side and the Chinese silk blouse with red and gold embroidery, and casually parting the crowd that was laboring under the hot sun on market day, just like a Moorish queen, idle and naked beneath her seven veils, along the fresh water-lined paths of her Alhambra.

Lacking holy oil, she was anointed with the arrogance of her cheap perfume; instead of a robe and crown, she paraded the impudence of her dark skin, and from the pedestal of her worn-out high heels, she treated the entire universe like a conquered vassal at her feet. If shooting stars came down from the sky, it was to bring her news of other wanderings, and for whom, if not for her, did the night watchman announce his rounds every hour with two mournful notes of his whistle? At dawn the robust aroma of coffee seeped forth from the pot and traveled to her bed to awaken her, and if the tuberoses disrupted the afternoon tranquillity with their oily smell of resurrection, they did it only to see her smile. Wandering troubles seeking consolation approached to drink her tears, the mist that flooded the valley cloaked her like a bride's veil, cat's eyes glowed phosphorescently when they looked at her, the days passed slowly to caress her at length, and if the great Río Magdalena took the trouble to funnel the abundance of its waters past Tora, it was only for the privilege of washing her feet.

"It wasn't her fault," says Fideo protectively. "So many people swore that they loved her that she believed it. Starting with you, doña Todos los Santos. You were the first one to confuse her."

"I did what I could to get her to open her eyes," Todos los Santos responds in self-defense. "One day I heard her say that the mockingbird sang so sweetly and so incessantly because it sang for her. Ay, my conceited child, I reprimanded her. Don't aspire to be a gold coin and don't have the impudence of wanting the world to love you; understand once and for all that *putas* are the other side of the tapestry, the rough side of life, and that it is the dark half of the moon that shines on us. Us? We are backroom tenants. They venerate us if they see us glow in the background and in the dark, but they squash us if we attempt to emerge into the light of day. Don't forget, girl, the great truth of *amor de café*: we *putas* are always at war."

"At war against who, *madrina*?" asked Sayonara, acting as if she didn't know.

"Against everyone, girl. Against everyone."

The *madrina* warned her, having guessed the harsh reality that the future was sure to bring: Girl, things aren't like that. But a pretty girl doesn't have to pay any mind and Sayonara kept strolling through life on a red carpet.

Things aren't like that, but today I suspect that Todos los Santos, the wise old woman, the holy celestine, wasn't right. That for once she was wrong because her young disciple, in the splendid egoism of her beauty, did come to be the very center of that whole universe, the privileged object of all love.

"Forgive me for saying this, Todos los Santos," I venture, "but in that specific topic, in that precise moment, it wasn't you, but she, who was right."

twenty-one

 Hired by the mayor, the gynecologist Antonio María Flórez had arrived in town with his wife, Albita Lucía, and their four children almost a year after the fiery riot that had reduced the clinic to rubble. When he saw the disastrous state of the facilities that were supposed to serve as his offices, instead of wasting time seeking official assistance or submitting bureaucratic claims, he set about the task of reconstructing the place brick by brick with his own hands to expedite his plans. He had decided to eliminate the coercive mechanism of the health card—which had already been abolished de facto by the riled-up women—and offer instead free, voluntary medical attention for the *prostitutas*. He had come to Tora to replace the previous charlatans in white lab coats, driven out of town by a ferocious collective vengeance, which one day took the form of a cruel joke and the following day became a threat or a serious hint, poisoning each minute of their lives until they were run off.

When he first arrived, Dr. Antonio María was the object of similar treatment. The girls, convinced that he too had come to make a fortune building up his business of disrespect and extortion, welcomed him the very first night by fouling the door to his house with the fetid corpse of a hanged cat, but that didn't frighten him off, nor did the campaign of vicious rumors that spread through the pueblo, saying he was a faggot, a squealer, an atheist, and a pimp. They circulated odious lies, that his feet stank, that he used to beat his mother mercilessly, and that he was so miserly that his children were on the verge of starvation. But Dr. Antonio María, a good man who was unscathed by the slander, continued diligently with his modest work as an amateur carpenter and lent a deaf ear to all the foolish babble. He was so tidy in appearance and in character that no one seriously believed the rumors about his reeking feet; since he turned out to be an orphan, the one about hitting his mother was spoiled; he admitted his atheism with such pride that no one dared to reproach him for it; the generous aromas that emanated from his wife's kitchen when she cooked made people doubt the deprivation of his children; and so forth. One after another the false accusations were eroded away without his even having to deny them.

But the anger of the women of La Catunga, goaded by the fresh memory of the disgrace they had suffered, refused to give up the sweetness of their revenge. The doctor had finished the basic construction stage and was beginning to install the windows in his clinic. One morning señora Albita Lucía was on her way to the main plaza, when from a high window the dirty contents of a chamber pot were emptied on her head. The affront was excessive even for the hardened patience of Dr. Antonio María, who would surely not have thought twice about it if it had fallen on him. But it was as if someone had punched him, this attack against the curly red hair of his wife, an abundantly freckled and vivacious woman with white, perfumed skin whom he adored as the sun of his days. So he made the instant, irrevocable decision to leave within twenty-four hours the town that had greeted them with such hostility.

They were going to leave on the noon train the following day. The doctor spent a night traumatized by the remaining bitterness of the undertaking that he would be abandoning before he even began it, and in the morning, while his family finished packing their recently unpacked trunks, he went to stand in the frame where the door to his clinic would have been installed, wearing his doctor's coat and with his stethoscope around his neck.

"Spread the word that at eleven-thirty I will hold my first and last consultations," he said to some passersby, and he didn't have to wait more than a quarter of an hour for patients to begin to appear.

It was then that Antonio María Flórez saw what would make him decide not to leave and would cause him to stay in Tora for the next ten consecutive years, until he became almost on a par with Santa Catalina, a saintly benefactor of the barrio of La Catunga: some unmistakable red pustules soaked in infectious pus and a few small, soft tumors, with gummy elasticity, on the thighs of three of the five women he examined.

"It is *treponema pallidum*," he declared. "This town is going to be consumed by syphilis."

The weight of that diagnosis reduced the seriousness of the incident with the chamber pot and the other injuries in the doctor's eyes, and it caused him to reflect on the fact that after all it is enough to speak words of forgiveness for it to be granted.

"I forgive you all," he said loudly, and raised his arms to the sky as he hurried to his house along streets that the fierce midday sun had left without a single soul.

He convinced his wife of the need to unpack once again, he enrolled his children in the only lay school in the pueblo, and from then on he dedicated all of his time to helping and consoling the women infected with the illness, advising the healthy ones on how to avoid infection and combating venereal disease with the tenacity of a fanatic, like that which Savonarola would have launched against the carnal splendor of the Renaissance.

Soon he realized that the elimination of pressure and blackmail had resulted in the surprising consequence that more than half of the women refused to visit the gynecologist's office.

"Why, Doctor," I asked Antonio Maria Flórez, when I had the opportunity to meet him. "How do you explain the fact that so many wouldn't come?"

"The majority out of fatalism, because they were convinced that no one dies before his time. They believed in those kinds of things, in deep-rooted, commonly held tenets, like fate is up to God, or when it's someone's turn it's his turn. I arrived in Tora when the *prostitutas* were still queens and señoras of position, but that didn't mean that deep down they didn't have a strong awareness of living in sin. And since they took for granted that sin implies punishment, they saw venereal infection as a debt they didn't have to get rid of, because in some way it was deserved. They dealt with the subject of infection like Russian roulette: They went to bed with this man or that one like someone who puts a revolver to his temple, and they pulled the trigger to see if they were spared or got a bullet. They couldn't grasp the idea that God could forgive them. Once I heard Fandango say, when she found out that her best friend had contracted syphilis, that now it was time to pay for a whole life of being in disharmony with heaven."

"It's curious, Doctor, that women so easygoing about sex would be so panicked by a gynecologist," I say to him.

"I find it fairly logical. To begin with, there is no one more full of mystery than a *prostituta*, and her state of health is one of the secrets she hides with greatest care because her livelihood depends on others believing that she's healthy. But there's something else that I don't know how to classify, and which constitutes the main obstacle: The gynecologist has to do with her thinking about what she is doing, treating it rationally, and they can't bear that. They work in prostitution as blindly as a man condemned to the firing squad who prefers to be blindfolded before he's shot. Also, to practice it they make use of faculties that are beyond reason, as I suppose happens with witchcraft. It is something that happens to them down there, under their skirts, under the sheets, always far from their faces. The further from their faces and their brains, the better. Many of them hate being kissed, especially on the mouth or the breasts, while from the waist down they give the client license to act more or less as he pleases. When they fall in love with a man, they incorporate their whole beings into the sexual act, but generally they behave like split beings: From the waist up is the soul and from the waist down, business. You must understand that as a gynecologist, you are the eye that sees, the one who uncovers what is hidden, warns of the risks, removes the blindfold with regard to sicknesses. That's why at first so many stayed away from me, because whether or not they wanted to, I forced them to integrate the two halves of their bodies through a process of reflection and acknowledgment that I've always felt was very painful for them. But it's normal; you can be a bullfighter or a fire-eater if you accept death as fate, but as soon as you put prudence and common sense in the mix, you flee in terror. The same thing happens with them. I think that's why for months my presence was much more uncomfortable for so many of them than that of the previous doctors, who simply swindled them, that is, they made a pact of blind complicity with the women. So great was their need to deceive themselves that they took pleasure in deceiving me, and for that sometimes it was enough for them to resort, a half hour before their appointment, to the old trick of bathing themselves by sitting on a washbasin, with warm water, lava soap, bicarbonate of soda, and a lot of lemon. With this procedure they cleaned the secretions and eliminated the odor, so that I would find everything in order and go on to the next. Why would they go to the trouble of deceiving me? You tell me, if the era of obligatory consultations and cards was over. I think they did it simply to avoid facing the truth. The women of La Catunga treated me very cordially, very affectionately, but they became nervous when they lay down on the examining table in my office. Petroleum had to grow scarce in the area and prostitution had to decline as a business before they would seek me out without apprehension, truly driven to heal themselves, to remove their bodies from the orbit of sickness, and to enroll it, so to speak, into the desired realm of health."

Dr. Antonio María was convinced that this peculiar mental universe of the *prostitutas* of Tora was directly rooted in their Christian upbring-

ing, because as he told me, among the Pipatón Indians a different attitude could be perceived. They sold their bodies to eat and to feed their
children and that seemed to be sufficient justification for them, without
getting so many knots in their heads.

"The *pipatonas* were my most assiduous patients," he tells me, "taking into consideration, as far as I knew, that they were also seeing their
own medicine men, relying on both my drugs and their traditional cures.
What is certain is that among them the illness struck with much less virulence than among the rest."

They had a clear and unfettered view of a profession that they entered and left according to their needs, and they didn't make a great distinction between the man who paid them to possess them and the one
who, outside of prostitution, possessed them without paying. They
needed to survive and that was that. Good, for them, was to stay alive;
and bad, to die; they didn't have a sexual ethic any more complicated
than that, or, more precisely, they didn't adhere so much to an ethic as
to a sort of biological determinism, according to which woman was
woman, *prostituta* or not, and man was man, no matter who he was. It
amused me to learn that for the Pipatón women the male body was comprised of head, arms, legs, trunk, and little trunk, and the female, of
head, arms, legs, trunk, and for-the-little-trunk.

Dr. Antonio María, who wasn't about to sit around waiting for a
frenzy of cankers and eruptions to sprout up around him, took on the
task of visiting house to house to pull the negligent and stubborn out of
hiding. Among these latter was Sayonara, who on the day of the uprising, while doing everything possible to make the flames lick the mus-
taches of the impostors, had sworn on the holy cross of Christ that she
would never again let a doctor, fake or documented, put his hands on
her, even if tuberculosis had her spitting blood or leprosy reduced her to
stumps. So, when she happened to see through the partially open window that Dr. Antonio María was knocking on her door in the mourning
tie he wore every day in honor of the marshal Antonio José de Sucre,
murdered more than a century earlier, with his leather bag filled with

implements, medicinal herbs, and bottles, and with his face shaded by the wide hat he wore to protect himself from the sun, she slipped out through the patio, and if she didn't jump onto the roof to fly away, it was only because Todos los Santos's hand managed to grab her by the ankle and hold on to her tenaciously.

"Come down from there, girl, it's for your own good."

"I'm not coming down and I'm not letting that man touch me."

"Bring me a rope!" ordered Todos los Santos. "This savage is going to let herself be examined if I have to tie her to the bed!"

"I tell you that I don't want to go near that man, *madrina*, because he has evil intentions. Don't you see the shamelessness in his smile?"

When I met Antonio María Flórez, I thought Sayonara hadn't been wrong to suspect his smile: It was true that in the middle of that austere face and neat profile were a set of rabbit's teeth more appropriate for a magician or a tango singer than for a gynecologist.

"You are wrong," insisted Todos los Santos to her adopted daughter, still holding her by the ankle. "His big-toothed smile makes him human. If it weren't for that he would be as dry and tight as a cigarette."

When the unruly Sayonara finally stood face to face with the doctor and was able to confirm for herself that his circumspect bearing, his professional demeanor, and the affable gray slate of his eyes counterbalanced the playful air of his outsized teeth, she changed her mind about defying him and agreed to lie down without underclothes and with her legs open and bent. But the doctor had barely brushed her thigh with his hand before he felt her jump, her nerves on edge, tensed to the point of bursting like the strings of a guitar. He tried to chat with her to relax her, to make her think about something else so she would lower her guard and allow him to examine her, but the girl was trembling from head to toe, electric and wild like a filly.

"We can't do it like this," the doctor said.

"Then let's not do it," she replied, standing up and covering her legs with her skirt.

"Come here," said Dr. Antonio María, who had understood that the

exam couldn't be conducted during this first visit, and he changed tac-
tics to calm her. She approached him and he put one end of his stethoscope in her ears as he placed the other on the left side of her chest.

"What is that echo?" asked Sayonara, pulling out the stethoscope
and taking a step backward.

"The beating of your heart."

Then she drew near again, let the doctor replace the earpieces, and
stood there, self-absorbed and perplexed, for a long time, glimpsing the
pulse of life that came and went, recurrent and obstinate, through secret
arroyos, flowing through the soft labyrinth of purple walls and resonat-
ing vigorously in her internal cavities.

"The beating of my heart!" she sighed, and from that moment on she
would never forget Dr. Antonio María, the first person in the world to
invite her to hear the deep rhythm of her own soul.

A week hadn't gone by when the doctor, about to leave his office
after a long day of work, found Sayonara perched on the front steps of
the clinic, waiting for him.

"You, here?" he asked, happy that she had finally decided to allow
him to examine her.

"I'm not here for that, Doctor, I've come to see if you would let me
listen with that thing again . . ."

They went inside; without anyone telling her, she lay down on the
examination table and the doctor placed the stethoscope on her heart.
Again she was awed, listening to how the tumult of her insides seemed
to come from the very depths of the universe.

"Tell me, Doc," she said after a while, looking at him with a heart-
melting seriousness and innocence. "Tell me, Doc, does one have
two hearts?"

"No, only one, here in your chest. Give me your hand and listen to
mine," he said, putting her hand on his own chest. "Tock, tock, tock . . .
it beats like a clock, just like yours."

"Then you recognize your heart because it beats, right?"

"Yes, that's right."

"And does it beat more when you fall in love?"

"Yes, I suppose so."

"But are you sure, Doc, that a person only has one heart?"

"Why do you ask me?"

"Well, because the other day I met a man from Campo 26, they call him Payanés, and I felt like I had two hearts inside my body, one in my chest, just like yours, and another here, down below," and the girl took the doctor's hand and placed it on her groin. "Do you feel how it beats? This is my other heart."

twenty-two

Olguita's soft presence peers into life through a discreet window, always from the side. If there was anyone who wasn't born to be a *puta*, it is she, the beatific Olguita, with her clear soul and a body atrophied by polio. Yet she knew how to prosper admirably in the exercise of the profession and had the gift of keeping, as persistent and stable clientele, a select group of lonely men who in the impeccable linen sheets of her bed found a trustworthy woman and an attentive listener; a woman who thickened the best *candil* with brandy on her wood stove and who with a delicate gardener's hand maintained an aroma of mint and basil, of chamomile and marjoram, on her patio that made one trust that the future would bring kind things.

Among the men who without realizing it found in Olga's arms the reason for their existence was a certain Evaristo Baños, a welder for the Troco, who was nicknamed Nostalgia by his fellow workers. He used to arrive on Fridays without detours, skipping the usual stops in the bars, and if he found her busy with someone else he would sit and wait on the steps outside her door without complaint, his elbows on his knees and his head in his hands. Once inside and free of his clothes, he officiated, with the luxury of repetition, over the same ceremony as always, which consisted of removing from his billfold a wad of family photos—mother, wife, and children, distant in time and space—to drop them one by one on the bed with his faith focused on them and repeating names and ages as if pronouncing an incantation against loss.

"And who is this little one?" Olguita would ask him, though she already knew it all by heart because they had gone over and over the same litany together. "Has the eldest finished school yet? How many months pregnant was your wife here? This spotted dog is called Capitán, right? And isn't this black dog Azabache?"

And so it went from Friday to Friday until one astoundingly hot Wednesday word came from the *petrolero* camp by way of Nayib, the street vendor. Stuck down in a well, installing a valve, Nostalgia had torn off his ring finger. Nayib himself had taken on the task of spreading the news from house to house, boasting of having been partially involved in the drama, because it was from his peddler's satchel that the eighteen-karat-gold ring that caused the accident had come—it had gotten hooked on a bolt just at the moment that Nostalgia, a robust man from Santander, was pulling downward with his full body weight.

"There's been an accident!" came the voice of alarm, and Nostalgia was lifted out by two fellow workers who took him to the hospital, caked with mud and with a frozen look on his face, less from pain than from confusion. His pupils were focused on a right hand that didn't seem to be his because it weighed less than the other and because it was wrapped in a towel soaked with blood.

"That's why the company has prohibited the use of metal rings or chains, loose shirttails outside of pants, or any other whim that lends itself to this kind of accident," said Demetrio the nurse, as he removed the towel, looking at the useless space where the absent finger used to be. He was surprised by the surgical cleanness of the cut and he sewed the stump with coarse stitches, as if he were mending a burlap sack. "That's why there is a rule that workers must wear shoes and not sandals, which leave the feet unprotected. But they don't follow the rules, so they have to face the consequences."

A massive female assembly congregated the next day at Olguita's house, and while they awaited the arrival of the mutilated man, they busied themselves by speculating on the fate of the ring finger.

"I say they should throw it to the dogs."

"They say the ring wouldn't come off the finger . . ."

"The ring should be given back to Nayib; Nayib should reimburse Nostalgia his money and the finger should be thrown in the river."

"To be eaten by the catfish that we will eat later? What a disgusting idea. It should be buried in some corner of the cemetery; it would fit inside a cigarette box."

"We could also preserve it in formaldehyde, as a memento . . . ," suggested Olga, who was sentimental and given to making the sign of the cross over things that had to do with blood.

"Bury it in your garden and plant a chamomile bush on top of it, so that it will grow really poisonous and deadly," proposed Sayonara, who always came up with ferocious initiatives.

"The things you say, girl!"

At that moment the women parted to create an alley of honor so that the mute Nostalgia could pass. He was coming to Olguita in search of an explanation and consolation, already aware that he had lost not only a finger and part of his hand but also the possibility of continuing with his career as a welder. The company had given him a bonus and a month's leave for the damages suffered, but it was public knowledge that at the Troco the injured stayed on to run errands, to do gardening, or for other tasks for low wages and even lower dignity.

"What do you think happened to the ring?" asked Nostalgia, who hadn't thought of asking about the finger's whereabouts. "I bought it to give to my woman someday; she's been complaining for sixteen years that we haven't gotten married. It must still be in the well, I guess . . . where would the ring be? Does anyone know?"

"Forget about the ring, Nostalgia," ordered Todos los Santos. "With your accident it has been proven once more that these barbaric lands only tolerate single men and that around here marriage brings calamity."

Neither the finger nor the ring ever appeared, and in time Nostalgia, who became a messenger for the Troco offices, forgot about them and his welder's dreams, and although for the rest of his life he kept on showing the photographs of his wife, his children, and his dogs to anyone who would let him, he never went back to find them. But that doesn't mean he turned into a pitiful man; he maintained the custom of coming down to Tora every week or two to receive from Olga, as a sort of consolation prize, a tender embrace between freshly ironed linen sheets.

twenty-three

 "Dress nicely and brush your hair, I am going to take you to see the other world," Todos los Santos announced one day to Sayonara and her four sisters, Ana, Susana, Juana, and little Chuza.

They put on their stiff organza dresses—the ones reserved for national or religious holidays—with frills and bibs and broad skirts puffed up with crinoline, like light-colored cotton clouds: baby-chick yellow for Sayonara, cotton-candy pink for Ana, sky blue for Susana, mint green for Juana, and white like the snows of days gone by for little Chuza. They greased down their hair and splashed on perfume, brushed their teeth, put on their stockings and shoes, and started walking behind their *madrina*, dressed up in their Sunday best on a Tuesday and advancing through briers and underbrush that threatened to tear the organza and that messed up their hairdos. In spite of everything, they proceeded carefully and elegantly like country people when they come into town for mass, because Todos los Santos had warned them that if they wanted to know the other world, they had to arrive with their dignity intact.

"So that no one dares to pity us," she said.

"This dress is scratchy, *madrina*," complained Susana.

"You'll just have to put up with it."

They reached a place outside of the fence around the Troco by walking along a path that Todos los Santos knew. They went down a hill and crossed a stream after taking off their shoes to keep them from getting wet, then sat on the rocks to dry their feet, put on their shoes again, brushed their hair, before finally arriving at their destination.

"Well, there it is. That is the other world," announced Todos los Santos, in front of a place where the thick vines that clung to the length of the fence had fallen away, and where, due to some oversight in security, there were no armed guards to scare off curious or ill-intentioned people.

Piled one against another and sheathed in their colorful organza dresses, like packages of bonbons, the five girls could see better than if they had a first-tier box, all five faces pressed against the stretch of wire fence to avoid the quadrangular frames, the five pairs of Asiatic eyes opened so wide and round that they lost their slant. From there they saw what their fantasies could not have even attempted to imagine: the mythic and impenetrable Barrio Staff, where the Tropical Oil Company had installed and isolated the North American personnel who held positions of management, administration, and supervision, and which was a reduced-scale replica of the American Way of Life. It was as if a slice of a comfortable neighborhood in Fort Wayne, Indiana, or Phoenix, Arizona, had been removed and transplanted in the middle of the tropical jungle, with its gardens and swimming pools, its well-manicured lawns, its mailboxes like birdhouses, the golf course, the tennis courts, and three dozen white, spacious houses, all identical and completely imported, from the bedroom furniture to the roof tiles and down to the last screw. In the background and on the top of a hill, dominating the barrio, rose a house built of pine called Casa Loma, the residence of the general manager of the company, with its ample rooms, its vestibule, terraces, and garages.

For a long time the five girls looked mutely at everything, and since they didn't see anyone appear there inside the fence, they thought the other world was a bewitched and deserted place like Sleeping Beauty's castle. It seemed as if the inhabitants had left suddenly, without time to take any of their belongings with them. A solitary towel lay abandoned at the edge of a pool, the translucent water still agitated by an absent swimmer, a tricycle overturned as if the child who had been riding it had fallen and run to look for his mother, a lawn mower that was waiting for the man who had just gone inside for a glass of water. These objects were gleaming, still unused, as powerful as fetishes, possessed of a well-being not belonging to the people who used them but rather to the objects themselves.

"Doesn't anyone live here, *madrina*?" asked Sayonara in a voice lowered out of fear of shattering the mirage, but at that moment the lawn-mower man came out of nowhere, started it up, and began working.

"What is that man doing, *madrina*?" asked Susana.

"He's cutting the grass."

"To give it to the animals?"

"No, he is cutting it because he likes it short."

"What a strange man . . . ," said Ana. "And why do they have those poor people locked behind this fence?"

"We are the ones who are locked away, the ones on the outside, because they can leave, but they won't let us in."

"Why won't they let us in?"

"Because they are afraid of us."

"Why are they afraid of us?"

"Because we are poor and dark-skinned and we don't speak English."

"Look, *madrina*, the houses are like cages too," said Juana, "they can't come out through the door or the windows."

"Those are screens, so the mosquitoes don't get in."

"The mosquitoes can't get in? And the other animals can't get in either?"

"Only dogs."

"Can the dogs come out?"

"If the people open the door for them."

"What is that woman doing?" asked Ana when she saw the owner of the towel stretch out on a lawn chair to sun herself.

"She is going to lie in the sun."

"Lie in the sun? Then she must have cold blood. Machuca told me that lizards lie in the sun to get warm because they have cold blood."

"No. She wants to lie in the sun to make her skin darker."

"But why do they do that," said Sayonara, "if they don't like dark-skinned people?"

"You have to understand them," said Todos los Santos. "They weren't born here. They are North Americans."

"Why did they come here?"

"To take oil from the land."

"Why do they take it?"

"To sell it."

"Oh! Is it a good business to sell land without oil?"

"What are those two doing?" asked Ana, pointing to a pair of women who were chatting at the door of a house.

"They are speaking English."

"Then how do they understand each other?"

"Because they know how to speak English. Inside there no one speaks Spanish."

"Someone should teach them . . ."

A group of children jumps into the pool to paddle around, a man starts washing his car, a woman picks up a hose and begins to wash her dog. Little Chuza, dazed, watched everything without missing a detail, but she didn't ask anything because little Chuza never opened her mouth.

"They wash dogs, they wash children, they wash cars . . . ," said Juana. "What clean people! And where do they get so dirty, if there's no dirt in there?"

"There is no dirt because they clean it."

"But why do they clean it if there is no dirt . . . ?"

"To keep busy and to kill time until they can return to their country."

"Look, *madrina,* they're barefoot. Don't they have shoes?"

"Yes, they do. They're barefoot because they like it—they keep their shoes in their houses."

"So they don't get dirty?"

"Maybe."

"What if their feet get dirty?"

"Then they wash them, like their dogs."

"But why would they wash a dog?" asked Ana, who never in her life had seen anyone wash a dog.

"So he won't smell."

"Do their dogs smell very bad?"

"All dogs smell the same."

"I heard something," said Sayonara. "Señor Manrique told me. He said that the floors of some houses are covered with wool, like sheep."

"That really is strange!" shouted Susana. "That must be one of Sayonara's lies."

"It's true," confirmed Todos los Santos. "They are houses with rugs."

"What crazy people!"

"And what are those people doing over there, *madrina?*" inquired Juana, tugging on Todos los Santos's skirt.

"They are playing a game called tennis."

"But they're not children . . . adults play too?"

"Yes," said Susana, showing off. "And the one who catches the ball in his hand wins."

"No, the one who throws it the furthest with the racket wins," corrected Todos los Santos. "The racket is that squashed basket they have in their hands."

"And inside there, in Barrio Staff," Ana wanted to know, "do people also die?"

"Yes, they do. Death is the only thing that strikes them whenever it wants."

twenty-four

A ball of rice. The critical events that occurred next origi-
nated with a soggy, cold ball of rice cooked in vegetable oil,
one of those balls without salt or God's mercy that the management of the Troco distributed among the workers at
lunchtime, and which they, not wanting to subject themselves to the
displeasure of sinking their teeth into, preferred to kick around in the
soccer matches they improvised in the building that served as their
dining hall.

That morning, sheets of indecisive rain undulated across the sky,
evaporating upon contact with the scorched earth, and the men of
Campo 26 worked reluctantly amid dense clouds of heat. Delaying his
appointment with death, Sacramento had decided to test the stamina of
his weakened legs in the open air after having been released from the
hospital. His unexpected recovery from an affliction lying somewhere
between malaria, amebic cysts, and yearning for eternity was not so
much due to the brown mixture, the white mixture, or the poisonous,
pink quinine, as to the life-giving power of a dream and the palpable effects of the object that provoked it: the trinket of hair that Payanés had

given him. Because as Olguita explained to me, nothing protects you with such loyalty nor transmits such vigor as an amulet made from the hair of the one you love, and the inverse is also true: An array of ills can be unleashed by a single hair from the head of someone who hates you.

"You don't have to be very sharp to realize the power of hair," she told me one day. "You only have to see how it continues to grow after death. As if that weren't enough, it's the only part of the human body that doesn't feel pain or decompose."

"Does it protect you even if the tuft hanging from your neck hasn't been cut for you but for someone else, and its owner doesn't even know that you are the one wearing it?" I ask her.

"One would suspect that under those conditions it would protect you less, but it would still protect you. Anyway, it worked for Sacramento, and he isn't the only one to have been saved by hair."

"Are you a living being or a suffering spirit?" a disconcerted Payanés asked his friend, who an instant earlier he had given up for nearly dead, as he saw Sacramento appear on skinny Emilia's platform with the uncertain step of Lazarus, who arose and walked, still shaken by a tremor from beyond.

"I'm still not sure," answered the resuscitated man.

"Are you well?"

"I am, which is saying a lot."

"It's a miracle! Without warning you've come back to life . . ."

"I wouldn't go that far, but at least the will to live has come back."

"It's incredible, I'd even swear that you've grown," said Payanés to hide his churning feelings, and he confessed to himself that he had been prepared for his best and only friend's death but not to see him alive again. "Before, I was a couple of inches taller than you, and now you must be taller than I am."

"They say the fever either kills or stretches," replied Sacramento, and he sat down off to the side to watch, worn out by the exertion of breathing among the healthy again and stunned at the velocity and precision with which Payanés and his new work partner fit and coupled the pipes. Pajabrava had replaced Sacramento and was a man with a persistent gaze and the air of an apostle who had the habit of locking his eyes on others until he managed to plant the seed of fear within them. Years of experience around the globe had made him a *petrolero trashumante*, as they call those who follow the pipeline on its journey from the jungles of Catatumbo to the deserts of Syria, going off, coming back, and going off again. Sacramento tells me that they called the man Pajabrava—slang for "avid masturbator"—because he never missed an opportunity to preach against the practice of masturbation, which was so useful in regions of lonely men. During his discourse, Pajabrava penetrated his listener with his discomforting drill-like gaze while he overwhelmed him with quotes from diverse masters of Eastern thought, until forcing him to admit that onanistic practices were responsible for man's perdition and his flagging will.

"You're so fast at your work, *hermano*," said Sacramento to Payanés, who glistened shirtless, bathed in mist and sweat, exhibiting the bleeding rose on his chest as if it were a medal, and who was so synchronized with skinny Emilia's bold metallic vibration that it almost seemed like a male coupling with a powerful and ferocious female. "You're ten times quicker than when we started."

"You see, now they call me Cuña a Mil, because I can fit a thousand bands an hour. I told you I was going to become the best *cuñero* in the country."

"Because you gave up the filthy habit of playing with yourself," Pajabrava started off with another sermon. "That's where your energy comes from. If you go back to messing around, you'll be no good for this work and all the good rhythm you've developed will go to hell. A worker who masturbates is worth less than a burned match. That's why we're the shit we are, look around you, a poor yellow crushed army of unredeemed jerk-offs."

"Jerking is the opium of the people," declared Payanés, parodying words that had been repeated around the camp lately.

"Jerkers of the world unite!" added an amused Sacramento, feeling once again like a member of the human race.

"Make fun of me, I don't care," responded Pajabrava. "But I'm warning you, each drop of semen that you waste is an ounce of vital force escaping from your body."

"You're right, we shouldn't waste precious semen. Let's go demand that the company provide each worker with a little jar so he can collect it properly."

"Good idea, *compañero*," said Montecristo, one of the other members of the team. "And they should put some barrels in the middle of the camp so all the men can empty their jars into them, and then they should consider the possibility of digging a huge lake to hold the barrels containing the entire nation's life force."

"And there would be a bonus for the worker who makes the largest individual contribution," said Macho Cansado, pantomiming a spasmodic ejaculation.

"The era of white gold has begun!" shouted Payanés, inspired by the band that had risen up against Pajabrava, whom no one had dared to stand up to until now because of his experience and seniority or perhaps out of guilt for the venal pleasures of lonely nights, or out of fear of being petrified by his cold, stiff gaze, like that of the walking dead.

But the unstable and heated spirit in the camp wasn't coming just from the evil eye that Pajabrava was propagating with his insistent morality. Some other undetermined discomfort was hanging over the men, like pepper in the air, an insect invasion, or excessive humidity, something that electrified the surroundings, an uneasiness among men who didn't know quite what they were doing there, as if suddenly their own pants were too big or too tight, as if what until yesterday was sufficient and good is today too little, too late, obsolete. A generalized nervousness was lurking around the 26 that restless morning, making the men talkative, susceptible, prone to joking, and unfocused.

Sacramento approached Payanés with a need for intimacy, for exchanging secret words that concerned only the two of them, or more precisely, that single secret word that belonged to them both and which they painfully shared on the margin of the contagious banter of the others, and it was none other than her name.

The act of including Sacramento as a character in this book forced me to ask myself how to come to understand and appreciate him in his unenviable role as a tropical Werther, so obsessive and unreal in his love that he belongs to another epoch, melodramatic and excessive when seen from the perspective of a new century which has walled itself up in its panicked fear of being ridiculous and has branded as ridiculous whatever is not imminently practical. How to get closer to Sacramento, to his grating custom of loving until death and his tendency to live dying. How not to diminish or disdain him for being excessive or out of place, and at the same time how to trust the honesty of his love, tenacious but self-sufficient, radical but suspect in its disinterestedness of the subject of that love. The theatrical purity of his idolatry moved me, but I couldn't escape the presentiment that the object of his fervor was a creature he himself had invented, which wasn't the girl or the *puta* either, but a nonexistent third woman halfway between the two.

"I can't imagine her, now that she's grown up," Sacramento said to Payanés, interrupting him in his work. "Please tell me what she's like."

"Well, she's like the rest of them, what do you want me to say? She has her little arms, her little legs, her little tits . . ." Payanés was avoiding the answer and at the same time evoking for himself the complete anatomy of that adolescent gone astray, from the smell of smoke and lavender lingering in her hair to her toenails, painted red like geranium blossoms.

Now I suspect that if Payanés, so formed from the clay of this world, could remember Sayonara in all her light and her smell, it was because he had seen her with the eyes of ordinary love, while Sacramento, on the other hand, adored her through eyes filled with ecstasy; he carried her embedded in the violet pores of his liver, which is the organ of melancholy, and that's why he sighed with hope by day and desperation by night.

Pajabrava climbed up to the tower's platform to perform the duties of capper and permitted Sacramento to reassume his own, but Sacramento functioned with such a lack of conviction and such inability that the rhythm of the work dropped.

"Payanés," Sacramento resumed the conversation, trapped in the spiderweb of his obstinacy, while he struggled to hold the pipe with the wrench. "Payanés, tell me if it's true that she smells like lavender."

"What?"

"Her, Sayonara, does she smell like lavender?"

"How should I know? I don't even know what lavender smells like."

"But you said the other day that she smelled like lavender . . ."

"Well, then, yes," he was forced to admit. "She smells a little like it. Why don't you be quiet now and put your head to what you're doing, you're going to slice off my fingers with this shit."

"Are you sure? I would say she smells more like smoke. If someone asked me, I would say that Sayonara smells like smoke. And like the mountain."

"Quiet, asshole, you're going to mutilate me!"

"This amulet that you gave me smells like the mountain, you know? Just like her hair. When I was a boy I used to get close to her to smell it without her knowing it and becoming afraid, because I thought that what people said must be true, that before she had come to Tora she had hidden in the mountains. They said that since the adults were killed by La Violencia, many children like her ended up as orphans, wandering around and living in caves. Then I thanked God that I didn't have parents, that way no one could kill them and I wouldn't have to live in the mountains."

"Damn it, Sacramento! Think about what you're doing. We haven't gotten anywhere in two hours, and Abelino Robles is going to be furious."

"I asked her if she had seen tigers when she lived in the mountains and she said yes, and she wanted us to pretend that we were brother and sister hunting tigers and we would hang their teeth around our necks. But I didn't want to play; I only wanted to think about her when she was an orphan, living in the mountains, terrorized by tigers."

"Fucking son of a bitch! You're about to crush me! Your fucking mother! That's it, it's over. I can't work like this anymore. Tell Abelino

Robles that you're still weak and that he should move you over to cleaning pipes."

Payanés was secretive about his love for Sayonara, focused as he was on the occupational hazards of his job, and I think that unlike Sacramento, who needed to talk constantly of his passion to assure himself that it still existed, Payanés was content to be quiet, sure that on the other side of the jungle the girl he desired was gently grasping, between her thumb and index fingers, the other end of that invisible thread of joy and anxiousness that he held between his teeth. Sacramento was a man molded by doubts, and Payanés, by reality.

"Today, I'll excuse your performance, boy," Abelino Robles, the gang leader, warned Sacramento. "But if you fail tomorrow too, you'll be a gardener, planting gladiolas with the other useless men."

Did anyone notice Sacramento's virginal paleness when by order of his superior he had to surrender the precision wrenches, abandon the platform, enter the area they disdainfully called *la olla*, the pot, where the dug-up pipes were stored, take a brush in his hands, and begin to scrub them with gasoline until they were free of mud and grease? Faced with that demotion to scrubber, anyone else would have burned with humiliation, anyone but Sacramento, who at that moment felt that planting gladiolas was the same as polishing Abelino Robles's shoes; kneeling down to scrub pipes was the same as being an oil magnate and shitting out the world's heart. He was pale, yes, and had dark circles under his eyes, but the anguish that was gnawing away at him was caused by something else.

After scrubbing for a while he couldn't contain himself any longer; he left the pot and climbed back up to the platform where Payanés and a new partner were sweating in the throes of pipe fitting.

"Tell me, Payanés, why did you have the amulet tied around your neck?"

"Ay, Jesús, give me patience! Where do you think I should have tied it? Around my balls?"

"Don't get like that, just tell me. You could have put it in your pocket, for example. Why didn't you just put it in your pocket? If a man doesn't love another man's woman, he has no reason to tie her hair around his neck."

Startled, Payanés's hand narrowly escaped being crushed between the pipes. He choked on his words and his guilt, not knowing how to respond, and he used the excuse of the racket produced by the chain as it passed through the winch to say that he couldn't hear what Sacramento had said. Then he was saved by the howling of the whistle indicating the rotation of shifts, and the seven men in the team hurried down the tower to head toward the dining hall. Payanés, to escape the awkward situation, went off on a tangent and started teasing Pajabrava.

"Tell me, master, do you think that nuns masturbate?"

"It is well known that during the cold nights in her cell, Sor Juana Inés de la Cruz . . . ," began Pajabrava's torrent of words, and his response could still be heard when they reached the dining hall to find that, in the midst of general chaos, balls of rice were buzzing through the air and landing on the large portrait of Mr. L. P. Maier, the general manager of the Tropical, who presided over the room from his fixed position high up on the front wall, and from which spot, despite the rain of projectiles peppering his image, he greeted the workers with a broad smile: bland, American, and Protestant.

It had just begun, in an unforeseen, unpremeditated manner, this violent jolt that would forever mark the lives of everyone involved in this story, and that from that time on would come to be known as the rice strike.

twenty-five

 For a while now, Sayonara had taken to visiting Dr. Antonio María Flórez's office almost daily, not for a genital exam—something she never agreed to, despite the doctor's insistence—but to help him with his duties. She demonstrated skill as a nurse and had a particular passion for sicknesses, which led her to insert her finger in every wound, to volunteer to give injections and remove sutures, to examine any rash, swelling, or suppuration she laid her eyes on, and to ask with insatiable curiosity about symptoms, remedies, and medicines.

"Sometimes I think, Doc, that men don't love me," was the surprising comment from out of nowhere that she made to Dr. Flórez on Wednesday evening, after they had seen the last patient and were preparing to close the office and leave for their respective homes.

"What do you mean, you who are so loved by all of them?"

"That doesn't mean anything, Doc. What I want is just one man who loves me, but really loves me. The way you love and protect your wife, you know?" she asked as she scrubbed her hands with disinfectant soap, erasing the day's chores.

Dr. Antonio María didn't answer her either yes or no, instead he simply stood behind her as she washed her hands with the honest movements of someone who is unaware of being watched. He looked at her as he had never allowed himself to do before, that is to say, with eyes that seek to possess that upon which they are resting, and with the painful tension of desire he studied those hands with their long fingers and almond-shaped nails, all the more amazing for someone like the doctor, whose own nails capped stubby fingers. Then, slowly, breath by breath, he noticed the soft line of her arm as it disappeared into her short sleeve, and then moved his eyes immediately to the seashell of her ear, which offered him the fascination of a small labyrinth of flesh, then on to the shining glory of her hair that refused to stay out of her face even though she had shaken her head, and it slid forward again, back over her shoulders, alive and untamed, to fall forward and mingle with the splashing water. And it should be said, because Dr. Antonio María himself acknowledges it today, that in that opportunity his eyes took minute notice of the arousing vibration of the girl's buttocks, caused by the energetic movements of her hands as she rinsed them.

An hour later the doctor was sitting at his kitchen table in front of a plate of *arroz atollado* and lettuce salad served by his wife, Albita Lucía, for whom the turbulence dancing in his mind didn't go unnoticed.

"You're coming from a place that you still haven't been able to leave," she said to him, and to cover up he asked her to pass the pepper, but he wasn't able to prevent her from reading the images that moments before had been captured in his retinas.

"Do you think that I wouldn't have liked to be a *puta*?" she asked him, tilting her head of brassy curls in such a delightful manner that it immediately yanked him away from his journey through someone else's woman and brought him back to the complacency of finding himself at home with his very own.

"Really?" he inquired, intrigued and amused, letting out one of those laughs that exposed his rabbit's teeth to the elements. "I never suspected that you would want to go to bed with a lot of men."

"I don't want to. If I were a *puta,* I would call myself Precious and I would charge so much that no man could afford me."

The next day Dr. Antonio María left the clinic earlier than usual, asking Sayonara to be sure to lock the door securely when she left.

"*Adiós,* child. I have to go now, because Precious is waiting for me at home," he said in parting. He hurried away from the clinic and didn't want to look back because he knew that Sayonara would be standing in the doorway, watching him leave, illuminated by the glow of loneliness that always surrounded her and that if he turned to look at her he would have been unable to resist the temptation to hug her tightly.

"Be gone, sorrow!" Piruetas was heard to shout as he came down the middle of the street with little dance steps and clowning around, with a bottle of white rum in his hand and clinging to a pair of very drunk girls.

"Be gone, sorrow," they say Sayonara repeated as she locked the clinic door.

twenty-six

I am trying to concentrate on fragments of information about the famous rice strike that I have compiled from the press of the era, from files and from union documents, but my head is speeding off in ten different directions at the same time, as if trying to take in everything with one fell swoop. Writing this story has turned into an already lost race against time and faulty memory, twin brothers with long fingers that touch everything. Each day they appear and momentarily stir up before my eyes glimpses and reflections of situations, of moments, of words spoken or unspoken, of faces that I recognize as invaluable, loose pieces of the great puzzle of La Catunga, which overwhelm me with their little voices shouting for me to pay attention to them and ordering me to document them in writing or else they will be swept away by a broom and become lost among the debris. I cannot keep up with this attempt to imprison a world that goes by in flashes like a dream remembered upon waking, elusive in its vagueness and hallucinatory in its intensity.

Just as it is with my own dreams, I alone have the opportunity to bring into focus this fragile and volatile kaleidoscope, made of insect's wings; only for me does the keyhole exist, inviting me to spy, while on the other side of the door the disappearance continues little by little, and the only things that will endure are those that I am able to capture and to pierce with a pin to affix them to these pages.

But the task is more devilish still, because I am also assaulted by the conviction that, contradictorily, the very act of inserting myself into a foreign and private story, of sniffing around what otherwise would have disintegrated, of clearing the dust from shelves where already little more than dust remains, accelerates the fall into oblivion, just as occurred in Fellini's film *Roma*, where the camera, as it enters an ancient *domus*, hermetically sealed for centuries, catches a momentary glimpse of some frescoes that vanish instantaneously upon contact with the devastating external atmosphere. The same camera that perpetuates the image of the frescoes is what has destroyed them, as if they were real only as long as no one looked at them. I sense that like those frescoes, La Catunga is self-sufficient, can conserve itself in its own oblivion, and lives only when others ignore it.

Yet, at the same time it doesn't exist if I am not here to bear witness. And because of that I persevere, I meddle, I violate the story's reserve. This morning, for example, I was awakened by the need to define an image that earlier had barely caught my attention, that of the painter who at some point had done the oil portrait of Mistinguett that provoked such displeasure in her. Had it been just an ordinary artist, or an unknown amateur, or was it possibly someone who had managed to endure in museums and reproductions? Did that painting still exist, the one in which Mistinguett said she looked like a chicken? Curiosity compelled me to get up at once and, without pausing for breakfast, drove me to Todos los Santos's house.

I found her up and about and particularly spirited, renewed by a sudden burst of vanity: She had cloaked her old age and her ailments in a showy, bright-pink nylon nightgown, had mounted upon her withered bun a tall Spanish comb encrusted with gems, and wore on her feet a pair of slippers made of rabbit skin dyed a soft shade of pink.

"You look very elegant, Todos los Santos."

"They are simply artifices to mask the weariness," she clarified, and I began to question her about the famous painter while she, all pink and vaporous, visited one by one the cages of the strange zoo of small captive animals, unpleasant like all zoos, that she kept on the patio, in the garden, the corridor, and the kitchen of the house she shared with Fideo and Olga.

"That portrait? Who knows where it ended up?" she answered, as she tried to focus her dull pupils on a bizarre, awkward bird that was looking at her with round, pearly eyes like a pair of shell buttons. Missing a leg, the bird was clinging with the remaining one to the old woman's finger, wings flapping painfully to keep its balance as she offered it a piece of plantain.

"What kind of bird is that, and who amputated its foot?"

"It is a *chuachí* and when they brought it to me, as a baby, it was already mutilated, the poor thing. His name is Felipe."

She told me that in spite of her reputation as a diva, Mistinguett was in reality a fat and wicked woman with large breasts, and that the painter, in contrast, was a timid and desperately fragile man, who from that day on never again made "modern portraits" of the girls because he had been discredited for making them look ugly, with wild hair and terrified eyes, as if they had been run over by a train.

"Except for the *pipatonas*. He did paint them in the modern style, because it didn't bother them," Todos los Santos told me, now feeding rice to a friendly parrot that was walking up her arm and shoulder onto her head to peck at the stones shining in her comb.

"And what is this meddling parrot's name?"

"He's not a parrot, he's a *guacamayeta*, and his name is Felipe."

"Are they all named Felipe?"

"No, that monkey's name is Niño."

"And that cross between a fish and a pig?"

"He's a *zaíno* and he's still just a baby. His name is Niño and he's my baby."

"Niño!" she called out, and Niño trotted over, and several other unclassified specimens who must also have been named Niño grew restless and turned to look at her.

"I suppose that painter left La Catunga to look for another place where his paintings would be more appreciated . . ."

"No, he didn't leave," Todos los Santos corrected me impatiently. "I already told you he stayed with the *pipatonas*, letting them take care of him and painting them for free in the modern style, and at the same time, to earn a living, he painted a series of landscapes in a more conventional style. Those we did admire, and we would buy landscapes from him every now and then."

As I was able to establish later on—only through hearsay, because I was never able to see any of his paintings—"the series of conventional landscapes" consisted of a few seascapes painted from descriptions he'd heard, several Paris street scenes—also improvised because just as he had never seen the ocean, he had never traveled to Paris either—and a few sunsets in fierce violets and dramatic oranges that turned out to be his greatest commercial success because they were widely admired by the *putas* of Tora, including Todos los Santos.

"That was art! That was inspiration!" she exclaimed excitedly, as she changed the water in the cage of a toucan with an enormous yellow beak. "He was short and had a pale complexion, but I have heard, although I wouldn't know from experience, that he was the happy owner of a powerful and oversized sex organ, something like this toucan's beak. His name was Enrique. Enrique Ladrón de Guevara y Vernantes, with more family names than a telephone directory, because he came from a distinguished family."*

But his landowning and aristocratic blood didn't save him from moral sorrows or physical calamities. On the contrary, he was chained to them by several generations of intermixing Guevara thieves with Vernantes ladies, and of Guevara ladies with Vernantes thieves, who chose

---

Ladrón is used here both as a family name and, below, as it is more commonly used, to mean "thief."

to marry among themselves to maintain their properties undivided and their lineage pure. With the lamentable result, unacknowledged by the family even in the face of the evidence, that defects and degeneration were twisting and deforming them until they began to produce circus freaks, whose physical rarities were attributed to the pernicious effects of supposed contracted illnesses and never to hereditary defects. Among these latter was Enrique, with his height of scarcely four and a half feet that was further reduced by the curvature of his misshapen legs. And as if his forsaken body weren't punishment enough, he was covered with, instead of hair, eyebrows, and beard, a fuzz like dried dandelion blossoms, more transparent than white, and only comparable in lack of pigmentation to his skin—a silk paper with a propensity for being damaged by the slightest accident—which was the insipid color of watery milk and tinged with bluish highlights from the underlying network of illustrious veins.

"So Enrique Ladrón de Guevara y Vernantes was an albino dwarf?" I said to Todos los Santos.

"For Mistinguett and the others at the Dancing Miramar he was an albino dwarf, as you say, and they disdainfully ridiculed his physical defects, but to the women at La Copa Rota, which was the lowliest cave of a café, he was always respectfully called don Enrique. But if you want to know so much, go ask Fideo; no one knew him like she did."

Fideo, skinnier than can be imagined, lies dark and shriveled like a dried prune in the hammock that is her deathbed, regurgitating memories and struggling to stay alive, because although she has wanted to leave this world for some time, her fear of death binds her to life. Sober and lucid only now, on the eve of her great, definitive drunken spree, she pulls out a contraband drop of enthusiasm amidst the miseries of her agony and smiles when I mention don Enrique's name.

"Ay, don Enrique!" she sighs, and catches her breath. "Ay, don Enrique . . ."

Fideo, the excruciatingly thin dancer at La Copa Rota, a drunk at the age of thirteen, fourteen at the most, and already filled with vices, initiated sometime earlier by force into the arts of hard love. "Dance, Fideo! Dance, skinny girl!" shout the barefoot *tagüeros* who frequent the place, sitting in the darkness on bundles of sorghum, oats, and rice, and she disrobes, takes a drink, and raises her arms, then half closes her eyes and undulates her wire-like waist, another drink and her dark body—almost a whisper, barely a shadow—turns golden in the reflection of candlelight while at her feet, which are encased in an old pair of white children's shoes, it rains coins. While the others pretend not to notice, one of the *tagüeros* stands up drunkenly, raises Fideo in the air as if she were weightless, and takes her behind the curtain in the rear, toward the back rooms.

There was no place for a creature like Fideo in the red and black velvet rooms of the Dancing Miramar nor on the less pretentious stages in dance halls like Las Camelias, Tabarín, or Quinto Patio. They wouldn't allow her in riffraff bars like Candilejas or El Cantinflas, or even in La Burraca, a late-night pool hall where schoolboys secretly went in search of old *putas* who would teach them how to love in exchange for a lemonade or a *mogolla*.

"Why?" I ask Todos los Santos. "Why did they refuse her entry everywhere? For being an alcoholic?"

"Partially for being an alcoholic, because in the better bars it wasn't proper for a woman to get drunk. From the first day they taught us how to pretend by drinking rum diluted with three parts of mint tea instead of straight rum. But the main reason she wasn't allowed in wasn't that, but due to a bad habit that Fideo had."

"And what was that habit?"

"She would cut men's faces, or scratch them with her fingernails. Fideo had had a devilish temperament since she was a little girl, and at the first sign of displeasure with her clients she would leave them scarred. They would complain to the owners of the bar, and when there were several victims, they would throw her out into the street."

For weeks Fideo would wander around looking for a new client, and when she found one, she would completely forget the lesson she had just learned; at the least provocation the claw would emerge and she would scratch again. And she kept going downhill from there, knocking on doors that were further and further away until she found refuge on the bottom rung, according to Tora's peculiar and rigid hierarchy: La Copa Rota, a grain store with a straw roof and a hard-packed dirt floor that during the day sold feed and at night became a bordello, with an open drum in a corner for a toilet and illuminated by gas lamps because it had no electricity. It was on the edge of a horse path a half hour from the pueblo, in the shadow of the thick jungle where you could already begin to feel the threat of tigers and the green breath of the vast humid expanse. A dozen *pipatonas*, recruited from a neighboring village, took care of the shabbiest clientele in Tora, a migrating barefooted population comprised of hunters, wood gatherers, *tagüeros*, and other poor jungle scavengers, who returned from their outings exhausted, malaria-ridden, and full of worms to seek comfort between the first pair of legs that welcomed them.

Where else would don Enrique and Fideo have met each other? Unacceptable specimens of their respective universes, each in his own painful way. Where else, if not in this exact spot, this last resort, situated on the margin of all human vanity, would their destinies meet, the violated and drunken adolescent and the dwarf artist and aristocrat? Only at La Copa Rota, of course, according to the centrifugal laws of marginalization; in that attempt at a bordello where the Pipatón Indian women worked as prostitutes without red lightbulbs, or green ones, or yellow, let alone white ones, assuming the electric wires had reached that far; having given up the nakedness without surprises, with which they had moved freely about the jungle, to drape themselves with tight outfits made of cheap fabrics that made them look heavy and shapeless like barrels, and wearing crooked high-heeled shoes that bruised their toes; adorned with fake gold rings and earrings, these women, for whom pure gold had been—so they say—familiar and noble like water and corn.

"Did Fideo like the paintings he made of her?" I ask Todos los Santos.

"Yes, she liked them, and they made her laugh. Don Enrique told her jokes while he painted her and was very clownish. He used to put a lit match near his ass when he was going to fart and a flame would come out."

Don Enrique distinguished himself with vast experience in matters pertaining to sex, which in comparison made the other clients of La Copa Rota appear innocent and illiterate. Because they arrived tired and starved for women, they would do their thing and then immediately fall asleep on top of the bags of grain, or they would leave and not come back, or they would come back when the women had already given up on them. But don Enrique rented one of the rooms at the back of the brothel on a permanent basis and became a member of the household, eating breakfast on the patio with the regulars and never seeming to be in a rush to do anything. In the mornings he would play dominoes or dice with Fideo, making her laugh with jokes about ladies who pee and gentlemen who poop. And in the afternoons he would paint. He painted her over and over again: lying down, standing, or sitting; dressed, undressed, or half-dressed; with red bows or perfumed flowers in her hair; taking her siesta or eating a mango or playing with the cat, as if his only happiness in life were painting her. And they toasted with little glasses of *aguardiente*, the strong licorice-flavored liquor. One for the model, another for the painter, two for the model, two for the painter, because they both drank shamelessly and in the same quantities.

When Fideo wasn't there, or was in a bad mood or didn't want to model, then don Enrique would be content to paint some drunk lying on a table or the boy behind the bar, who knew how to dress up like a fairy, a gypsy, and a beauty queen, but most of all he painted the *pipatonas*, staring off into space while waiting for clients, nursing their babies, or weaving straw baskets as they sat on the dirt floor waiting for clients.

He even painted the owner's cat several times and Fideo decided that those were his best paintings. He also enjoyed watching the women dance, holding one another close, and other things that they did but didn't talk about afterward out of shame. Fideo and the *pipatonas* brought him the news, massaged his legs, forever aching, with petroleum pomade and electric liniment, and forgave him for everything because he was an artist, and artists had the right to invent crazy things and to be different from everyone else. They liked to smooth his hair with their horsetail brushes and they called him Angel Hair, convinced that his exceptional hair and his strange body contained happy omens and were a symbol of something good, because without a doubt God had exerted himself to the maximum to produce such a unique and comical creature.

"You're so blond, don Enrique!" Fideo would praise him when she was in a loving mood, and she would caress his pale down. "I'd like to have a child as blond as you."

"Fideo never hurt don Enrique, as she did other men?" I ask Todos los Santos.

"She scratched him a few times, but nothing of much consequence. She wasn't lacking in motives, because don Enrique was always chasing her around, trying to stick his equipment where it didn't belong. Who knows where he learned so many strange things and dirty games, maybe in the palaces of the nobility, where he lived as a boy," Todos los Santos tells me, and Fideo, from her hammock, lets out a lively Ay!

Without even trying, Fideo knew how to cultivate her own style, hormonal, hurtful, and crude, and she raised the bar slightly on what was permissible by disrobing and exhibiting her wounded soul and her malnourished body, by marking men's faces for life, and by vomiting abundantly when she got carried away with the *aguardiente*. In a world of prostitution where the most daring acts were dance contests, Fideo was a scandal and an invitation into transgression, and Tora still remembers her as a skinny, ferocious girl with a hoarse voice who would climb up on the tables and shout:

"Bring me a man who loves me and a tiger to scratch my ass!"

One day don Enrique had confessed to the girls that he had been born a dwarf because his mother and father were first cousins, and that other horrors occurred in his family that no one wanted to talk about. Then they understood why their don Enrique, instead of living with his own people, so wealthy and elegant, had chosen to share miseries at La Copa Rota: because he himself was one of those horrors that wasn't talked about by his family. But here he could forget about his shame and his ugliness, because he knew that they liked him just as he was, little and white-haired, wicked, kind, and playful.

As I am writing, I realize that La Copa Rota was the place destiny had also reserved for Sayonara—almost as thin as Fideo, almost as Indian as a *pipatona*, and as forsaken by God as either of the two. Then I think that a good part of the heart of this story lies in the journey she must have taken to elude that fate. Or perhaps not to elude it, because anecdotes aside, the Asian princess, the chosen one, *la novia oscura*, the universally loved, even and especially she—and therein the intensity of her passion—belongs to that incandescent center of the world that is and always will be La Copa Rota wherever it is found: indivisible nucleus, heart of hearts, living flesh, nut. Everything else on this earth is red velvet, circus lights, and sophistication. I thought of these ideas in the heat of my writing, but afterward, much later the same day, in the freshness of nightfall, when I watched a barren chicken named Felipe settle down to sleep on the pink rabbit skin–clad feet of a drowsy Todos los Santos in a corner of her kitchen, I realized that things gently explain themselves and that there is no need to ramble on.

twenty-seven

Everything seemed to indicate at the time of the rice strike, which would go on to mark a before and an after in the history of Tora and its people, that Sayonara was a girl of fragile love and momentary enthusiasms, incapable of settling her volatile heart for very long on any single soul. She had something about her then that was elusive, an incapacity for committing, a difficulty in seeing into the future or fixing her eyes on what was really in front of her.

Her refusal to open herself to others was especially evident in her relationships with men, close to her body and far from her interest, and this prompted frequent scolding from Todos los Santos, who reprimanded her inability to put her heart into the task of serving her clients.

"You are with them but you don't seem to notice them," the older woman would say to her. "You don't listen to them, you don't pamper them. You treat them like ghosts. I don't know how long your bad habit of going around self-absorbed will last. It's as if the rest of us are invisible."

Once, señor Manrique, who never stopped flattering Sayonara with requests for her time and demonstrations of his senile love, had asked her to iron his dark-blue suit, and in a moment of carelessness she had burned it. Another time she inconsiderately dismissed an engineer from the Troco, who had waited an entire afternoon without moving an inch just for the opportunity to be with her, with the excuse that she was tired. She publicly berated a rich landowner, who suffered greatly because of his fondness for her, for robbing land from others at gunpoint. "Go home, don Tomasito, or I'll tell your wife about you," she once said, ridiculing a married man who had approached her surreptitiously.

"You forget that you're a working woman, not a spoiled girl, and you have an obligation to lend your services with courtesy and according to professional standards," Todos los Santos said to her, perhaps without realizing that it was precisely that rude and inconsiderate way of offering them her beauty that fired men up and drove them to fall in love with her.

But as I have been told, it wasn't an attitude toward men specifically but toward the world in general. Some have described her to me as egotistical, but egotism doesn't fit with the tenacity with which she committed herself to her work on behalf of her sisters, not allowing herself to rest until she had rescued them one by one from abandonment. Which doesn't mean that when she had them by her side once again, she stayed close to them and helped them with their daily affairs. Far from acting as a mother to Ana, Juana, Susana, and Chuza, from the very first day Sayonara left that role up to Todos los Santos, and what's more, in their presence she became one more little girl—always the younger sister with the heartrending memory of her big brother?—and just like the others she fought over silly matters, she did bad things behind Todos los Santos's back, she allied herself with one in opposition to the rest, she made them all cry equally.

Todos los Santos was not in agreement with this division of labor and always resented that Sayonara had left her with the hard work of administering authority over those creatures that were frequently unmanageable, especially in the first days, when they were recently arrived and, due to their touching timidity and defenselessness, irritated her with habits like hiding food under their beds, burying foreign objects in the patio, and, the most inconvenient of all, raising their skirts and defecating in any corner as if they were animals.

Sayonara was always closer to little Chuza than to the other sisters, and she would take the child with her to the washing rocks at the river, to the market, to the Patria theater, to visit friends, perhaps because the child's muteness made her the ideal companion for an older sister who didn't have ears for anything but her own internal voices. Little Chuza, in turn, worshiped Sayonara as one should only do with the saints in heaven. She wouldn't lose sight of her for an instant; she would clown around and do somersaults to get Sayonara's attention. Enraptured, she would watch her older sister as she brushed her hair, or dressed, even when she shouted in fits of anger, or sang with joy, or was quiet and absent. Little Chuza lived to idolize her sister, and lacking words, she would cover her mouth with both hands, trembling with admiration.

Those who knew her when she first came to La Catunga say that Sayonara was very personable as a young girl, but they complain of the evanescent disposition she later developed. Once, an epidemic of cholera spread through the region, and the air, reverberating with microbes, filtered threateningly through the windows. Alarmed, Todos los Santos temporarily shut down the business and closed her house to outsiders to prevent the contagion from reaching the children, whom she forbade to drink water that hadn't been boiled or to eat raw fruit or vegetables, caramels, or any other food that wasn't prepared at home. Despite the precautions, Susana showed signs of having contracted the illness, a fever so high it made her glisten in her bed and gave her a looseness of the bowels that wasn't helped with the traditional extract of *corona-de-Cristo*, nor with Dr. Antonio María's new pharmaceutical prescriptions. In an emergency operation, Tana took Ana, Juana, and Chuza to her house in order to move them away from the source of infection, and Todos los Santos stayed home with Olguita and Sayonara to watch over the sick child, who in addition to the previously mentioned maladies was racked by a series of vomiting spells that doubled her over, nearly pulling her heart through her mouth, and made them fear dehydration. While the two older women wore themselves out in the kitchen with poultices and medicinal soups, they asked Sayonara to take a rag and clean the floor of the room, soiled with vomit, and when they returned they found her there, paralyzed, with the rag in her hand and looking at the smelly mess without having lifted a finger.

"What's the matter with you, *señoritinga*-who-steps-so-delicately? Are you repulsed by your sister's vomit?" Todos los Santos fumed. "Give me the rag, I'll clean it up."

"I'm not repulsed, *madrina*," Sayonara answered without batting an eye and handing over the rag, "it's just that I'm noticing a strange thing. Have you noticed that whenever someone vomits, they vomit carrots? Just like this, chopped into little pieces, even though they haven't been eating them . . ."

"Your sister is dying on us and you sit there philosophizing," barked Todos los Santos.

Susana's illness turned out not to be cholera but a bout of food poisoning due to overly sterile conditions and a lack of street germs, and today, so many years after the danger has passed, Todos los Santos laughs as she describes to me Sayonara's impertinence.

"But I assure you at that moment we were not amused," she clarifies. "We almost killed her for going around, like she always did, contemplating her navel while the rest of us were breaking our backs to keep the world from crashing down on top of us."

Did some secret call pierce her armor to resonate within young Sayonara? Did she demonstrate attachment to anything? An object, a photograph, anything, maybe a stuffed animal?

"With gifts Sayonara was like a little child," Todos los Santos tells me, "before they were even unwrapped she had already forgotten about them. She never demanded anything for herself, not even her share of the money she earned. She gave it to me without counting it and I distributed it in this manner: a quarter for household urgencies, another quarter for basic needs, a little for our enjoyment, and the rest I would deposit in a savings account in her name. When I asked her to look, even just out of curiosity, at how much she had put away, foreseeing the day she might have to touch that money, she would reply yawning: Ay, *madrina*, don't talk to me about numbers, they get all mixed up in my head and give me a headache."

She never gave up her somnambulant passion for going out at night in her sleeping gown to contemplate the immensity of the sky.

"I don't know how many times she made me expose myself to the cool night air to repeat the story of the music of the spheres," sighs Todos los Santos. "She had learned it by heart exactly as I had told it to her the first time, and if I changed a detail she would call my attention to it immediately and make me start all over again from the beginning, until I had recited it perfectly."

I also inquire about Sayonara's fascination with poetry. I want to know if it perhaps opened some route to her most intimate thoughts.

"When she was little she led me to believe that she would be a devoted reader," confesses Machuca, "and I had the hope of finding in her a great companion in the love of literature. But it didn't turn out that way. And not because she didn't read, the problem was that she always wanted to read the same things. That's wrong, read: She was always asking to be read to, because what she really loved was to listen. But as I told you, always the same, like a scratched record. She would come and ask me to tell her, over and over, the stories of Ophelia's drowning, the guillotining of Marie Antoinette, Joan of Arc burning at the stake, the shooting of Policarpa Salavarrieta. Always suffering heroines with tragic endings. She never tired of that. But, oh, when I would try to convince her to let me tell her about something new! Or if I invited her to read Shakespeare on her own, or Tirso de Molina or any of a number of sublime authors out there, forgotten by young people today. She only wanted to hear the same stories, over and over again."

There were two dates that were awaited by Sayonara with joy and anxiety. The first was Tuesday, the day the mail arrived at the post office, when she would go to claim her postcards from Sacramento without fail, even during the periods when they didn't arrive with any regularity. The second, the last Friday of every month.

"The very day she made the promise to Payanés," Olguita tells me, with as much fervor as if she were telling her own story, "Sayonara hung on her door an illustrated calendar with galloping horses, a gift from the foundry Mora Hermanos, on which she circled the last Friday of each month. And that is saying a lot when you take into account that she never wore a watch nor had any interest in whether it was Monday, Thursday, or Saturday, and I don't think she ever even learned the names of the months of the year in order. There are people who are aware of every second, but Sayonara wasn't one of them."

She seemed constantly shaken by an internal agitation, as if squeezed into a pair of pajamas made of nettles and spurred on by some rush to get who knows where. But at the same time she showed an appalling disdain for the time of day. For her, days undulated eternally and without urgencies—at least concrete, exterior urgencies—and she was always surprised when darkness fell, as if she hadn't been expecting it.

"What? It's already night?" she would ask, and she would protest when Todos los Santos would wake her in the morning. "What is it, *madrina*? Is it morning already?"

She would stuff herself with candy at odd hours and then not eat a bite of lunch. She would go shouting into the street when the whole barrio was taking a siesta and would fall asleep in the middle of parties. She wouldn't accept dates or commitments with precise schedules, and if she accepted them she wouldn't honor them. She was like the fishermen on the river, Olguita tells me, who lie in the shade to wait for the rising tide to fill their nets with fish. Sayonara was waiting too, standing at the edge of life. But what was it that she awaited so anxiously? Great advents, I suspect, but I can't be sure, perhaps because for her too they were never manifested as anything precise.

It is only clear to me that her waiting was not patient, not placid or resigned, and if she didn't know tomorrow's date, it was because what she yearned for wasn't coming tomorrow or the day after or even next week, but it forced her to wait, to allow time to pass and the wind to blow. Meanwhile, she was inwardly tense and anxious, and the fact that her desires had no name of their own, far from mitigating them, made them overwhelming. What was inside the impenetrable mind of that child, pushed by the world into an adult existence? For long periods there were lagoons of water so still they seemed frozen, and every now and then intense high tides appeared that didn't correspond with the vagueness of the moons unleashing them.

I think I can imagine Sayonara well as a young girl, when she arrived in La Catunga, bony and with scraggly hair like a hungry cat already determined to become a *puta*. I find decipherable the adolescent who discovers her own beauty in the mirror and starts to make use of the fascination she exercises over others. I am not surprised by the girl who has burning eyes because she saw her mother burn. I know about the strength of her character when it was put to the test; about her cleverness in measuring strengths, diving in at first to pull back later; about her incendiary irreverence. However, I must admit that I am perplexed by the young woman who emerges later; though more admired, she is more self-absorbed, allowing herself to be looked at without seeing anyone, as available to men as she is oblivious to them, and holding herself in the circular path of her own time frame, without building solid bridges to the world around her. Was she preparing herself, perhaps, and storing energies?

Every now and then I ask myself to what degree Sayonara's spirit and sensibility weren't blinded by her crushing past. How could she cry for her brother without bleeding to death? How could she remember her mother without turning to ash? How could she love without rekindling the horror? There are sights that can destroy you, and the worst death is rarely your own. In this country marked by violence, we have learned that one of two things can happen to a child who witnesses the atrocious death of family members: Either he is carbonized or he becomes illuminated. If he is carbonized he is reduced to half a person, but if he is illuminated he can become a person and a half. In Sayonara, the approximation of one of those two opposing destinies was beginning to present itself, but it still wasn't clear which.

twenty-eight

 "We've already told you about *mister* Brasco, remember? He was a friend of ours who was fond of Sayonara and liked to talk to her about snow and the cold storms of his land, because he was a foreigner from far away. We called him Tell-me-why because of his habit of going around asking things, and we also called him the Hanged Man, because of what happened to him during the rice strike."

A very tall blond man with white skin, long as a gust of wind and uncommonly thin. *Mister* Frank Brasco knew what it was like to have a thick rope around his neck, everything in him bracing for death, counting the minutes and confused by the possibility, unforeseeable a year earlier, of ending his days hanged in a country that he wouldn't have even been able to locate with any precision on a map. And all because the men of Camp 26 got bored with having to swallow their pride crammed up in nasty balls of cold rice.

"What's going on?" Payanés tried to raise his voice over the shouting as he entered the dining hall, beginning to feel carried along by the wave of a collective anxiousness that he had been unaware of until now. "Who can tell me what's going on?" he insisted, in the middle of the melee of rice balls whizzing overhead to end up splattered on the wall.

If he had been more experienced, he might have guessed that the redoubled blood flow, the ants' nest of expectations vibrating in the air, and the sparkle in the men's eyes were the announcement of the arrival of the great rebellion, which returned cyclically to involve Tora in its fury, like summer in other hemispheres.

"What's going on?" asked Sacramento in his quieter, convalescent tone.

"We're fed up with this shitty food," responded a man who was actively involved in the fray.

"But why today and not before, if we eat the same thing every day?"

"These gringos think they're smart," came the answer. "Again today, lunch is just brown sugar in hot water and rice balls. It's not even fit for prisoners, *hermano*, they have no right."

"At least in here we get rice balls. Out there they don't even have that . . . ," said Sacramento.

His words came from a world that was before the loss of candor, but that wasn't how they sounded. Just the opposite, they provoked ire and mistrust and the other men yelled at Sacramento, calling him a scab, a sellout, and a strikebreaker, and in the midst of the tumult they might have broken his skull if old Lino el Titi Vélez hadn't stepped in. Lino el Titi was a leader of earlier strikes who still wore the crown of his faded union glory.

"I will vouch for this boy. His words are innocent and do not come from ill will," said Lino el Titi vehemently, whose love and extracurricular life had transpired entirely among the bars and beds of La Catunga, and so he had known Sacramento from the days when he was a baby with no one to change his diapers and had to teach himself how to walk, grabbing hold of the brickwork on a corner of Calle Caliente.

"You're content with very little," he said to Sacramento when the others had moved away. "Even the dogs won't eat these rice balls. The other day I gave one to a hungry stray that sniffed it and turned up his nose at it. What do you think they eat in the manager's dining hall? They give the gringos eggs and milk, and fruits and vegetables, hot, healthy food that you could really use, boy, because this jungle is sucking up your soul."

"Well, it's true that the balls are pretty damn bad," acknowledged Sacramento. "But what if the gringos get mad and decide not to toss us even the balls?"

"They can't starve us to death because they need us to work," Lino el Titi told him, before disappearing into the din of the minuscule battle.

Payanés, who had heard the dialogue, grabbed a ball of rice in his right hand. He did it just to participate in the fun, just because, with the shyness and remorse of a child who has stolen an apple. But he was immediately overcome with a powerful urge to throw it with all his might, he, a responsible and peaceful man, unassuming and well intentioned toward authority, who until now had felt only gratitude for the opportunity to work given him by those foreign bosses who smiled down from their photographs and decided his fate from their pool with blue reflections in their walled neighborhood. If before he felt only gratitude and submission, suddenly today, with that ball of rice in his hand and sensing the pulsing indignation of the others, he found more than enough reason to fuel his own. For the first time, he realized that the world, kind perhaps for others, had reserved a hostile face for him, and he decided that he wanted things to be different, he, Payanés, who knew how to block out suffering with such valor, or, depending on how you looked at it, with such cowardice. He, who looked down upon the complainers, who didn't know discontent, who disdained pain to such a degree that he was incapable of detecting it even when it was inflicted upon him, who didn't allow himself to dream except when he was asleep. Today, he suddenly allowed himself to be swept along by the furor and began to resent deep in his bones the chronic dampness of his hammock on those suffocating jungle nights, nights so short they afforded no rest. And he detested the loneliness of his endless days among so many men who, despite the crowded conditions, couldn't keep one another company. He felt a tiredness that he had never allowed himself to feel before, and for the first time since he had left his distant city of Popayán, he allowed himself the luxury of longing for those people that he hadn't seen since.

"Well, yes, damn it. I'm fed up too," he admitted. All of a sudden he felt like demanding repayment from life for all the hardships and pettiness he'd had to endure, and throwing in the face of the Tropical Oil Company all the aches that the excessive work had burned into his muscles, driven until they cramped, and the deafening noise of the machines that cluttered his skull and dried out his thoughts, and the galley slave routine that he had so good-naturedly accepted, and above all the black weight of that sky that surrounded him every night far from the embrace of that girl who wouldn't tell him her name but who made him a promise at the river, and he hated the fat men reeking of alcohol who were at that very moment kissing her on the neck, and he also hated, with a rebellious poison, those foreign bosses he had never even seen, and he blamed them for the heavy absence he felt and for the unsatisfied waiting he had to endure as he paid thirty days of forced labor for the dream of a single encounter of love. Then he tightened his hand on the ball of rice and threw it against the photograph on the wall with the fury of someone taking a step toward the galvanized lands of risk, knowing that there is no turning back.

What Payanés did not realize, not even at the instant that his ball smashed against *mister* Maier's undaunted smile, was that he was living the first moments of what from then on would be the forever famous rice strike, the fifth and most violent of the so-called primitive, or heroic, strikes by the Tora union, which regained its strength when it was least expected, meaning when the projectiles had died down, spirits had calmed, and the rice scattered all over the floor made the dining hall look like a church vestibule after a wedding.

It was then that a belligerent and vociferous group who weren't ready to call it quits on the ruckus, among whom were several maintenance workers—famous for their excesses—clustered around Brasco, the North American engineer who held the post of general supervisor and who was the only manager willing to mix with the Colombian workers and maintain any kind of personal relationship with them.

Too skinny and way too tall, Brasco experienced problems with the coordination of his own height: He walked as if perched on stilts and was unable to prevent his neck and arms from undulating as they stuck out from the collar and sleeves of his baggy shirt. He had already been warned by his superiors about the danger of not maintaining distances, and they had even told him they would cancel his health insurance policy if he persisted in his habit of visiting local *brujos* and healers. But he refused to imprison himself in that exclusive world of *norteamericanos* that he considered a concentration camp. That's why he would join the workers at lunchtime and sometimes late at night, when they sat around a pot of coffee, under a riot of stars and cicadas, to tell stories of ghosts and spirits who wander around doing things that an Anglo-Saxon like him found improbable.

"But tell me why . . ." He always began his sentences with those words, and the workers nicknamed him that, Tell-me-why. Tell me why Mohán carries girls off to the bottom of the river if he could make love with them more comfortably and without getting wet on the shore?

"*Míster* has already started with his tell-me-why's," they would laugh. "Well, because he lives down there and that's where his sumptuous palaces are."

"But tell me why Luz-de-la-Ciénaga eats little children when there are so many pigs and chickens and fish . . ."

"Because if he doesn't eat children he's not scary, *míster* Brasco, and his stories wouldn't interest anyone, not even you."

According to the testimony of old workers at the Troco who took active part in the rice strike and with whom I have been able to discuss the events, Brasco was the only one of the company managers who at the hour of the ruckus didn't take refuge in the golf club, which besides having green lawns was also, and above all, an authentic concrete fortress designed for these eventualities, although it had been camouflaged beneath the warm color of the bougainvilleas.

"We're not going to do anything to you, *mister* Brasco, we just want you to taste this garbage, to see what you think," said one of the men that surrounded him, corralling him into a corner.

"Okay, I'll taste it, but don't push me or touch me," he told them. "You're right, it's pig slop, from now on no more rice balls," he promised, and the workers applauded as they returned to their places to continue their lunch now that the uproar was over. The last few uninspired projectiles flew overhead. Pajabrava stood on top of a table to harangue, taking advantage of the opportunity to add followers to his anti-masturbatory crusade. Others played soccer, and the matter wouldn't have gone any further—one more among so many harsh moments without serious consequences that occurred daily in the midst of the work stress at Campo 26—if at that moment a spokesman for the management hadn't communicated over the loudspeakers that law enforcement officers were already on their way to the camp, that if the revolt didn't cease there would be reprisals against the instigators, and that the workers should immediately liberate Mr. Brasco, who was being criminally detained as a hostage, or the company would have no choice but to respond with force.

The festive air of a few minutes ago froze with the stridency of the declaration, and the mere mention of reprisals and the presence of uniformed officers burned their spirits triple what the rice balls had. Frank Brasco, who had already left the dining hall, was the first to be surprised by the inopportunely timed threats and was on his way to the golf club to report that the incident was already over and that he was safe and sound when he was detained by the same maintenance men who had corralled him earlier.

"You're not going anywhere, *mister* Brasco. Nobody wanted to take you as a hostage, but now they have forced us to. You heard for yourself that it was their idea, and since things are the way they are, we have to listen to them, because you have become our only guarantee."

"At that moment I felt afraid. For the first time in the two years that I had been working at the 26 I was afraid," Frank Brasco tells me as he shovels the snow from the entrance to his cabin in Vermont, where I have come to interview him. "The men from operations were decent and proper and I felt safe with them, but there were some barbarians among the men from maintenance. They had a reputation for being unpredictable in fights with the bosses, and it was precisely one man, Mono Nieves, and another they called Caranchas, both radicals from maintenance, who were taking me hostage. It was to my disadvantage that they had found me at a particular moment when I was behind the dining hall where the others couldn't see us, and I knew that being caught between those two irrational parties was going to be difficult, on one side the managers and on the other Mono Nieves and his men, who had just been handed on a silver platter the perfect opportunity to start an imbroglio."

"Don't worry, boys. I'm going to the office to tell them there's been a misunderstanding. You'll see, with a little goodwill everything will be cleared up," Brasco tried to say, but at that point Mono Nieves and his men had already hatched plans in their heads.

"But tell me why you have to do this," Brasco began.

"There is no tell-me-why that can save you," interrupted Nieves. "You come with us and forget about asking questions."

Meanwhile, in the dining hall, the tension had become unbearable for the more than two hundred men who knew they were cornered in a building that would soon become a trap with no way out. From the loudspeakers came threats of the siege of the camp if the workers didn't release engineer Brasco at once, "deliberately captured as a hostage by the group of rebels in the dining hall."

"Where is Tell-me-why?" Lino el Titi Vélez started shouting, trying to take control, but the engineer had disappeared and nobody knew where he was.

They tell me that traditionally in critical situations like this, with the imminence of disaster, the old union spirit for fighting is reborn. It had been dormant for a couple of years after a slew of debilitating strikes that ended in deaths and massive layoffs, and the old leaders, among them Lino el Titi, came out of their slumber to roar again like shaggy beasts, and their roars were recognized by the multitude. They declared themselves in permanent assembly and set midnight as zero hour to declare the strike. Someone produced a pen, another a sheet of notebook paper, and five veterans, swept up by the sudden enthusiasm and already having forgotten the punishment that had previously paralyzed them, sat around a table. Minutes later, one of them, nicknamed Bollo de Yuca because his mother had been selling balls of yuca at the entrance to the camp for years, read out loud the sheaf of petitions they had just improvised, which began with the demand for the immediate withdrawal of law enforcement officers.

The second demand got right to the heart of the matter and centered on the rice: "The workers of Campo 26 are fed up with the abominable quality of the food that the Tropical Oil Company provides for us, in particular the abhorred and inedible greasy rice balls, which we demand be replaced by decent, good-quality rice, and which should be accompanied by a portion of meat or vegetable, and in no case shall rice again be accepted by the workers as the sole lunch ingredient, as has happened so often in the past." To this stipulation they added a detailed list of the daily humiliations that had been poisoning the men's spirits for a long time, demanding potable water in the camp to halt intestinal infections, diarrhea, and dysentery; clothes-washing facilities near the barracks, because the men had nowhere to scrub their clothes; a section in the cemetery in Tora so that the workers' mortal remains would have a Christian burial and wouldn't be just dumped into any clearing in the wild jungle; and lastly, a sufficient number of latrines, because the existing ones, numbering one for each fifty men, forced them to make lines that were so long that the majority chose to relieve themselves behind the bushes, creating unclean and unhealthy conditions.

Over the loudspeakers, the management threatened to intervene if engineer Brasco wasn't delivered to the front door of the hospital within the half hour. But how were they supposed to return him if they didn't know his whereabouts? Then Mono Nieves, Caranchas, and the rest of the maintenance crew leadership appeared and confessed to the strike committee that they were holding Brasco and they would free him in exchange for the demilitarization of the area.

"We have Tell-me-why and we also have control of the power plant, which we have just seized. We will put ourselves at your disposal if you give us three seats on the committee," proposed Mono Nieves.

"They sat down to work out an arrangement among themselves whose terms I didn't really know the details of," Sacramento tells me. "And when they reached an agreement, Lino el Titi started to give orders on forming committees for guard duty, food, and I don't know what else. One of those orders was directed at me, a man who could be trusted, he said, because he had known me since I was running around in diapers. He named me as a member of a security squad and assigned me the mission of going with the men from maintenance to where they had hidden Tell-me-why and sticking with him twenty-four hours a day, or until ordered otherwise."

"You better kill yourself," said Lino el Titi, "before you let him escape or let anyone harm him. There are two orders, both equally important: Don't let him escape and don't let him die. Do you understand?"

"I understand."

"Do you have a friend you trust who can accompany you?"

"Yes, Payanés. He's been my traveling partner for months now."

"Are you sure he won't betray you for any reason?"

"Sure enough." Sacramento began to feel again the burning memory of Sayonara's hair being tied to his best friend's neck.

"Then take him and have him help you watch the gringo. Nobody else should know where you are."

Caranchas took Sacramento and Payanés to a small toolshed tacked onto the power plant. Dark and humid, it was where they were hiding Brasco, who awaited word on his fate in sorry condition. He was the color of a corpse, this man who was normally pale, his blue eyes injected with blood and his hands tied behind his back, his whole suffering body stretched out, feet on an oil drum and neck encircled by a rope hanging from one of the ceiling beams.

"If they try to rescue you by force," the three men guarding him warned, "we'll give your drum a good kick and it's good-bye, *míster*. Good-bye forever."

"So, they had Tell-me-why in the gallows," Sacramento explains to me, "and concerning his fate, nothing had been written yet."

How did the events unravel from that moment on, how was the committee divided between the moderates from operations and the radicals from maintenance, how did the situation get out of control for the workers: these are things that Sacramento and Payanés, because of their being locked up with the candidate for hanging in that suffocating shed, didn't learn about until several days afterward.

"Caranchas had said that we were to wait there without taking our eyes off *míster* until he came with instructions. But hours passed and it seemed as though everyone had forgotten about us. From far off came shouts from the crowd, but it was just noise and we couldn't make out any of the words: It was impossible to tell if they were the voices of friends or enemies. So Payanés and I waited blindly without hearing anything, locked up in that hot place, resentful and mutually distrustful because of the jealousy between us, without knowing whether the armed forces had entered or not, with our gringo standing on the drum and measuring the increasing voltage of the threats against him by the three men from maintenance, who were getting drunk off a bottle of *guarapo añejo* that was also souring their mood and fueling their arrogance."

Every now and then, one would leave the hiding place to try to find out something, then return with fragmented and contradictory news. The troops already have us surrounded; a lot of workers are fleeing the camp through the rear into the jungle; we have already declared a strike indefinitely; the management declared the strike illegal; Lino el Titi and a commission are negotiating the release of *míster* Brasco; the gringos said that they won't negotiate and that we can do whatever we want with Brasco; Lino el Titi is not in charge anymore; Mono Nieves has been wounded and now Caranchas is commanding the revolt; Caranchas says everything's screwed up and that the only order is to loot and destroy the camp.

"You don't know what it's like to have a rope around your neck for four hours, without understanding what's going on outside and fearing that at any minute they'll kick the drum out from under you and that you'll just hang there, like a sausage in the cupboard. My body became numb from holding the same position for such a long time, while my head, sticking out from the other side of the rope as if it weren't mine, was spinning a thousand revolutions per minute. Fortunately, I trusted Payanés. I knew him well because we shared a fondness for skinny Emilia, the camp's oldest and most prized piece of machinery, and on several occasions he had joined me during the periodic repairs that had to be made on her. Sacramento, however, I was seeing for the first time, but I sized up his character and something told me that although he was just a kid he could also be trusted. As for the trio from maintenance, I was dead, but I figured that as long as Payanés and the kid stayed with me, my neck had some chance of being spared from the noose. There was, however, a sort of rivalry between those two that worried me. It was as if they felt uncomfortable with each other."

"Even then the tension was noticeable?" I ask Brasco.

"Yes, it was noticeable; don't ask me how I knew, but it was evident. At that point I didn't know that a woman was the cause, so I imagined all sorts of things, like they had different ideas about what to do with me. Believe me, when you are in the gallows you get very paranoid. . . . Had I suspected that the trouble was over a woman, I would have been a little calmer."

At some point Brasco told them he really needed to urinate.

"That, you're not going to be able to do," responded one of the drunks after studying him for a minute. "We can't untie your hands and we're not in the mood to grab hold of your thing. Everyone assembled here is too macho for that. Ask for something else, water, a cigarette, anything, and we'll be happy to help you out, but there's no solution for that other little problem."

"It's urgent," insisted Frank Brasco. "Don't make me go through the shame of wetting my pants. Payanés, please, untie my hands."

"I will untie them," decided Payanés, and he also released his neck from the noose. "But, *mister* Brasco, don't you try to escape."

"It's a deal," promised Brasco. Once free he attended to his needs behind the door, then asked permission to rest a little. "I've been standing for too long," he said, as he sat down on the ground, and his guardians didn't say a word.

"Okay, back to your position, *mister*. If Caranchas comes in here and finds us like this, cuddling on the floor like brothers taking a siesta, he'll shoot us all," said Payanés after a good while, and Brasco heeded him.

As if a premonition had driven Payanés, barely two seconds later Caranchas returned. He was soaked with sweat, gasping as if he had been running, and frowning as if he had a toothache.

"Your compatriots have abandoned you, *mister* Questions," Caranchas blurted out. "They say they don't negotiate or compromise, and they won't be blackmailed on account of your kidnapping. They say you could never be trusted and that you're probably our accomplice. They also say that for some time they've been warning you and despite that you got mixed up in this and dug your grave with your own hands."

"That's not true; I don't believe you, Caranchas. I don't believe they're saying that."

"If it's not true, then why don't they withdraw the troops? There they are, three hundred yards away, aiming their guns at us from the fence, and any minute now they're going to come in and seize the camp. You're not worth shit to us, *mister* Tell-me-why," shouted Caranchas, more disillusioned than angry. "We were wrong about you. Anyway, we're not letting the troops in, even if we have to blow up the camp to keep them out."

"The man spoke with such disenchantment," Brasco tells me, the snow glistening on his shovel in the Vermont air as he throws it aside, "I would have sworn that the next thing he was going to do was kick the oil drum out from under me to put an end to the comedy of errors. But he didn't do it. He simply left and I just stood there, with the rope around my neck, suddenly very tired and horribly confused."

Then Payanés said he would go out to verify what Caranchas had said about the closeness of the troops and he came back in a few minutes to confirm that it was true.

"Groups of workers are arming themselves with sticks, bars, and rocks, and they're getting ready to mount resistance," he reported, then he showed us the ground coffee beans that he was holding in his hand and a pair of tin cans for preparing it. He built a fire on the other side of the door, boiled some water, threw the coffee in, and then he poured it from one can to the other, filtering it through the cloth of his shirt. He approached Brasco with the steaming liquid, whose hands were still tied, and held it as the American drank, sip by sip, blowing on it first so he wouldn't burn his mouth.

"But tell me why," Brasco murmured, "why do things have to end up like this . . . ?"

"Drink your coffee and don't ask us questions, *mister* gringo," Payanés advised, "because we can't answer them."

"So what do we do now?" asked Sacramento worriedly.

"Now we lock Sor Juana Inés in her cell so she can please herself," answered Payanés, who for a while now had been mulling over the secrets that Pajabrava had said about the nuns.

"I'm serious. I wish I could find old Lino el Titi to ask him what we should do!"

"If there's a strike, we have to support it," mumbled one of the drunks.

"Of course, you idiot, but how? On one side we have Lino el Titi and his men, on another we have Caranchas and his men, and on yet another we have drunks like you. And you're all proposing different things."

"Let's arm ourselves with sticks and go out to see who confronts us," said another man, more drunk than the first, and then he fell asleep, conquered by the *guarapo*. His two friends stood up and went out to participate in the melee.

"A single shot would have been enough to ignite the wells and engulf the whole camp in flames," Brasco says to me, "and lacking faith I gave myself up to Mohán, Patasola, Luz-de-la-Ciénaga, and to all those ghosts they had been telling me about. If they can't save us, I thought, no one can."

"Let's loosen that rope necktie, *mister* interrogator, we're leaving," Payanés suddenly said to him, removing the noose from around his neck and untying his hands. "You too, Sacramento."

"What for?" asked Sacramento. "I'm not moving until Lino el Titi gives me orders."

"We're going to defend Emilia until Titi comes and tells us what to do. We're not going to let anyone hurt her, no matter what side they're from. If they get too close, it will have to be over our dead bodies."

Outside, night had already fallen, the world spun black, and in it reigned a chaos heavy with foreboding. The great rice uprising had just begun.

twenty-nine

Night was falling so softly that part of its darkness melted into foam before settling. Sitting in rocking chairs, the women chatted on the patio while upon their heads, shoulders, and laps soft black flakes fell, piling up until they were completely covered. Tana warded off melancholy with the false luxury of her fake jewels. Olguita, always looking for someone to protect, was knitting a scarf for a night watchman, a lover of hers, who coughed because of the damp night air. Sayonara soared far away as she braided and unbraided her lustrous mane, dominating God knows what anxieties in that incessant doing and undoing. Ana and Susana searched for the three bright stars that formed Orion's belt. Sitting at her older sister's feet, little Chuza lined up a long row of pebbles on the ground. Todos los Santos served *mistela* in delicate pink cups. And Machuca fanned herself with the lid of a pot while she told a story from centuries earlier that half intrigued them, half annoyed them, because according to her, it involved real facts about pagan whoring.

The story took place, as Olga remembered it, in a lost, nameless country where all women, regardless of rank or age, had to go once during their lives to the temple of the goddess to give themselves to the first stranger who solicited their love, without denying anyone. They would adorn their heads with garlands of gauze and daisies and offer themselves in honor of the deity. The men, in turn, were to circulate there, also willing to give themselves to any woman for that one time. There were rich women dressed in brocades and attended by servants, beggars covered with rags, beautiful young women who were quickly chosen and could then return home free of the commitment, and ugly women that no man looked at and who had to remain there for two or three years, sitting among the multitudes that filled the temple, before they were able to fulfill their obligation. And there were as many handsome men who were pleasing to the chosen woman as there were deformed or sick men who filled her with horror.

The women of La Catunga listened to all of this openmouthed and confused, and when Machuca finished her story a silence so great fell upon the patio that you could hear, almost, the frozen humming of the three stars adorning Orion's belt.

"That is the strangest story you've ever told us." Todos los Santos's voice emerged from the darkness. "I think it's pure invention."

"Wasn't there another temple where the men sat for the women to come and choose?" asked Ana, who now participated in the women's conversations, although no one took the trouble of answering her.

"How dare you, Machuca, say that they gathered in the temple," said Tana angrily, who was orthodox in her convictions. "Only you would believe that, you're so corrupt and such a heretic. And what temple could it be? It can't be God's temple . . ."

"It was the temple of the goddess."

"There are no goddesses, you know that. Except Virgin Mary, who is pure and chaste, and doesn't go around offering to raise her skirts."

"They chase us out of the church when we go to pray," someone was heard to say, "don't even talk about going there to find a man."

"There were goddesses before," Machuca assures the others. "And things were different. Everything was different, because women were in charge."

"Well, I prefer the world the way it is now," countered Sayonara, who always took a contrary position. "What if a disgusting man with an ugly face appeared, or one with bad breath, or rough skin, and you weren't allowed to refuse!" She burst out laughing. "What good did it do for women to be in charge if they couldn't refuse an ugly man. I would cover my face with my hair so the man would pass right by me and go bother the next woman."

Now the others were amused too. Suddenly everything seemed funny and they laughed so hard that they tossed their heads back and hit their legs with their palms, as they usually did when they were really happy.

"You say that now, because you're young," preached Todos los Santos. "It's worse if you have to wait three years because nobody wants you."

"Oh, no," countered Sayonara again. "It's always better to be alone than to be in poor company."

"You don't know what you're talking about. You don't know loneliness. It really has rough skin."

While Olga is telling me about what they talked about that night, which would be nearly the same as this one if Sayonara were still here, I try to decipher the mystery that lies beneath contact with the skin of a stranger. To not refuse a man you didn't know? To give yourself up to the unknown, to allow yourself to be taken, would it be burying yourself or saving yourself? What hidden dimensions would be opened, of terror and of pleasure, of discovery and of loss?

"Is it difficult to have an unfamiliar man so close?" I ask, now that I find them sitting in rocking chairs in the middle of another patio like that one, decades later, shrouded by an identical darkness, under the same three stars that mark the belt of Orion, the celestial hunter who this night, just as on that one, wanders the ether, pursuing beasts. When they hear the question they look at each other and the laughter returns and the palms hitting the legs, and they are girls again.

"Sometimes the client turns out to be a fool and things get nasty," replies Machuca, the pen pusher, who is still wearing half-sleeves of black cloth on her forearms, the ones she uses at the town hall so that her blouse doesn't get stained when she writes.

"Tell the truth," goad the others, "tell her, Machuca, that you liked it. And how!"

But Machucha doesn't tell; she plays innocent.

"You have to learn to be there without being there. To train your mind to disengage from what the body is doing. You don't let them touch your face, not to kiss you at all, because the only thing they end up doing is messing up your hair and your makeup," asserts Tana, and my head is filled with the memory of so many paintings of Christian martyrs who turn toward heaven their serene faces, untouched and illumined, while their bodies, subjected to torture, melt in fear.

"And the body," I ask, "doesn't it feel any desire or pleasure?"

"The desire for the client to finish quickly and the pleasure of him paying you so you can come home with food from the market," says one of them, and they all laugh heartily.

"Remember Pilar, the island girl," growls Fideo, in a man's voice from her invalid's hammock, now that she can speak because she has decided to recuperate, just to be contrary, since everyone had accepted her death as a fact. "One day Pilar announced that she was leaving because she couldn't put up with their breaths. That's how she said it: 'I can't put up with their breaths anymore.' She gathered up her stuff and left."

"That isn't funny; I understood what she meant," says Todos los Santos. "To know the breath of a stranger brings an uneasiness that is sometimes too much to bear. I'm not talking about garlic breath or the smell of alcohol or cigarettes; those breaths smell like things, they're always the same. The unbearable breaths are the ones that are particular to the person, to his private affairs."

"But is there any case where a woman enjoys it?" I ask again, although I have heard here in Tora a phrase that is repeated so often that it has become a saying: Men pay to feel and we charge because we don't feel.

"You tell her, Machuca . . . tell her why they call you the Glutton."

"I didn't become a *puta* to flee from misery," says Machuca, "or because I was raped. They didn't drag me into the profession or deceive me into it; I came to it out of sheer pleasure and enjoyment. Why should I lie, I always knew how to enjoy parties, money, *aguardiente*, tobacco, and above all other earthly pleasures, the smell of a man. The warmth of a man, you understand? I'm not one of those women who cries about the life that fate gave her. I enjoyed my youth and spent it going out on the town until I had nothing left but crumbs. And the bed? The bed was my altar, strangers were my fiancés, and the sheets were my wedding dress. That's why these women think I'm a *bruja*, a witch, and I can only say to them: Maybe you're right, and I hope there's a God somewhere so that on Judgment Day I can shout in his face that I did what I did because I did it in honor of lust and because I wanted to."

"You see? She is a *bruja*," laugh the others. *"Bruja rebruja, puta reputa."*

For Olguita there were no unknown men, because she only had to look them in the eyes to know them, whether they were cross-eyed, one-eyed, or blind or were hiding some trick of love behind their silky eyelashes, or whether the most beautiful, unfaithful blue sparkled in their pupils; all she had to do was speak to them affectionately to know them.

For others, like Tana and Machuca, all men were passed over because they had never found the man who would live on in their dreams. Others more unfortunate still, like beautiful Claire, found him only to lose him later.

"There is no worse torment than that of a whore in love," brays Fideo with a midnight voice. "Others come, always others, while the one she waits for keeps her waiting."

Speaking of Mary Magdalene from biblical times, Saramago mentions the deep wound that is "the open door through which others enter and my beloved does not." Among the prostitutes of Tora, it was the pain and festering of that wound that threw them, at three o'clock in the morning and at a corner called Armería del Ferrocarril, under the old train cars passing noisily and leaving behind traces of rust, and at times of blood.

Todos los Santos believes that Sayonara didn't suffer the rigors of that wound through which happiness escaped and death entered. She assures me that hers was another pain, which even she herself didn't recognize as pain, and which didn't push her toward death but unleashed in her a ferocious appetite for life. She had an itch in her soul, Todos los Santos tries to explain to me. Sayonara, to whom they all returned, whom no man abandoned or stopped loving, she who knew how to love many, to be happy with many, to find herself in many, she, *la bienamada*, the well loved, nevertheless had a misfortune: her incapacity to surrender herself to the blessing of a single love.

She loved good men who loved her well, and yet others came to erase those footprints and open new paths in her heart. Any of them would have been enough for her to have approached peacefulness, but she preferred to fill herself with open spaces that became yearnings for new loves: noble gentlemen, faithful in their ways, who deposited their fervor in her and who nevertheless in her eyes were nothing more than moments, honest but fleeting, of a longer and much more complicated journey.

"Do you think, as a mother, that it was possible for a man to make your adopted daughter love him?" I ask Todos los Santos, and expect the worst, because I know how irascible she gets when I force her to speculate. Yet she surprises me with her doubt.

"I have often asked myself that very same thing."

A while after Sayonara's arrival in La Catunga, during the period of training and apprenticeship, when she was still the girl and not yet Sayonara, Todos los Santos was worried about not being able to find a crack from which to look inside her tortoise's heart, always hidden and withdrawn into its shell. Was there anything or anyone in the world that could stir her up? A memory that could awaken her longing? Some unconfessable desire that she wanted to ask of the Sacred Heart? Had her many past hungers convinced her that the only worthwhile pleasure was a plate of rice with lentils?

"I was afraid that being so dry of emotions, my adopted daughter wouldn't be able to manage very well as a lover. Because to go to bed without love you have to know how to love, and those who think otherwise don't understand anything," the old woman tells me. Coiled around her shoulders is a silver fox, very dead and very forties, that she has rescued from the trunk where she keeps her memories among mothballs. "To sweeten her insides I began to give her a cup of hot milk with five teaspoons of honey daily. Then, seeing her act so strangely, I thought I had gone a little too far with the honey. But a few years later I realized that the error had been just the opposite, too little honey. Until I came to believe that eight or nine spoonfuls was the minimum dose to make her character well tempered."

"And today, have you reached a conclusion?"

"Maybe Sayonara loved too much, or maybe she couldn't love. I still don't know."

"It's the same thing that happens to all of us," says Machuca. "We professional women divide ourselves into a hundred loves and we don't know how to content ourselves with the joys of one single love."

thirty

 In the capital, I dedicated myself to inquiring what happened to the life and paintings of don Enrique Ladrón de Guevara y Vernantes. I learned that during the first two years of his life in Tora, his family was unaware of his whereabouts—or preferred to ignore that they were—and gave him up for lost, or at least well hidden. Until the day that a friend of the family who was passing through the oil city on business brought back news of him.

"What is Enrique doing in Tora?" asked a maternal uncle, Alfonso Vernantes. "How does he support himself?"

"He paints," answered the friend. "I saw several of his paintings. Your nephew Enrique paints women who reek of syphilis."

They went to look for him, found him, pulled him kicking and screaming from Fideo, and committed him to an insane asylum, according to some versions, and according to another, they sent him out of the country, all with the greatest stealth to avoid scandal or gossip. When I returned to Tora, I told this to Todos los Santos, who already knew.

When they took him out of La Copa Rota, did don Enrique kick with his short, arthritic legs, did he beg with his sharp dwarf's voice, did he order with the haughty voice of the wealthy that he be left in peace, and was it all useless? Perhaps. I will never know for certain how that scene happened, that tearing away, because when I ask Fideo, the only eyewitness, she becomes catatonic and I realize that I will only injure her further if I continue throwing memories in her face.

"It wasn't easy for Enrique to live among those people who are so different from us," says his sister, María Amalia, an elderly lady, intelligent and kind, with whom I chatted one afternoon as we had tea. "Or to live in that miserable place he chose. In one of his letters to my mother he confesses it, he says that every day away from home requires of him struggle and determination."

"Did your mother know where he was?" I ask.

"Of course, she always knew, but she never let anyone else know. They took Enrique out of there after my mother's death, because they wouldn't have dared to while she was still alive."

"Why didn't your mother ask him to come back, if he himself had confessed that it wasn't easy for him to live there?"

"Because my mother, who adored him, was well aware that for Enrique it would be even harder to make a place for himself in our family. Do you know what it means to be a dwarf among such proud people? If you ask me what the best thing my brother found in that other world was, I would say that it was invisibility. There he felt invisible, without witnesses to his deformity. That is priceless."

After the committing of don Enrique—or his deportation, whichever it was—Alfonso Vernantes, the maternal uncle, personally traveled to Tora with the inquisitorial task of gathering up every last painting, to destroy the evidence of the passage of his family name through a world of infamy. If the painting was a seascape, sunset, or Paris scene, he paid little for it. He offered a better price if women appeared, if they were naked it rose higher, and when he had gathered five or six he would burn them on a pyre. In Tora they still tell stories of those strange negotiations, like the one about a small drawing of two girls embracing on a bed, for which don Alfonso paid a fortune.

Nothing makes you more vulnerable than having the task of guarding a secret that is already public knowledge—as all secrets tend to be—or easier prey for whoever decides to take advantage of that weakness. Only a few days passed before Piruetas smelled the opportunity of a lifetime and joined forces with a photographer friend who dabbled in painting, to begin producing a series of obscene paintings that they signed with don Enrique's name and presented to don Alfonso as if they were original works by his nephew.

For a few weeks don Alfonso fell blindly into the trap. He saw in Piruetas and his photographer friend two irreplaceable accomplices for his delicate mission, because they were astute and discreet and because they could do what was forbidden to him: circulate among the lower echelons, scouring dangerous bars and prostitutes' hovels in search of incriminating evidence. During that time, Piruetas and his accomplice lived the high life at the expense of the Ladrón de Guevara y Vernantes's scruples, until don Alfonso discovered he was being duped. In his haste to swindle, Piruetas grew so bold that he began to produce paintings that were more and more ordinary and slipshod, to which was added a dispute with the photographer friend over money matters that caused a rupture between them. So, from then on Piruetas assumed the artistic labor himself and without assistance from anyone: he, who had never held a pencil in his hand, not to mention a brush.

"This can't be Enrique's," don Alfonso finally said one day, suspicious. "It's too awful."

"It's modern painting, don Alfonso, and you just don't understand it," replied the pseudo-painter in defense of his scrawling.

But even don Alfonso, who because of disgust and ethics barely looked at his nephew's paintings, even don Alfonso himself, they tell me, in spite of being blinded by propriety, saw enough to realize the difference and drive off the impostor.

"Where can don Enrique be?" I ask Todos los Santos. "Still locked up in his asylum, or off in some remote corner of the world?"

"He died some years ago from syphilis, as do all those who have known true love."

"Strange," I say. "No matter what his sister says, I think he found his chance for happiness at La Copa Rota."

"Happiness, no," she contradicts me, she who refuses to let a hollow phrase pass without filling it with cruel realism. "Let's say that at La Copa Rota he set down his fate, and that if he wasn't happy, at least he found his light."

"They say that some men take refuge in bordellos seeking the same thing that monks do in monasteries."

"Is that from some book?"

"Probably."

"No wonder. Books are filled with shit like that."

thirty-one

 "These women don't understand how things are," Olguita tells me later, when we are alone. "They think they do but they don't. Trust me when I tell you that Sayonara did know how to love, and that she loved Payanés from the very beginning and to the point of delirium."

"Then why did she do things the way she did?"

"Because the paths of the heart are not straight, but snaking and twisting, and they let us see where they begin but not where they end. But that's getting tangled up in conclusions of a story that begins plain and simple: Payanés was the first unknown man that Sayonara was able to get to know. In him she found bread for her hunger and water for her thirst."

"He has the sweetest skin I have ever known," Olguita swears she heard Sayonara say. "But not sweet like sugar, sweet like an old pain. The sun keeps it brown from the waist up, but it is reduced in color on the rest of his body. What I miss most is his chest, his big chest with the rose tattoo, soft and bulky but only a little, just enough to be strong like the chest of a man and kind like the chest of a woman. Deep within his eyes nests a sadness, a sort of helplessness in that mixed yellow color, a yellow burning with green: the eyes of a stray animal. His hair, which is also of a double color, sometimes seems black as night and sometimes shines with silver threads."

"That's called gray hair."

"Well, he has gray hair then."

"Why would he have gray hair, when he's so young?"

"He has suffered, you see."

"Some women focus on the look in a man's eyes," Olguita tells me. "Others like men with an elegant style. There are those who complain if men are knock-kneed or flat-assed, or have tangled eyebrows or stooped shoulders. Many girls want to see them in leather shoes or boots and turn their noses up at cloth shoes, because they are a sure sign of poverty. Any woman appreciates a powerful male member and most prefer a sweetly drawn smile with healthy teeth. Once I heard that you shouldn't sleep with men with only one ear, because if you get pregnant most likely you'll give birth to a deaf child. And so on. But Sayonara fell in love with a chest, and she said that in Payanés's chest she had found her happiness and her reason for living."

Like gusts of air in an empty house, the breaths of many strange men blew on her neck. Her life was tangled up in that sleepy haze of foreign bodies that passed through her bed, one after another, in the procession of their indifference. Her bedroom was conquered territory, the camp of any army, and her white sheet was the flag of her purchased love. Her naked body accepted with indolence the rubbing of skins that were odorless, or that smelled of distant places, and on which neither her touch nor her eyes wanted to linger. Until suddenly, without warning, came the contact with the skin that somehow awakened her, giving her the touch that her fingertips, alert at last, demanded, and in the skin of that stranger she felt the exact temperature that reminded her of happiness.

"My man tastes like moss, like a manger, like the Christ Child," announced Sayonara. "He tastes like Christmas."

"Hush, girl, that's sinful talk!"

"He smells delicious, like a forest perfume with a good smell, and he also smells like a horse. I like that about him, that he has a strong horse smell. The smell of horse sweat, which is the same as the smell of desire."

"Girl, such things you say!"

"Do you know what a *petrolero* smells like after ten hours of forced labor under this strong sun?" Todos los Santos asks me. "No, you can't imagine. He smells like pure race, *mi reina*. He smells like the whole human race."

"That depends on the color of his skin," adds Olguita. "The whitest ones, the ones with more European blood, are the ones who smell the worst."

"Cover me with your skin," Sayonara asked Payanés, and he spread over her and clothed her and made himself more hers than her own skin, and he blanketed her with his chest, that foreign chest, which in a simple, miraculous instant made itself so familiar. And so comforting. A chest like a roof that shields and protects, and there, outside, let the world end, let it rain sparks and let God do whatever he chooses.

Olguita, the hopeless romantic, tells me tales and I don't know whether they're true or imaginary. She tells me, for example, that Payanés slept holding Sayonara with the yearning of an orphan that she knew how to calm for a while, and that his sleep lasted only the second it would take for him to relive that memory the following day, the same, eternal second that it would take for his eyelids to close and then to open again.

"Is this how long a stranger's love lasts?" Sayonara asked, watching him leave. "Is there a love more intense and aloof? Is there another possible form of love?"

"A lot of poetry, a lot of poetry," groans Todos los Santos as she reads this. "I don't see anyone around here who is willing to tell the hard truth, which is that skin that is too familiar is no great gift, first because it starts turning gray and then little by little moves toward invisibility,

old and worn like a shawl that is used every day, until finally, now inti-
mately known, it becomes as unfamiliar as the leather in your next-door
neighbor's shoes: just skin, any old skin. But you all don't listen to me
and you keep on weaving your own versions, so it just doesn't seem like
anyone around here is interested in the truth."

thirty-two

CRIMINAL HANDS BURN LA COPA ROTA was the headline that appeared one day, after the forced departure of don Enrique, among the items in the *Vanguardia Petrolera*, which circulated daily in Tora. It was never proved who did it, but according to reports the fire happened at seven o'clock one morning in August when there were no clients in the place. Awakened by asphyxiating smoke, Fideo jumped out of bed and ran, tripping over people because several women were sleeping on the floor, and seconds later they were all seen fleeing as the expelling archangel saw Eve, naked and barefoot and shouting obscenities. They managed to safely escape the scorching flames, and a while later, although more choked by the smoke, so did the owner of the establishment, the bar boy, and the cat. But the hut, whose straw roof had caught fire first, was engulfed by the dry summer wind that whipped up the flames and reduced it to a pile of ashes, with a half drum enthroned in the center: the one that had served as the toilet, and the only object spared for memories.

You might be thinking that this is the third or fourth time that fire has crept into this story to reduce reality to nothing. It doesn't seem accidental to me. As a Colombian, I know that I am delineating a world in perpetual combustion, always on the verge of definitive collapse, a world that despite everything manages, only God knows how, to hang on with fingernails and teeth, blazing in its final, reckless flashes as if there were no tomorrow, and yet another dawn soon fills the sky and here below the delirium gains new energy, scatological, impossible, and the new day travels along a thread of anguish toward a too predictable end, announced by the din of men and women banging on their empty pots with spoons.

And yet at midnight, against all odds, our peculiar apocalypse is once again postponed. Maybe because of that we are so dead, and at the same time so alive: because each sunset annihilates us, and the dawn redeems us.

"Where did Fideo end up, since after the fire there was no place for her?"

"Everything that goes up comes back down again," Todos los Santos tells me, "and sometimes, very seldom, but it has happened, what goes down comes back up."

Many of the regular clients of the Dancing Miramar and the other prestigious clubs, especially the younger ones, had allowed themselves to be attracted by the temptation of coarse love and had begun to frequent La Copa Rota, where they gathered to watch Fideo shining in her sickly light, embodying the hoarsest voice of the underground, the lowest of the lowly depths, humanity stripped of its skin, split open and displayed for sale, like meat on a carcass.

The barbaric separation from don Enrique broke the soul she didn't have, and if she was a wild beast before, afterward she became a cruel wild beast who, when she couldn't bite others, chewed and destroyed her own paws. To see her expose herself, naked, talking filth and biting flesh, made men horny and ignited their virility, so they riled her up and gave her alcohol, gave her alcohol and riled her up, and she went along with it because she could no longer find herself except in the open wound where her heart had been.

"Ay, don Enrique!" sighed Fideo from her invalid's hammock.

The more turbulent the aura surrounding her, the stronger the aroma she expelled, and the deeper she fell, the higher her prestige grew. Until Negra Florecida, owner of the Dancing Miramar, resenting the loss of regular clients and eager to regain them, decided to give them a little of the medicine they were asking for, and she took advantage of the fire at La Copa Rota to offer Fideo work at her establishment. Even today it is rumored in Tora that behind that misfortune was a match struck by order of Negra Florecida herself.

That is how they came to compete for men's love in the same arena, Sayonara and Fideo, angel and demon, life and death and a whole list of dichotomies, and the once harmonious world seemed to split in half, or at least it felt in people's hearts.

Fanaticism sprang up, uncompromising, between *sayonaros* — nostalgic for old times — and *fideístas*, revelers who lived for the moment. And although the two women had an identical smell, which was merely human, they said Sayonara smelled of incense, and she was venerated for her air of child *puta*, unattainable and sheltered in her way of being there without being, for remaining unsullied by the many hands that had touched her, while they said that Fideo smelled of musk and they sought her out because she was just a plain whore, committed to the profession without offering resistance, without holding back, baring her insides in public and not keeping a single gesture or secret or memory for herself. Well, perhaps a memory, just one, but a delicate and kind one: Ay, don Enrique!

I try to communicate to Todos los Santos what I have been deciphering and she laughs.

"Don't get me tangled up in words," she insists. "The difference is that with Sayonara you had to love her, and that with Fideo you only had to pay her. That's it."

"Fine, you in your way and I in mine, we both think the same," I defend myself this time. "And now tell me, did each resent the presence of the other? Was it hard for Sayonara to suddenly find herself with competition and to see her hegemony at risk?"

"How should I put it? They were both too lost in their own worlds to worry about the other."

They worked under the same roof, but they belonged to worlds that never touched, each one playing for all she was worth to maintain supremacy over her own, but with no awareness of the size of what was in play. Also, in their roles as infallible lovers—and both were, each in her own way—they demonstrated their inability to feel jealousy, because neither recognized the existence of a rival; what's more, for them a rival couldn't exist because both knew that, in terms of her own pleasure or loss, they had already won, forever, the bloody poker game that was their peculiar way of understanding love.

There is a piece of information that, while literary, seems like it could be verified with a historical or sociological examination of that period: the beginning of Fideo's tenure at the Dancing Miramar, since it coincided with two more measurable and less allegorical worldly events—the outcome of the rice strike and the spread of syphilis to epidemic levels—and marked what could be called the end of innocence for La Catunga. And the loss of innocence brought with it the pain of seeing the familiar become strange and opened the door to loneliness, which translated into the skin of strangers seeming unfamiliar and covered with thorns. And it wrought misery, which came when people aspired for more, disdaining the dignity of poverty.

Fideo's entry at the Dancing Miramar was the symbolic event that marked the beginning of the dissolution of La Catunga as it had been known until then: a simple port, open without suspicion to the winds of crazy love, the transparent surface of a lake before it is stirred up by the wind.

thirty-three

At night all cats are brown, and that night all men were cats. With feline and furtive steps they traversed the extreme tension of the 26, all around them a night hermetic and strangely devoid of noise for the first time in seven years—the quiet, heavy machines like enormous animals dreaming in the mist—because the rebels had extinguished the power plant and blocked the valves in and out. With technology forcibly silenced, the human voice took possession of the camp, newborn and still testing its own strength in the form of anonymous shouting that at times ebbed and at times surged, and it was also possible to hear tremulous breathing and other slight noises produced by figures who were crouched in anticipation of something, who were moving toward somewhere, who were protecting themselves behind barricades of oil drums.

"Despite my nervousness I was thinking about her," Sacramento tells me, "and by saying that I'm not telling you anything new, because I have never been able to think about anything else. I cursed myself for not having sent her postcards again, since she enjoyed receiving them so much, but at the same time I forgave myself by reflecting that I hadn't done it, not because I had forgotten or out of laziness, but because of my confusion about words; since I had confirmed what I suspected, that the girl and Sayonara were one and the same, I lost the sense of how I should write to her, especially in the ticklish area of how to address her: Adored fiancée? Señorita? Dear girl? My beloved? I got all tangled up in those meditations on grammar while the revolt in the camp was growing, and vigorously. Payanés, the gringo *mister* Brasco, and I went to find Emilia. I lit the way with a company-issued lantern in my hand, holding it far out from my body so it wouldn't reveal too much in case someone decided to shoot at me. The other two men thought it would be prudent to put out the lantern because mistrust and confusion were alive and palpable in the darkness. I didn't want to extinguish it because its greenish light calmed me, but they convinced me, so we continued on in the dark, sniffing our way uncertainly, until we found our tower."

"At first, spokesmen from management harangued over the loudspeakers, threatening reprisals against the striking workers and attacks from the troops," I am told in a bar in Tora by don Honorio Laguna, an old welder who was also present the night preceding the strike. "But then somebody smashed the speakers and we didn't hear anything else from the enemy, nor did we know the color that things were starting to take. We began to see groups organizing with tools and iron bars urging the seizure of flash points like the pumping stations, the warehouses, and the UCD plant. And there were others who were saying we should rig the machines, by which they meant remove some vital piece so they would explode when the scabs tried to start them up again. Or that we should cap the pipes, and some even proposed attacks against the golf club with all those foreigners inside."

"I had wild ideas that night," Sacramento tells me, "and I let myself get carried away by the suggestion that we should arm ourselves so we could crush the skull of anyone who crossed our path. Because we were sure that under such crazy circumstances there was no Lino el Titi to step forward, or anyone else with authority to give us better orders."

"It's well known that Sacramento had lost heart that night, having decided to join the participants of the last judgment. What I mean," says

Machuca, "is that he was already anticipating the personal catastrophe that was about to befall him. He must have sensed that the world was going to end for him, so it would be that much better if it just ended for everyone."

But he couldn't make any headway down the road to annihilation because Payanés was obstinate and had a different plan in mind. He kept on repeating that they shouldn't join the mob who were fucked anyway, that they weren't going to destroy the machines that were their only guarantee of sustenance; instead they were going to defend skinny Emilia from anyone who tried to damage her.

"He talked about that tower as if rather than a framework of steel it were a woman, exposed and solitary, in the midst of all that vandalism," says Sacramento, "and I was bothered by his way of referring to something as if it had a soul."

"Look at her," exhorted Payanés, "my Emilia, tame and quiet beneath the stars, and more loving than ever."

"I wanted to check, so I turned to look at the stars," says Sacramento, "but the sky must have been stormy, because I could only make out five or six, nothing in comparison to what the nights of a *petrolero* are like, dotted with stars, as the song goes. So I told Payanés not to exaggerate, that it wasn't the time for it."

"Sacramento and Payanés spent the night perched like monkeys in the tower, airing, through questions and accusations, the rivalry that had unsettled them and to which both of them avoided direct reference in order to mask the real issue," says Machuca. "Every now and then they would throw stones down below against suspected threats, but they did so blindly in the pitch dark and without really intending to hit anyone. With them was Frank Brasco and later they were joined by old Pajabrava, who also climbed up to ensconce himself in the tower."

"It hurts here, señor apostle," said Sacramento to Pajabrava, sinking his index finger in his left side below his nipple. "Here, look, right here, it burns like the devil. You who know so much, can you tell me why when I think about a certain girl my heart hurts like this?"

"That's why they put it in your chest," Pajabrava told him. "As Yahweh revealed to Samuel, the heart is the organ of pain and of love, which are one and the same. They say that when you see it consumed by flames it's a sign of divine fervor, and when it is pierced by an arrow it means that it's repentant. If it is pierced by a knife it is enduring one of life's extreme tests, if it is lanced with thorns it is bearing the torment of a human love, and if it is bleeding it has been abandoned."

"Well, then, mine must have fire, arrow, knife, thorns, and bleeding, all at the same time, because it hurts like hell," said Sacramento, who forgets about piety when it comes to expressing the furors of his spirit.

"After hours with that rope around my neck I suddenly found myself free and miraculously alive and that cheered me up," Frank Brasco tells me, as the fire in his hearth warms the interior of his cabin in Vermont, "but I was struggling to understand the situation. The overall one, of course, which was chaotic, but also my own. The executives of the Troco, my compatriots, had abandoned me by refusing to negotiate for my life. So, one thing was clear and another unclear; it was clear that I had no allies and it was unclear who my real enemies were. The only one who proposed something concrete in the midst of that disorder was Payanés, who wanted us to defend Emilia, and it seemed right to me because I too felt affection for that great prehistoric hulk. In lieu of a better strategy, we entrenched ourselves with a good supply of projectiles to throw from the tower; that way we could prevent anyone from getting close enough to damage her and at the same time cover our backs. Night was in my favor, because it hid the fact that I was one of the gringos, whose heads the mob was demanding for being exploiters and imperialists. I was a renegade gringo, cast off by the rest, of course, but the rebels didn't know that, so that with the light of day things were going to get more complicated for me. But there was still time before that happened and I thought, as they say in Colombia, Morning will come and we'll see."

Morning came and they saw. Outside the fence, surrounding the camp like a ring of steel, the army's Fourteenth Brigade had taken up positions under the command of General Demetrio del Valle with all three hundred twenty of its men armed and wearing camouflaged uniforms.

"That same night the news of the insurrection at Camp 26 reached La Catunga and it brought us out of the bars," relates Machuca. "We heard about everything, the flying balls of rice, the kidnapping of Frank Brasco, the resurrection of the veteran Lino el Titi as union leader. Then we *putas* gathered and decided to head over there with food and provisions, in the spirit of solidarity and knowing that the striking workers must be starving. When we approached, well into the morning, we found that the troops had the camp surrounded. The boys were fenced in like the famous warriors of Masada and it turned out to be true that they were howling with hunger."

Then the professional women, nurturing and generous, elbowed their way up to the fence and showered the other side with bread, oranges, *panela*, plantains, bacon, and canned food, which the workers greeted like manna from heaven, since they'd had nothing in their stomachs after their breakfast the previous day, before the revolt erupted.

"Tell her, Machuca," urges Fideo. "Tell her about Payanés and the beans."

"The workers built fires, heating up the food in tins, and then ate heartily," Machuca begins telling me, "while on the other side of the fence the troops, without food, watched them with faces like beaten dogs. So Payanés said: Do you want some? —offering part of his beans to an adolescent soldier who vacillated between accepting or not, between hunger and suspicion."

"Don't touch that!" shouted the captain to the young soldier, who stiffened upon hearing the order. "It's probably poisoned . . ."

"How can you say that, *hermano*, do you think we're inhuman monsters?" said Payanés indignantly. "Are you going to call me a murderer for feeling sorry for this boy who hasn't had anything to eat? Think about it, *hermano*, the workers are people and so are the soldiers; there's no need to tear each other apart . . ."

"You are subversives from the guerrilla . . . ," the captain tried to justify himself while the soldier hastily devoured the beans like a hungry child, because deep down that's what he was.

"They're good, these beans," he acknowledged. "If they're poisoned, well, the poison suits them. To your health!" the boy shouted to the men inside the fence, and they, following Payanés's example, shared their bread with the soldiers only a couple of hours before events would lead them to a cruel confrontation.

The members of the battalion threatened to enter the camp, take it by force, and squash the rebels, but they hesitated. They put off the decision, as if giving themselves time, since they knew that once inside they wouldn't be able to shoot because any stray bullet could ignite the wells and unleash hell. In the meantime the workers were reinforcing themselves. The strike committee was gathered in some secret corner; Lino el Titi resumed control and decreed that the strike must continue until victory or death. And this news, which spread like wildfire, caused the initial fear, confusion, and chaos to yield to greater fervor, worker unity, and a feverish determination to fight.

"Victory or death?" said Brasco. "You people speak in hyperbole. I would propose victory, or a reasonable alternative."

"We made history," says don Honorio Laguna, the old welder, and a few big tears of pride pour from his left eye, because the other one is false.

"It was then that he saw them, and in that instant he felt the full weight of his pain," Machuca tells me.

"Who saw? Who did he see?"

"Sacramento. He saw those two."

On that dawn of historical repercussions, Sacramento was floating in an air magnetized by Sayonara, as if sealed in a cave of solitary bliss. He turned to look toward the place where a cluster of women were causing a commotion by passing food over the fence. Among them he recognized the girl, although she was already a woman, dressed for combat in an oriental blouse with its tight row of cloth buttons covering her heart. She still had the same bearing of an undomesticated animal he had noticed the first day he had seen her, and her shiny hair was gathered at the crown of her head in a ponytail that fell wildly down her back.

"First I saw her, then I recognized her and then I suddenly realized what she was doing . . ."

Sayonara was extending her delicate fingers with their almond-shaped nails through the holes in the wire fence to touch the thick hand of a worker who was none other than Payanés: separated by the fence and the presence of the armed forces but joined together by a shared look, dissolved in the sweetness of their encounter, hypnotized and dormant in the timeless moment of their contact. Their index fingers sought each other with pleasure and confidence, unaware that the mere touch would bring rebirth and give new impulse to their story, unaware that salvation would be won if the connection was made—fingers intertwined—or disaster if not.

"Sparks, *mi reina,*" sighs Olguita. "Between his index finger and hers sparks and stars emanated to illuminate the sky."

"I only had to see how they looked at each other to know everything," Sacramento tells me. "I felt a sharp pain in my gut and a great desire to fall dead; then came a nausea, like a sour mouthful, the quiet taste of death. What was life for them was death for me, and every time I tell it I kill myself again as if I am reliving it. The world was paralyzed for me and it became night in the middle of the day, as if the images had fled and all that remained around me was a nothingness frozen in black and white, while I burned over hot coals. Jealousy? No, it was jealousy that had burned me earlier, but now it was worse, because as I told you it was pure death, but a wrenching one, not a gentle one. With the passing of the hours my panic dimmed and I faded away to ashes, and the only thing that remained alive in me was the memory of unbearable pain. I was there but I no longer had bones, or flesh, or eyes, or hair: I was a mass of dazed pain that walked without knowing where."

Sacramento didn't notice when the troops violently pulled the *prostitutas* away from the fence as the women tried to hang on to the wire with hands like hooks. Nor does he remember the many hours of being blocked off without communication from outside, which prevented them from receiving food and forced them to eat iguanas, *chigüiros*, cats, and other domesticated animals; nor did he know when Lino el Titi, demonstrating the power of his old charisma and newly recovered leadership, said that any worker who damaged a machine would pay with his life.

"Faced with this last measure, Caranchas and the men from maintenance confronted him with his error, warning him that he would have to settle accounts if the company brought in scabs and reactivated production, thus thwarting the strike," don Honorio informs me. "But Lino el Titi, being a *petrolero*, the son of a *petrolero*, and now the father of three *petrolero* sons, could not tolerate the idea of damaging a means of production which, he believed, would give substance to the families of his grandchildren and great-grandchildren tomorrow. He was a straight man, Lino el Titi, incapable of comprehending that others played crookedly."

Besieged by hunger and the psychological war being waged by General del Valle, who kept airplanes flying low over the camp, and resolved to continue the strike clandestinely in Tora, the workers, through their strike committee, agreed to abandon the installations without committing industrial sabotage in exchange for the troop's agreement to allow them to leave peacefully, without aggression, firings, or reprisals. Despite his great anguish, Sacramento does remember the exodus of men passing in single file through a double cordon of defiant troops, the unbearable tenseness, the sensation of expecting a shot in the neck at any moment, the certainty that one of the soldiers aiming at them would shoot and unleash a massacre.

That was when Lino el Titi, surrounded by the strike committee and a group of bodyguards, appeared out of nowhere and approached Sacramento, distinguishing him as someone in the leader's full confidence.

"You know Machuca, right?" he asked Sacramento. "When you get to Tora look for her and tell her to dig out the mimeograph machine, oil it, and fill it with ink, because the strike bulletin is going to circulate again. You will be in charge of it. The committee members will send you the content, we'll figure out how, and you will be responsible for seeing that a thousand copies are printed daily. Machuca knows how to type, how to use the mimeograph machine, and how to do things quietly. Is this your friend?" he asked, referring to Payanés.

"That's Payanés," responded Sacramento, spitting out the word "Payanés" as if he were saying "Judas," but Lino el Titi didn't notice the subtlety.

"Well, then, you, Payanés, you'll be in charge of distribution, which must be handled in secret," he ordered. "You'll give the bulletins to the neighborhood leaders and they will give them to the block coordinators, so that they can be circulated to everyone. That way at least eight or ten people should read each copy. Is that understood?"

"*Sí*, señor," said Payanés, puffed up with pride, barely able to believe that he had been honored with such a responsibility. "Yes, sir, don't worry, we will do everything exactly as you say, but I have one question, señor: Who are the neighborhood leaders and the block coordinators?"

"They know who they are, they know from the last strike, and they will come forward ready to do their part as soon as they see the first bulletin passing from hand to hand. The bulletin is the heart of the strike," Lino el Titi informed Payanés, before he disappeared majestically, surrounded by his guards. "As long as the bulletin goes out, the strike will remain alive."

"Payanés urged me to identify myself to the troops as a North American functionary, so they would release me as was my right and I could spare myself a lot of anxiety," Frank Brasco tells me, "but I wasn't eager to do that. First out of anger at my people, who had given me up for dead, and then out of solidarity with the Colombians, because I felt closer to them and because their claims were based on reason and basic worker rights. So I covered my head with a straw hat and hid my mouth and nose under a handkerchief, as I saw others doing, and I left the camp pressed against and hidden by the mass of workers."

Then all at once what had been expected occurred: the burst of betrayal from the soldiers' rifles and the workers' response with bottles of sulfuric acid and phenol, with the tragic result—which could only be tallied three days later—of eleven dead workers and three burned soldiers. It's a good thing don Honorio describes this to me, because Sacramento, who was lost in the unconsciousness of his immense sorrow, doesn't remember it clearly; he didn't even hear the shots, he says, because inside him the voices of desperation were shouting even louder.

"We made history," don Honorio assures me, and tears trickle down the furrows on the left side of his face.

I have in my hands a copy of the sixth strike bulletin, printed in faded purple letters stiff from the rigor mortis that attacks paper over the years. This same piece of paper must have passed through Payanés's hands fresh from the mimeograph machine, its ink still damp, and he must have given it to Sayonara, his accomplice, his beloved, his efficient and unconditional helper in the risky task of clandestine printing and distribution, at a moment that must have made them feel like protagonists not only in their own personal drama but also in the history of their nation, which for an instant sat them in its lap.

"The cocktail of collective enthusiasm, solidarity, and fear was so explosive," Frank Brasco tells me in Vermont, "that you could say that we were all in love with everyone, that we didn't need to drink to get drunk and that we didn't need physical contact to make love."

I understand his words: They allude to a communal eroticism that electrifies the air in certain exceptional moments, inviting people to believe that happiness is possible, that life is generous, that you can subdue loneliness and isolation, that one has in his own hands the ability to assure that today will be followed by a tomorrow, and that tomorrow by a day after tomorrow, in a dazzling succession of futures that we Colombians have never experienced. So, although they barely had time for kisses between events and to embrace between tasks, during those thundering days Payanés and Sayonara were given the privilege of living love in that splendid and fruitful place in which it moves beyond itself, casts itself upon the affairs of the world and becomes contagious.

Never had they been so young, so beautiful, or so happy as then, nor had they ever been so convinced that they would love each ever forever and that they would never die.

Machuca, distinguished woman of letters, master of graphic duties, lieutenant under Lino el Titi, and supervisor of underground operations, has kept this copy of the Boletín de Huelga number six safely stored for years among photographs, love letters, foreign money, magazine clippings, and other prized mementos.

"This sheet of paper," she tells me, "represents perhaps the most important thing we have done in our lives."

The chronicle of bulletin number six began with the arrival of the striking workers of Camp 26 in Tora, where they went into hiding because the strike had been declared illegal and therefore punishable. To camouflage himself among the crowds, given that he was being pursued by the law with orders for his capture, Lino el Titi, already consecrated and on the verge of becoming a legend, bleached his hair yellow and shaved his mustache, with the result that people who saw him pass would say: There goes Lino el Titi with yellow hair and no mustache. So he decided instead on a disguise consisting of a cap and dark glasses. There goes Lino el Titi with a cap and dark glasses, they said then.

Infected with rebellious passion and led by Machuca, the *prostitutas* of La Catunga went on strike with legs crossed in solidarity with the *petroleros* and stayed out of the café. They traded dangly earrings and diadems for red rags that they tied around their heads and took to the streets, along with the general populace, to participate in the manifestations that arose on every street corner and to join protests and massive acts of resistance in support of the list of demands. And, out of an extra sense of civic concern, they demanded an aqueduct and sewers in the neighborhoods of Tora, which were burning with thirst and drought. Repression sharpened its nails and selected its victims. The arrested, nearing a hundred in number, were kept under the rays of the sun and the chill of the moon on the baseball field, which had been converted into a temporary prison. And during a brutal siege, General

Valle's men beat Chaparrita to death and left Caracoles paralyzed on one side of her body, for the simple crime of having hidden several strikers under their beds.

To prevent solidarity with Lino el Titi and the rest of the members of the strike committee, the army issued, on behalf of the oil company, the written order that the townspeople not "shelter in their homes persons who are not members of their family, or persons of dubious or bad conduct who would compromise the good name of the family." Despite this mandate, Machuca, for years the soul mate and mistress of Lino el Titi, hid him for a week in her big oak armoire, among plush robes and feather boas and facing a window that was open to the street twenty-four hours a day so that anyone who passed by could see and not suspect a thing. Acting as if she were taking clothes out of the armoire to dress herself, once a day she gave Titi a plate of food and received from him a full basin and pages of writing scrawled by the light of a lantern that were to orient the strike activity with precise instructions and general politics. In the darkness of night, Machuca would rescue him from the armoire and hide him in her bed, beneath her large, matronly body. She would whisper news to him and transmit messages from the other members of the committee, and with delicate movements that barely altered the sheets, she made love to him until he was exhausted. To the song of the blackbirds she put him away again in the big oak wardrobe, where Lino el Titi, in the company of extra-large bras and baby-doll nightgowns, and pressed between inexplicable winter coats impregnated with camphor, spent the day ruminating, sleeping, and writing instructions, recommendations, and sermons as heated as he himself must have been closed up in that hiding place without ventilation.

"Under those conditions he wrote strike bulletin number six," Machuca tells me. "He did it in his usual style, so instinctively in tune with the general feeling that he began by saying, 'The people and I think that . . .' or 'The people and I feel that . . .' Confidently he spoke of 'a voice that vibrates and does not tremble,' of 'a life for humans and not for animals,' or of other ardent notions in that tenor. I don't remember clearly anymore. Then he slid the sheet through the gap between the armoire's doors and I hid it between my breasts to take it to Payanés, as I had done with the five previous bulletins, but this time on the way from my house to Adela Lightfoot's, where the mimeograph machine was hidden, I was detained, and although they didn't find Lino's paper, they did prevent me from delivering it."

The barrio leaders were already waiting to pass it along to their block coordinators, and so were the neighbor women who would distribute it under plantains and heads of cabbage in market baskets, and the children who would post themselves on the street corners to look out for the enemy. The mimeograph machine had been oiled and filled with ink and was ready to chew through the stacks of paper, Payanés was impatient to begin the work, Sayonara peered out from the doorway to see if Machuca was approaching, as did the band of horn blowers and timbal drummers who offered themselves as volunteers to cover the noise of the printing with the blasts of their music. All of Tora tense, awaiting their bulletin to prove that the strike was still alive, that in spite of all the repression the leaders hadn't given up, that in spite of the difficulties victory was within reach. But Machuca, detained at the baseball field, never arrived.

"Give me a pencil, beautiful," Payanés said to Sayonara. "I'm going to write this blessed bulletin myself."

"How could you think of such a thing! How do you know what instructions to give out?"

"You'll see."

A few hours later the sheets were being passed from hand to hand, raising the strike to its highest peak and rekindling the energy of the townspeople, who still remember with emotion that its content was reduced to three words, or more precisely to a single word repeated three times: *Rebeldía! Rebeldía! Rebeldía!*

But if the workers counted on discontent to unite the masses, the company knew how to use contentment to divide them, and it began to offer promotions, bonuses, and privileges for those who returned to work ignoring the union authority. "A free house for the worker who starts a family," promised one of the flyers circulating around Tora to encourage modernization, moralization, and the return to normalcy, which ultimately landed in Sacramento's hands, good, tormented Sacramento, who from the moment he saw another man with the woman he loved had been writhing in an agony of jealousy and rancorous suffering, keeping himself on the margin of the collective exaltation. I don't dare ask him when or how he made the decision to present himself at the personnel office to put himself on the list of candidates for subsidized housing, because I know it's a subject that hasn't healed and still festers in his conscience, in the memory of Tora and in the disgust of Todos los Santos, who still recriminates every time she remembers the incident.

"As a result of the virulence of the strike," don Honorio Laguna explains to me, "the company management had begun to reconsider its position. They realized that to have rootless men piled up in barracks with a hammock and a single change of clothes as their only belongings and with a *puta* as their only love, or in other words with everything to gain and nothing to lose, was to be confronted by bitter enemies that were impossible to manage. On the other hand, a man with a house, a wife, and children, which sizable burden the company helped him to support, would think twice before risking his job to join the fight. At least that's what the Tropical Oil Company decided: that it was time to modernize its structure to better control the untamed personnel that it kept caged up in the *petrolero* camps."

"Sacramento knew that only by setting up a home far from La Catunga would he be able to separate Sayonara from prostitution," Machuca tells me. "That's why he ran to sign up on the list. And also to get back at Payanés: An eye for an eye and a tooth for a tooth, you betrayed me in matters of love, so I will betray you in matters of work. It was clear that he did it for her and only for her, but that wasn't a valid excuse for the others."

Because it turned out that with the help of scabs and through sentimental weakness of the workers in not damaging the equipment to make it unusable, the company was able to partially resume operations in Campo 26, giving the coup de grâce to a workers' movement that it had already weakened through violence.

"We workers hadn't counted on the eighty survivors of the killing spree at Orito, who had arrived in Tora two weeks before the strike, looking for a *petrolero's* salary," says don Honorio; "or the forty-some families made homeless by the flooding of the Río Samaná; or the group of recent arrivals from Urumita, Guajira, who offered themselves for work; or the one hundred sixty Pipatón Indians recently expelled from their ancestral lands by the Troco itself in its project to expand operations; the displaced from who knew where, the one hundred twenty-seven from somewhere else, the thousands of unemployed who proved to be more than willing to accept any job without imposing conditions."

"Not to mention the Sacramentos who betrayed us out of anger," comes the poison-filled voice of Todos los Santos.

"Don't judge, Todos los Santos," responds Olga, and for the first time since I have met her I detect harshness in her voice. "No man knows another's thirst."

"One thing has to be cleared up," announces Machuca, "which is that Sacramento was never a rat. He didn't sneak in to work behind the strikers' backs to help break them and benefit from the situation. That never even occurred to him. His only error was to put his name on the list to receive a house, but given the circumstances, that was an error people considered criminal."

The strike bulletin, which appeared every day come hell or high water, had become the visible testimony of the fact that the strikers didn't give in and continued the struggle in hiding. Dodging threats, beatings, and arrest, they managed to circulate fourteen bulletins, but when the fifteenth was in the process of being created, General Valle and his men descended upon Adela Lightfoot's house, arresting her and the band of musicians, seizing the mimeograph machine, and destroying pots and pans, utensils, and papers—saying it was *"guerrillero* material" they had found inside. They didn't lay a hand on Sayonara or Payanés because the two managed to escape across the roof and then later to hide in separate locations. That day, for the first time since the strike had been declared, people kept waiting for the bulletin and interpreted it as a clear signal that things were going badly.

"It's true that the rice strike achieved almost none of its demands and that it ended in failure," recognizes don Honorio Laguna, as he drinks the last sip of his coffee, "but it was a valiant, dignified failure, and that's fairly close to a victory. Well, one thing concrete was achieved, and that was that at the 26 they never gave us balls of rice for lunch again," he adds in closing and laughs at his own joke.

thirty-four

 During the strike, Frank Brasco, having completely forgotten, you could say, about his identity as a North American engineer and a high-ranking employee of the company in conflict, installed himself among the people of Tora. He tacitly declared his feelings toward the striking workers and supported them in practical ways by lending his services as a nurse to dozens of wounded men, a skill he had learned in his youth through a stint with the International Red Cross; and in legal and formal ways that couldn't be classified as anything other than humanitarian aid. In addition, in his few free moments he would take Sayonara to eat snow cones at Isaías's bar, the only way of giving her a tangible and comparative explanation of the nature of snow.

The company, of course, censured him by demanding his resignation, which he submitted at once together with a long public letter. Unfortunately I have not been able to find a copy of it because not even he himself kept one. In it, according to what I've heard, he offered a shrewd analysis of the imperialist enclave and its effects on the local populace.

But his compatriots did not forgive him, nor was he able to free himself from the sensation of belonging to a nation that mistreated and abused others. Neither worker nor boss, neither North American nor Colombian, neither a man of the tropics nor a man of the poles, he was driven by a chronic restlessness and an implacable unwillingness to align himself with his own people. And perhaps it was that inability to find himself on one side or the other that drove him to take final refuge in the winters of his native Vermont, making the decision, after his retirement, to watch from there the days of his old age pass and never to leave it again.

"Maybe because being in this snow is enough like not being anywhere," he says to me. "In the Colombian green I found passion and the difficulty of living, while the winter white of Vermont offers me the benefits of rest. It covers me like a sheet and lets me remember in peace."

thirty-five

 After the strike, Tora, as short on water and choked with the stench of open sewage ditches as always, remained submerged in the nostalgia of what it could have been but wasn't. Drowned in the painful immobility of its failure and the renewed proof of its impotence, the city saw itself additionally divided into two jealous and resentful halves: the families and friends of the striking workers who remained faithful to the bitter end on one side, and on the other, people aligned with those who wavered and allowed themselves to be tempted by the company's lures, offers, and enticements. The workers who weren't fired, among them Sacramento and Payanés, returned to work under conditions that were equal to or worse than before. Those who had fallen were honored with speeches and floral offerings. Three-fourths of those arrested and detained at the baseball field were freed and the other fourth were tried by a war tribunal and condemned to long sentences at the island prison of Gorgona.

After escaping from Adela Lightfoot's house on the day it was invaded, Sayonara took refuge among a group of women who were scrubbing clothes at the public washing facility and so managed to go unnoticed, but she lost track of Payanés. When she returned to Todos los Santos's house, she received the information that he too was safe, and after another week she learned that he had returned to work at Camp 26.

"I'll wait for him here, then," they say she announced, and she prepared to allow time to run its course and to temper the agony of uncertainty. "I'm sure my days of joy are behind me," she said. "Will remembering hurt less each day, or more?"

Until finally, after a stretch of anonymous Mondays and the dissipation of lost Thursdays, as if born out of the intensity of the waiting, the last Friday of the month arrived in La Catunga and Sayonara was aware of it, even before waking, in the smiling wind that entered her window dragging along chirps and small shivers, as if it blew from a country of birds. She took refuge in the light cave of her sheets to dream about the man who had promised to return, and she drew him toward her with the obstinacy of her thoughts and the pulsating of her feminine parts, stretching the minutes of her awakening to allow the tickle that had begun to stir her eyelids to descend along her neck and bubble across her breasts, small and tight like a nut when they were exposed, but now, with the nearness of her beloved, spongy and welcoming and replete with promise.

Now fully awake, she confirmed contentedly that in the deepest recesses of her being, in the middle of the curve of her hip, there where so many men had foraged without leaving a trace, an untouched space grew warm and damp, anxious to receive, seeking a tenant like a magnet drawing metal.

She rose without anyone having to beg her, contrary to her custom of lounging in bed until the fifth or sixth time her *madrina* called her to breakfast. And she had already crossed the patio, scattering the chickens, and had bathed using gourds filled with clear water from the cistern when she heard the first shout, "The chocolate is ready!" that on any other day would have found her lost in the mists of morning slumber.

"Sayonara! Your breakfast is getting cold!"

"No, thank you, *madrina,* not today."

"Come! The *arepas* are burning . . ."

"Forget the *arepas, madrina,* not today."

"Did you feed the canaries?"

"I'm coming."

"Didn't I ask you to pour boiling water on the latrine? It reeks and it's clogged."

"I'm coming, *madrina,*" she said, but she didn't move. She kept brushing her long hair with slow strokes, letting the brush sleep in her hand and her mind soar with the memory of the joy that was to come, while she went about, without really noticing, the impossible task of matching the different rhythms of her own being.

"There are mysteries in this life," I hear Todos los Santos reflect, "so remote that the human mind can't even begin to touch them. One of them is the magic of electricity, another is the composition of a rainbow, and another, more impenetrable still, is the Immaculate Conception. But none is as astounding as happiness. You," she points at me, "you who have studied at a university, do me the favor of explaining that human vice of placing your entire joy in the hands of someone else. That's what my girl Sayonara did with that *petrolero* who they called Payanés and about whom we knew so little. She gazed at him as if she were under a spell and clung to his love like a baby to his mother's breast or a ship-wreck victim to the plank that saved him, as if she really needed him to survive, and without thinking or consulting she gave him the blossoming branch of her hope. My girl who had everything, who never lacked a mother's care, or the attentions of men who loved her, or physical beauty, or health, or food on the table, nothing. Nothing, nothing, nothing. Why did she have to go looking for what she had never lost? Who can explain that mystery to me? Maybe you, who, as you say, studied at a university?"

"I must be lovesick, because my body hurts from wanting him so much. If I don't touch him, I'm going to die," Sayonara confessed that morning to Olguita, saying it just like that, because the rare alchemy that makes your happiness rest in the hands of someone else was operating in her with an irrevocable simplicity.

Around three, Todos los Santos came upon her adopted daughter cleaning her teeth with ashes, as she herself had taught her. Then she watched her squeeze some clothing and other objects into some boxes and put on the puffy yellow organza dress, braid her hair with silk ribbons, and dress up her sisters too. Ana in chrysanthemum pink, Susana in sky blue, Juana in celery green, and little Chuza in immaculate lily white. During the remainder of the afternoon Todos los Santos watched as Sayonara soared along on the breeze of her anxiety, looking at everything with the already absent eyes of someone who is not going to come back and scurrying all over the house as she moved various articles, without rhyme or reason, from here to there and from there to here. Todos los Santos didn't ask any questions when she saw Sayonara drag a heavy clay pot from one end of the hallway to the other, nor when she decided to rescue a Chinese folding screen from a trash heap, not even when she freed the Nativity shepherds, forgotten since December, from their wrapping to place them, offhandedly, on a shelf with the other porcelain objects.

"Christmas is over, to hell with the shepherds!" exclaimed an annoyed Todos los Santos, returning them to their box. "You'd better not get used to chewing anxiety," she advised her adopted daughter, "which is a stubborn vice, like that of horses who chomp on air in the stable and then don't want to eat anything else. You're as skinny as you are because you feed on sheer nerves."

"My God, girl, what are you doing?" asked Olguita, upon seeing Sayonara in such a crazy state.

"I don't know if he'll come for me, Aunt Olga. Maybe he doesn't remember . . ." was how she responded, and she kept on with her endless running about, sheer purposelessness that calmed her anxiety and mitigated the back and forth of an uncertainty that said yes when coming and no when going. Is he aware of the date? Will he be able to come? Will he want to? And the inclement seesawing in her chest, pounding her ribs, coming and going and saying yes, no, yes.

"Sayonara! There is a client at the door and he wants to know if you . . ."

"Not today, *madrina*, tell him I can't today."

"But it is don Anselmo . . ."

"I can't."

"Not Anselmo Navas, not him. It's the generous don Anselmo Fuentes!"

"Tell him tomorrow."

"He says it has to be today, because tomorrow he's leaving for Valledupar . . ."

"Well, then tell him to have a nice trip, and that as far as I'm concerned he might as well leave today," and the whole time she was caught up in that useless motion, unable to control the trembling in her hands that prevented her from getting a grasp on reality.

"I already told you, *madrina*, I'm not available for anyone today. Another day, with pleasure. Not today."

She mopped the patio tiles, then swept the kitchen and once again mopped the already clean patio, her energies fixed on erasing the day once and for all, on throwing out the hours that stretched out before her like dead cows and which separated her from the only thing that interested her and gave her a reason for existing: the awaited, definitive hour, the hour of their reunion.

Will he come? Will he not come? No one saw Sayonara approach the river's edge, only herons sweeping through the air without disturbing it. The water breathed tamely like an animal in a stable and in the sky the afternoon died a natural death, without bloody reds or sudden bursts of orange, only a luminous mauve that faded into a series of increasingly tired grays. No one was coming.

Unaware of their oldest sister's anguish, the other girls entertained themselves by striking palm fronds to the cadence of a children's rhyme:

I looked for paper and pencil, *tibi-∂í,* to write a letter to the wolf, *tobo-∂ó,* and the wolf answered me, *tibi-∂í,* with a howl of love; first Juana with Ana and Susana with Chuza, then they changed partners, in an amusing synchronization of hands, arms, and voices.

That man approaching step by step, his silhouette dressed in white, could it be him? Or not? It was.

But it wasn't his customary gaze, it was as if he had been expecting to embrace a solitary woman and not crash into that image that unfurled into five, she and her sisters, she and her quadruple reflection, from old-est to youngest, and, as if that weren't enough, with luggage and para-phernalia scattered around the gathered family.

"Where are you moving to?" asked Payanés from a distance, and Sayonara could only respond with a slight gasp that seemed almost like a hiccup, but that had a cataclysmic impact within her, causing a mo-mentary paralysis of the principal organs and a brusque rush of blood to the upper half of her body, leaving the lower half limp as a rag.

"I have waited for you, hour after hour, for thirty days and thirty nights," Payanés said to her when they found themselves face to face, but more than an affirmation, his words were a reproach.

"And I for you."

"What about your sisters?" he asked.

"I brought them with me," she stuttered, stating the obvious.

"But why?" insisted the *petrolero,* who was anticipating the delights of his appointment for love.

Sayonara was stunned by that question she hadn't expected and whose response seemed so clear, so beyond words, that she had no idea how to answer it. Why had she brought them? Why hadn't she come alone, as it should have been, to the only anxiously awaited meeting of her entire life? She, the beautiful whore, the seductress, the favorite dis-ciple, why was she behaving with the dull-wittedness of a novice? She looked at her sisters beside her, as lonely as she herself and equally ig-norant of their own loneliness, and her heart shrank at the armadillo-like timidity in those four pairs of eyes that almost didn't dare rest on what they were looking at and that gave up on everything beforehand, because they knew nothing in this world could ever belong to them. And yet they were waiting for something, who knew what, so nice and extraordinary, that the future was about to give them on this unique day.

"I brought them with me because I am myself and my sisters," she said finally, as if wanting to cry without being able to, as if wanting to avoid weeping but failing.

But Payanés wasn't a man to go around acquiring family responsibilities in the name of love. The last Friday of every month, that's what they had agreed on from the beginning and he was willing to stick with that to the end. But nothing more. Don't ask him for a permanent home or a quiet heart, because he couldn't give them; only an arm for working, another to embrace, and a road in front of him, as they often say in this land of the rootless.

"But didn't you yourself tell me, Todos los Santos," I ask, "or were they Olguita's suppositions, that Payanés longed for his own house when he entered the patio of your house? Didn't he see in you a mother and in Sayonara's sisters, his own sisters?"

"It's possible. And that in Sayonara he had found the memory of a first love, that too might have been. But for someone like him, it's one thing to carry the weight of longing for a family and something altogether different to carry the weight of a family," she clarifies. "When they come to Tora, all men are fleeing from commitment and they become enthralled with speculation, which ties them down much less."

"What's wrong with you?" Sayonara asked her beloved.

"Since we failed in the strike I've been in a devil of a mood, thinking and rethinking about where we went wrong. I can't concentrate on anything else."

"I thought that tonight you and I could swear our commitment to love each other forever . . . ," Sayonara ventured, aware that she had never before said anything that so challenged both the risk of pretentiousness and the sense of the ridiculous.

Payanés, who looked at her with blank eyes as if she were speaking

German, must have thought that the pompous yellow organza dress the girl was wearing was a most appropriate costume for such a stilted discourse. The words "commitment" and "forever" had meaning for him if they were associated with something eternal, such as the metallic solidity of skinny Emilia, but not with the unprotected candor with which this girl had come to give him her life and to dump her sisters on him as part of the package.

"Well, if it can't be forever, then it will be never," Sayonara lashed out angrily and capriciously at a silent Payanés, because she didn't know how to accept anyone's disagreement.

"You have to realize that for being a *puta*, Sayonara had strange ideas," offers Machuca. "And an undesirable temperament, of course, because there aren't many clients willing to put up with fits and demands."

"That's true," adds Olga, "for a *puta*, Sayonara was a pain in the neck. Besides, it's not fair to imagine in Payanés a hardheadedness that didn't exist. He is a good man, you have to say that, and he was truly in love. It must also be true that the breaking of the strike had damaged his spirits and weakened his convictions, because the same thing happened to all of us. After that fiasco, even the air was poisoned."

"Commitments forever are fine for boleros and soap operas," interrupts Todos los Santos, "but they had no place in La Catunga. My foolish girl liked to go around repeating foreign ideas and fancy phrases she learned from other places. Imagine," she said, scandalized, "talking about forever in this troubled land where we don't even know what's going to happen in the next few hours . . ."

"Precisely because of that," says Olga. "Because of that, precisely."

"Only moth eggs are forever," adds Fideo, who it seems woke up today in the delirious phase of her illness.

"You should know that in Popayán . . . ," began Payanés, but Sayonara rushed to interrupt him to talk about something else, anything else that would make noise, because she knew that what he was about to say to her would break her heart.

"In Popayán . . . ," insisted Payanés, determined to confess but impeded by difficulties, as if each syllable were a huge rock that he had to carry on his shoulder, and Sayonara saw that an unburdening was coming at her from which she wouldn't be able to protect herself, and in that instant of painful revelation, before the words reached her ears, she also understood why Payanés never spoke about his yesterdays, as if he had just floated in on a pink cloud. And she knew then what everyone except she had suspected; what her *madrina* had guessed a long time ago and why she had kept saying: "Don't ask him any questions. Go to see him on Fridays and charge him hard cold cash for your love, but don't get involved with him or ask him any questions. Hope stays alive as long as you don't ask, because answers destroy it."

"In Popayán I left children, and a wife too. Not the wife I would like to have, but the one I have . . ." Payanés squatted at the river's edge, conflicted and sort of dazed from the exertion of having spoken the truth, and he started throwing flat stones in the water to make them skip across the still surface. The Río Magdalena, which had once ignited its waters to receive them, a bonfire that consumed but didn't burn, now passed in front of them tame and bored, an apathetic witness of their fateful encounter, without showing off laundresses, or turtles, or old musicians, or anything like herds of pigs coming down to calm their thirst.

"Sayonara was stunned by the bluntness of the blow," Olguita tells me, "and she couldn't find a way to digest the bitter cake. And she felt ridiculous in her braids and ribbons, her highbrow words, her doll's dress, and her packed belongings. But of course, since after a while Payanés was still absorbed with his stones and gave no sign of communication, she began to pace around him, trying to move closer but without daring to."

The fine thread that bound them had been broken and she couldn't find a way to mend it, although she was now willing to forgive in exchange for very little, and if that wasn't possible, then in exchange for next to nothing, anything, just so that he would allow her to approach the clean smell of his white shirt, or lean her head against his big chest, or trail her index finger along the open petals of the rose tattoo, or to imagine the security of his muscles beneath the cloth of his trousers.

"What are you doing?" she finally dared to ask, but Payanés didn't even turn to look at her.

"Bread and cheese."

"What?"

"Nothing. That's what we call this way of making stones dance across the smooth water back at home, 'making bread and cheese,' " he said with the insipid voice of disenchantment, and watching roll across the ground, like decapitated dwarfs, all the treasured desires of those lonely nights in the *petrolero* camp.

"Ay, *amor mío*, let me close my eyes and rest against you even for an instant, because life is so heavy and I can't bear it anymore," Sayonara wanted to implore, but she knew she wouldn't receive a response and any plea would sink to the bottom of a sea of strangeness.

"Shall we go?" she murmured hopelessly, knowing that her quarter hour of happiness had already passed.

"Go where?"

"Anywhere . . ."

"So where are we going to go, with all these girls and all this stuff? Look, Sayonara, or whatever your name is, you can't demand anything from me . . ."

"But I'm not demanding anything." She wanted to retract her words and erase the traces of her unfounded illusion, but it turned out that she and the four girls, all five dressed in colorful organza as if they were wrapped in gift paper, with their three bags and two boxes, weren't a demand but a supplication, an unconditional and mute offering to someone who would love and protect them.

Meanwhile, in the patio of her house, Todos los Santos, who was feeding *auyama* to a captive tapir, sensed the disaster that was about to occur; she smelled it in a fetid gust that rose from the river.

"Ay! my innocent girl," she lamented out loud, though she was only heard by a *guacamaya*, a few parakeets, and the tapir, "how many times have I told you that a *puta*'s love isn't love for life but only for hours. How many times do I have to tell you that the unattainable girl smells like roses and one who gives herself away smells like filth. Get hold of yourself and endure the lash—we'll see if you learn next time."

What came next was the awkward ending of a ridiculous scene. Walking along without destination or conviction, lugging the boxes, they decided to stop at a parody of a fair unloaded from a cart and anchored to the foot of the train station, illuminated by anemic lightbulbs and animated unsuccessfully by the monotonous melodies of three musicians with a propensity for yawning. It was an ephemeral monument to artificial happiness: a suitable mausoleum in which to give a third-rate burial to a love story with such a calamitous ending.

The girls won trinkets throwing darts at a cardboard clown, bought gummy caramels that got stuck in their hair, took off their shoes, and got their frilly organza dresses dirty. Payanés, who didn't know whether to think of them as treasures or monsters, as always occurs with the children of others, made an effort to behave himself and treated them to a double order of tutti-frutti popsicles and roasted corn with lard and salt. He bought each one a stuffed animal, and after a while, barely opening his mouth and looking somewhere else, he said good-bye with a laconic "I'm going." And Sayonara, who understood that it was a farewell without reprieve, watched him depart through the underbrush that closed around him in shadows, feeling the dizziness of a slight death sicken her heart. But, in spite of everything, she didn't lose the illusion that at the last minute he would turn his head and at least say to her, "I'll see you. A month from today, by the river, I'll see you."

"And did he say it?"

"No, he didn't say it. He left just like that, without saying another word."

thirty-six

 The girls were already beginning to feel sleepy, hugging their stuffed animals and convinced they had known happiness that night at the fair, but Sayonara didn't want to go back to the house to ruminate in the darkness of her room on the hollow echoes of that "I'm going" that had left her bleeding inside.

She just stood there, incapable of letting go of the already extinguished light from the bulbs, as if hypnotized by the persistent singsong of the long gone musicians and with the same expression of confusion as a child who invites another to play with her new toys and suddenly finds them faded and broken. As if holding in the folds of her skirt tops without strings, dolls without arms, and kites that don't fly, she couldn't shake her astonishment at seeing her spells and charms inexplicably useless and disdained.

The fury of a woman scorned or the authentic desire to die? Both, together and intertwined. Her pride wounded and crushed to her roots, with a pain in her chest as if from broken ribs, Sayonara obeyed the first stirring of her feet, which wanted to take her to foolishly and blindly finish off the night of her despair at the Dancing Miramar, where there would be no lack of men in love with her to keep her occupied while she left behind this twisted and bitter-tasting day. Already on her way, though, she was assaulted by a doubt that made her stop short. What if she ran into Payanés in the middle of Calle Caliente, forgetting about the past in the arms of Molly?

"The mere thought made her burn with fury," Olguita tells me. "A dangerous thing. When a *prostituta* burns with jealousy and allows herself to get swept away by her temper, it seals her fate. Believe what I'm telling you; we've seen it happen a thousand times."

Payanés unburdening himself to Molly: reason enough to go and kill her, the *muy puta* Molly Flan. There's no reason that vengeance has to be only Fideo's privilege, and how sweet it would be to kill Molly, but what for, after all, if it wouldn't do any good anyway; the best revenge would be to go to Popayán and tear out that wife's eyes, although thinking about it again, what did that poor woman have to do with it, there on the other side of the world breaking her back to raise a few kids while her husband is over here running around having fun with a couple of lost women and a *vallenato* trio. The only worthwhile thing would be to go for that bastard's jugular, to tear him apart with your teeth, scratch his face until he was marked forever, give him a good kick in the balls, and shout in his face the four cardinal insults: bastard, liar, traitor, murderer of my dreams.

It was a vulgar but rhythmic bolero, easy to sing, in reality sung so often that it was already part of the folklore of La Catunga and of other red-light districts around the planet. From then on everything would be foreseeable: poetry of degradation; cold, hard anecdote; a script of misery that other women have already written. Drunk, Sayonara would threaten to throw herself under the wheels of the train, then she would reject that dramatically excessive exit and opt for singing *rancheras* with a wounded howl while hanging from the neck of some other drunk.

The following night she wouldn't even appear at the Dancing Miramar because everyone would already know that that stage no longer belonged to her, that the most sought after *puta* in Tora had dropped in category and was no longer at the level of the select clientele, of the nights of champagne or the décor of mirrors and velvet, and keeping a stiff upper lip, she would have to make do with joining the cast of a cheaper bar.

"Every girl in this profession knows there will always be a cheaper bar," Machuca tells me, "and another and another still as you move further from the center, the hill barely inclined so the fall isn't too noticeable. And she consoles herself by thinking there are many years and many steps that she can roll down before she hits the bottom, to what is rightfully called the bottom of the bottom."

"That night Sayonara tempted fate," Todos los Santos tells me, disturbed by the memory. "She walked a long while on the edge of her decisions and was a step away from taking the nefarious one, the one without recourse, the one waiting for her with its door open. The all too familiar door that awaits every woman of the profession at the end of the alley. But no. Not her. She hadn't been born to be a tango lyric. I knew it from the first day I saw her, when she was still a flea-ridden child: This one will be saved by her pride. Do you remember I told you that, the morning we met, when you first started coming around here asking questions?"

"No more yellow dresses," declared Sayonara, as if canceling with one fell swoop the vestiges of her childhood. "To hell with hair ribbons."

She tore off the puffy sleeves and the lacy collar, ripped off the frilly layers of tulle that covered the ample skirt, and released both braids, closing her eyes to feel the caress of her newly freed mane, which glided down her back like tumbling water. An absurd amount of hair for so small and sad a woman. Just like her mother's and the only inheritance that remained from her. With the sheen of astrakhan fur and blue fox-tails, the mass of hair invaded the night, billowing, and when the breezes grew stronger it undulated, long and free, silky and magnificent, like a river in the wind.

As if taken by the hand of a guardian angel, the winged creature that by means of theatrics and distractions dissuades its protected souls from heeding the call of the abyss, Sayonara refrained from going to Calle Caliente and headed back toward the Magdalena. When she reached the river's edge, she allowed herself the luxury of doing what any woman without a *prostituta*'s courage would do under similar circumstances: she burst into tears.

It occurred at the hour in which the silver phosphorescence of the *yarumos* glistened, those beautiful trees of the moon, but she wasn't in the mood to notice the landscape. As Ana, Juana, Susana, and Chuza closed their eyes, tiny sleeping bundles curled up in tulle and sheltered from the sky beneath some bush, Sayonara gave in, without suppressing hiccups or sobs, to an uncontrollable, inconsolable, magdalenic weeping, as she had never allowed herself before nor would allow afterward, surprised at the salty taste of her tears and by their burning nature, like that of holy water, reddening her cheeks as they coursed down them. She let them fall, drop by drop, without thinking of anything more specific than her own sorrow. In all the sorrows of yesterday and today molded into one, without name or face, one big, soft sorrow like a breast that feeds and consoles, old familiar sorrow, so bitter but when all is said and done so much her own.

"She cried all night, she, the inconsolable one, until the weeping calmed her. There's a reason people say," Todos los Santos explains to me, "that it is good to cry out sorrows. It means that you rid yourself of pain through your eyes in its true consistency, which is water. Why do you think tears are salty? Because they are sorrowful water. That's why."

A girl's tears that fell into the river, which also performed its role, forgiving, baptizing. To understand better: The Magdalena sucked up the suffering and bristled with compassion. So, against a background of moonlight on the *yarumos*, the girl's silhouette became cleaner and lighter as the waters clouded, grew sad, flowed more hesitatingly. Until finally, on the verge of dehydration, Sayonara decided that it was enough. I am myself and my tears, she was able to recognize for the first time since she was born, and she stopped crying.

Over the nocturnal fields wandered large and imprecise beasts that exhaled warm breaths, and the waters of the river became polished and compact: a mass of darkness that invited one to walk upon it. From where did such an enormous flow of living waters come? From where so much liquid running through its bed? Rain, sap, milk, blood, snow, sweat, and tears, the Magdalena was fed by the effluvia of nature and the moods of men.

Although the night prevented her from seeing the dead bodies carried along by the current, Sayonara felt them pass, inoffensive in their slow, white transit. They flowed past one by one, embraced as a couple, or sometimes in a chain, holding hands, transformed into foam, porous material that floated, peaceful, pale, finally impregnated with moonlight after having spilled onto the shore, so long ago now, all the uneasiness and pain in their blood. Sayonara, the girl of good-byes, placed her feet in the water to be near them and contained her panic as they brushed her ankles in passing, got tangled in her legs with the viscosity of algae, and sent her messages in their peculiar language, which was a gurgle of organic substance disintegrating in shadows. Later, when the moon hid and the sky was bursting with stars, she didn't want to leave the river or remove her feet from the water because she knew that the silent pilgrimage also carried with it her loved ones, her burned mother, sweet Claire, her beloved brother, flowing down the Magdalena purified at last and converted into gentle memories, after so many years of suffering and making her suffer, stalking her like ghosts.

"That's why they don't let themselves be buried," Sayonara finally understood. "That's why they look for the river, because underground, alone and quiet, they die, while in the current they travel, they can look at the sky all they want and visit the living . . ."

She also knew: I am myself and my dead, and she felt less alone, as if the millions of steps between herself and them had evaporated.

Todos los Santos tells me that only at dawn the next day, a Saturday and the day of the fiesta of San Onofre, did Sayonara return to the house with the four girls and their belongings, and that as soon as she saw her adopted daughter enter, with the shredded dress, her hair wild and her eyes ravaged from all the crying, she realized that it was true: Something serious had happened to her. Something serious and definitive.

"I didn't dare ask her," the old woman says to me, "because she had already lost the habit of answering me. I would say things to her a dozen times without receiving an answer, as if she were deaf by her own will, or as if answering would exhaust her tongue."

She took Juana and Ana aside and interrogated them in a severe tone, commanding them to tell her whether someone, or something, had hurt her, but the two girls swore that no, they hadn't seen any attack or accident.

"I served her breakfast, waiting for the words to come on their own, but they didn't come. I saw her bitten by lost love and marked by loneliness, everything in her weariness and injury like in a draft mule. Then I decided to ask her, committing all my understanding to interpreting her response, and I was surprised that her voice came easily, without my having to beg, and sweet again, as it had sounded once when she was a child:

"'Life hurts a little, *madre.*'"

Todos los Santos felt that Sayonara was serene—wounded and mistreated, but serene, and like Moses, saved from the water: the victor over her own phantoms. That is how the *madrina* knew that during the night her adopted daughter had been doing the same thing that snakes do, when they rub against rough rocks to slip out of their old skin and exhibit a new one.

"Finally," Todos los Santos says to me, and a minuscule brilliance lights up her blind eyes, "when I thought that nothing would change, Sayonara left behind the slippery and self-absorbed skin of her adolescence."

thirty-seven

 "I put her in that life, and it's only right that I separate her from it" was the credo that Sacramento imposed on himself as a mandate, and he was a faithful crusader, willing to do anything to see his cause triumph. Now, in addition, he had a powerful ally in his quest to save the woman he adored, because the Tropical Oil Company had made the profitable, corporate decision to redeem all the *prostitutas* in the area.

The exchange of salary for love opened the door to immoderation and irrationality: desire, which burns, also consumes wealth and doesn't leave anything in return, except renewed desires. And neither the company, nor progress, nor order could find a way to derive benefit from that vicious circle, or at least that was the explanation of the problem according to the enveloping syllogism of don Horacio Laguna, with whom I am having a conversation at the old-fashioned café El Diamante.

"Capitalism can't grow healthily like that," he tells me, "and that's why the gringos who managed the company declared themselves the enemies of promiscuity, at least of ours, the Colombians'."

Although they offered houses, education for their children, health subsidies, and even access to a commissary where they sold meat below the prices in the plaza, the majority of the workers refused to jump through that hoop, as a matter of principle and due to ancestral fondness for the vice of sweet love. But not Sacramento, who saw the new policy as his key to the future.

While brigades of Franciscans of uncertain Mediterranean accent, wrapped in rough brown robes, looking as if they had escaped the Middle Ages, landed in Tora to minister courses in premarital preparations, other brigades, also wearing hoods, except over their faces, ran through the streets harassing the populace and punishing *a posteriori* its "friendship with the strike's bandits." One afternoon when Sayonara was returning from the port of Madre de Dios, where she had traveled for three days to entertain outside clients, she suddenly had a bad feeling that made her hasten her steps. She reached the house gasping to find an opaque look of sterile fury on the faces of Todos los Santos and Susana, who sat immobile on the sidewalk next to the front door, displaying the humiliating desolation of their recently shaved heads. Together with seven other women from La Catunga, they had been forcefully and cruelly sheared, with ugly scratches on their skulls and loose strands of hair here and there that had escaped the ravages of the shears.

"They told us they were shaving us so we would learn. They didn't do anything to Juana and Chuza because they weren't here when the hooded men invaded," Susana told her, and Sayonara couldn't speak a word because a knot of indignation choked her.

"And Ana?" she was finally able to ask, not having seen her sister.

"She still has all her hair, but she's not here. Yesterday she went away with some soldiers that wanted to see her dance."

"My poor sister! This life surrounded by *putas* has thrown her to the dogs!" wailed Sayonara, out of her mind and throwing herself upon Todos los Santos in attack, but the others pulled her away, reminding her that you don't touch your mother even with a rose petal, so she started smashing her knuckles against the walls and kicking the doors. "My poor sister, broken and raped, all because of me and this life of *putas* where I brought her. The bastards took her away!"

"They didn't take her away; she went of her own free will."

"Lies! How can you say that, *madrina*, on top of everything else and as if it were nothing?!"

"Just yesterday we went to find her at the temporary camp that del Valle set up in Loma de Tigres, because we had been told they were keeping her there. We organized more than twenty to go demand her return, her and four other girls from the barrio, but when Ana came out herself, and we all heard her words, she told us she wanted to stay. It did no good to beg her, or threaten her, or reason with her. She said she didn't want to come back, and she didn't."

A painful and prolonged sound escaped from Sayonara's mouth, more the howl of an animal than a human cry. The loss of Payanés had carried her toward a high, severe pain, you might even say almost elegant if you take into account that the absence of love creates an intensity comparable only to that of its presence. The sadness that invaded her now had, however, a muddy and base nature, and it was nothing like the lofty penitence of golden needles of the earlier one. But added together, the one sublime and the other despicable, they pushed her to the limit of her own hope, where she discovered that something had died in her, which made her think vaguely of a punishment from God which must be accepted. It was then that Sacramento appeared with the plans for the future workers' barrio in his hand and the signed promise of a house in his pocket. He proposed marriage in a church, offered to take her and her sisters out of La Catunga and to give them a more dignified and secure life, and Sayonara, without thinking twice, said yes.

"I would say she didn't even think once," muses Olga, "but it was to be expected, because it is well known that Sayonara's fate is guided by a racing star with a capricious course."

"Are you going to live in a house that comes from the same people who vilify you?" Todos los Santos asked her, indignant and incredulous, as her hand, operating on its own, went over her stripped skull as if taking stock of the damage.

"Even if it were the devil himself, as long as I can get out of here," replied Sayonara. And just then an insipid, misty rain began falling from the sky, but not completely covering the sun, and a faint rainbow was cast across the river, like the flimsiest of bridges.

"San Isidro, patron of celestial phenomena," Olga tells me she prayed at that moment, "protect this child from the attack of her whims, which drive her from place to place without her being able to master them . . . ?"

"My girl was sick from hoping too much," Todos los Santos explains to me, demonstrating a tolerance today that it seems she didn't at the time. "I kept telling her that you can't expect so many things, because life isn't one of the Magi who will come bearing gifts."

"What was your name before you came to Tora?" Sacramento asked his bride-to-be later. "That's what I want to call you, your real name, the regular one, and that's the one I have to give the priest who is going to marry us."

"I don't think you'll like it . . ."

"Tomasa? Herminia? Eduviges? Come on, don't be afraid, tell me, any name will do; it doesn't matter if it's ugly."

"My name was Amanda."

"Amanda!" Sacramento was shocked. "But that's a name for a *puta* too . . ."

"To you it would seem like a name for a *puta* even if my name were Santa Teresa de Jesús, *hermanito*."

"Hush, don't tell me anything else. Everything I discover about you is a new dagger that I have to carry around stuck into my body."

"If we're going to go on like this, you'll be more wounded than the Virgen Dolorosa, who had to bear seven daggers, all in her heart."

"Her name is Sayonara, understand?" exploded Todos los Santos, coming out of her room, where she had sought refuge, "and you are no-body to come around and take away her name."

"No, *madrina*, my name isn't Sayonara. I have a name just like every-body else, the one my mother and father gave me when I was baptized, and today I am going to quit being a *puta* for the good of my sisters and because I want to go back to using my real name. Even if it hurts, *madrina*, my name is Amanda Monteverde."

"Amanda Monteverde," repeated Todos los Santos, as if surrendering, and in the instant that she spoke those two words an abyss opened between her and her adopted daughter.

"It's not bad blood, Olga. Or at least it's not all bad blood. There's something wrong here, something outside of the law, and it's going to have an ugly backlash," said Todos los Santos when Olguita pointed out that it took deep bitterness not to congratulate a daughter on the day of her wedding. "But if marriages for love are bad enough themselves, what can we expect from one contracted out of disenchantment? That Sacramento is going to pay for this, the meddling nincompoop."

"Can't you forgive the desire for happiness of a boy who has never had anything in his life, not a mother, or a roof, or affection, or even a name that isn't an offense?"

"Sacramento himself is the one who is going to suffer on account of this bad idea, you'll see. And he's going to make us all suffer, because with this marriage he is opening a door that leads to who knows where."

"Stop being so proud, Todos los Santos. The problem is that you raised Sayonara to be a *puta* and you can't bear the fact that she's decided to be something else."

"Something is wrong, Olga; I know it even if I can't put my finger on it."

What dress was the bride going to wear for the improvised ceremony? The yellow organza number, speculated those who were betting on the matter, but they didn't know she had torn it apart and sworn on the shreds that she was no longer a child. So?

"So it was her combat attire, what else?" Olga says to me. "Gold earrings, tight black tube skirt, and pure silk blouse: like a Chinese princess. Or, rather, Japanese."

As was to be expected, the priest didn't approve of the outfit: Being the first time in years that he had let a lost woman enter the church, he wanted the ceremony to be instructive, so he sent for a lace veil, long and white, and he asked her to cover herself with it. And so, as they still tell the story in Tora, the very beautiful Sayonara, from that day on better known as Amanda, was married: dressed as a *puta* underneath and in white on the outside.

Very beautiful, yes, but it was a somewhat literary and unreal beauty, like a classic heroine. Her sisters, friends, and coworkers in La Catunga preferred not to enter Ecce Homo, as it had long since been declared off-limits to them, and they waited for the bridal couple outside the church's front door with their hearts flooded with ambivalent emotions, somewhere between hopefulness and disenchantment. Todos los Santos, with her eyes sunk deep in mourning-black sockets, was wearing a baseball cap to hide her recently inflicted baldness. Tana was visibly and deeply moved and glittered with jewelry. The girls in organza, of course, as with any big occasion. And Olga in dark glasses to hide her emotions and the swelling caused by her tears. Machuca was absent because even bound and gagged she couldn't be dragged to the church.

"Life is a failure," sighed Tana, who was prone to speak in tango lyrics.

"It can only be lived," Todos los Santos corrected her. "There are no successes or failures; it can only be lived."

"Sayonara is leaving us," said Tana, who never learned, starting to weep again.

"She was never completely here."

Finally the bridal couple emerged, their union blessed, but no one threw rice, there were no bells ringing or firecrackers exploding. Instead, in the middle of that dull, colorless afternoon, Piruetas suddenly appeared, wearing a queer's little cap, a bright-red handkerchief around his neck, and a tropical shirt featuring blue palm trees on an orange background, and as Sayonara was removing the veil to return it to the priest, he caressed her with his eyes from head to toe with the slimy, lubricious gaze of a randy old man.

"Even if the *puta* wears white, she's still a *puta*!" Piruetas shouted, and kept on walking, leaving everyone stunned and disgusted in the cold wake of his shadow.

"We're leaving Tora," said a pale Sacramento, and trembling with rage over the affront, he tore up the contract for subsidized housing and threw the pieces into the air. And right there, outside the church door, he made the impromptu decision to leave and communicated it to his wife and the sparse crowd.

"To go where?" asked Sayonara.

"Where nobody knows you or can throw your past in our faces."

"What about the house, Sacramento? The house they were going to give us?"

"The only house waiting for us here is shame."

"To their wives, who demand a lot, men give little. And to us *putas*, who ask for nothing, they give us nothing," grumbles Fideo from her hammock sickbed, waking and immediately falling asleep again.

thirty-eight

 For a few days now Todos los Santos, who has begun the move toward the great dazzling hereafter, smoking-cigar and all, with foxtails around her neck and pink fur slippers, has begun calling not only her numerous and varied animals Felipe, but also the people around her.

"Come here, you, Felipe," she orders me, "and listen to what I am going to tell you about my girl Sayonara's wanderings: When taking the balance of how we have lived, measuring the sum of our days honestly, the rest of us always opt to remain, clinging to the crumbs of our survival; while she was the only one who could really leave, without fear, without a guaranteed return, in the full glory of her blossoming and vigorous life. And in a horrendous display of egotism, and hardness toward others too."

I ask Todos los Santos how many times, honoring her own name, Sayonara said good-bye.

"You can't just count the times she left," she replies, "but also the times she wanted to leave, which were innumerable."

<h1 style="text-align:center">thirty-nine</h1>

 "Ay, Payanés, when did you become my nightmare . . . ?" Everything about Sayonara was turning into pain: the pain of Payanés, whom she loved and didn't have, the pain of Sacramento, whom she loved and didn't love, and the pain of being herself.

"Remember when they pretended to be the traveling brother and sister, and it brought such happiness to the days of Sacramento's and Sayonara's childhood?" Olguita asks me. "Well, it became their reality. After the wedding they had no choice but to pack their belongings and start traveling, this time for real but also to escape, like they did when they were children, to that country without memories, which is the land of nevermore."

The continuous passing of migrating birds was their only guide during those months of flight stitched together in one postponement after another of any arrival, heading south amidst hardships that found them each day farther away, following the brown heron and the spoonbilled duck, the *paco-paco*, the white heron and the ruffled grouse, and so many other creatures that fled through the air and whose names they never knew. They became inhabitants of the road and they followed the whims of its turns and cutbacks without stopping to rest, one behind the other and the other behind one as if they were still following each other on make-believe horses around Todos los Santos's patio, fed by the urge to leave and without reaching a decision to stay anywhere. And so, aboard that escape train, their days unraveled.

Rescued by Sacramento's love through the bonds of marriage did Sayonara, the young whore from Tora, become Amanda, the one who was to be loved, Amanda, the *radionovela* star? Did she embody the miracle of the outlaw who becomes good through a little affection, the flower rescued from the dirt, the protagonist of the nightmare that became a dream and the dream that became reality?

"Useless words!" exclaims Todos los Santos indignantly. "Can anyone call days that were filled with bewilderment happy? Days that drove my child Sayonara, the same girl who was always dreaming of love, to seek joy trailing behind a man, and if that weren't error enough, behind a man she didn't love? I would also have to say: days of hardship, separated only by the arid string of good-byes and the passing one by one of countless hours of anguish."

Life is inclined to encourage with promises and to dazzle with magic tricks, but no, it didn't grant a miracle or the life of a *radionovela*, because from the very day of the wedding the mask of mirrors was removed to uncover something resembling a face. Forcing Sayonara to embark on an uncertain journey, made of confused love and shattered dreams, which left her no other choice but to dull herself with exhaustion on the long marches so that she wouldn't have to recognize that she couldn't recognize herself. Or that she could only find half of herself in the skin of that new woman who wanted to be called Amanda, while her other half missed having a place in this world. And it wasn't that Amanda didn't do everything possible, that she didn't struggle to pull Sayonara from the tangle that confused her steps. The same obstinate determination that Sayonara had invested in becoming a prostitute, Amanda now dedicated to the task of turning herself into a lady, because her life was, today as yesterday, one long, courageous search for existence, and if one door closed, she found the strength to go through another, even if it opened at the totally opposite end of the hallway.

"No one can invoke the hackneyed 'it has been written' in the name of my girl, that credo of fatalists of every sort," says Todos los Santos, "because she liked to do whatever she wanted."

For Amanda there were no writings that dictated her fate, holy or profane. But to reach past her own star and to transform herself was a difficult task in which Sayonara wouldn't help her because she refused to step aside, obstinately holding on to existence and fueled by the ferocious torrent of a will to live and a longing for death that had been awakened in her on that afternoon of love by the river. Nothing could dissuade her, not Payanés with the meager surrender of his affections, nor Sacramento with his excessively vehement demands for devotion, nor even Amanda herself in her rush to find roads less steep.

"Where does the soul of a woman go who loves one man and marries another?" Olga wonders out loud. "In my opinion it is divided in two, and both become lost in the waters of confusion."

"There weren't two, but three women in her," argues Todos los Santos, "Amanda, Sayonara, and she herself. Sayonara loved Payanés; Amanda married Sacramento; and she loved only herself."

"Sayonara complained that no man loved her well," Dr. Antonio María Flórez once told me, "but it was really the other way around, as I saw it. She could never bring herself to fully love anyone. That girl reminds me of a paradoxical poem by the master Pedro Salinas. 'Why the rush to make yourself possible, if you know that you are what will never be?'"

Todos los Santos asks me to read her what I am writing and I do.

"Too many words," she protests. "The life of a *puta* will always be identical to the life of any other *puta*, even if it is the life of a woman with showy plumage, like Sayonara. In matters of men, we *mujeres* of the profession can only choose three categories. Only three because no others have been invented. Those we call the tormentor, the lottery, and the client, the latter of which is the most advisable and the one I recommend, because he pays you and goes away, letting you get on with your life; you can keep on playing if-I-have-seen-you-before-I-don't-remember. The other two stripes, the lottery and the tormentor, are both pure trouble and sorrow."

"The lottery is the shining knight who finally comes to you," says Olguita. "He's the lover every woman waits for, convinced that one day he will come to take you away and marry you and sweeten your life with conveniences, eternal love, flattery, and gifts. With Sacramento, Sayonara got her lottery, or at least that's what she thought."

"Lottery, grand prize or golden cage, which are its other names," says Todos los Santos, "because it strangles with the finest noose, made of love, and presses against your neck like a pearl choker, or like the amulet of braided hair that Sacramento once tied around his neck and still wears. Did Amanda choose to compromise in marrying him? That's her business. We all warned her not to do it but she, of her own free will, locked herself in that tower and threw the key into the moat."

"And the tormentor," continues Olga, "is the man who makes you suffer because he makes you fall in love with him but he won't commit, or he commits only partially, like Payanés, who was just like the thorny rose he had had tattooed over his heart: a rose of pain and a compass rose, pointing in all directions. Payanés, like any self-respecting *petrolero*, gave you two gifts, the open road and the pain of freedom. And, if there's anything a woman of the profession knows about, it's freedom, but she also knows how much it rends the heart. A lover who promises you affection the last Friday of every month and complies religiously is something worth celebrating. As long as you don't resent that in addition to the comforting Friday, God has created three others, plus four Mondays, four Tuesdays, four Wednesdays, and a lot of et ceteras for a grand total of three hundred sixty-five days in a year during which you have to deal with the ups and downs of your lonely heart."

Torn between Sacramento and Payanés, her greatest prize and her greatest punishment, what happened, asked Olga, to Amanda's broken heart? Was it destroyed by her inability to choose? What is most likely, perhaps most certain, is that she harbored the suspicion that well-being, if it existed at all, must be hidden somewhere between those two extremes.

Sacramento, Sayonara, and her three remaining sisters formed a rickety caravan that moved forward along the paths of displacement, and Sacramento, who had always put his love into what aroused the most suspicion in him, now turned the corner on his old torment and learned to doubt to the point of agony that which he truly loved. And at the same time, to finish tangling the skein, he insisted in distancing Amanda from Tora to save her from the assault of memories, without suspecting that memories, with their light feet, would arrive before them anywhere they went.

Behind the couple, like the colorful and fluttering tail of a kite, ran the three girls, Susana, Juana, and little Chuza, now going through periods of hunger, now filling up on pineapples or mangoes gathered from the fields they crossed, now desperately longing for their sister Ana, their mother, Todos los Santos, and their many aunts, only to forget them completely moments later, so attached to the idea of pursuing their fate beneath the immense sky, as yesterday they had been to taking shelter beneath a safe, familiar roof.

Nine days after embarking upon that crossing with neither shipwreck nor guiding star, they entered the misty forests in the mountains of Amansagatos, famous because no one has been able to determine whether the rain there is perpetual as it falls or rises, since it never reaches the ground before it is already ascending again, and evaporating. Once there they stopped near a stand of cedar, *guayacán, amargoso,* and other trees that thrive in humid environments, where Sacramento, on the recommendation of an acquaintance, obtained temporary work at a sawmill. On his first day of work, Amanda was stirred by a desire to properly fulfill her obligations as a new wife, and after the disgusting chore of plucking a chicken, she then inexpertly stewed it and ran downhill through sheets of rain and dense vegetation to take lunch to her husband, since she had heard that it is necessary for an honest woman to feed her husband well and without fail, because he provides protection and sustenance. When she appeared, as if on a stage in a theater, in the intense light that fell from above onto the cut clearing, Sacramento, upon seeing how beautiful she was and knowing that she was his, felt a sudden jolt of happiness flooding him inside, and a kind of foam like the head of a beer swelled his masculine pride.

"But I wasn't the only one who turned to look at her," he remembers uneasily, because in order for him to feel humiliated, his woman didn't need to cast her eyes on another man, it was enough for another man to cast his eyes on her.

What caused the bitter taste was Amanda's arrival, with all her radiant youth enveloped in white light, the lunch pot held in one hand, her soaked dress licking her body, and her wild tresses dripping wet, and all of the workers spread throughout the clearing stopped what they were doing, axes frozen, to pierce her with their eyes, like pins in a tailor's pincushion.

"It was always the same," Sacramento tells me in an anxious tone, as if begging me to understand him. "As soon as she would appear, no matter where it was and even though they didn't know her, men would begin to act strangely. They would straighten their backs, wipe their sweaty hands on their shirts, cough to bring attention to themselves. I don't know how else to describe it, but it was strange. As if they were communicating in code or in some secret male language the fact that she was there. That she, the beauty, was there bewitching them, even though she wasn't doing a thing, making them anxious, leaving their desire and memories scorched."

Sacramento grabbed her forcefully by the wrist, almost hurting her, and pulled her aside, shaken.

"How dare you come here like that, with your clothes wet, don't you see that you're leading them on, half naked like this?"

"But it's pouring rain, Sacramento, what do you want me to do? You're all wet too, *hermanito*, what's the matter . . . ?"

"Don't call me *hermanito*, I'm your husband. You want to know what's the matter? They already know, that's what's the matter . . . ," he said with a choked voice, as if relaying the worst of news.

"They already know what?"

"About your past."

"They don't know anything. What are you talking about? Nobody has said anything and we haven't even told them our names. It's you who are going to give us away, because you think about it so much that they're bound to hear your thoughts . . ."

"Well, if they don't know yet, they're going to guess from your brazen manners. Go home now," he ordered her, then he made her promise never again to appear in the clearing, not even to bring him food.

"Fine," she said, resigned, "but you're going to die from hunger down here, and I, from boredom up there."

"I prefer to die from hunger than to let them look at my wife like that. It's a matter of honor," he said to her, and it was the first time Sayonara had heard that word, "honor," which would eventually draw so many tears from her.

The next morning, Amanda and the girls stayed up on the patch of the mountain they had been allotted to scratch away the overgrowth and see if one day they would be able to reap a meager harvest; and meanwhile Sacramento went down the mountain to the sawmill to earn his daily wages. In the evening, stung by fleas and by resentment, he returned to their rented room, four walls of rough-hewn planks, exuding dampness and rootlessness.

"What did you do all day?" he asked his wife.

"I caught a *zaíno* and a lizard and roasted them so you would have some hot food."

"What happened, you didn't bring me any lunch?"

"But you told me . . ."

"All the men's wives brought them lunch, everyone's but mine, and I was so hungry. The other workers must have thought that I have a wife who has fun while her husband works and goes hungry . . ."

The dialogue was so ridiculous that Amanda burst out laughing, because she still laughed then, unaware of the scope of her melodrama, and Sacramento, in spite of his indignation, couldn't avoid laughing too at his own excess.

Then, already lying down, she allowed herself to be overcome with tenderness and gratitude toward him, as she watched him cover the cracks between the planks with clay so that the girls, who were sleeping, wouldn't be troubled in the night by the wisps of mist or cries of night birds. For a moment, as the Coleman lantern buzzed cozily, Sayonara enjoyed feeling that fear remained outside and the girls were floating peacefully along in their dreams. And calming the obsessive, burning memory of Payanés, she let herself be soothed by the idea that like this, like now, she was okay, and that it was comforting and pleasing to have a husband.

"*Hermanito,*" she sighed, and fell asleep contentedly.

Sacramento lay by her side and just looked at her for a long time. "Your face is so pretty," he kept saying to her, but around midnight he still couldn't calm or contain himself or refrain from awakening her.

"You weren't having fun, were you?" he asked her.

"When?"

"Today, at lunchtime."

"In this dead place? How do you think I could have fun in this dead place?"

"With other men . . ."

"No, Sacramento, I spent the day hoeing with the girls, and we didn't have any fun."

"Did you think about him very often? Do you miss him?"

"Payanés? I try to forget him, Sacramento, but you keep reminding me about him." Sayonara turned her back to him, covered her face with her arms, and pretended to cry to see if she could escape his renewed attacks of jealousy. And when Sacramento saw that olive-skinned back, reflecting the warm glow of the Coleman lantern, he began to kiss her shoulders as he asked for forgiveness. "That roasted lizard you cooked for me was very good and I'm a thankless husband," he rattled on. "Forgive me, *mi vida*, how could I have mistrusted you," his voice becoming gradually more unsettled until it turned into reproach again. "No jealousy or anger, because I forgive you for the step that you took. Such a dark fate, such an ungrateful road. Such false promises. The wounds of ungrateful love, weaving through the familiar empty words spoken out of sheer spite, until they turn into insults. You go from hand to hand, everyone is talking about you. Your lips deceive me, lying, betraying . . ."

"Enough, Sacramento! Hush now, you're going to frighten my sisters. Stop all this silliness, I want to go back to sleep."

Then he embraced her trembling with love and misgivings, and she let herself be embraced, but the dream of that other embrace came to her forcefully and she couldn't help that it hurt to rest her head against the chest that wasn't her beloved's.

"Like animals that want to bolt and go back to the stable," Olguita says to me, "that is how a woman in love thinks: always struggling to escape from everything else to be able to return to the memory of her beloved, the only place where she can find comfort and rest."

I want to ascertain Sacramento's feelings in those days toward Payanés, and I ask him if he thought too often of his friend.

"I couldn't forgive his betrayal," Sacramento confesses. "But at the same time I couldn't forgive her for having separated me from my best friend, and I blamed her for our misfortune. Today I regret hurting her with the accusation, but at the time I let myself get carried away with a question that had no answer, whose fault was it, hers, his, or perhaps mine; or was it life's?"

For Sacramento, who fluctuated between seething with jealousy and mourning his lost friendship, Payanés didn't just pursue him in his thoughts, he also laid traps in the physical world.

"I thought I saw Payanés everywhere," he says. "He was crouching behind every tree until I might let down my guard so he could go to her. And those eyes of his, yellow streaked with green, which you don't see in these parts, but I saw them in the faces of all the men who looked at her. And at the same time, how I missed his presence as a brother from those days of sharing bread, pick, shovel, and even shoes, knowing that my luck would be his too, sharing together the rocks in the road or the coins of our daily pay! But I couldn't forgive him for having tried to take her away from me and I wondered if despite the marriage he hadn't taken her from me anyway."

That night rife with bird calls, after hours of filling his lungs with her breath and feeling its sweetness when he inhaled it and its poison when he exhaled it, Sacramento got up, prepared some strong coffee on the little stove, and sobbed dejectedly over the steaming cup. As dawn broke, Amanda and the girls were surprised to find their belongings gathered up and the pair of suitcases packed and knotted with rope.

"We're leaving," announced Sacramento. "We need to go further, to where the shadow of your bad reputation doesn't reach. And I'm warning you now, so that we don't fall into the same quagmire again: I don't want you going around like a wild filly. No bare feet or hair blowing in the wind."

Sayonara listened distractedly as she softly sang the profane verses with which the barefoot missionary women taught her mother her first words in the white man's language:

> I wonder at this ruffling,
> The wind in my tresses fair.
> Perhaps consumed with love,
> It sings and celebrates my hair.

Couplets that her mother sang to her when she was young? Or that she never sang being what she was, an Indian, a Guahiba, shy about singing and lazy about speaking Spanish.

"Don't sing that anymore," Sacramento scolded her, jealous of everything, and now even the wind. "You must try to not be so obvious; don't show your true colors so they won't notice you."

"Fine," she said, resigned, still not suspecting how deep she could tumble down that path toward total renunciation. "I'm going to buy a real pretty clasp, or maybe some nice ribbon, and if you want I'll tie my hair back so no one will see it."

"It would be better if you just cut it off . . . ," he grumbled, and she, ignoring him, started singing the verses again.

"Sacramento had always been, by natural inclination, a soul given to extravagant behavior," Todos los Santos tells me confidentially, as if I didn't already know. "But the insecurities of that troubled love drove him even further and set him on a path of obsession tending toward cruelty, and the more he suffered, the more he tortured."

Everything he adored in Amanda, everything that bewitched him about her, was also a target for his scorn.

He wanted to tear out that particle of lunar material encrusted in Amanda's forehead, which had accidentally landed between her eyebrows and radiated like a talisman, like a prearranged signal or a soft, wordless revelation, and made her an object of passion for men. Sacramento needed to extirpate it, whatever it was—malign tumor, philosopher's stone, or golden nugget—because the hypnotic power of that woman, who was public before but now, according to words sworn at the altar, had become completely his, was concentrated in that tiny meteorite and not so much in charm or beauty, intelligence or carnal attributes, to say nothing of the gift of seduction, because the bare truth was that Amanda, or Sayonara, had no other gift as appealing as that special way of hers of seducing by not seducing.

Don't wear earrings anymore, they're too suggestive, ordered Sacramento, and she obeyed in order not to hurt him, but the secret wasn't in the earrings. Don't walk like that, it's provocative, but the truth was that she walked with the same rhythmic cadence as any woman from the tropics. Don't be so haughty when you answer, because your rebelliousness ignites desires, and she tried to please him but she still ignited them even when she was silent. Don't laugh, because your laughter is an invitation, but she invited when she was serious as much as she did when she was laughing. Don't look men straight in the eyes, because you challenge them with your gaze, but even when she kept her eyes on the ground no one failed to notice the stone, or the patina, or the gift, or whatever it was: that glimmer of moon and silence, of shadow and awe, with which she cast her spell.

"Don't try to take that from her, it's not her fault, she was born that way, lustrous," Todos los Santos had uselessly warned Sacramento.

Seven months after the wedding, Machuca chanced upon the married couple in Villa de la Virgen del Amparo, a stately city of rigorous architecture and rigidly moral people that since the eighteenth century had had its own coat of arms, a royal warrant from His Majesty Carlos III, and a cathedral with authentic lepers in its entryway.

Machuca the heretic, who had been born—and who would have thought it?—in this hallowed place, had returned to her homeland for a couple of days to renew her identification documents in order to be able to vote in the coming elections, and she tells me of her surprise upon spotting Sacramento, who had gone back to his initial profession of being a cart man and was busy running errands around the market plaza. Machuca hugged him effusively and asked about Sayonara, and he greeted her formally, distantly. He confessed that in order to supplement the family income, Amanda had taken a position as a domestic servant in the home of one of the most traditional families in Villa de la Virgen del Amparo.

"They hadn't helped themselves with the money that Sayonara had accumulated in Tora working on her back, because how was Sacramento going to endure such a blow to his pride," Olguita tells me. "He told her that it was dirty money, wrongly earned, that he was no pimp or kept man and he preferred to die of starvation than to have to touch it."

"That was a relief," says Machuca. "At least the girl didn't sacrifice her savings struggling to save that deformed marriage, which was all screwed up from the start."

"But I am going to ask you a big favor, señora Machuca," she tells me Sacramento explained to her with elaborate circumlocutions, "which

is that you don't approach Amanda too much, and please don't be offended by my asking this, because I have nothing but respect for you,
but as you well know customs are not the same everywhere, and it so
happens that the people who hired Amanda are very high-class and
scrupulous, and if they come to suspect, of course I say this to you with
no desire to injure you, as I have been explaining, if these people come
to suspect what Amanda's prior economic activity was, they would
surely kick her out, and again I beg you to forgive my impertinence and
the abuse of confidence; I'm sure you can understand."

In spite of Sacramento's warnings, Machuca made her own inquiries
about Sayonara's exact whereabouts, and wrapping herself up in a
threadbare shawl to hide her unmistakable appearance as an old *prostituta*, she knocked at the door of the house, passing herself off as a beg-
gar seeking a crust of bread. The door was opened by a very skinny,
taciturn young woman, sheathed in an austere blue dress, like a novice's,
her hair hidden beneath a handkerchief tied around her head, whom
Machuca didn't recognize at first as Sayonara.

"Come back at noon, that is when we distribute soup to those in
need," she was told by the blue shadow that had been Sayonara the magnificent, and who stepped back in alarm when the indigent woman in the
threadbare shawl grabbed her hands.

"Is that you, Machuca?" she asked, suddenly recognizing her friend.

"He goes down to the river every Friday, to look for a certain girl . . .
I only came to tell you that."

"Payanés?" Amanda dared to ask, lowering her voice as if she were
speaking a sacrilege.

"There are those who swear they have seen him even on Wednesdays, and on Saturdays. Alone, throwing stones in the river, wearing
cologne, dressed entirely in white, with all of his pay in his pocket, waiting, always waiting."

"They say that?"

"They say that."

"Tell me who he is waiting for . . ."

"You know very well . . ."

"Tell me . . ."

"For a girl, who, before she left him for someone else, was called Sayonara. It is said that he who waits loses hope, but that's not the case with him. His seems to be a hope goaded on week after week by an infinite patience. Every time they tell him you got married in a church, wearing a white veil, he says the commitment you have with him is before and above any other."

Fearing the displeasure of the lady of the house, who was wary of strangers and suspicious of any words whispered behind her back, Amanda hurriedly said good-bye to Machuca, acting as if she hadn't listened to her. But she had. She gathered up her confidence, folded it over twice with great tenderness as if it were a fine linen handkerchief, carefully put it away hidden against her heart, clinging to it to stay alive during those times of transit through the lands of nothingness.

"Where are you, Payanés, who is kissing you . . . ? If not me, who is embracing you . . . ?" She gave in to a sighing that was half killing her, half reviving her. "Don't force me to bear so much unfulfilled desire gnawing at my heart . . ."

I have in my hand a small testament of what happened in those days of languishing sadness. It is a note hastily written in pencil by Machuca to Todos los Santos, three or four days after her encounter with Sayonara. Months afterward, they would make peace and everything would go back to the way it had been before, but due to some yes-it-is-no-it-isn't, the friendship between Machuca and Todos los Santos had frayed during the period following the strike, marked in all of La Catunga by reticence, arguments, and strained nerves. So, even though they had stopped speaking, Machuca wanted to alert her old friend about Sayonara, whom she had seen surrendered to an unhealthy resignation. After a formal salutation, she wrote: "Several days ago I chanced upon your adopted daughter, who, as you may know through news from other sources, resides with her husband in Villa de la Virgen del Amparo, in this same *departamento* of Santander. I found her in good health and free of material contingencies, but I regret to inform you, *comadre*, that something must be done, because there is nearly nothing left of our girl's former happiness." Underneath, in black ink and in Todos los Santos's handwriting, appears a kind of reply, jotted down after she'd read the letter, and directed at no one in particular: "Nothing can be done. We must simply wait until life, which once brought her here, brings her back again."

forty

We are going through strange days, with little talk and even less understanding, due to the bad taste provoked in Sacramento and the old ladies by the constant recollection of events subsequent to the wedding. My questions have stirred up bitter memories and now I can't find a way to penetrate the wells of silence inside of which Sacramento drowns in feelings of guilt, Olguita in tears, and Todos los Santos in recriminations. And as if that weren't enough, winter, or glass weather, as the fishermen on the Magdalena call it, has made the temperature drop in Tora by a few degrees, and the arrival of the cold—in reality a slight diminishment of the heat—has brought with it another inconvenience, Todos los Santos's lack of bladder control, which causes her to become soaked every now and then by the lukewarm moisture of her own urine. Too proud to let anyone know what has happened, she keeps rocking as usual in her chair on the patio, feeding her animals, or napping in her bed.

"Come on, mother. We're going to change our clothes, because we've had another accident," Sacramento says to her, delicately using the plural conjugations of the verbs and helping her to get up.

"You too, son?" she asks. "Has this foul weather weakened your kidneys too?"

We couldn't drive away the cold from her with the hot water bottle or the foxtails that she makes us wrap around her throat, or the famous pink rabbit-skin slippers that she keeps on her feet night and day.

"Be still, there's nothing to do," she tells us, swatting away our attempts to care for her. "Let's just wait for winter to go away and take the intemperance with it, and meanwhile we'll swim in urine. Nothing else can be done."

However, I think we have discovered a more or less effective way, if not of curing this small catastrophe, of at least anticipating it. Todos los Santos, taciturn and withdrawn, has begun every now and then to break the long silences that overwhelm our conversations with an explosive cascade of words which are sometimes scolding, sometimes advice or warning, but are most often simply nostalgic digression. The content varies, but the form, always torrential, alerts us, because her urinary incontinence, by some curious anatomical symbiosis, is usually preceded by verbal incontinence. In these circumstances she mentioned for the first time the episode that she refers to as the elephant. When the thing with the elephant happened . . . and she's off and running.

"Seen from above, all human life seems like a tangle of whims, becauses and for-no-reasons, and only by intense scrutiny and through searching for its meaning over the long term do you begin to find a pattern. Even those who are most caught up in the foolishness are clear about their motives for doing what they do, and there is no chance occurrence that isn't, in and of itself, a known result," she began saying a little while ago, as the rest of us rushed to place a basin under her skirts. "Forget about the basin and grab your notebook so you can write," she ordered me, "because today I feel the need to talk."

"Keep talking," I say, "keep talking, I'm recording it in my memory. What were you saying about motives?"

"At night, we old people go to bed not to sleep, but to brood and ponder, and this morning, almost as the alarm began to ring, I realized clearly why Sayonara had married. She was trying to recover her name."

"What are you saying?"

"The name that you carry is the sign of the life you have lived, and if you want to change your life, you must begin by changing your name. Sayonara had to go back to being Amanda to be able to make her visit . . .'"

"What visit? To whom?"

"To her father, who was still alive, and even today the news of his demise hasn't reached us here. You cannot go before your father saying that you have buried the family name that he has conferred on you and that you also changed your baptismal name for another that sounded prettier. That is in poor taste. Amanda must have imagined, speculating about the eventuality, that when she saw her father again and he asked her: 'What have you done with your life, daughter?' she would be able to look him in the eyes and say to him, without lying too much: 'I got married, Father; I am a married woman who has fulfilled her duty to take care of her sisters and teach them by good example.' However, being Sayonara, she would have cast her eyes on the ground, ashamed, silent, in such a way that her father would become suspicious."

"Around here few adversities are as feared as parental rage," interposes Sacramento, "and much is done to prevent it. Or to pacify it, if it has already been unleashed."

"So how did Sayonara know where to look for her father?" I ask them.

"She had been making inquiries for some time," replies Sacramento, "and she knew exactly where he was."

Her source of information was a gentleman named Alfredo Molano, a wanderer by profession and very up-to-date on news about rambling and ramblers, who was known to have brought the news that Abelardo Monteverde, her father, was working as a merchant selling a variety of goods in the town of Sasaima, that he was still married to the same white woman, had educated her children, who were now grown, and was raising the new brood of little ones that they had had together. With that information in hand, Amanda took it into her head to go and find him.

"So what did that man do for you, apart from abandoning you, for you to be going to thank him?" Sacramento said to try to dissuade her.

"He gave me my being," she answered, just like that; five dry, withering words that may not have meant much, but that didn't offer any room for argument.

"He is going to leave Sasaima," she said. "I have a feeling, if I don't go now to look for him, I won't find him."

"All the more reason. I don't know what your hurry is to go digging up sorrows."

Nothing could be done. Sayonara was burning with an urgency that didn't allow delays, an itch that made her stand up when she sat down; it woke her up if she lay down, tightened her throat and suffocated her appetite.

"She understood it as a mandate," Olguita tells me, "or a mission she had to accomplish. She thought she should go to look for her father, as if her fate were demanding it."

"Shoo, Felipe!" Todos los Santos drives away one of the Felipes, in this particular instance a quadruped with black fur, similar to a small pig, who is trying to eat her slipper.

"What did Amanda expect from her father?" I want to know.

"We all yearn for paternal approval," responds Todos los Santos. "Even the worst sinners are afraid of living without it. Why? Because it's human nature, and also her nature, Sayonara's. She needed to know that her father didn't condemn her for what she had done. If you ask me, I would say that was precisely why she stopped doing it."

"What did Amanda expect from her father?" Sacramento echoes my question. "That's exactly what her father wanted to know, as soon as he saw her."

About to board a bus, because just at that moment he was hurrying to depart for Venezuela, don Abelardo Monteverde rubbed his eyes incredulously when he recognized his daughter Amanda—a ghost the past had vomited up without asking permission or giving warning—standing on a corner of the market plaza in Sasaima, her hair and the dark blue suit that she wore then, like a novice's, soaking wet, and hidden behind her, also very wet and biting their nails with shyness and fear, were the three younger sisters, in organza and crinolines. Wiping from his forehead the copious sweat caused by such an unforeseen and embarrassing situation, don Abelardo didn't ask what had happened to Ana, he didn't know which was which, he didn't inquire where they had come from, how they had survived in the intervening years, or even where they were going. Nor did he ask if they were hungry, or why their clothes were wet, and he never learned that they had traveled two days by bus, enduring stops and searches from first the army, then the *guerrilleros*, and then seven and a half hours by foot, along rugged paths and in the rain, to find him.

"You've found me at a bad moment, daughter," he said to Amanda, addressing her because she was the eldest. "I don't have any cash in my pocket and I'm about to leave on a trip. What do you need?"

"I only want your blessing, señor *padre*, for me and for my sisters."

"That's all?"

"*Sí*, señor *padre*, that's all."

"Well, that being the case, there's no problem," said don Abelardo Monteverde, with his shirt open across a chest that was sparsely covered with hair and an enormous belly hanging over his tightly cinched waist, and he raised a fat right hand to bestow his blessing upon them.

"May God protect you," he said four times, ceremoniously, touchingly, while being rushed by the bus driver who kept honking his horn to hurry the passengers because darkness was rapidly approaching.

Don Abelardo, his boot already resting on the bus's running board, hesitated for a moment, holding back from his lips the *hasta lueguito* he had ready to end the surprise visit by these daughters, so remote now in his memory and his affections.

"Wait a second, I'll pay you for the delay," he said to the driver, and then he signaled for the girls to wait for him where they were standing. He crossed the market plaza in huge strides, took out a ring of keys, opened a door, and went into a house that must have been where he lived, or was perhaps his warehouse.

Several minutes later he returned with a porcelain elephant under his left arm and a length of cloth in his right hand.

"Take this, *mija*," he said to Amanda, handing her the elephant and the cloth and looking at her for an instant with a foolish expression that, forcing things a bit, could have been interpreted as tenderness. "Accept this from me, so you don't go away empty-handed."

Then he gave each one a kiss on the forehead: the clumsy and rough kiss of a man who never kisses. But a kiss nonetheless, the pathetic, shaky, and guilty gesture of someone who might have wished for things to be different and was seeking forgiveness.

"Forgive me, *mija*," he said to Amanda with a trembling voice, as if he were dangerously close to breaking into tears, "but I can't do anything else for you all. I have a wife who would get angry, I have other children and a lot of obligations, I have another life now . . . you must understand . . ."

"Don't worry, señor *padre*. I want you to know that life, thank heaven, has treated us well and that we are leaving here grateful for these gifts, which are very pretty."

Sayonara never again went looking for her father, perhaps because she had already obtained from him the blessing she thought was so necessary to move forward with her life. The elephant . . .

"I can understand that someone would want the Holy Pope's blessing," Fideo interrupts me as I am writing the previous paragraph, "but, what the hell good is a blessing from a man like Monteverde, so loutish and coarse?"

"You only have one father . . . ," I tell her.

"That's a lie," she replies. "You only have one mother; the father can be any old son of a bitch."

Continuing: to move forward with her life. The elephant still exists, although its tusks are chipped. It sits on a corner cabinet in Olga's house, and I am looking at it now. Meanwhile, Fideo is looking at me.

"Don't think it's one of a kind," she says. "A lot of people around here like to decorate their houses with elephants just like that one. You also see a lot of clowns. And ballerinas. A lot of porcelain ballerinas. But nothing beats the elephant as decorative material."

Fideo is right. Over the years, I have seen elephants like this one in the living rooms of many homes, and I wonder how it could happen that, among the infinite variety of objects with no precise use that exist throughout the whole country, there is one in particular that manages to stand above the others. It makes one think of a certain suspicious repetition, a certain persistence of a model that is imposed for some unknown reason, despite its gratuitousness. In other countries an example of these kinds of insistent objects, almost fetishes because of their ubiquitousness, might be plaster gnomes planted among the flowers in the garden. Here in Colombia, the elephant beats the gnome by a wide margin.

First, because it is seen in greater numbers, and second, because plaster gnomes come in different versions—with white beards, with black beards, with red caps, without caps, with a lantern in their hand, without a lantern—while the porcelain elephant is always the same in its gray sleekness, its soft breast like a matron's, with a black, diminutive eye on each side of its face, the invariably chipped tusks, the partially open mouth revealing a pink, fleshy interior, the powerful foreleg bent and delicately balanced on a white ball of dubious interpretation, which could be a faded globe or a large balloon. Or maybe an elephant egg?

I hold the pachyderm in my hands for a while and then return it to the shelf. How strange paternal love can be, I think, and how strange the means chosen to express it.

A serene silence lulls the house. For a couple hours now Todos los Santos has been sleeping calmly in her rocking chair, without wetting herself.

"Are you gone?" she asks me, opening wide her blind eyes and try-ing to look at me with her fingertips.

"No, Todos los Santos, I haven't gone. I'm here, beside you."

"Ah! Since you were so quiet, I thought you had already gone. Come closer and give me your hand, that way when you're quiet I won't lose you."

forty-one

At a certain distance from Todos los Santos's house there flows a gully of stinking, black waters. When the wind blows in this direction, the smell reaches here. The gully carries along decomposed organic material, broken toys, used sanitary napkins, syringes, bottle caps, cotton balls that may have been used to cleanse infections, the remains of a mattress, pieces of blue plastic, yesterday's paper: life, that is, in the intimacy of its residues and its dirtiness. But the water that runs through that gully sounds the same, stone by stone, as the water that flows clean along other estuaries.

"The lesson that can be derived there," deduces Todos los Santos, "is that there is no bad that is not good nor good that isn't also bad."

The lesson isn't clear to me, but I take advantage of the favorable climate to ask her about related matters.

"Explain to me, if I am not boring you, Todos los Santos, when *prostitución* is a sin and when it isn't."

"There is a lot of rationalizing out there on the subject, but the consensus is that it is always a sin."

"But an absolved sin when the woman suffers in bed," clarifies Olguita, "and a condemned sin when she enjoys it, in which case she will surely go to hell when she dies, because she has not paid, like everyone else, her debts to the beyond."

"If I could ask the genie in the bottle for a wish," rants Fideo deliriously, "it would be for enormous tits that I could jerk a man off with."

"What a stupid way to waste a wish. Everyone has his own wishes! Before going to bed, Sayonara would stand before the Sagrado Corazón and ask him for a strange blessing," remembers Todos los Santos. "She would stand there and repeat out loud, every day, the same phrase: Jesus, may you keep murderers from killing tonight, so the people in the world can sleep without fear."

We were talking on the patio and drinking lemonade, we in our rockers, the Felipes in their cages, and Fideo shaking in her penultimate death throes, all drowsy from the heat and the smell of vinegar filtering through the air today somnambulantly, impregnating the still hours of the afternoon.

"Let's go back to the parable of black waters and clear waters," I ask Todos los Santos.

"Ridiculous!" she replies. "The only thing that matters is we are splashing around in our shit in this town because neither the authorities nor the oil company have been capable of constructing a sewer system."

forty-two

 One of Amanda's obligations in Villa de la Virgen del Amparo, according to the agreement stipulated from the beginning with her *patrona*, señora Leonor de Andrade, was to accompany her every evening to six o'clock mass. While the cathedral's interior was the kingdom of overbearing colonial saints floating in incense smoke and the stink of withered lilies, outside in the square, a boisterous, pagan court of merchants, which in biblical times would have been driven away with lashes of a whip, had set up camp. There were lepers who hung around the temple awaiting the eventual miracle of their healing and who in the meantime extorted the consciences of the worshipers by exhibiting the horror of their wounds and mutilations; and there were lottery ticket sellers with their sheets of winning tickets pouncing on the devout multitudes, knowing that those who pray the most also bet the most.

It was there, in the midst of the anguished, afflicted throng that assaulted her as she left mass every afternoon, where one day Amanda discovered Fideo among a scruffy group of low-class *prostitutas* who were waiting to be taken to a male penal colony in the jungles of Guaviare, where they would lend their sexual services, according to the generalized practice that upon becoming too old or sick to work in the urban centers, *putas* were recruited by *chulos* to serve prisoners, border guards, brigades of rubber harvesters, liberal *guerrilleros*, advance squads of *tagüeros*, and others exposed to the harshest desolation and isolation known to man.

"Will you give me some money to buy a drink, girl?" Fideo asked Sayonara, taking her by the arm, recognizing her as she passed by.

"What are you doing here?"

"Life goes on. Give me some money for a drink, I said."

"A drink! You should be asking for medicine, Fideo. I can tell just by looking at you that you're very sick."

"I may be sick, but you're half dead. Look at that nun's costume they make you wear."

Amanda convinced her to come to her *patrona*'s house at noon the following day, to accept the charity of a good bowl of soup, and Fideo accepted the invitation for the rest of the week and the following one as well, because the *chulo* who was coordinating the *putas*' trip to Guaviare kept looking for reasons to delay it and to keep squeezing them: The women had to give him additional money for land travel, an extra sum for river travel, a portion for the dentist who was going to go ahead and extract rotten teeth so that they wouldn't complain of toothaches once it was already too late.

So, in the company of tramps, street urchins, and begging monks, and between spoonfuls of corn chowder or potato soup, Fideo and Sayonara exchanged information about their respective troubles.

"Tell me about don Enrique," Sayonara asked. "Was he really a dwarf?"

"A dwarf with a big *pipí* and an even bigger heart."

"You have to go back to Tora, Fideo, to have Dr. Antonio María treat you, before the sickness in your blood kills you."

"Don't feel sorry for me, look at yourself. My problem is just malignant syphilis, but your illness is mental, which is more injurious and less pardonable. Go back to your *madrina*, you have a place there. Or are you happy playing the part of the dubious wife who deserves the punishment of a slow death?"

"Each of us has to deal with her own calvary," responded Sayonara, to justify her resolute decision to stay where she was.

In truth she had other motives she didn't confess: In the painful process of renouncing her own existence, Amanda was little by little carving out a peaceful place where she could begin to understand Sacramento. Being decent turned out to be a more arduous, inclement proposition than being a mere *puta*, but she was determined to conquer it, and Sacramento was responding to her progress with better treatment and less ambivalence, and, as always, with his gentle dedication to the girls, Susana, Juana, and Chuza, whom he provided with an education, familial affection, and a kind life.

Hidden in the blue dress of the wayward novice, Sayonara's body was letting itself be domesticated and locked in its cage, her name crouched behind the name Amanda, and her eyes took refuge deep within their sockets, while her whole being and all of her desire wandered miles from there, searching for a trace of Payanés along the waters of the Magdalena.

Amanda received, whether she wanted to or not, free daily lessons in proper comportment and decency from her *patrona*, distinguished mistress in such matters, and if as Todos los Santos's disciple she had learned how to be a person, as doña Leonor's employee she had earned the opportunity to learn how to be no one. If before she was encouraged to be beautiful, friendly, and trusted, now revealed to her were the secrets of invisibility, humility, insubstantial presence, and the faintness of a shadow.

Doña Leonor's two unmarried daughters, Nena and Márgara, lived with her and it didn't take Amanda long to understand that in the eyes of their mother the two did not enjoy the same moral approval. Nena measured up, but Márgara failed to: for receiving telephone calls at all hours; for maintaining relations with men from classes beneath her own;

for not properly understanding that "honor is more fragile than glass" and that "it is not enough to be, one must seem"; for wearing tight and improper-colored dresses; and, what seemed to most unnerve her mother, for not controlling her scandalous laughter, while her sister Nena, from a young age, knew only too well that it was preferable to barely smile.

Amanda learned the Ten Commandments so that she could put them into practice, and Sacramento breathed a sigh of relief, resuscitating little by little his battered honor and allowing himself to look others in the eyes again, and the unmentionable past became evanescent, and even, for moments, forgettable.

Amanda also learned to look back with new eyes. She had always heard her friends and fellow workers in La Catunga called *mujeres*, or at worst *putas*, but not in an offensive way; now she knew that they were also shameless adulterers, hussies, *busconas*, loose women, *pelanduscas*, *fufurufas*, and *pelafustanas*. If as a *puta* she knew that sex could be boring, now, as a decent woman, she had heard that it was also filthy. And she could see herself in a distant mirror once when she heard doña Leonor say:

"I found a little Indian woman for the necessary duties; I hope she doesn't turn out to be a thief . . ."

Everything went well as long as Sacramento didn't get angry, which occurred at increasingly less frequent intervals, but from time to time the incubus would begin to growl at him again and to show its claws, especially on those nights when he failed in his attempts to make love to his wife.

"How do you expect me to behave like a man if you destroy my manhood with your conduct? For the others you would dress up, wear perfume, you would wear high heels, and now that you live with me you don't even brush your hair . . ." He would blame her and open up again, like a wound in his memory, the fascination with that woman she had been before he had forced her to become someone else.

"Damned if I do, damned if I don't," Amanda weakly protested. "It would be best if I just died, or maybe I have already died and I just haven't realized it yet."

Nevertheless, life was bearable thanks to the softer tone it had been assuming, in which being awake was very similar to a slow, grayish dream. Until Leonor de Andrade's youngest offspring came home on vacation. He had long eyelashes, studied law in the capital, and his name was Rodrigo; and Amanda made the imprudent mistake of mentioning him to Sacramento.

"That boy Rodrigo makes me laugh," she told her husband. "He knows how to pull coins out of his ears."

"When jealousy is unleashed it is important to tie it up again quickly, with rope, a gag, and a straitjacket, so it doesn't cause too much damage," pontificates Todos los Santos. "But when he thought that that boy Rodrigo had taken notice of his wife, Sacramento gave free rein to his feelings of jealousy and let them run wild and wreak havoc, like stallions from hell."

"Let's go back to the jungle," proposed Sayonara, trying to calm him. "At least there is nothing but monkeys out there and you would have no reason to be jealous of them . . . maybe . . ."

"But nothing made any difference," Olga tells me. "There was no salve that could soothe Sacramento's fury, and each day, from the moment she left for work, he would follow her and spy on her, to see if she breathed, if she spoke to anyone, if she walked anywhere, completely forgetting about himself and his own job as a cart man."

"I will quit working in that house," she suggested, "and look for another job where there are no men to make you uncomfortable . . ."

"There will be men in every house."

"Come on, then, let's go to another pueblo. Melones, Delia Ramos's sister, lives in San Vicente Chucurí, and she's given up the profession and now she runs a beauty salon where they style hair and do manicures. She'll take us in."

"No. Your bad reputation has already reached there."

"Then to Medellín. I have an aunt named Calzones there . . ."

"Calzones, Melones, *putas* and more *putas*; they're all *putas*. Isn't there a single decent woman left in the world? Do you know what they say about me? That I married Sayonara, the *puta* from the Miramar," shouted Sacramento from the bottomless anguish of his black-and-white universe: heaven with Sayonara and hell without her, or rather torment with or without her. She could be only one of two things: goddess or trash, or both things alternatively with no intermediate possibility.

"It would be better if I just killed you and then myself," he declared, adopting a language of love that seemed like a report from the emergency room of a hospital, because he couldn't string two sentences together without including the words "blood," "poison," "wounds," "dagger," "sacrifice."

"Hush, Sacramento, you're scaring me," she said to him. "You're starting to talk like those heroes and martyrs . . ."

"No one will ever love you as I do."

"It would be a relief," she muttered, and she endured, endured, endured, until one day she got tired and fell wildly into a limitless exhaustion; hurricane winds blew once again in her heart, suddenly tearing her from her circumstances, and she accepted, in a single stroke of reason, that old, familiar certainty that life is somewhere else and flows through other streams. The irrepressible force of whim and of why-not, which is the principal motor of those who have an indomitable will, surged up in her again, blunt as a mandate, and without tempering her rage she threw a pot of boiling milk in Sacramento's face, burning his chest with the liquid and opening a gash in his forehead.

"If this is a marriage, then marriage is not a good invention," she said, free now of any hint of docility. "I'm leaving Sacramento, *hermanito*. I'm leaving forever."

"Then he," Olga tells me, "recognizing the return of the real Sayonara and without daring to ask her to stay, warned her, 'If you go, I'll die,' but she went anyway, although she knew that this time Sacramento wasn't exaggerating that much."

"At that very moment my adopted daughter's time for returning began," Todos los Santos tells me. "My girl went running to find Fideo, and she said: 'Let's go, right now.' "

"What about your sisters?" Fideo wanted to know.

"Sacramento promised me he would take care of them."

"But how am I going to walk? Can't you see the condition I'm in?"

"Give me that ring you're wearing."

"I can't. It's the last thing I have that was Enrique's, do you think it's some cheap trinket? It has an engraved coat of arms and is made of pure gold, a lot of karats . . ."

"Give it to me." Sayonara took it from her, and after a while she came back saying she had traded it for an old but sturdy burro.

forty-three

 "During those times in Villa de Virgen del Amparo," Fideo tells me, "Sayonara lived clinging to her longing for Payanés. 'Come back to earth, girl,' I advised her when I saw her flying so high; 'come down from that cloud.'"

The more insistent and deep-rooted in her the memory of him grew, the more it began to fade. The first thing she lost was his head: How did he look at me, out of the corner of his eye or straight on? She couldn't say for sure. He has big ears, half the size of a frying pan, Fideo teased her, but Sayonara recalled them as being perfectly sized, and pink. What came from his mouth, words of love or silence? With the distance of time they both sounded the same. Were his kisses really that deep? Or were they inventions? His skin was a true gift, even with clothes on, of that she was certain.

"Wherever you put your hand on him you find a lot of man," she sighed.

Was his hair very dark? Dark and light, black and white, both mixed. And what was it that had been beating in his forehead: the promise of bliss, or had it been a forsworn good-bye from the very beginning? She couldn't tell for sure, even when he had been with her, the memory of which is now blurred into the long string of symmetrical days.

After his head, his arms were forgotten and the imprint of his embrace became nebulous, and she lost the sensation of his neck in spite of that time when he turned his back; his legs also evaporated, and she could no longer distinguish them from the legs of other men, not to mention his feet—so absent were they that Sayonara convinced herself that when they were making love, Payanés had never removed his socks. Even his hands faded and the last traces of his caresses turned into smoke. But his chest remained, Payanés's chest, and it became as immense as the universe.

"In the memory of that chest," Fideo assures me, "Sayonara built her home."

A chest opened in embrace, protective like the chest of God or of any other father, as old as an elephant and soft like a bed, and warm: without cracks where the wind could slip through. Not the narrow chest of a boy, not a chest covered with hair, or wounded by a spear near the heart; not one of those sharp, lean chests like the ribs of a ship, or the muscular thorax of an athlete, none of that; not the chest of a general, loaded down with medals. But a spacious chest, sufficient, familiar and wise, ample like a hangar; abundant with milk and honey like the breasts of a woman; a chest with the dim light of a church and the well-being of a stove, with thick stone walls, high ceilings under friendly heavens, and a big wooden door that opened just enough for her. That chest.

"I say," says Fideo, "that she confused the memory of what it was with what she wanted it to be."

A chest that gives itself to you without your having to ask and that doesn't make you wait, that doesn't fear, doesn't frighten, doesn't delay; a chest that doesn't hold back, or measure, or stop, or mistrust, or calculate; our house, a generous chest like a banquet; crypt and castle, a cave of sleeping mammals, while outside the winter roars and blows: a flowery bed.

"Too much wishing for things that don't exist in this real world. What you're looking for is not a man, girl," suspected Fideo, "but to die and go to heaven."

"Maybe."

forty-four

"One day she told me about Lucía," Fideo tells me. "She told me she had been tangled up with that woman for a good while."

There were alienating months during which Amanda lived twenty-four hours a day with a woman she had never seen nor ever would, but whom she came to know better than a sister. It was Lucía, the wife Payanés kept in Popayán and who had been, according to him, the reason for his distance, for the rupture, for the tantrum that night by the river and all the turns that fate later took as a consequence. Sayonara, who didn't know her real name, began calling her Lucía, a name she thought sounded cold, caustic, sonorous, and haughty. She could well have won easy points and gotten the early advantage by baptizing her Ramona, or Chofa, or Filomena, but she suspected that it would be an improper tactic and an imprudent approach to ridicule or minimize her adversary.

"So it was Lucía," says Fideo, repeating Amanda's words.

Before she knew it, she was having breakfast, lunch, and dinner with this Lucía; she even gargled with her, but gargled with cyanide, because she was being poisoned, and if she didn't leave Lucía's side day or night, even though she hated the woman, it was because after all it was only with her that Amanda could vent her feelings and because she hadn't found anyone else with whom she could maintain that uninterrupted, circular, and useless dialogue on the man doubly absent: for one and the other, because of the fault of one or the other.

"Here we are, tearing each other's hair out of love for him," said Sayonara to Lucía, "and he's probably out there somewhere, with Molly firmly planted on his lap."

The more force she applied to erasing Lucía from the map, the more persistent she became, and the more present, until the day came when Amanda felt that the faceless, ageless woman had installed herself permanently in her kitchen, always there, invoked by her and sitting on a stool, like another tenant except invisible to Sacramento and the girls, with her disheartening message on the tip of her tongue, sometimes resentful and tearful, other times furiously demanding what belonged to her, but always invincible in the tenacity with which she had determined not to go away, even though her hostess called her *bruja,* nightmare, pain, that woman, her.

"All that was missing was for me to serve her a cup of coffee every morning," Amanda said to Fideo, and she also told her that she finally understood that she thought more about Lucía than she did about Payanés, and probably even more than did Payanés himself, who in Amanda's eyes was becoming less her old love and more the actual husband of that phantasmagoric Lucía.

"It's me who is giving him to Lucía," Sayonara said to herself, alarmed, and she decided to make peace with the woman, give back her human qualities and her right not to be a miscreant or a succubus, and she stopped wishing for her character to be sour or for her to have sagging tits and bad breath.

Simultaneously she gave Lucía the peremptory order to leave her mind and license to exist out there, in her own environment, so that they wouldn't have to continue stepping on each other's toes or beating on each other like a couple of boxers fighting over the close quarters in the ring, the gold medal, and the single portion of air. From then on she ig-

nored the other woman's company, even though she had become so necessary, and she said *adiós*, hopefully forever, and while at first there was
an absence, later she felt strong without Lucía and satisfied at having
unencumbered herself of that dual and unbearable alliance, of complicity and rivalry, with a stranger.

"Of course, from time to time Lucía returned," Fideo tells me, "but
more faintly and only to make courtesy visits. She would sit silently on
her stool, drink her black coffee, say thank you, ask permission to withdraw, and she would return to Popayán, her native city."

forty-five

From the first moment, when I first saw the photograph of Sayonara, I had the feeling that she had died under violent circumstances. Just as I had guessed that she was a *prostituta* from her crudely plucked eyebrows and her soft, cold gaze that was like the touch of silk; just as I suspected — erroneously — that her name was Clara, in contrast with the dark light she radiated; and as I remember having thought that she possessed the sort of beauty that opens the door to death.

I have followed the occurrences in her life, trying to record her slight footprint and her uncertain trail. The Girl, Sayonara, and Amanda: I have witnessed three different people and I haven't been able to fully integrate them into a true and definitive identity. And I would only be able to do it poorly, as I am convinced that not even she could do it.

"I am divided inside, Doc," Dr. Antonio María tells me that he heard her lament once, "and each of those who live in me pulls in her own direction. I'm tired, Doc, of all the pulling, it is nearly tearing me apart, and I want to rest as one single person."

"We're all like you, divided," the doc tells me he said to her, "but when we are one and able to rest, it's because we're dead."

I have wanted to understand the passion of the woman who was not called Sayonara in vain and accompany her along the paths of her recurrent farewell. I wanted to know what her problem was, but it seems to be a given that the problem is always something else, and that behind the motives that drive someone, another motive often lurks. Life is debated in deep waters while words and explanations slide across the smooth surface.

That's fine, I think. That's how it should be. That the memory of Sayonara stays where it should be, in the interlinings of supposition and expectation, half veiled and half revealed by the recollections that others have of her. Or of them. Of those three: Amanda, the Girl, and Sayonara. And as for me, it is enough to reach the end of her story delicately. With just enough coherence and without forcing things, without excessive literary adjustments and without trying to clarify the mystery of her trinity. I should allow her stele to extend among the shadows, plural and slight, refraining from calcifying it by exposing it to the light of day.

Now I want to retrace the steps she took among her people on that decisive and rain-swept day, the day of her return to Tora, when they saw her arrive just as she had left, her hair dripping water, wearing the black skirt with the slit up the side and the Chinese blouse with its tight row of buttons and its domesticated dragon.

"Just as she had arrived, yes, but with the difference that she now breathed more deeply," Todos los Santos corrects me, "but that was noticed only by those of us who loved her. What I mean is that there was something new about her, a gift she had acquired during her absence, which was maturity. A splendid maturity, without hurry or stridency, sweet and serene like the morning star."

"Sweet and serene?!" laughs Olga. "You compare a Malaysian tiger like her to the morning star?"

They tell me that the return trip was hard and slow, and full of surprises.

"Hard and slow and full of surprises, *sí* señor, just like life," says Olguita philosophically, and she bursts out laughing again.

"Hush, Olga," scolds Todos los Santos, "stop repeating things, you sound like an echo."

Sayonara led the burro by its halter, with Fideo draped across the small wooden pallet on the animal's back like a sack. The sick woman, feeling uncomfortable and annoyed in her burning and ulcerated skin, was in a foul mood, and she attacked with such surliness any attempt to help her that on more than one occasion Sayonara had to threaten to abandon her for some passing Samaritan to deal with her excesses. But the threatening didn't do any good. Fideo calmed down only when she slept, overcome by the numbness and swelling of her appendages, but she became herself once again with every bump along the way to shout to the heavens, with a pathos that to Sayonara seemed out of place:

"Ay, don Enrique, take me with you!" she howled. "Have mercy on me and take me to where you are, because down here they're all a bunch of bastards!"

"Ungrateful woman," responded Sayonara.

"Anyone who thinks that on top of all this I have to be thankful can go fuck his mother! Thank you, God, for these *bubas* as big as chicken eggs? Thank you, Virgin Mary, for these stinking pustules? Who the hell do you want me to thank?"

"At least that man who came by to offer you some water. You didn't have to curse him; he was only trying to help."

"To help! The miscreant . . . he's probably the brother, or the cousin, or at least the friend of the bastard who gave me this plague."

From a distance, before the first roofs appeared, Sayonara spied the eleven blue flames from the refinery's smokestacks, rising against the drizzle above the tops of the tallest trees, and her eyes, recognizing her home, grew watery as she watched the slowly rising columns of thick smoke. Then she looked again.

"What strange columns of smoke," she commented.

"What's strange about them?" growled Fideo.

"They rise strangely into the air."

It seemed as if they stopped midway up to expand toward the sides, swelling into fat clouds, puffing up oddly to create an additional cap on a sky that was already charged with electricity, thereby rarefying the air and somehow altering the look of the familiar, turning it into a simulation of its former self.

"Things have changed down there, Fideo," Sayonara warned her. "We are not returning to the same place we left."

"Things always change, don't think you're so clever."

In reality the signs of strangeness had been visible, sporadically, for a couple of hours now, since the travelers came across the first hut. At the edge of the road, just there, covered with sticks and pieces of plastic, with three sheets of tin for walls and a burlap bag as a front curtain, barely a yard high, so that a person fit inside only lying down. Next to the hut, sitting on a rock, waiting, was a very poor woman with her breasts exposed and her lips painted red. Fideo had a fever, and to protect her from the drizzling rain, which had soaked her and was making her shiver, Sayonara had the idea of asking the woman's permission to let the invalid rest under the makeshift roof until the rain stopped.

"Get out of here!" shouted the painted-mouthed woman, throwing a rock at them. "Clients are already scarce enough! Get out of here, you infected women, before you scare away the few clients left!"

A little further along, the road emptied onto a highway, now asphalt, and Sayonara, Fideo, and the burro started walking along its edge, hugging the cliffs so that they wouldn't be struck along a curve by one of the vehicles that nearly scraped them as they sped past, and so that they wouldn't die under the wheels of the trucks filled with soldiers and weapons.

"Pretty, this asphalt," said Fideo, suddenly in a peaceful mood. "It shines very nicely."

"It reflects the lights from the cars, because it's wet," said Sayonara, but it would have been better if she had remained silent, because Fideo, irascible again, answered her with pedantry.

And then, again, familiar places glistened with hints of unreality, when by the edge of the highway, one after another and at intervals, enormous advertising walls appeared, on which the company, through slogans, tried to motivate the workers, or the male population in general, to leave behind the risks of a roaming life and illicit love to form a family like all other law-abiding families. A man without a home, urged the wisdom in the signs, is like a saint without a robe, like a bird without a nest, like a nest without a bird, like a house without a roof, like a roof without a house, like a head without a hat or vice versa: all things abandoned, undesirable, or incomplete.

"Listen to that, the Troco is insisting on officiating over wholesale marriage," said Sayonara, and she hadn't finished speaking before they spied in the undergrowth, just beneath one of the walls, another hut similar to the previous one but a little more solid and decorated all around with a colorful synthetic garland. This time the owner was a young fat woman, squeezed into a pair of tight slacks, and as they hurried on so as not to hinder her, Sayonara and Fideo saw a driver and his helper climb down from a sixteen-wheel Pegasus that stopped in front. Next, they saw the driver and the fat woman enter the hut and could discern, through the cracks between the sticks, what they were doing in there while the helper waited his turn outside, trimming his fingernails with a nail clipper.

"The other woman handles the pedestrians and this one, the motorized clients," noted Fideo.

Mingling in the sad air, odd bits of Victrola music came floating through the rain, making Sayonara quicken her pace and preventing her from stopping until she reached the lookout point from which one can view the fair, serpentine Magdalena, whose waters at that instant were being drowned by the last rays of the sun. She could contemplate the city of Tora in its entirety, motionless against the great current but overflowing on the other three sides as if it had decided to grow against all human reasoning and against the will of God. On the far side of the river the downpour was stronger and the view into the distance merged into washed grays, as if another country lay in that direction.

She crossed the Lavanderas bridge just as, one here and another there, the colored lights in La Catunga were turned on, licked by the rain and very diminished in number, but still blue, red, green, and festive, like Christmas Eve.

"There aren't as many lights now," Sayonara said to Fideo.

"Why shouldn't there be, if the *putas* have taken to the mountains and work in huts. Slow down, girl, you're pounding me! Ay, don Enrique! Tell this merciless girl to slow down, she's finishing me off!" shouted Fideo, bouncing around like a sack of corn because Sayonara could no longer withstand the frenetic beating of her heart, which was running wildly toward the encounter, and following her heart, she had begun running also, right down the mountain.

Before they reached the first streets, the rain had already stopped, and Sayonara, hiding behind a wall, removed her soaked clothes and put on her combat attire, complete with earrings and high heels, and she wanted to put Fideo in a clean flowered cotton robe.

"So you'll arrive looking pretty," she said, but Fideo, more offended than if she had been slapped, retorted something about how pretty did she think a sack of pus could be. But, finally, she let Sayonara brush her hair, dry her face, and fit the robe around her, and despite the torment in her groin she sat astride the burro, very erect and composed as a matter of pride.

Then they went, before anything else, to look for Dr. Antonio María at his clinic. They found him standing in the doorway, aged and with his rabbit's teeth even more pronounced than before because his cheeks had become hollow.

"This pueblo has been defeated by morality and its Siamese twin, shame," the doctor told them, after giving them a cursory greeting, happy to see them but too distressed to express it, and he went on, burning and uncontrollable, with his discourse. "They consider syphilis an obscene illness and they call its propagation and that of other venereal diseases the plague, without differentiating. Any serious illness of the body is the plague and is impure and censurable, whether it's smallpox, Chagas disease, skin infections, yaws, leishmania, blue bloater, or even common wounds or serious-looking injuries. The generalized philosophy is that any sick man is a victim, that all *putas* are sick, and that any sick woman is a *puta*. The *prostitutas*, and in no instance the men who go to bed with them, are the source of infection, the origin of evil. The current credo is that the sick women must be exterminated and the *putas* must be eradicated, and according to what I've heard, some fifty *prostitutas*, or suspected *prostitutas*, have been locked up at Altos del Obispo in a detention camp with barbed wire and military guards. Others have moved to the cemetery to work double shifts, offering their love at night on the graves and earning a few extra centavos during the day as hired mourners. Meanwhile, the community of the healthy holds firm to its crusade and boasts of its inflexible conduct, because they take for granted a correlation between the plague and moral degradation. No one, especially not the *prostitutas* themselves, wants to know anything about the scientific explanations or methods of prevention, because it is more dramatic and seductive, more useful for the self-pity they've always clung to, to believe that the illness is an expression of divine anger because God is an advocate of monogamy."

"Could you give us a glass of water, Doc?" Sayonara timidly interrupted his sermon, and only then did Dr. Antonio María notice the travelers' absolute exhaustion and Fideo's deplorable state of health.

"Excuse me, please!" he begged, truly ashamed. "Come in, come in, inside you will find a bed and food for both of you."

"How are Precious and the children?" Sayonara asked, smiling, and the doctor, who at first didn't know who Precious was, quickly remembering his wife's words, laughed and answered that they were healthy and had moved to the back part of the clinic to live, out of fear of those who came to harangue at the house while the doctor was away, working.

"So, Doc," asked Sayonara, "are they getting rid of the *putas* in Tora?"

"There are more than before, only more wretched. The men who marry don't stop . . ."

"La Copa Rota was a palace compared to what we saw today," interrupted Fideo.

"Those who marry don't stop seeing them because of it, and the *prostitutas* are also sought out by the new arrivals, the multitudes who are being displaced by the violence in the countryside."

"Well, Doc, I have to be going before it gets too late, because I've brought my *madrina* some *arequipe en totumo* and she won't eat sweets after nine, because she says it causes insomnia," said Sayonara as she prepared to depart. "I leave my sick friend in good hands. I'll come back around eleven to take the night shift."

"No, not tonight. Rest today and tomorrow, and I'll wait for you on Wednesday, if you want. Precious and I will take care of Fideo. She'll be with two others, Niña de Cádiz and Gold Teeth, who are staying here until they get better—"

"Until they get better or die," Fideo interrupted again.

"Who are here until they get better, so she won't be alone. What about the burro, are you taking it with you?"

"The burro belongs to Fideo."

"Then leave it, it will be a help in carrying water. Wait, girl," the doctor said at the last minute, taking her by the arm, "let me look at you. It won't take more than five minutes. Don't be irresponsible or obstinate; look how, morality aside, the infection is spreading, and if the illness is treated in time it's better than if—"

"No chance, Doc," Sayonara cut him off sharply, "there's no need for you to examine my body, or to put your mirrors and fingers inside me. I know how to look at my own body and I assure you that my *chocho* is as fresh as a rose."

A HARD DICK DOESN'T BELIEVE IN GOD, the subversives had written in large, irregular letters on the facade of the Ecce Homo, and Sayonara crossed the central plaza with suspicion, sniffing this and that unfamiliar item like someone returning to a place he has never been. She saw more police walking around; more boys wearing dark glasses; fewer couples dancing in the cafés; more trash in the street; people quieter, more elegant, better dressed; others more tattered and hungry; many without a roof or work, standing around on street corners with their children, with nothing to do except wait.

As she passed in front of the Descabezado, Sayonara felt the pinch of a bad memory, or a premonition, or maybe it was the cloying, perverted smell emanating from the municipal slaughterhouse. A few seconds later she ran right into the person she least wanted to see, that scoundrel Piruetas, who was moving through the crowd with nervous little jumps in his white shoes, with a portable display case hanging around his neck, on which were displayed a variety of concoctions and herbs for an improved love life, and the infamous Pomada de la Condesa to restore virginity, a very solicited gift in those times of counterreform.

"The more prohibitions, the greater the proliferation of pornographic businesses, and who better than Piruetas to squeeze the juice from that fruit. When the vein of falsified paintings ran out," Sacramento tells me, "he dedicated himself to the sale of a stimulant that beat all the others in Tora, which he invented, produced, and promoted himself: pepper suppositories."

"That's why Piruetas prances through life," laughs Todos los Santos. "Just like that, sort of like a tight-assed Punch, as if holding a pepper suppository between his buttocks."

"In addition, he sold condoms made from animal intestines," Sacramento continues, "also patented by him and promoted as the modern solution against pregnancy and infection, but infamous among users for being uncomfortable, slippery, and of dubious efficacy."

"Start suffering, men of tender heart: La Hermosa has returned!" proclaimed Piruetas in falsetto when he saw Sayonara passing, and faces unknown to her turned to stare at her.

"Go eat shit, you creature of ill omen," she retorted, driving him away with her hand. "Last time you tossed a compliment at me you turned my life into shit, and I still haven't recovered."

Although she hadn't noticed it, many eyes had seen her, had followed her step by step, had caught her scent from the very moment she set foot back in the pueblo, and now Piruetas's announcement spread from house to house: She had returned.

For the second time the child *puta* took the pueblo; Sayonara, the *puta*-wife; Amanda the bride dressed in white; the wife now without her husband and once again dressed for night; the beauty challenging the world as she did in those other times, those that people wanted to forget, come hell or high water.

"Maybe if she had come back with her hair covered up and her body hidden in the sad, sober novice's dress that she wore in Villa de la Virgen del Amparo," speculates Machuca, "maybe."

And as if her reappearance weren't enough, she had come dragging astride a burro the exemplary and resuscitated image of sin with all of its consequences: Fideo, covered with cankers, some hidden and one displayed in the place that most terrifies and offends others, the middle of her face. Sayonara hadn't finished telling Piruetas to go eat shit when she detected in the surrounding multitude the subtle, spasmodic, and frighteningly synchronized reflexes of cattle the instant before they stampede. In the midst of an unforeseen paralysis of air, a sudden, dark, collective choreography took shape into which she tried to integrate herself without knowing why, perhaps out of mere survival instinct.

"This is why I came back to the pueblo, to face my destiny," Todos los Santos tells me that Sayonara was able to understand in a sparkle of final lucidity.

Seconds later she was imprisoned by a human barrier, forced into the front row just across from where a spontaneous band of wrathful citizens was sacrificing a thin man, of short stature, in a white, unbuttoned shirt, the tail of which hung outside his pants.

"So they didn't fall upon her?"

"Hush your mouth and knock on wood," said Todos los Santos as she rapped on the table with her knuckles. "They got another Christian soul and not her, because as Fideo said the other day, Sayonara carried that black bird around on her shoulder, but she kept it pacified and fed it from her hand. But she didn't miss a single detail of the incident, and that man's passion and death were so embedded in her that for several days afterward she kept repeating, like an automaton, that he was small and skinny, that his shirt was hanging outside his pants, and before he expired he tried to say something no one understood. He was a *zapatero*, you know? What you would call a shoe repairer. A humble craftsman with an eccentric name, Elkin Alexis Alpamato, originally from Ramiriquí, in Boyacá, who had lived in Tora for three and a half years. We all knew him because we took our shoes to him to repair. When a heel wore out, twisted, or broke open, there was no one like him to restore it with new leather and a reinforced metal tap. He alleged that high heels were one of the seven greatest inventions of civilization and that together with the silk stocking had been Eve's true sin in paradise, the real apple of damnation. 'Alpamato,' we would say, 'make these heels ready to strike sparks on the pavement tonight,' and he would, because he liked to deliver."

It took sixty seconds to kill him and they did it by kicking him, in the single, fulminating lashing out of an uncontrollable centipede, a swift and voracious assault by starved sparrows on a crust of bread. After the beating, he stood up in a last attempt at decency, leaned against a wall, tried to find his last voice, and then fell again, already dead, a poor bloody rag without guilt or redemption. Sayonara watched the killing without taking her eyes off the victim, as if seeing again something she had already seen, what she had always foreseen, as if she were a witness of something that was supposed to occur but didn't, as if it weren't that man but she herself who should have died that night, at that predetermined hour and in the desolation of that street corner.

"She had to witness such a horrifying scene the very day she came home," Machuca tells me, "as if the city itself had decided to bring her up to date on the new times that had settled in around here."

"What had the *zapatero* done?" I ask. "Why did they kill him? Who killed him?"

"Regular people; don't think they were murderers or professional evildoers. Small-business men on Calle Caliente, enraged by the evictions."

Never before and never again were the four sources of power in such agreement, nor did they act in such synchronization. Public health measures were preached from the pulpit, the Tropical Oil Company performed marriage counseling, the Fourth Brigade decided who should be pillars of morality, and the mayor, who was the representative for Tora in the National Conservative Directorate and the fellow party member of Senator Mariano Azcárraga Caballero, the ingrate who drove beautiful Claire to her grave, was the individual who singled out those who deserved scorn and punishment for breaking ethical, hygienic, labor, and public order laws.

One of the central aims of this four-party strategy was the leveling of the red-light district, because they wanted to build on that land barrios of family housing in the image and likeness of the Barrio Staff, but in a squashed, Creole, and proletarian version. They professed to want to do away with the *puterío* and the red-light districts. But what it really boiled down to was that everything that had to do with poverty looked red to them, as if the poor barrio and the red-light district were one and the same. After one of their evictions, on the day Sayonara returned, the victims descended on the plaza, pushing in front of them anything they could, movable or immovable.

"But why the shoe repairman? What had he done?"

"Nothing. He hadn't done anything."

He only tried to calm the crowd to prevent them from vandalizing, but the level of discontent had grown so acute that it was his unfortunate fate to become the scapegoat and receive their wrath.

"Of course, Sayonara would have given a different explanation for the events," Olga informs me. "If you had asked Sayonara, she would have told you that the shoe repairman, without knowing it, had swapped his fate for hers."

After the crime, for a few eternal minutes, the city was submerged in a rare lethargic silence and absence, as if everyone had run inside their houses or their own hearts to hide from the horror, and it was during this span of otherworldly stillness that Sayonara walked down Calle

Caliente and entered La Catunga, feeling foreign inside her own body, looking at this planet with the eyes of a stranger and trembling with apprehension as great or greater than that first time, so many years ago. Then she saw Sacramento again, the boy, sitting on his cart with his curly eyelashes and his strawlike hair, warning her that anyone who entered that place could never leave.

She looked for Todos los Santos's house and found nothing but rubble. She went back, looked again, but she found nothing, and then she asked, Olga assures me, whether she might be dead after all, and whether the episode with the *zapatero* had been one of those pitiful lies that the dead tell themselves to palliate the irreversibility of their situation.

Moving forward with some difficulty due to her high heels and the tube skirt, without light from lantern or moon, Sayonara persevered, balancing herself among the mounds of rubble and thinking she glimpsed here and there traces of her past: This bit of dust was oranges from breakfast, that brick is from the afternoon you told me, those dirt clods were coins in my pocket, that pile of clay . . .

"Aspirina's collar!" she suddenly shouted, because there was Aspirina's collar with each and every one of the fake diamonds, glittering and real in the middle of that pile of nothing and inviting Sayonara to restore her faith in her own existence.

She didn't find much else to celebrate, no patio, no window, no sky on the other side of the window, no mirror next to the cistern, no canaries in their cages, no pigsty or stand of plantain trees, no grain store on the corner, no Dancing Miramar with its dancing contests and red velvet decor. What to believe, the collar, which was there, or all the rest, which wasn't?

"And my mother, Matildita Monteverde? And my *madrina*, Todos los Santos?" she asked out loud in the darkness.

"About your mother, I don't know anything," a human voice answered her, coming from she didn't know where. "About your *madrina*, I can give you a message. After the eviction came the demolition, and Todos los Santos went to Olga's house to live."

"So they didn't knock down Olga's house?"

"No. The improvements haven't reached that far yet. This part here is not called La Catunga anymore but La Constancia, and they say that soon it's going to be a respectable barrio."

Sayonara expressed her thanks for the information and moved away from this second stage of her past, which the bulldozers would soon be leveling, just as the first, that of her childhood, had been devoured by flames, and just as the third, that of her marriage, had already started to haunt her from the quiet side of her memories.

Olguita's patio smelled of everything, the good and the bad, of aromatic herbs growing in pots, of enticing food browning in the oven, of the urine of domesticated animals, of the stench of the gully that ran nearby with its black waters tumbling over rocks. Todos los Santos was dipping a quadruped afflicted with mange in benzyl benzoate when she saw Sayonara approach, and the days of waiting had been so many and so long that she didn't know whether it was really her or merely the incarnation of her memory. She couldn't greet the girl, or manifest her great joy or ask anything, because she understood that her adopted daughter, who looked pale and undone, didn't want warm welcomes or answers, she only wanted to tell about the horror of the lynching once and again and again, as if freezing the scene in words could prevent it from happening.

"Is it true that sometimes someone else dies for you?" was her very first sentence as she entered. "I have the sensation, *madrina*, that a *zapatero* has just succumbed to a death that was meant for me."

"As much as Olga and I argued with her, we couldn't rid her mind of that fanaticism," Todos los Santos tells me. "She swore that she had seen the ray of death descend from heaven straight toward her and then veer away at the last second to strike Alpamato."

Without listening to explanations, Sayonara went into the bedroom and walked straight up to the Master, the young, tormented Jesus Christ with his exposed heart who knew, like her, what it was like to offer a neighbor your entrails; the same Christ who had filled the days of her youth with terror and with solace, the one who during so many hours of her work, as she lay in bed, had illuminated with burning lamps the minimal truth of a lonely and naked girl, rendering her invulnerable by bathing her in his red-black glow.

"Señor *mío* Jesucristo," she implored, kneeling before the painting, "patron saint of the broken, take the soul of your servant Alpamato, now that you have thrown his body to the wild beasts. If it is true that he died instead of me, following your holy example, thank him for me. Tell him that the day will come when I too will have to accept the death of another and that I hope to do so then with as much generosity as he has just done for me."

"What is happening in this pueblo, *madrina*?" she asked as she went out to the patio.

"Strange things. Boys kill cats and skin them, some people leave their homes and no one ever hears from them again. I'm telling you, things are happening. The other morning, in the middle of Calle Caliente, doña Magola's peacock turned up stabbed to death."

"A peacock stabbed to death? Who would want to stab a peacock to death?"

"I don't know, maybe the same person who skins cats. And the girls?" was the only thing Todos los Santos was able to inquire. She didn't even want to ask about Sacramento, because she blamed him for the misfortunes of the family and all of Tora.

"The girls are fine, back in Virgen del Amparo. Sacramento is taking better care of them than if he were their father. I came alone, *madrina*," Sayonara announced, "and I don't plan to go back to him."

"You do everything backward," said her *madrina* reproachfully. "You stop being married just now, when wives are going around puffed up with pride and *putas* have to hide to avoid animosity. Give me that papaya, how much is that *guanábana*?—that's what the ladies say when they go to the market, like that, pointing at the fruit with their stiff fingers so that you'll notice the brilliance of the band of gold on their hand," she said. "And they buy inexpensive meat at the commissary with a card that certifies them as the legitimate spouse of a company worker. You'll see them, they devote their entire afternoon to a foreign pastime they call a canasta tea, which consists of playing cards and swallowing little cakes and sweets."

"You're too hard on them," chastised Olga, who felt congratulatory because of Sayonara's return and offered *mantecadas* and *pandeyucas*, because for them there was no better way to express affection than by showering others with an abundance of food. "Married women also scrub the floor and put salt in the soup and suffer disillusions, just like us . . ."

"Hush, Olguita!" said Todos los Santos to silence her, "you shouldn't make any concessions whatsoever. Like I said, the wives gobbling cake and wine, and the *putas*? The *putas*, who feel out of style and cornered, have had to invent a whole repertoire of tricks in bed just to survive.

"To be sought after, professional women found it indispensable to know how to juggle, fence, and display other exquisite talents difficult to even imagine before, and now lost is the girl who isn't able to perform agilely and without fuss such feats as the double bowl, the golden shower, the dead dog, the angel's leap, the big suck, the dyke dip, the garage door, the drop of milk, and any number of exotic acts invented by mankind, even reaching the extreme of shaving pubic hair to guarantee the clients, ever more demanding and coarse, that they were free from lice.

"Machuca? Since she can't hear us, Machuca decided to paint her nipples purple . . ."

forty-six

 "He was a Mexican telegraph operator, and he called Sayonara *mi guadalupana* because he compared her to the Virgen de Guadalupe, also Mexican and with hair as long and beautiful as the Virgen del Carmen's and Sayonara's own," Todos los Santos tells me of a man named Renato Leduc, who was brought to Tora by life's winding road. "That's what he called her, *mi guadalupana,* and since he also wrote her verses, the day he decided to return to his country because of her indifference he left her a farewell poem that I still have. I will show it to you if and when I find it, because it was such a long time ago. . . . It was before the rice strike, during the golden era of the Dancing Miramar.

After digging through boxes, sacks, and drawers, Todos los Santos presents me with the following poem, typewritten and signed by the telegraph operator Renato Leduc:

> *Jovian pain of losing*
> *adored things.*
> *Pain that oft*
> *costs your life,*
> *and oft costs naught.*

I once told you: I love you,
as I had never said before
nor ever will again so true.
I said it to you in desperation
because I knew that very soon
another would say it too.

I said it in desperation,
but I have nothing to regret.

I loved you so, I loved you
because in your eyes so fair
was a piece of infinity;
because of your chestnut hair;
because of your mouth
barbarously naked
I loved you, I loved you so . . .

But so many people loved you
at once,
that I told myself: it is implausible
to plead
—if so many people love her—
things she does not need.

I thought of killing myself
then,
but I didn't, because
I asked myself, why?
Lost in pain and grief
I let my beard grow
because that limpid love so brief
from it derived such merriment,

since virgins have always found
—or so they say—in beards much amusement.

Jovian pain of losing . . .

Apart from being a poet, there is little I am able to find out in Tora about the author, who defined himself as a bureaucrat of the lowest level. I know that when he arrived here he lodged at the Casa de Huéspedes, belonging to Conchita la Tapatía, a fellow Mexican, and that during the many nights in which they shared reminiscences of their motherland over glasses of Vat 69, he told her that he had trained for his profession at the Escuela Nacional de Telégrafos in Mexico City, which occupied an old building on Calle Donceles, next to the women's insane asylum, and that he had started working before he turned thirteen—before he even had hair on his balls, he said—to help support his widowed mother. That before he arrived in Tora he had passed through Paris, where the *puticas* in the Latin Quarter taught him how to speak French; that he was fiercely anticlerical and *aluciferado*, a term he himself used, meaning "possessed by the devil"; "a man who had lived a great deal," as Todos los Santos said; a man who was stuck on Sayonara from the first time he saw her through the window of the telegraph office in Tora, who became her most assiduous and starry-eyed client, and who weekly left in her hands nearly the entirety of his scant weekly salary.

"You can't offer your heart to a woman like that," admonished his Colombian best friend, a giant of a man named Valentín.

"For a woman like that, I have nothing but heart," Renato replied.

"Love me," Leduc begged Sayonara.

"I can't love you. I look at you and I don't see you."

"You have an empty pot where other women hold their feelings," the telegraph poet told her, and she realized that he was right, in part.

Then, enamored and in pain, he quit his job, packed a trunk with

all of his books and his two changes of clothes, wrote the final poem, ti-
tled it "Romance of the Lost," sent it to the addressee in an envelope, and
returned to his Mexico, where he was heard to say that he had left
Colombia to flee the indifference of a distant lover bent on remaining
a *puta*.

forty-seven

The day after her return to Tora, Sayonara shook off her exhaustion by sleeping until the middle of the morning, and when she arose she found her *madrina*, Machuca, and Olga whispering suspiciously in the kitchen.

"Are you going to tell me what you are up to?" she asked them. "Since last night you've been plotting something behind my back and it's time for you to tell me what it is."

"We're going to tell you, we already decided that. It's bad news. About your sister Ana."

"Did she die?"

"No, but that might have been preferable." They kept beating around the bush, without daring to be specific.

From the moment of her arrival, Sayonara had been asking about her sister and they had answered her evasively. We don't know, it seems that she lives on a *finca* near the village of Los Mangos, she left a telephone number but no one ever answers there, and when they do they say she moved somewhere else. Then, because of the deception and the delaying, Sayonara pitched a fit, one of those demoniac rages with eight legs and two heads that spits poison from its mouths and fire from its tail, one of those boundless bursts of anger that hadn't possessed her since adolescence and that still gave them something to talk about in Tora.

"Either you tell me now, or I'll tear apart this house and everything in it."

They told her. Ana was the mistress of General Demetrio del Valle, commander in chief of Tora's campaign of moralization and shanty eradication, who, because he was married civilly and in the eyes of the church to a rich lady from Anolaima and didn't want to be found out, kept Ana closed up in a house next to the garrison and had spread the word that she was a cousin of his from the country whose education he had charitably offered to sponsor.

"I'm going to get her out of there even if it costs us both our lives," announced Sayonara, and without further delay she started off.

"Wait," suggested Todos los Santos in a softer voice, so as not to unleash the storm again. "Let her make her own life just as you have made yours. Besides, the way things are right now, it's better to be the mistress of a gorilla than the wife of some man who's dying of hunger."

But Sayonara wasn't there to hear her, and a few hours later she was clambering across the garrison's tiled roofs, then broke a window and climbed through it.

"Del Valle pays for my private English and dressmaking lessons," Ana told her. "He has given me a television, a record player, and a collection of LPs. He brings me marzipan fruits made by nuns and bottles of sweet wine from Oporto, and as if that weren't enough, in bed he prefers sleeping over messing around. Does it look like I'm suffering, sister?"

"And the wrongs that the military has done to our family? Have you forgotten the atrocious way they caused the deaths of our mother and brother? And the wrongs they have done to our people, back in Tora? Have you forgotten?"

"No, *hermana*, I haven't forgotten, and sometimes the anger makes my blood boil and I see red, and at those times I hate del Valle and want to strangle him with my bare hands. But then he brings marzipan, turns on the television, falls asleep like a little orphan, and I forgive him. If you saw him without his hat, with his four hairs plastered against his skull, he wouldn't seem so ferocious to you. But I promise you one thing: If some day the anger overcomes the forgiveness, I'll put strychnine in his *café con leche*. Or if some day I get tired of marzipan and studying English, I'll take off through that window, *hermana*, the same one you just came in by, and I'll go straight to Todos los Santos's house."

Several times I have made notes in my notebook that I should inquire about an enigma, which is: On what do Olga and Todos los Santos actually live? Finally I get up the nerve to ask and Olguita tells me that when the savings that Sayonara had left for her sisters ran out, Sacramento took charge of the situation. Persevering in the lumber business, he managed to finance the girls' education as well as special treatment for little Chuza, who he still takes to Bucaramanga once a month to see a speech therapist, because although she's now married, she still hasn't spoken a word.

"Also," Olguita tells me, "that good Sacramento sends Todos los Santos a voluntary monthly stipend, despite the fact, spiteful old woman, that she still hasn't forgiven him. To think the only thing that getting married did for him was to acquire the obligation of maintaining the bride's family in perpetuity. He ended up paying with interest for those seven coins he received that day when he delivered her to Todos los Santos for training!"

"Olguita also provides income," Sacramento adds. "Just as you see her sitting there, the old girl is still an active professional who hasn't lost her original clientele. Only those who die desert her, and not even them, because she visits them at the cemetery."

Yesterday, which was Saturday, Olga and Todos los Santos were busy preparing lunch because Sacramento, Susana, Juana, Chuza, Machuca, and Tana were visiting.

"Here I come, don Enrique! Get ready, here I come!" shouted Fideo suddenly, when we weren't paying her any attention because we were involved with the stuffed chicken and the onion salad, and when we ran to her side, we saw her make a final struggle to sit up in her hammock, call out once more to don Enrique, and die.

And yesterday the women decided that I had to say the final words of farewell at the burial, and this afternoon, a glass-weather Sunday, we dug the hole under the same *guayacán* tree and the same sky that shelters Claire. I saw many other graves in the middle of that meadow with the view of the river, barely marked with a wooden cross and maybe an epitaph: "Here lies Molly Flan," "Finally at rest, Delia Ramos," "N.N. new victim of the plague," "La Costeña, love forever, your friends," "María del Carmen Blanco alias La Fandango," "Eternal glory for Chaparrita, heroine of the Rice Strike," "Teresa Batista, tired of war," "This is Melones, sister of Delia Ramos."

When the moment arrived for me to speak, all the women looked at me as if I were the prima donna at a municipal theater performance. Then I placed a wreath of white roses in don Enrique's name on the grave and said a few words that made some of those in attendance cry but disillusioned the rest, because just as they were beginning to be inspired, I had already finished. In matters of love, I said, everything is expectations and bets, some become shipwrecked, others somehow end up sailing smoothly, and in the midst of so much dreaming and foolishness one thing is certain: Fideo got closer than anyone to what is perhaps real love. She knew how to give it, she received it with open arms, and she kept it alive until the day of her death, and hopefully also from now on, amen.

forty-eight

The disaster that was spreading through the streets stopped at the doors of the houses and inside them reigned something similar to everyday tranquillity, to the continuous quiet of things. It is worth saying that despite everything, water was carried in the same buckets, the stove was lit with the same wood, the canaries still sang, and life clung to the tiniest ordinary things in its search for happiness.

"The events in La Catunga sound very appalling now that we're telling them to you," says Todos los Santos, "but at the time, just like now, they were part of our everyday routine and we didn't really notice them. Ah! So-and-so was taken by the virus. Ah! They found a common grave with so many bodies. Ah! Lino el Titi's son was tortured to repay his father's union-related sins. That's what we would say and what we still say, ah! all blessed day, but as one would say ah! I forgot to pick up the blue dress from the cleaners. The war is like that, more scandalous when you talk about it than when you are living it."

"Because you tell it all at the same time, but you live it event by event," clarified Olga.

A little war, blind and without name, like all of ours, came down the river and went through the streets; tranquillity took refuge in the patios of the houses and the great tribulation was borne inside everyone. The memory of Payanés and her hopes of being with him in the future was the lamp that warmed Sayonara's vast loneliness. It was the cornerstone of her thoughts, which at every turn bumped into him in the heights and depths of hope and despair, in sparks of joy and moments of mourning. Olguita and Todos los Santos watched Sayonara dedicate her days to the ceremony of waiting, busying herself with the minimal rituals of all of those who in this world do nothing but wait, trembling with impatience: thinking, praying, and cultivating a hernia from so much effort.

"But what was she waiting for? What was it exactly that she was waiting for?"

"Ay, *mi reina,* the same thing she had always been waiting for, for the month to end and for the last Friday to arrive . . ."

"She went to the clinic every day to care for Fideo, who was improving little by little with the injections of penicillin mixed with benzoin that Dr. Antonio María gave her," says Olga, "and the rest of the time, Sayonara waited. And she plucked daisy petals, which is classic in these cases, since the daisy is recognized as the most convenient flower, because it only knows how to say yes or no, he loves me or he loves me not, that's all, so that if it is not to be, then let it be no for once and for all, so I can just die and get it over with, without further delay, because a person in love can't bear anything in between."

"And she constantly questioned me," adds Machuca. "I had become her informant and adviser and she interrogated me as if her joy depended on the words that I would have the grace to speak. 'He's going to come,' I assured her. 'He's going to come, you'll see.' "

"How do you know, doña Machuca? Why are you so sure?"

"I've already told you, because he's been seen looking for you lately. And since you are so eager to see him, why don't you go and look for him? You know where to find him . . ."

"Don't even think about it, doña Machuca. I could never do that. Why don't you just tell me about Emilia again?"

" 'Ay, *niña*! Don't you ever get tired of it?' I asked her," says Machuca, "and I would repeat the news of how they shut down Campo 26. How the old workers and the strikers were discriminated against with the argument that their experience wasn't worth anything now because the company valued personnel who had studied in technical institutes, and as part of the modernization process they were getting rid of obsolete machinery. How they had sold skinny Emilia for junk and several people had heard Payanés say that anything they did to Emilia they were doing to him, that if Emilia was no longer there, then he didn't have a commitment to the Tropical Oil Company anymore, or any reason to stay on at the Campo."

They also heard him say that he was going to look for better oil regions in Catatumbo, or around Tibú, where they had begun to recruit, or if not there, then in Cusiana, where they were laying pipe, or in Yopal and Orocué, in the far reaches of the Llano, the western plain; that maybe he went to look for work in Saldaña, where they were drilling, or in Tauramena, in the Casanare jungle, where a contracting company was looking for welders and pipe fitters.

"They say that Payanés is going around saying that he is willing to go anywhere that the voice of the pipe calls him, and that if it's necessary he'll follow its trail all the way to Saudi Arabia. They say that before he leaves he will come looking for you."

"Then I will go with him," Sayonara swore to Machuca.

"And what are you going to do when hunger strikes you?" Todos los Santos wanted to know.

"I can mount a show of exotic dances and he can sell tickets at the entrance, or I can sell outside a movie theater the *empanadas de pipián* that you taught me how to make. I can do housework as I learned in Villa de la Virgen del Amparo, like ironing shirts and polishing parquet floors, or I could work as a hairdresser. Maybe I would become a *puta* again, you never know . . ."

"And you would go off again like that, with one hand in front of you and the other behind you, without knowing if you would find a roof to shelter you at night?"

"I would go like that, *madrina,* because you know that life in this pueblo is no bed of roses, and because I don't need any more protection than his loving chest."

"Ay, *Virgen santa!* An umbrella in a hurricane would protect you more than his loving chest. And the remaining matter of that wife of his in Popayán, have you solved that?"

"That will be dealt with, *madrina,* along the way."

"Along the way, along the way! The way to sorrow is where you'll be heading again . . ."

"What are you saying, Todos los Santos?!" says Olga indignantly. "As if there were any ways in this life that didn't lead to sorrow. But it's still worth the trouble of following them; no, child, don't be discouraged."

One by one the slowest hours of the century filtered past and Say-onara was barely surviving her own hopefulness, always besieged by the certainty that something—or everything—was in play; that something—or everything—could be won or lost. Until the last Friday of that last month of the year dawned, brushing lightly against first the smokestacks at the refinery, then the tops of the highest trees, next the roofs of the houses, and finally the naked backs of the sleeping women, to find Say-onara already bathed and dressed and finished with breakfast, kneeling before the Christ with the blond beard.

"Today is the day, Señor Jesús," she prayed, "and I have come to ask you for something: Either you make that man love me, or you give me the courage to forget him. One of the two. All-powerful Señor, you who take everything and give everything, allow us to love one another until the end of our days, which isn't much to ask, since the lives of humans are short. I won't demand a commitment from him, or marriage or any other word, just true and clear proof. Send me a signal: If Payanés can't offer me great love, then don't let him appear today at the river. If it is otherwise, then give him swift feet, Señor, so he will arrive quickly."

"Careful, girl," Todos los Santos told her, listening to Sayonara's prayer from the doorway, "don't ask for supernatural announcements, they are almost always deceiving. Understand this, girl, you were born to be a nun or a *puta,* because no man exists who can put out that fire of longing inside you, or calm such a jumble of hopes."

"Don't teach me to resign myself, *madrina,* because I don't want to learn. It's already too late in life for me to accept defeat. I want to die peacefully knowing that I loved and was loved, and I assure you that it is not going to be a lack of faith that interferes with my efforts. Señor Jesús," she began to pray again, "help me to prove those wrong who believe that this is a valley of tears, amen."

They took stools, umbrellas, and cold drinks and sat at the edge of the Magdalena to wait, in respectful silence, as befits great occurrences. Sayonara was wearing her tight skirt and silk blouse, but she had traded her spike heels for some sandals, in case things turned out well and she needed to walk a long distance.

"Do you think you can make it all the way to Saudi Arabia in this suffocating heat?" one of the women joked, and they all laughed nervously.

Toward ten that morning they saw a group of people walking toward them and Sayonara's heart stopped, but they turned out to be pilgrims on their way to the sanctuary of Las Lajas.

"Have you come across anyone?" Todos los Santos asked them.

"Because of the stifling heat today, everything is very quiet," they responded.

Between that hour and eleven-thirty, the women didn't notice anything worthy of mention, and later they saw moving down river, at more or less regular intervals and for a period that stretched until noon, a pair of men fishing from a *chalupa,* a few fur merchants, and a *champán* rushing in an injured woman. Nothing more. Except for Sayonara, all of the women withdrew to eat lunch and came back down later with a plate of food that she wouldn't even taste. The afternoon heat put them to sleep at their watch posts, all but Sayonara, who remained painfully alert. Five o'clock came without event and discouragement began to invade the women, except for Sayonara, who ran to brush her hair and rinse her face with cool water.

Toward six-thirty a serene apocalypse of fires began to softly descend, one of those sunsets in Tora that, as Olga says, are so beautiful they hurt; one just like that other one with pink hues that Sacramento sent on one of his postcards of hopeless love; or copied from that bloody sky that convinced beautiful Claire of the sweetness of death; or like the ones that don Enrique painted to please his clientele, adorned with birds in flight and a glimmering horizon: a sunset just like those that Todos los Santos is able to contemplate in spite of not being able to open those other heavy eyelids that have been born under her eyelids.

"Here he comes!" Olguita suddenly shouted, and everyone stood up in unison, as if they had heard the national anthem. "Here he comes! He looks strong and handsome, all dressed in white!"

But she hadn't finished her announcement when his image vanished, like an inopportune cloud in the middle of the rays of the sunset.

"In white, yes, like a phantom," grumbled Todos los Santos, trying to lower the volume on the scene. "Don't embellish or exaggerate, Olga, you only saw his ghost. To me, Payanés is slippery, one of those who goes through life without underwear on under his trousers. You notice that he doesn't even have a name, Payanés, the man from Popayán, because his presence is nothing more than a gust of freedom. Which is what this girl has always pursued deep down," she said, but Sayonara, in agony, wasn't listening to her, "but she disguises her impulse and tries to make an appearance of refuge, of a loving chest, of protection, of paternal love, of anything: This girl only loves her own flight."

"But that is love," Olguita, the cripple, defended her, pounding her withered, steel-clad legs against her stool. "To run off using someone else's feet!"

"It's him," said Sayonara, now without the shadow of worry, shrouded in an old dignity and a new security, as if she had just deciphered some serious riddle or the key to something profound, and they knew the hour of the myth had come: the *puta* and the *petrolero*.

It is true that in a strict sense she was no longer a *prostituta* and he was no longer a *petrolero*, but maybe one day they would be again—he a *prostituto* and she a *petrolera*, as a favorite poet of Machuca's named Rafael

Pombo would have said—but if that didn't happen it wasn't a waste, because the sworn truth was that the women saw them depart, with the eyes that God put in their heads, together up along the Magdalena, one behind the other and the other behind the one, and both following the trail of life, or, better still, the force that pulls life from outburst to outburst without letting us know where it is carrying us, he dressed in white, with the rose incarnate wounding his chest and his profile facing forward, and she with her hair in the wind, gazing backward, clinging to what she is leaving behind and with the aura of death's beloved child reverberating around her more now, but it had surrounded her as long as they had known her. United at last, the *puta* and the *petrolero*, joined as one in the warm rapture of an embrace, while before them stretched the road to an uncertain future, like any worthwhile future.

"That is how we watched them depart in the scent of a legend and along the edge of the river, while we cried bittersweet tears and wished them 'God be with you' with waves of our handkerchiefs," reports Olga, letting out a round, translucent sigh.

"As an old, experienced woman, I know these things," continues Olga, "and I assure you that Sayonara left with Payanés and that she has been happy with him. And unhappy too, of course, but you can't take that away from her, the troubles of love aren't troubles. She has been happy for all of us because we deserve it, after so much activity and struggle."

"Me? I still write postcards to her, because I had confirmation that she appreciated receiving them," Sacramento tells me. "With everything else, including the marriage, I wasn't able to do anything except bother her, but my postcards cheered her up, as she told me herself. Since I don't know where to send them, I keep them here, in this shoe box, so I can give them to her the day she returns."

"Because she is going to return," Todos los Santos assures me, wrapped in her silver fox, as she caresses a Felipe with soft fur sleeping in a ball in her lap. "My girl will come back sooner or later, because the turns in her road always pass by my house."

ACKNOWLEDGMENTS

This book would not exist without the interest that has been invested in it, day to day, by Thomas Colchie, my adviser and literary agent; his wife, Elaine; and María Candelaria Posada, my old university classmate and, through entire lives of closeness, my editor today. I thank them and also Jaime González, Samuel Jaramillo, and Bernardo Rengifo, dear friends who read, reread, commented on, and added their bits to the manuscript.

For their kindness and thorough, factual knowledge, I thank Juan María Rendón, Alberto Merlano, and Marco Tulio Restrepo, directors of Ecopetrol, the firm that financed a portion of the research for this novel.

I thank also Rafael Gómez and Carlos Eduardo Correa S.J., who will know how valuable their generous and intelligent advice was when they read these pages, and Antonio María Flórez, the Spanish doctor who told me of his conversations with prostitutes in the health clinic of a Colombian pueblo in *tierra caliente*. Álvaro Mutis, for a certain sentence among those that appear here and from whom I heard it. Leo Matiz for the rights to the evocative photograph that appears on the cover. Sofía Urrutia, who made me aware of "La maison Tellier," the story by Maupassant that was key in finding the tone for this novel. Graciela Nieto, who will be surprised when she encounters, from the mouth of one of the characters of this fiction, an anecdote from real life that she related to me. María Rosalba Ojeda, my right hand for domestic matters and other urgencies. And as always and for so many reasons, my son, Pedro, my sister, Carmen, and my mother, Helena.

In Barrancabermeja, I thank don Marteliano, a former worker at the Tropical Oil Company, and the Pacheco family, with its three generations of oil workers. Hernando Martínez—Pitula—a former worker at Ecopetrol and today a taxi driver, who was my guide through the city. The many people that I had the opportunity to interview, among them Jorge Núñez and Hernando Hernández, current president of the oil workers union. Monseñor Jaime Prieto, bishop of Barrancabermeja. The legendary Negra Tomasa, William Sánchez Egea, Manuel Pérez, and don Aristedes. The *Japonesa*—who told me her entire life story. Amanda and her sister Lady, Gina, whose help was so valuable, Abel Robles Gómez, Dr. Orlando Pinilla of Bucaramanga, the civil leader Eloisa Piña, señora Candelaria, a resident of the barrio Nueve de Abril. Librarian Jairo Portillo. César Martínez, Luis Carlos Pérez, father Gabriel Ojeda, and Gustavo Pérez.

Wilfredo Pérez, a catechist and a good man, who was killed by the paramilitaries in May 1998.

In Bogotá, Gustavo Gaviria, whose conversations were so revealing, and Guillermo Angulo, for making me aware of the poetry of the Mexican Renato Leduc and the miracles of an old love of his and of the writer Manuel Mejía Vallejo, named Machuca. Dr. Eduardo Cuéllar Gnecco. Moisés Melo, director of Editorial Norma, for his comments. For their valuable texts on Barrancabermeja and Santander, Virginia Gutiérrez de Pineda and Jacques April-Gniset. Alejandro Santamaría for introducing me to Father Carlos Eduardo Correa. Dr. Ignacio Vergara, the analyst of the fictitious characters in this novel and the previous one. Marie Descourtieux, for the books and texts on prostitution she sent me from Paris, and the memorable Scottish poet Alastair Reid, who laughed with me as we created the conversation about snow that appears here from the mouths of the gringo Frank Brasco and Sayonara.

The Colombian Ministry of Culture, for giving me a grant that aided the writing of these pages.